The Last Word

Also by Elly Griffiths

THE DR RUTH GALLOWAY MYSTERIES

The Crossing Places   *The Woman in Blue*
The Janus Stone   *The Chalk Pit*
The House at Sea's End   *The Dark Angel*
A Room Full of Bones   *The Stone Circle*
Dying Fall   *The Lantern Men*
The Outcast Dead   *The Night Hawks*
The Ghost Fields   *The Locked Room*
The Last Remains

THE BRIGHTON MYSTERIES

The Zig Zag Girl   *The Vanishing Box*
Smoke and Mirrors   *Now You See Them*
The Blood Card   *The Midnight Hour*
The Great Deceiver

OTHER WORKS

The Stranger Diaries
The Postscript Murders
Bleeding Heart Yard
The Man in Black & Other Stories

NON-FICTION

Norfolk: A photographic journey through the land of Ruth Galloway

ELLY

Griffiths

The
Last
Word

QUERCUS

First published in Great Britain in 2024 by Quercus
This paperback edition published in 2024 by

QUERCUS

Quercus Editions Ltd
Carmelite House
50 Victoria Embankment
London EC4Y 0DZ

An Hachette UK company

A CIP catalogue record for this book is available
from the British Library

PB ISBN 978 1 52943 347 0
EB ISBN 978 1 52943 345 6

1

Typeset by CC Book Production
Printed and bound in Great Britain by Clays Ltd, Elcograf S.p.A.

Papers used by Quercus are from well-managed forests and other responsible sources.

For Daria Miskevych

Read your own obituary notice; they say you live longer.

James Joyce, *Ulysses*

Chapter 1

Edwin: a eulogy from a dead man

Monday, 4 April 2022

There are some advantages to being the oldest sleuth in the country, thinks Edwin. For a start, you don't have to be at your desk early. His morning routine now includes yoga stretches and deep breathing. In for four, hold for four, out for four. Then he breathes through alternate nostrils and finishes with a deep sigh called 'the ocean's breath'. If he's really organised, he will have put his porridge on first and will be able to sit down and eat it at perfect Goldilocks temperature. The porridge is made according to his late neighbour Peggy's specifications. It's not very nice but Edwin sees it as a tribute and perhaps a penance. Next is Wordle, an online word game once ubiquitous amongst members of 'book twitter' but now, as far as Edwin can tell, only played by the dogged few. But Edwin persists because he has got to preserve his winning streak in the face of understated, but deadly, competition from his friend Benedict. After completing the puzzle Edwin walks to Benedict's Coffee Shack to share the results (especially if he has guessed the word in fewer than four tries) and read the papers, an activity he regards as essential for any well-informed private investigator.

Today, Edwin arrives at the Shack at twenty minutes past nine. The commuting crowd has gone and the mothers and babies have not yet arrived. It's a sunny spring day and the kiosk, with its rainbow bunting, looks cheerful and welcoming. Benedict is looking out for Edwin but, as he sees his friend approaching, withdraws inside, to make the coffee and probably to hide the fact that he was anxious. Benedict is a great worrier.

'Five,' says Edwin, when he gets to the counter. 'One of those infuriating words where there were too many options. I had "slack", "black" and "flack" before I got "clack".'

'I got lucky early on,' says Benedict, with the modest look which says he got there in three, or even two. 'Your usual?'

'Thank you, dear boy.'

While Benedict prepares the best flat white in Shoreham-by-Sea, Edwin sits at the blue picnic table and opens *The Times*. His favourite paper is the *Guardian*, although he has a guilty soft spot for the *Telegraph*'s book coverage, but *The Times* is best for his other not-so-secret obsession: the obituaries.

Today there's a bumper crop: three, including one deceased he knows (knew) personally. The first is a trade union leader who died at the age of eighty-four, which, given his own age, Edwin now considers untimely ripp'd; the second a pop star who sadly seemed determined to act out the clichés of that profession; and the third is a producer Edwin worked with in his BBC Radio 3 days.

Charlie (Chips) Walker

BBC producer famous for his bonhomie and long lunches.

Bonhomie is one word for it, thinks Edwin. Chips could be good company but, if you got on the wrong side of him, his sarcasm could make you wither inside. 'Are you trying to bore the listeners to tears?' he once enquired of Edwin, who had been so shocked that his own eyes had started to water.

Chips Walker, the veteran broadcaster and producer, was responsible for introducing a whole new audience to classical music with light-hearted TV shows such as Very Verdi *and* Mostly Mozart. *Chips, who died of prostate cancer aged 85, studied at the Royal Academy of Music before joining Radio 3 as a trainee. He went on to present the Sunday evening show before turning his hand to producing. With his second wife, Margot Emsworth, he set up the production company Counterpoint which was responsible for a series of shows based on well-known classical composers . . .*

Edwin, a quick reader, has skimmed through awards, illnesses and another wife before Benedict puts coffee and a brownie in front of him.

'Who's dead?' Benedict sits opposite him.

'Producer I once knew . . . bit of a monster, if truth be told . . . leaves a wife and five children. Five! He was always extravagant. Wonder what the *Guardian* has to say about him . . .'

It's more of the same, with perhaps a little less Verdi and more BBC. He skips to the end of the piece. Unlike the *Times* obituaries, which are unsigned, the *Guardian* credits the writer.

'This is interesting,' he says.

'What?' Benedict cranes his head to read upside down. Edwin turns the paper.

Charles 'Chips' Walker, broadcaster and producer, born 19 February 1937, died 3 April 2022.
Malcolm Collins died in 2021.

'Eighty-five,' says Benedict, doing the maths. 'That's no age,' he adds, seeing Edwin's face.

'No,' says Edwin. 'The obituary writer, Malcolm Collins, is also dead. He died last year.'

'I suppose that often happens,' says Benedict. 'They write obituaries long before people die. There must be hundreds for the Queen and I bet she's outlived countless journalists.'

'She'll live for ever,' says Edwin. 'It's odd, though, isn't it? We're reading a eulogy from a dead man.'

Benedict doesn't look as though he finds it that odd but his attention is diverted by the arrival of a stunning blonde in designer running gear. This, much to Edwin's – and even Benedict's – continual amazement, is Benedict's girlfriend, Natalka.

Natalka stops at the bench to kiss Benedict on the cheek and perform some rather theatrical stretches. Benedict hurries away to prepare her signature cappuccino with cinnamon. He'll draw a heart in the foam too, Edwin knows. Edwin's not exactly an expert on living with women – he's known he was gay since prep school – but there is such a thing as being too romantic. Still, Natalka doesn't seem to mind and she and Benedict have been together for over two years now. Their relationship has even survived her mother moving in. Edwin thinks this has put a strain on the couple, though. Not least because Benedict gets on so well with Valentyna.

It seems that it's Edwin who is the reason for Natalka routing her morning jog in their direction.

'News,' she says, bending one leg back in an uncomfortably jointless way. 'We've got a new case.'

Natalka and Edwin are partners in a detective agency. It was Natalka's idea. In fact, Edwin suspected Natalka of suggesting the enterprise to give him that dreaded thing – an *interest*. He imagined Natalka saying to Benedict, 'We must give Edwin an interest, something to keep his brain alive. It's not enough to do the crossword and that Wordle thing.' Benedict had been dubious. 'Finding Peggy's killer was heart-breaking. And dangerous,' he said, during one of the planning meetings at the Shack. 'Do you really want to go through that again?' 'We won't be dealing with murder,' said Natalka, though Edwin had thought he detected a note of disappointment in her voice. 'It'll probably be women wanting to catch their husbands cheating.'

The agency was first in Natalka's name. NK Investigates. And it really did give Edwin an interest. He loved trailing people, old enough to become invisible, taking surreptitious pictures on his mobile phone. He even liked lurking in cafes, eking out a flat white while erring husbands flirted only a few yards away with women they had clearly met online. Eventually Natalka suggested that he become a partner so Edwin invested some of his BBC pension and the K and F agency was formed, standing for Kolisnyk and Fitzgerald. Natalka had first suggested F and K but, written down, that looked too much like the F-word with the middle asterisked out. It would have been even worse if they'd added C for Cole but Benedict still refused to join. 'I've got enough work running the Shack,' he said. But Edwin knew that, despite loving crime fiction, Benedict was squeamish about the real thing. Work at K and F all but disappeared during the pandemic but now that they are picking up a few cases again Natalka runs the business side along with her care agency. She's a born entrepreneur, Edwin thinks.

'Another Jolene?' says Edwin. This is their rather unkind name for the deceived wives although, in the country and western song, Jolene is actually the scarlet woman who is threatening to steal the unnamed man.

'No,' says Natalka, pausing impressively before starting on the other leg. 'A murder.'

'Murder?' Benedict puts the coffee carefully on the table. Please notice the heart, Edwin begs Natalka silently.

'Nice heart, Benny,' says Natalka, taking a sip. 'Today I got a call from a woman who thinks her mother has been murdered. The mother is an author, Melody Chambers.'

'Famous?' Edwin reaches for the papers. 'Will she have an obit?'

'You and your obituaries. I wouldn't think she's in the papers. She's a romance writer. Love and all that. You know.'

'I think I vaguely remember,' says Edwin. 'It'll probably be in the *Guardian*. They like women more than *The Times* or the *Telegraph*. Yes, here it is.'

He shows the page to Natalka.

Melody Dolores Chambers, author. Born 17 May 1952, died 2 April 2022.

'Only seventy,' says Edwin. 'Not quite, in fact.'

'I expect she died of old age,' says Natalka. She's probably joking but it's hard to tell from her face sometimes.

'Author of *And There You Were*,' reads Edwin, 'which was made into a film starring Nicole Kidman. It says here she died of a heart attack. Look, obituary by Malcolm Collins. The dead man.'

'I've just been talking to her daughter, Minnie,' said Natalka. 'She read that article about us in *Sussex Life*. She wants us to investigate.'

'She thinks her mother was murdered?' says Edwin. 'Does she have a suspect in mind?'

'Minnie says that she and her sister Harmony think Melody's second husband killed her.'

'Melody and Harmony,' says Edwin. 'Oh dear.'

'You'll have to be brave,' says Natalka. 'Minnie is short for Minim.'

Minim Barnes (née Chambers) lives in a large house on the outskirts of Brighton.

'Mummy loved music,' she tells them in her vast, uncomfortable kitchen, 'Daddy too. That's how they met. Singing in a choir.' She dabs her eyes with a Sussex seabirds tea towel.

'Alan's tone deaf, of course,' says Harmony who is perched on a stool at the catafalque Edwin believes is called a kitchen island. He's sitting on a high stool too and wonders if he'll ever be able to get off. Natalka, who had leapt up on hers, now says, 'Edwin knows a lot about music. He used to be on BBC Radio 3.'

'Really?' Both Harmony and Minnie turn to Edwin with new interest. They are not very alike, the sisters. Harmony is tall with dark hair pulled back into a severe ponytail. Minnie is smaller with blonde hair in what Edwin (showing his age) would call a pixie cut. Harmony is forty-five and Minnie forty-two.

'I presented a show for a few years,' says Edwin modestly. *Forgotten Classics*. Six o'clock on Sunday evenings. The ironing slot, they called it. Edwin still irons his shirts though Natalka tells him that people don't bother these days. 'We buy things that don't need ironing, or we just wear them with the creases.' He's a forgotten classic himself now.

'I'm sure Mummy and Daddy listened to it,' said Harmony. 'Alan listens to Planet Rock.' She shudders. Well, that settles it, thinks Edwin. Alan definitely did it.

'Daddy loved opera,' says Minnie. 'Especially Wagner.'

'I'm an Italian opera man myself,' says Edwin. 'Verdi and Puccini in particular.'

He always suspects Wagnerians, though there were plenty of them at the BBC.

'Alan likes heavy metal,' says Minnie. 'Tells you everything.'

The sisters' case is that Alan Franklin, Melody Chambers' second husband, killed his wife by replacing her blood pressure tablets with poison of some kind. 'He's a pharmacist,' they said in chorus, as if this explained everything. Edwin, who has a very good relationship with Dervish, who runs a chemist shop on the seafront, thinks that a lot more evidence is needed. Other signs of guilt include being fifteen years younger than his wife, having long hair and encouraging her to write a new will.

'It's not about the money,' says Minnie, putting two cups of professional-looking coffee in front of Edwin and Natalka. Benedict himself couldn't have produced better foam. Edwin takes a sip, worrying a little about caffeine overload. He usually restricts himself to one flat white a day.

'We're both comfortably off,' Minnie continues, 'with families of our own.' Edwin believes this. Minnie's house is a solid Victorian end-of-terrace near leafy Preston Park and evidence of Minnie's family is everywhere: a row of wellington boots in the hallway, football kit on the washing line outside, a 'Mum's Planner' stuck on the fridge, a palimpsest of scribbled handwriting. A small dog, who could have had 'family pet' written on its fur, watches them from what looks like a day bed.

'We don't need the money,' repeats Minnie. 'But Mummy always said she'd leave the house to us. It was *our* house. *Our* family home.' Despite the pixie cut and the designer leisurewear, Minnie suddenly sounds like a teenager.

'And now it goes to Alan?' asks Natalka.

'According to the new will, everything goes to Alan,' says Harmony. 'The house, the car, the boat. Even Frodo, Mummy's dog, belongs to him now.'

'I understand this must be very distressing for you,' says Natalka. Her accent often makes this sort of remark sound sarcastic but she manages to strike the right tone here. Both sisters lower their eyes as if to emphasise their distress. 'But do you have any evidence that Alan wanted to kill your mum?'

'Mum' is a nice touch, thinks Edwin, though he noted that both sisters used the posher, and more old-fashioned, 'Mummy'. It's what he had called his own maternal parent, although their relationship hadn't been the easiest.

'Oh, we've got evidence,' says Minnie. In a dramatic move, she produces a notebook from a concealed drawer in the catafalque. 'She wrote about it. I found this in her desk.'

Chapter 2

Natalka: first person

'It was all there,' says Natalka. '"I think my husband is going to kill me. I can't tell anyone. He watches me all the time. I'm scared of him."'

'Did the daughters show the notebook to the police?' asks Benedict.

'Apparently so,' says Natalka, 'but Alan – the husband – convinced them that it was fiction. Something she was planning for a new book.'

'Do you think that could be true?'

'I suppose it could be. And the sisters *hate* Alan. I think they'd believe anything of him. But I think it's worth Edwin and me talking to him.'

They are interrupted when Valentyna comes in with two bowls of steaming borscht. As often happens these days, Natalka is filled with so many emotions that she feels dizzy. On one hand, it's wonderful to have her mother here, cooking food that tastes of home. In the dark days of the Russian invasion in February, all

Natalka wanted was to get her mother out of Ukraine. When, after a panicky coach journey through Poland and her first-ever flight, Valentyna arrived at Gatwick, Natalka hugged her mother and vowed never to be parted again. This feeling intensified when, a few weeks later, Natalka's brother Dmytro made the journey in the opposite direction, leaving the safety of Scotland, where he'd lived since being released from a Russian prison, to join up and defend his country. Natalka – torn between pride and fury – was happy to have at least one family member where she could see them.

But . . . it's a one bedroom flat. Natalka and Benedict moved in on 3 March 2020 and, as Covid-19 swept the country, were instantly locked down together. It was a difficult time. Natalka was running the care agency almost single-handed. Many carers left, worried about their own families, but some stayed on, literally risking their lives for the people in their care. Natalka took on the clients that were left without carers and Benedict, Coffee Shack boarded up on the beach, stepped in to help. 'We've got to keep the old people out of hospital,' Natalka said, 'that's where people are dying of this thing.' All day long Natalka and Benedict cooked, cleaned and toileted. From behind their masks they chatted with clients who were terrified of the killer disease that had stopped their friends and families from visiting, leaving them prisoners in their own homes. When they got home, Benedict and Natalka took off their scrubs (bought by Natalka from a secret source because protective clothing was in short supply), showered and changed. Quite often they made love at some point in the process. Then they watched comfort TV reruns together: *The Office*, *Friends*, *Bake Off*.

Now, things are almost back to normal. All restrictions were lifted in March 2022, although Covid remains rife in the UK. It's still a struggle to find enough carers but Natalka is able to spend more time with the detective agency. One of the worst aspects of lockdown was not seeing Edwin. Natalka remembers standing outside Seaview Court and shouting up to Edwin on the balcony. He had seemed cheerful enough. He wore a different hat every day and demonstrated his mastery of various yoga moves. 'Be careful!' Benedict shouted, as Edwin teetered on one leg in tree pose. 'Namaste,' Natalka had said, bowing to him. 'What will happen if Edwin gets Covid?' Benedict said, almost every night. 'He'll die,' Natalka had answered. She has always believed in facing things head on.

But Edwin survived. He regularly claims that, at eighty-four, he's the oldest detective in the country but in Natalka's eyes he's invaluable. He can sit in a café for hours, carrying out surveillance, deploying his age as a cloak of invisibility. Yet his mind is as sharp as ever and his client reports are so beautifully written as to be almost poetic. He's even rather good with technology, although he persists in talking about the 'interweb'. Natalka should be happy: both her businesses are doing well and she hasn't had to resort to the rather dodgy Bitcoin business that gave her an income when she first moved to England. She's no longer worried that the Ukrainian mafia will track her down – she thinks they have bigger issues at the moment – and she feels settled in her life. She likes Shoreham, she enjoys running the agency and, by some miracle, she and Benedict have emerged from lockdown with their relationship intact. And yet, sometimes Natalka is almost nostalgic for the days when the streets were empty and her family only available via Zoom. It's great knowing that her mother is safe, living with them and cooking labour-intensive meals every night. Natalka loves speaking

Ukrainian with her, remembering old jokes and songs. The food is pretty good too. It's just that, with Valentyna sleeping on a sofa bed in the sitting room, there's nowhere for Natalka and Benedict to relax in their own flat. There's their bed, of course, but, even there, Natalka feels constrained. Benedict, the ex-monk, is surprisingly keen on sex and doesn't seem to be deterred by the maternal presence in the next room. Natalka wishes that she could feel the same.

'Borscht,' says Benedict. 'дуже смачний.' He is learning Ukrainian via Duolingo.

'You are so clever, Benny,' says Valentyna. 'Isn't he clever, Talia?'

'He's a genius,' says Natalka. She knows she should be happy that her boyfriend and her mother get on so well but, sometimes, their mutual admiration society makes her want to throw things at them.

Benedict starts to clear the table but Natalka grabs her notebook.

'Leave it. I'm in the middle of a case.'

'What is case?' says Valentyna, putting sour cream and chives on the table. 'Is it *murder*?' Natalka definitely gets her interest in crime from her mum.

'It's a woman who murdered her interfering mother,' she tells Valentyna.

Valentyna laughs delightedly at this but Benedict hastens to say, 'No, it's a writer who died recently. Her family think it might be suspicious.'

'You must ask Edwin,' says Valentyna. 'Edwin knows all writers.'

'He certainly thinks he does,' says Natalka, moodily spooning up soup.

Natalka had been afraid she would like Alan Franklin and, though she carefully maintains a neutral attitude, she feels a certain affinity with the long-haired chemist that she didn't experience with his stepdaughters.

'I don't think of myself as a stepfather,' says Alan, in the kitchen of the rambling house in Steyning. 'Just as well because they hate my guts.'

It had been slightly embarrassing asking for the interview but Alan had made it easier by saying, 'Have Minnie and Harmony asked you to investigate me? I thought they would. They're desperate to pin Melody's death on me. Shock, I suppose.'

To be fair, Natalka can see why the sisters feel angry to have lost this house. It's beautiful: stone, double-fronted, with bay windows and a large, rather overgrown, garden. The kitchen is a perfect mix of country cottage – Aga, pine dresser – and futurist laboratory – shiny blue units, marble counters, spotlit island. Natalka sees Edwin looking nervously at the bar stools by the latter. He seems relieved when they sit down at the scarred pine table.

A ginger spaniel who has been frisking around their feet jumps up and sits on Alan's lap. He tilts his head back to avoid the nose lick. Whatever the sisters might say, Melody's dog seems very happy with its new owner.

'He's called Frodo,' says Alan, reaching round the dog for his mug of tea. 'Melody's choice, not mine. He really misses her. I do too.'

'Do you mind telling us what happened?' asks Natalka.

'Like I say, it was a shock. Melody had just come back from the gym. She was very fit, exercised more than me. She was here, in the kitchen, getting some food for Frodo, and she must have fallen . . . I found her lying on the floor, Frodo licking up the food that had fallen onto the floor. I tried CPR but she was already dead . . .'

Alan's hand is shaking when he puts the mug back on the table.

'Did she have any heart problems?' asks Edwin. 'Was she on medication? Goodness knows, I take so much that I rattle . . .'

This isn't quite true. To Natalka's knowledge, Edwin takes statins and believes in the efficacy of an aspirin every day. But he is, in her opinion, rather obsessed with his own health, which might prove useful on this case.

'She took pills for blood pressure,' says Alan. 'But it wasn't dangerously high. She exercised, she wasn't overweight . . . The girls – God knows why I call them that, they're fully grown women – seem to believe that I replaced the tablets with rat poison, or something similar.'

'Was there an inquest?' asks Natalka.

'No.' Alan's voice takes on a steelier edge. 'There was no need. Cause of death was myocardial infarction. No suspicious circumstances. Whatever Cagney and Lacey would have you believe.'

Edwin laughs but this cultural reference means nothing to Natalka.

'What happened to Melody's blood pressure pills?' she asks.

'I put them in the medical waste disposal at the pharmacy,' says Alan. He gives a rather saturnine grin. 'Very suspicious behaviour, I'm sure.'

Natalka doesn't like his tone. This is serious, she wants to tell him. And, besides, disposing of the pills might be something a responsible pharmacist would do but it could also be seen as suspicious behaviour. Natalka is sure that Harmony and Minnie would take this view.

Edwin obviously decides on a change of approach. 'How did you and Melody meet?' he asks.

'At the pharmacy,' says Alan, the warmer note back in his voice. 'She came in looking for something for RSI. Repetitive strain injury. You can get it from typing too much. We got talking about her writing. She came back the next day – she admitted later that it was on a pretext – and I asked her out on a date. The rest is history. Mel was so . . . so much fun. The age difference didn't matter at all.'

All the same, this is said rather defensively. Natalka wonders whether Alan has had to justify his marriage many times before. She decides it's time to get tough.

'Harmony and Minnie showed us something Melody had written. It says that she was scared her husband was going to kill her.'

This time Alan laughs outright. It sounds genuine too. The dog barks in agreement.

'That was an idea for a novel. Fiction. She always scribbled bits in exercise books.'

'A novel about a wife being afraid of her husband?'

'Yes. Why not?'

'It's in the . . .' Natalka snaps her fingers, irritated that she can't think of the word. 'It's written in the . . .'

'In the first person,' supplies Edwin.

'Look, Mel was a writer. I don't know how she wrote her books. She didn't discuss her work with me. We had our own spheres of interest. I didn't ask about the books. She had her author friends for that.'

'Did Melody have many local author friends?' asks Edwin.

'Yes,' said Alan. 'They'd meet regularly. She was rather upset, actually, because one of them died a few months ago. He was a journalist . . .'

'Was his name Malcolm Collins?' asks Edwin.

Alan stares at him over the dog's topknot. 'How the hell did you know that?'

Took the words right out of my mouth, thinks Natalka.

Chapter 3

Benedict: a double life

Benedict tries never to feel resentful. It's a waste of energy and, besides, probably damaging to the soul. He remembers Brother Damian, who'd been his confessor in the monastery, quoting from the Book of Job, 'Wrath killeth the foolish man and envy slayeth the silly one.' Silly seemed a very unbiblical word, he'd thought at the time, but maybe it's right for how he is feeling now. He's silly to feel jealous of Natalka and Edwin because they have a possible murder case to investigate whilst Benedict's – self-appointed – role is to serve coffee to the early-morning dog walkers and office workers, none of whom seem very grateful for their mindful cappuccino. Benedict tries hard to make small acts special, perfect in their own way. 'The Little Way', St Thérèse of Lisieux put it. 'Miss no single opportunity of making some small sacrifice, here by a smiling look, here by a kindly word . . .' But it's possible that St Thérèse never had to serve coffee to a thirty-something in cycling shorts who can't be bothered to take his headphones off.

Benedict is very aware of his own faults – Natalka calls it 'being morbid' – and he knows that amongst them is an unhealthy fascination with murder. As a teenager he'd had a serious Agatha Christie habit. Once he tried giving the books up for Lent only to weaken on Palm Sunday – of all days! – and open *The ABC Murders*. Whilst training to be a priest, he'd turned to Charles Dickens and Wilkie Collins. He justified them to his conscience (an annoyingly intrusive presence) as Literature but, really, he was obsessed with the detectives: Inspector Bucket in *Bleak House*, Sergeant Cuff in *The Moonstone*, the intrepid Marian Halcombe in *The Woman in White*. When he entered the monastery, he gave up fiction altogether. At the time, it had been harder than giving up sex (which, to the young Benedict, had been a purely theoretical concept). He traced the first stirrings of his Doubts to buying a copy of *Gaudy Night* by Dorothy L. Sayers at Waterstones in Bradford, whilst supposedly on his way to a retreat. He remembers the shop itself, as beautiful as any cathedral, appearing like a cornucopia of temptation. The recently published crime novels, women in red coats walking through a succession of moody landscapes, seemed altogether too sensational but the classics section, tasteful oranges and greys, had a reassuringly academic feel. And, after all, *Gaudy Night* was set at Oxford. Practically a textbook.

When Benedict left the monastery, he moved to Shoreham, bought the Coffee Shack (with help from his parents) and rented an attic room overlooking the harbour. It was a lonely existence enlivened by one thing: television. Every night, wrapped in his duvet, Benedict would watch endless episodes of *Murder She Wrote*, *Monk* and *Midsomer Murders*. He learnt to distrust vicars, visiting historians and once-famous actors whose characters had no obvious link to the plot. When, together with Natalka and Edwin, Benedict had actually investigated a real murder, he'd thought that his life would change for ever. And it *has* changed. Being in a relationship with Natalka is the most wonderful thing ever to happen to him. Every day, he has to remind himself that this beautiful woman is smiling at *him*, is going home to *him*, that he can see her brushing her teeth or doing yoga in her underwear. It's surely enough excitement for one earthly lifetime. Except, it isn't.

Lockdown had been terrifying but, for Benedict at least, it hadn't been dull. He'd had to shut the Shack but that meant he could help Natalka on the front line, with the care agency. The days had been long and exhausting but he was buoyed up by the feeling of doing good and also supporting the woman he loved. He hadn't been able to see his friends or family but being alone in the flat with Natalka had been the opposite of lonely. They'd watched TV, cooked strange meals, developed an obsession with an online yoga teacher called Adriene. But, when lockdown finally ended, Natalka was a detective again and Benedict was back to serving coffee. Should he have joined the detective agency? At the time, straight after Peggy's death, it had seemed wrong to be seeking out the sort of criminals who had taken his friend's life. When Natalka protested that they would be mainly dealing with divorces, that seemed almost worse. Benedict is idealistic about marriage in the way that only unmarried people can be. He'd taken the high-minded line that he would carry on with the lowly, yet necessary, work of providing sustenance to the caffeine-loving citizens of Shoreham.

Benedict passes over a takeaway cup to a customer who is having an animated conversation with an unseen auditor. 'Thank you,' says Benedict loudly. Passive aggression is probably a sin but not, he thinks, a serious one.

'Benedict?'

For a second Benedict wonders if he's gone back in time or strayed into *Midsomer Murders*, because he finds himself staring at a clerical collar. His eyes move upwards and he sees a cherubic face split by a wide grin.

'Richard! What are you doing here? I thought you were in Surrey somewhere.'

'I came to see you,' says Richard.

'To see me?' This seems both flattering and slightly worrying.

'Have you got time to talk?'

Benedict scans the promenade but it is suddenly completely empty, seagrass blowing like tumbleweed.

'Let's have a coffee,' he says.

Benedict first met Richard Fraser when he came to the monastery on retreat. Richard was then a Church of England vicar who had been overwhelmed by an inconvenient compulsion to become a Catholic. 'Everyone will say it's because I don't like women priests,' Richard said to Benedict one day as they worked together in the kitchen garden, 'but that's not it at all. It's just, I'm a pre-Reformation person really. The Catholic Church is where I belong.'

Benedict, who was beginning to despair of ever finding a place where he belonged, had been impressed by Richard's conviction. He was prepared to disrupt his life – and the life of his whole family – on the strength of his belief. Because Richard was a married man with two children. In theory, the Catholic Church welcomed former vicars, and respected their marriage vows, but, as Richard's wife Madeline told Benedict, 'There's no role for us, Catholic priests aren't meant to have wives, let alone teenage children.' In his gloomier moments, Benedict wondered if anyone really had a role in life but he supposed that Madeline, a GP, already had her vocation. At any rate, five years after the conversation amongst the herbs, Richard became a Roman Catholic priest.

Benedict and Richard have kept in touch over the years, first via email then by sporadic WhatsApp messages. Richard had been supportive when Benedict left the order – 'God has other plans for you' – but, what with the demands of Richard's parish and the rigours of lockdown, it had been almost three years since they last met in person.

Benedict makes them flat whites and they sit at the table. He puts some brownies on a plate, remembering Richard's sweet tooth.

'Delicious.' The first one is gone in two bites. 'Don't tell Madeline. I'm meant to be on a diet.'

'You look fine to me,' says Benedict. But, in truth, his friend is slightly rounder than he used to be which, combined with his almost-bald head and full-cheeked face, makes him look a bit like a large baby.

'So why did you need to see me?' asks Benedict. 'And why the full metal jacket?' He gestures to the dog collar.

'I'm going to a meeting at Phil's later.' Benedict knows that this refers to the St Philip Howard Centre in Crawley. It's funny how stuff like that comes back.

Richard takes another brownie, looks at it sadly and then takes a bite.

'I don't suppose you heard that a vicar called Don Parsons died recently? There were obits in some of the papers.'

The word 'obit' reminds Benedict of Edwin, sitting at this same table and leafing through the broadsheets. *Not a bad haul today* . . .

'I didn't hear,' he says. 'I don't really read the papers any more.'

'No one does. But Don wouldn't have had any obituaries if he hadn't been living a double life.'

'Really? Wife and kids?'

'C of E vicars are allowed those. Even a few privileged Catholics are. Although I've heard all that's stopping. We married priests are too expensive. What with having to pay us a salary.'

Benedict knows that Catholic priests, unlike their Protestant counterparts, don't receive a salary, relying instead on parish offerings at Christmas and Easter. It's no wonder that some priests get quite evangelical about these.

'Tell me about Father Don's double life,' he says.

'Don had a very successful career as Donna Parsons, a romantic novelist.'

'You're joking.'

'It was secret for a long time but he was outed a few years back. Didn't seem to affect his – or Donna's – sales. I knew Don well. We were at the seminary together and our parishes weren't far apart. He was a quiet chap. Looked after his mum until she died, obsessed with his obscenely fat cat. You wouldn't think he could come up with some of the stuff in the books but . . . we all have our hidden sides.'

Benedict's not sure that he does. The thought makes him rather depressed.

'Why are you telling me all this?' he says. 'I mean, I'm sorry about your friend, of course, but I'm more of a crime reader.'

'That's why I'm here,' says Richard, licking brownie crumbs off his fingers. 'I think Don might have been murdered.'

*

'What did he mean, "murdered"?' asks Natalka.

'Murdered as in unlawfully killed,' says Benedict. He's slightly irritated that Natalka seems less interested in Don/Donna than in Melody Chambers.

'Ah,' says Edwin. 'Found the obit.' They are in the sitting room of Edwin's flat in Seaview Court. Natalka prefers meeting here because there's no chance of her mother appearing with Ukrainian snacks but Benedict finds the place slightly sad, despite Edwin's tasteful furnishings and his plentiful supply of classy biscuits. Maybe it's because it reminds him of Peggy, who once lived across the landing.

Edwin seems quite happy, though. He loves hosting meetings and always supplies pens, pencils and notebooks. Now he puts on his glasses and reads aloud from his iPad, font size approximately 50.

'This is from Monday's edition of *The Times*. "'Vicar who led double life.'"'

'That's what Richard said,' interposes Benedict. 'He led a double life.'

'Well, it's not a very original phrase, is it?' said Edwin, slightly sniffily in Benedict's opinion. 'Anyway, this is what the obit says: "To his parishioners in Morton St Mary's, The Rev Donald Parsons, who has died aged 62, was known as a quiet, kindly presence, devoted to his cats and his allotment. But the Church of England vicar, who died of a heart attack last week, had a secret. Writing as Donna Parsons, he penned a string of bestselling romantic novels including *Red as the Rose*, *A Country Girl* and *A Deadly Bargain*" . . .'

'Penned,' says Benedict. 'That's a word that only appears in newspapers, never in ordinary conversation. "Bedded" is another one. And "dubbed".'

'Do you want to hear this or not?' says Edwin. He scrolls down the page, using forefinger, not thumb. 'Parsons' pseudonym was discovered in 2019 after he won an award from the Romantic Novelists' Association. The subsequent backlash was said to have deeply affected the very private vicar . . .'

'Who wrote this?' says Natalka. 'Is it Malcolm Collins?'

'*Times* obits are unsigned,' says Edwin.

'Who's Malcolm Collins again?' says Benedict. He's conscious of the conversation drifting away from him as he looks out of the window. Not a very rewarding activity because, despite the name, Edwin's flat does not have a sea view.

'He's the man who wrote the obituary for my ex-colleague, Chips,' says Edwin. 'And predeceased him. We learnt this morning that Malcolm Collins was a friend of Melody Chambers.'

'Really?' says Benedict. 'Did he live in Sussex then?'

'Apparently so,' says Edwin. 'He and Melody used to meet regularly, along with some other writer friends.'

'Do we know how Malcolm died?' asks Benedict.

'Alan, Melody's widower, thought it was a heart attack.'

'Like Melody,' says Benedict. 'And Don Parsons.'

'People die from heart attacks all the time,' says Natalka. 'In my business, I know.'

Natalka often says things that make her sound like a hired assassin.

'But these were all youngish, fittish people,' says Edwin. 'Might it be worth investigating?'

'My friend Richard definitely thought there were suspicious circumstances with Don,' says Benedict, getting to tell his story at last.

'What suspicious circumstances?' asks Natalka.

'Well, for a start, he told Richard that someone was trying to kill him.'

This, at least, makes Edwin and Natalka concentrate on him.

'Don wrote Richard a letter before he died. It said something like, "I'm scared, they're trying to kill me." Richard was worried. He rang Don at once but it was a landline – don't think he had a mobile – and there was no answer. Next thing Richard heard, Don was dead. He feels terribly guilty.'

'Of course he does,' says Natalka, 'he's a Catholic.' She was brought up in the Orthodox Church but no longer practises anything except yoga.

'To be fair, I think anyone would feel bad in that scenario,' says Edwin, an enthusiastic, though slightly freelance, Catholic.

'Richard went to the police,' says Benedict, 'but they said they were satisfied the death was natural causes. He wants you to investigate. He heard about the agency somehow. Maybe the *Sussex Life* piece.'

'We are getting a reputation,' says Edwin, with some satisfaction.

'Richard assumed I was part of the agency,' says Benedict. 'I told him I wasn't but said I'd pass it on to you two.'

'Is he paying?' says Natalka.

'Of course.'

'Then investigate we shall,' says Edwin, opening his notepad.

Chapter 4

Harbinder: the blonde assassin

Through the glass walls of her office, DI Harbinder Kaur surveys her team with dissatisfaction. It's not that they're a bad lot. DS Jake Barker is irritatingly prone to standing with his legs wide apart and addressing his colleagues as 'mate' but he's a decent copper for all that. DS Kim Manning, currently eying her lunchtime sandwich, is always reliable, both for good work and for a good laugh. DC Victoria 'Tory' Hamilton-Fletcher is a pain but she's not completely unintelligent and her cutglass accent is sometimes useful when talking to more prejudiced members of the public. DC Patrick Connolly is gently cruising towards retirement but he was very helpful to Harbinder when she first started the job, explaining everything from the London Underground to the intricacies of the stationery ordering system.

It's not the personnel that's the problem; it's the fact that there are so few of them. Harbinder's Murder Investigation Team (MIT) is currently investigating a stabbing that might well be a hate crime, two drugs-related deaths and that of an elderly woman whose daughter thinks she might have been killed by a ghost. Harbinder could do with at least two more DCs but her boss, Superintendent Simon Masters, says that she's lucky to have a team at all, 'what with everything that's going on in the Met'. Harbinder takes this to mean the number of officers suspended for being part of WhatsApp groups full of racist and homophobic messages. This makes Harbinder feel that her superiors should value her – a British-Indian gay woman – even more and, quite often, it makes her want to resign from the force altogether.

Her phone buzzes. *Natalka*. Harbinder hesitates. On one hand, Natalka is always interesting. Harbinder's girlfriend, Mette, describes her as 'the blonde assassin'. On the other, she's probably ringing because she wants something. Or she's been arrested.

'Hi, Natalka.'

'Harbinder. How goes the crime fighting?'

'Very slowly. How's the private investigating?'

'We have a murder case,' says Natalka. And Harbinder can hear the excitement in her voice. She disapproves slightly – murder is not a game – but she understands.

'Tell me more?'

'Two writers who may have been killed.'

'May?' The word 'writers' reminds Harbinder of the previous case involving Natalka, a memory that stirs all kinds of emotions: interest, unease and a slight sadness.

'Deaths recorded as natural causes but the families think there was something suspicious. Both people wrote about being scared.'

'Wrote where? In their books?'

'No. One in a notebook and one in a letter.'

'Does anyone write letters any more? Or have notebooks?'

'These people do. Anyway, I need your help . . .' *There it is.* 'I've tried the local police but your friend Nigel . . . Nathan . . .'

'Neil.'

'Neil. He just isn't interested. He says there's no case to solve. No suspicious circumstances.'

Harbinder can imagine the conversation. When Harbinder used to work with Neil at West Sussex CID, she formed a strategy of pretending that he was a woodland animal: small, cute but ultimately harmless. It stopped her wanting to strangle him when he raised difficulties and objections. All the same, he's not a bad bloke. It was Harbinder who first encountered Natalka and she was aware that, in taking on the Peggy Smith case, she was bending quite a few rules. Neil hadn't approved but he'd gone along with it. But he wouldn't appreciate Natalka turning up again with her wild Slavic beauty and stories of foul play.

'I can't help you,' says Harbinder. 'I work in London now, remember?'

'But you could research the people involved. You're a detective inspector. You've got a *team.*'

'A very depleted one at the moment.'

'If I give you the names, will you just look them up?'

Harbinder sighs. 'I'll ask someone to run them through the database. See if there are any previous convictions. That's all I can do.'

'Thank you. You're a star. How's that sexy Great Dane of yours?'

'Mette's fine, thanks. How's Benedict? And Edwin?'

'They're both well. Edwin's a new man now we've got a proper case, not just stupid divorce stuff. Murder agrees with him.'

'Be careful,' says Harbinder.

'I'm always careful,' says Natalka, with a laugh that sounds slightly unhinged.

It's not until the afternoon that Harbinder has time to approach Laura, one of her civilian data analysts.

'Can you run these names through the database?' she asks. 'Melody Chambers, Alan Franklin, Donald Parsons.'

'Melody Chambers?' says Laura. 'Didn't she write *And There You Were*? I loved that book. The film's great too.'

'I don't have much time for reading,' says Harbinder. Although she does have a weakness for horror novels, anything involving killer rats or haunted brownstones in New York.

'It's all about finding the perfect man and then – spoiler alert – he's a ghost.'

'I hate it when that happens,' says Harbinder. She's out to her colleagues but allows herself the odd hetero joke.

Laura laughs. 'Talking of ghosts, wasn't she an author too?'

'You've lost me there, Laura.'

'The old lady in Kensal Rise, Eileen O'Rourke. The one who the daughter says was murdered by the ghost of Jack the Ripper. She was an author too.'

There it is again. Authors, in Harbinder's experience, mean trouble.

Chapter 5

Edwin: retreat

Now that Edwin has a serious case, he decides to vary his routine slightly. He still starts his day with the sacred trilogy of yoga/porridge/Wordle but now Edwin fires up his computer before saluting the dawn and, by the time he makes it to the Coffee Shack, he has made a breakthrough.

'Got it in four,' he tells Benedict, by way of greeting. 'I don't approve of American spellings, though.'

'I agree,' says Benedict, frothing milk. 'Took me six goes. I almost gave up.'

'And lose your streak?' says Edwin. 'Never.'

They sit at the table. It's a cold spring day and Edwin is glad that he put on his warm jacket and scarf. He's also wearing a deerstalker-type hat, as a nod to his detective duties. Benedict compliments him on it.

'Thank you, dear boy. It was a present from Peggy, years ago.'

'Dear Peggy. She did like her crime novels.'

'Yes. I'm afraid she wouldn't approve of Melody Chambers and co. Speaking of whom, I've found a link between Melody and Don Parsons.'

'Really? That was quick.'

'It wasn't that difficult. I just looked through their Instagram accounts. Melody's was full of pictures of Frodo, her dog, and Don's – or Donna's I should say – was mostly cats. But, last year, they both posted about going on retreat.'

'On retreat? Were they religious then?'

Edwin laughs. Just when you think Benedict has joined the real world, he comes out with something like this.

'A writing retreat, Benedict.'

'Oh.' Benedict flushes and Edwin feels sorry for the laugh. Two dog walkers approach the Shack and Benedict goes to serve them. This gives Edwin time to find the picture on his phone, not easy when your hands are cold. Benedict returns with two brownies. Edwin refuses his because he's watching his weight.

'This is the place. Battle House. It's not far from here, near Hastings.'

Benedict takes the phone and enlarges the picture.

'Looks a bit grim.'

'Maybe that's the point. No distractions. It's really just a house in the woods. Maybe an old farm building. I've looked and it takes six people at any one time. Retreats are led by a writer called Leonard Norris. He was quite successful in the eighties but hasn't published anything for a while.'

'You *have* done a lot of research.'

'I was up early. Anyway, what do you think?'

'What do I think about what?'

Benedict is being obtuse today, thinks Edwin. No wonder it took him six tries to find the word 'favor'.

'Shall we go there?' says Edwin. 'Pretend to be writers. Check the place out.'

Edwin walks quickly along the walkway by the beach. This is partly to warm himself up and partly because he's irritated with Benedict. He'd expected his friend to be excited at the idea of infiltrating the writers' retreat. He knows that Benedict yearns for excitement and this is real detective work, going *undercover*, for heaven's sake. Edwin has checked and there's availability in two weeks' time, after Easter. It's billed as a 'writing weekend', as opposed to a retreat, which might be even more interesting. Natalka wouldn't be interested in attending and Edwin doubted that she could pass herself off as any sort of writer – she's too glamorous, for one thing – but he'd thought that Benedict would jump at the chance. Edwin had imagined travelling there together, in Natalka's car or by train, getting their story straight on the way, checking in and assuming the guise of two aspiring authors. He had already decided that he would be a crime writer, in honour of Peggy. But Benedict had been oddly reluctant. 'What good would it do?' 'We can look for clues,' said Edwin. 'After all, Battle House is the only thing that links our potential victims.' 'Can't we just go there openly?' protested Benedict. 'Why do we have to pretend to be writers?' Honestly, thinks Edwin, turning sharply inland, some people have no imagination.

Edwin crosses the bridge that leads over the estuary into the town. On a sunny day, it's a lovely view, the sun shining on the water and on the windchimes adorning the houseboats. But, today, the sky is grey and the glass panels on the bridge are smeared with bird shit. The tide is low and the boats sit miserably on the mud banks. He wraps his scarf more tightly round his neck. 'There is a tide in the affairs of men,' thinks Edwin, who prides himself on having a Shakespeare quotation for every occasion, 'which taken at the flood, leads on to fortune.' Isn't there an Agatha Christie book called *Taken at the Flood*?

Edwin's spirits, momentarily dampened by his shortcut through the graveyard of St Nicholas Church, rise when he sees the brick façade of Shoreham Library. It's one of his favourite places. Peggy used to work there and had many friends amongst the staff. Edwin and Peggy visited every week, perusing the 'recently returned' shelf with expert eyes. The loss of the library had been one of the worst things about lockdown, even though Edwin attended several very interesting Zoom events. Today he's booked a session in the computer room, just for the change of scenery. After all, it's thanks to the library's Silver Surfer course that he's the modern detective he is today.

The main library is quiet, just a couple of students working at the tables and a woman sitting in an armchair reading a Lisa Jewell book whilst pushing a baby buggy to and fro, presumably to keep the occupant asleep. Edwin doesn't recognise the young woman behind the desk so he doesn't stop to say hallo, just signs into the computer room. It's a large airy space containing four bulky desktops, spaced well apart, possibly a legacy of Covid. All but one is occupied, two by young men, one of whom is wearing a turban. Edwin wonders if he's related to Harbinder and then chides himself for the possibly racist thought. Not all Sikhs are related to Harbinder but, then again, it's possible that all Sikhs in Shoreham are. The third computer-user is an elderly man who looks as if he could do with some Silver Surfer lessons. Edwin nods to his fellow techies, takes off his jacket, hat and scarf and sits down at the empty workspace.

He logs on and types 'Battle House' into the search bar.

Retreat into writing. Relax during the day, enjoying the peaceful views and the ancient woodland. Share your triumphs and disasters around the fire in the evening. Prize-winning author Leonard Norris is always on hand to help or for one-to-one coaching sessions.

Edwin enlarges the picture of Leonard Norris. He's a grey-haired man, probably in his fifties or even sixties, with a slightly anxious look around the eyes. 'Prize-winning' is stretching it a bit. Norris was longlisted for the Booker Prize in 1992 for a novel called *The Hopes and Fears of All the Years*.

Edwin clicks onto 'images'. The house, grey stone with a slate roof, stares back at him, aggressively symmetrical. The windows are small and deep-set; Edwin is not sure how much of the 'peaceful view' they will reveal. Besides, the woods surround the house on three sides and Edwin could almost swear the trees are moving closer as he looks. Burnham Wood coming to Dunsinane.

On the testimonials page Edwin reads: 'So calm and peaceful. Melody Chambers.' And directly below: 'Just what I needed. Donna Parsons.' He scans down until his mouse comes to a quivering halt by another name.

'The last word in retreats. Malcolm Collins.'

Chapter 6

Benedict: no such thing as fiction

A flurry of customers prevents Benedict from watching Edwin walk away. But he imagines him striding into town, deerstalker moving through the Wednesday people: the retired and the unemployed, the café owners putting out tables, squinting anxiously at the sky, the homeless gathering in church porches, the mothers pushing buggies, the aimless and the clandestine. Benedict knows that Edwin was disappointed in his attitude to the retreat. He wishes that he could run after him and explain but it's nearly lunchtime. Benedict has got to make sandwiches.

Sometimes Natalka comes for lunch but today Benedict knows that, after sorting out the morning's care schedules, she's going to talk to some of Melody Chambers' friends. He makes the sandwiches and wraps them in cellophane. The wind has picked up and crisp packets blow along the promenade. Benedict doesn't think many people will stop for an al fresco lunch. The guilty feeling intensifies, even though he cleans the coffee machine as a penance. Benedict knows Edwin wants them to go to the retreat together.

He wants them to pose as aspiring writers, concoct elaborate cover stories and devise a cunning code so that they can discuss their fellow scribblers. 'This book is very Ngaio Marsh, don't you think?' He wants them to read their work aloud, talk longingly about getting an agent and spend a fortune on writing journals.

There's just one problem with all this. Benedict *is* an aspiring writer. Though he has never told anyone, Benedict has completed two crime novels. The first, *Death in the Cloisters*, has currently been rejected by fifteen literary agents. The second, *The Abbot's Secret*, is languishing on his computer and he has started a third, *Flat White Murder*, hoping the move away from the monastery will make his work more commercial. The trouble is, having killed the coffee shop proprietor in the first chapter, he has nowhere else to go and no one to tell the story. The attempt to invent a Harbinder-esque detective has fallen flat because Benedict has no real idea how the police go about solving crimes. He could ask Harbinder, of course, but he cringes at the thought. 'Are you Shoreham's Agatha Christie now, Ben?' Also, he thinks that, having investigated a previous case involving crime writers, Harbinder is now probably prejudiced against the genre. Natalka would be *too* helpful, offering plot ideas and probably insisting on the inclusion of a beautiful Ukrainian. Edwin would criticise his grammar. No, it's easier for his writing to remain a secret for now.

Benedict wonders idly what his parents would say if they knew. They'd be impressed if he actually got a book published. Correction: they'd be impressed if he got a book published *and* it was a bestseller. Otherwise, Hugo, Benedict's financial wizard brother, would create a spreadsheet proving that, once the advance had been earned out, and after agent's fees and bookshop reductions,

Benedict's earnings amount to approximately twenty-two pounds and thirty-six pence. Benedict's super-capable sister, Emily, would sigh and ask when he was going to join the real world. Benedict's family had been shocked by his decision to become a monk. They were Catholic but only in the most tangential sense – palm crosses at Easter and midnight mass on Christmas Eve. 'You shouldn't take it so seriously,' Benedict's mother told him when he expressed a wish to give up meat for Lent. Well, typically, Benedict had taken it far too seriously but, when he left the monastery, his parents seemed disappointed all over again. They had helped him buy the Shack but having a barista son was not the same as having a barrister daughter.

The arrival of Natalka had helped. Hugo had actually exclaimed, almost angrily, 'How did *you* find someone like *her*?' Benedict's parents had been delighted to see him with a beautiful and intelligent woman. True, she ran a care agency, which wasn't something that impressed them at the rotary club, but she was an entrepreneur in her own way. But, recently, Benedict has noticed a faint impatience even with his trophy girlfriend. His mother had started mentioning marriage and grandchildren. Hugo and his equally scary wife, Celia, had produced two, and even Emily found time in her schedule for one. Only Benedict was letting the side down again.

Edwin's obsession with Malcolm Collins, the writer who predeceased his subjects, has made Benedict wonder how his own obituary would read.

'Benedict Cole was born in Arundel in 1987. His father, David, was a civil engineer who worked in Dubai for long periods of his career. His mother, Angela, was an ex-nurse who, upon marriage, devoted herself to her family. Benedict's school career was undistinguished. He didn't shine academically or athletically like his older brother Hugo, who became a city banker, or his sister Emily, a barrister. The family were Catholic but, even so, Benedict's parents were shocked when, aged eighteen, he announced his intention of becoming a priest. After studying at the seminary in Wonersh, Benedict was transferred to Rome where he made the decision to become a Benedictine monk. After six years, Benedict left the order to run a coffee shack on Shoreham beach . . .'

What would come next? The personal stuff usually comes at the end. 'Benedict is survived by his wife, Natalka, and their three children: Edwin, Maria and Valentyna.' But that is far too presumptuous. Benedict has never broached the subject of marriage with Natalka, who often says that she disapproves of the institution, despite possessing an ex-husband. And she'd never name a daughter after her mother.

'Benedict was in a relationship with Natalka Kolisnyk, who was far too good for him. She eventually left him for an Italian racing driver. Benedict continued to run the Shack, where he was a well-known local figure known as Crazy Benny, until his death at the age of eighty-three.' But that's far too morbid and, out of respect for Edwin, he ought to make himself live a little longer.

'Benedict Cole's first novel *Flat White Murder* was a *Sunday Times* bestseller. His "Coffee Shack" books were made into a successful TV series starring Andrew Scott and Nicola Walker. Benedict is survived by his brother and sister and several nieces and nephews.'

That was better, if still a bit sad. The good thing about writing a book must be that something of you survives, even if only in charity shops. Benedict loves finding old crime novels on second-hand stalls. But, without a book and without a wife and children, what will be left of the essence that is Benedict Sebastian Cole? It's possibly a godsend that a customer disturbs this reverie, even if they are requesting something called a caramel latte.

It turns out that not all Benedict's sandwiches are destined for the food bank. At two-thirty, Natalka turns up, flanked by two women.

'Lydia and Cecile.' Natalka performs brief introductions. 'They were Melody's writing friends.'

Benedict provides one hummus wrap, one tuna mayo sandwich and one roast beef salad (Natalka). The women already seem to be fast friends but Natalka gestures for him to join them.

'Lydia writes crime fiction and Cecile writes children's books. They both belong to Melody's writing group.'

'What a successful writing group,' says Benedict. He had a vague idea that such groups were for people who wanted to get published and somehow never achieved it.

'It wasn't really a writing group,' says Cecile, who has short blonde hair and (disappointingly) no trace of a French accent. 'It was more of a support group.'

Both women laugh. Lydia, who has wild curls of dark red hair, says, 'We meet every week for coffee and once a month for a meal. But it's more a chance to complain about our publishers, agents and husbands. It won't be the same without Melody.' She takes a sad bite of her wrap.

'Did Melody complain about her husband?' asks Benedict.

'That's what Natalka asked,' says Cecile. 'But she never did. Melody and Alan seemed very happy together. He was always very pleasant when we went to their house. He'd cook the meal and then make himself scarce. Very tactful.'

'I'll tell you who Melody did complain about,' says Lydia. 'Her daughters. Crotchet and Quaver. Goneril and Regan. Whatever they're called. They were always wanting something.'

'Like what?' says Natalka.

'Like money. Like Melody dropping everything to look after their kids. I mean, she had a job to do. Being a writer doesn't mean you're free all day.'

This sounds like something Lydia has said many times before.

'Why would they want money?' asks Natalka.

'To go skiing, to fund their husbands' business schemes,' says Cecile. 'You name it. To be fair, Melody hardly ever gave in. She wasn't a pushover.'

'Do you think there was anything suspicious in her death?' asks Benedict.

'It never occurred to me,' says Lydia. 'And I'm a crime writer. But real life isn't like the books. Melody had a heart attack. It happens.'

Benedict agrees that it does. Always suggestable, he feels that his own heart is beating faster. He asks if the two women have heard of a writer called Donna Parsons.

'I don't think so,' says Lydia. 'What sort of thing does she write?'

'Romance,' says Benedict. 'Donna was a pseudonym for Don Parsons, a vicar.'

'I think I heard about that,' says Cecile. 'Haven't men taken enough from us without stealing our names?'

'I suppose it was fiction,' says Benedict.

'There's no such thing as fiction,' says Lydia. Which seems the opposite of what she was saying a few seconds ago.

★

Benedict is closing the shutters on the Shack when Edwin appears, still in his deerstalker.

'Hallo.' Benedict is very pleased to see him. 'Shall I open up again?'

'No thanks, dear boy. I've had enough caffeine for the day. Guess what I've found out?'

'What?' Benedict envies Edwin his look of achievement. His eyes gleam, although this could be cataracts.

'Malcolm Collins went to Battle House too. I had a look at the comments on the website. Well, that was too good a clue to miss so I contacted an old friend, Basil Hopkins, who used to work for the *Guardian*. Basil remembered Malcolm well. He was the arts correspondent for a time and often ended up writing obituaries for writers, musicians and artists. Basil says it's normal to have these things ready in advance, especially if the person is sick or old. Then you just update them on the day. He said the most important thing is checking that the person is actually dead.'

'I can see why that would be important.'

'Basil was the one who actually completed the obit for Chips Walker, you remember, the producer I knew? But Malcolm had written most of it. I suppose he knew that Chips was ill. Even though he was only eighty-five.'

'No age,' says Benedict obediently.

'But the interesting thing is that Malcolm died in November 2021. And, just before he died, he went on a retreat. Guess where?'

'Battle House?'

'Got it in one. And Basil said that Malcolm came back buzzing with ideas for a book. He got the idea that it was based on someone he'd met on the retreat. But, a few weeks later, Malcolm was dead.'

Edwin looks at Benedict, head on one side.

'Oh, all right then,' says Benedict. 'Let's book our writing weekend.'

Chapter 7

Harbinder: don't forget the dead

Harbinder is not really sure what she's expecting when she knocks on the door of the house in Kensal Rise. She can hear Mette's voice, amused but also slightly disapproving: 'You don't drop everything just because the assassin wants you to.' 'I'm just following up on a lead,' Harbinder had protested but she knew this wasn't the whole truth. Natalka had sparked her imagination – often a dangerous thing for a detective – but she had also reminded Harbinder of the suspicious death that had first introduced her to the Shoreham crew. It had been a complicated and difficult case but it had also provided the impetus for Harbinder to seek promotion and move to London. That path had, ultimately, led to Mette, so Harbinder feels she owes Natalka something. Or is she just missing home and her friends?

Harbinder first visited the house on Shirley Road two weeks ago. Eighty-year-old Eileen O'Rourke had been found by her daughter, lying in a pool of blood on her kitchen floor. It had certainly looked like a crime scene and the attending officer had, in Harbinder's opinion, been quite right to call in CID. Harbinder had classified the death as 'unexplained' and there had been a full crime scene investigation. But, when the post-mortem results came in, they pointed to natural death. Heart attack, bloodshed caused by Eileen's head hitting the terracotta tiles as she fell. Case closed. But, before the files were stamped – electronically these days – Eileen's daughter, Felicity Briggs, turned up at the police station to claim that her mother's death was caused by 'evil vibrations' from her latest book, *My Name is Jack*, an 'autobiography' of Jack the Ripper. Felicity ended up talking to DS Kim Manning, which was lucky for her, because Harbinder's DS is a compassionate woman with long experience of eccentric witnesses. Kim had listened and taken notes. Eileen had received some criticism on social media after the book was published but, apart from one distressing encounter with an angry reader in a shop, there seemed no evidence that anyone had wished the author any real harm. Felicity hasn't been in contact again since the 'natural death' verdict but the words of Laura, the data analyst, about the woman killed by a ghost, have made Harbinder curious enough to meet the daughter. She's surprised by how normal she seems, a forty-something blonde in leggings and a soft grey hooded top that looks expensive. Felicity is now living in her mother's old home. Harbinder doesn't blame her. She's a great peruser of the property press and she knows that the handsome three-bedroom terrace house is worth approximately a million pounds.

Harbinder introduces herself. 'I believe you spoke to DS Kim Manning a week or so ago?'

'Oh yes,' says Felicity. 'She was nice. I mean, I could tell she thought I was nuts but she was nice about it.'

'Why don't you tell me what you told her?' suggests Harbinder.

Felicity looks surprised but she leads Harbinder into the beautiful kitchen (open shelves, exposed brick, bifold doors into the garden) that was also, of course, the place where Eileen was discovered in a pool of blood.

Felicity offers coffee and goes to crank up a professional-looking machine. As she does so, a white fluffy dog pads into the room as if sure of its reception.

'Cute,' says Harbinder. She's not very keen on dogs. Her parents have a German shepherd who seems to dominate their lives. But this animal *is* cute. It's the creature's entire *raison d'être*.

'He was my mother's,' says Felicity, without much enthusiasm. 'He's called Willoughby.'

'Hi, Willoughby,' says Harbinder. The dog wags its excuse for a tail and goes to stand meaningfully beside its monogrammed bowl. Felicity tips in some biscuits and places a minuscule coffee cup in front of Harbinder. She can hardly get her fingers into the tiny handle.

'You told DS Manning that you thought your mother's death might be linked to her books,' she says, thinking this might be the most tactful way of putting it.

Felicity obviously sees through this because she laughs. Willoughby barks.

'I told DS Manning that I thought Jack the Ripper's ghost must have done it. I must have been going a bit mad. I'm sorry.'

Harbinder waits. Is this trail really going to end in such a disappointingly sane way?

'The thing is,' says Felicity, 'her last book was so different from the others. Mum wrote about true crime but always from the victim's point of view. That was her thing: don't forget the dead.

But this last one was written in the killer's voice. In Jack the Ripper's voice! It was horrible. Gruesome and misogynistic. I couldn't believe Mum had written it. But, of course, it was her bestseller.'

'God bless the great British public.'

'Yes, exactly. They can't get enough of that lovable Victorian butcher. The book sold really well. It was published a few years ago and it paid for all this.' She gestures at the granite and brick kitchen. 'But, almost immediately, Mum started to get all this social media interest. Lots of things on Facebook and Twitter. Well, some of them I agreed with. Articles by feminist academics saying that we should be talking about the dead women, not the killer. But some were horrible. Threatening to kill Mum. That sort of thing.'

'Did your mother keep records?'

'No. I don't think she would have known how to save a tweet or a Facebook post. There were a couple of actual letters and she shredded them. Why keep negative emanations around the place, she used to say. But, that's just it. It *was* negative. It was as if the whole house was poisoned. I know it sounds stupid but I used to think I could see the Ripper's shadow on the wall. Just over there.'

Harbinder doesn't turn to look but it's a close thing.

'Was your mother upset by the media interest?'

'She said she wasn't but I think she was. She bought a security system. She'd lived alone since my dad died when I was twenty but she started to say that the house was too big for her. I mean, Mum was tough. She'd been a journalist for years, working on all sorts of cases. It took a lot to spook her but I think she was spooked.'

'Did she think she was in danger?'

Felicity is silent for a moment, looking into her miniature coffee cup. 'I don't know but, when I saw her body on the floor, covered in blood, I thought: he's killed her.'

'He?' says Harbinder although she thinks she knows who they're talking about.

'Jack.'

'Jack the Ripper?'

'I know it sounds mad but it was all because of him. His malign influence. He killed her. Not in a literal sense but the effect was the same. Blood and death.'

'When you spoke to DS Manning, you said you thought that someone had actually murdered your mother.'

Felicity smiles but she looks embarrassed. 'I think I babbled on about Jack the Ripper himself doing it. I'm sorry to have wasted DS Manning's time. She must have thought I was mad. But it was just such a shock. I couldn't believe it. I mean, Mum had angina but she took pills for that. I never expected her to have a heart attack.'

Harbinder sympathises – she knows she expects her parents to live for ever – but, all the same, angina does seem a likely contributing factor.

'Can I ask you something?' she says. 'Did your mother know a woman called Melody Chambers? She was a writer too. Of romance.'

'I don't think so,' says Felicity. 'Mum didn't have many author friends. She thought of herself as a journalist, said literary types looked down on genre fiction. I've got a friend who's a crime writer and she says the same.'

'So she never went on a writers' retreat?'

Felicity gives her a curious look. 'What's this about? Are you saying that Mum's death *could* have been suspicious?'

'There's no reason to think your mum's death was from anything other than natural causes,' says Harbinder. 'I was just interested because Melody Chambers died recently. I'm looking for people who might have known her.'

'Died? Was she murdered?'

'I can't say any more. I'm sorry.' Harbinder stands up. 'Thank you for the coffee. I'll leave you in peace now.'

At the door, she asks if Felicity is now living permanently in Shirley Road.

'Yes. It's a really interesting area. Great shops. Very well connected.'

Harbinder notes that Jack the Ripper no longer casts his shadow on the wall.

Felicity had given Harbinder a copy of *My Name is Jack* and she takes it into the station as a curiosity. It's a hardback with a lurid-looking cover showing a man silhouetted in a doorway, the blood from his dagger forming the words of the title, spot-varnished drops dripping from the final K.

'Jack the Ripper?' says Jake. 'He was a famous artist. I watched a TV programme about it.'

'I don't think anyone really knows who he was,' says Harbinder.

'I love true crime books,' says Tory. 'It's one of the reasons I joined the police.'

Harbinder can believe this. She lives in hope that one day Tory will regret this decision.

Kim's reaction is the strongest. She turns the book over so she can't see the cover image. 'I bloody hate books about Jack the Ripper.'

'Why?' says Tory. 'I thought you were from the East End?'

'That's why I hate them,' says Kim. 'You know you can go on a Jack the Ripper tour? Actually go on a tour to see where the women were murdered. There's a Jack the Ripper museum too. No mention of the women he killed. Does anyone remember their names?'

Harbinder assumes this is a rhetorical question until Kim says, 'Anyone? One of their names?'

'Weren't they all prostitutes?' says Tory.

'Mary Ann Nichols,' says Kim, 'Annie Chapman, Elizabeth Stride, Catherine Eddowes, Mary Jane Kelly. And there's no evidence that they were prostitutes – or sex workers as I'm sure you were told to call them, Tory. And, even if they were, did they deserve to die? Did they deserve not to be remembered?'

Kim looks so fierce that Tory mutters something and backs out of the break room. Jake says, 'Chill out, Blondie,' and follows before Kim can retaliate. Harbinder is left alone with her sergeant.

'Sorry,' says Kim. 'I just feel strongly about it.'

'Don't apologise,' says Harbinder. 'You're right. Tell me, what did you make of Felicity Briggs?'

'She was obviously highly emotional,' says Kim, 'but that was understandable. She'd just found her mother dead on the kitchen floor. She said that it was all to do with that book.' She gestures at the hardback, still face down on the table. 'But she also said that someone had been hanging around the house in recent weeks and that her mother had been confronted by a woman in a bookshop who told her that she was a disgrace to feminism. I followed it up and Eileen, the mother, hadn't reported anything. I even went to the bookshop – it's called The Owl Service and it's very cool – and they couldn't remember the incident. Then the post-mortem came in and it was natural causes so I didn't go any further.'

'Fair enough,' says Harbinder. In fact, Kim had gone further than she needed to, further than Harbinder would have expected of her.

'Do you have any doubts about Eileen's death?' asks Kim. 'Is that why you went to see Felicity?'

'No,' says Harbinder slowly. 'I don't have doubts exactly. It does sound like a natural death. Eileen suffered from heart problems. It was just Natalka – my friend from Shoreham – mentioning another author's death. I wondered if they could be connected.'

Kim looks quizzical but, then, she has never met Natalka. Harbinder goes back to her office, taking the book with her because the sight of it seems to upset Kim so much. She, too, keeps it face down and, at some point in the day, starts to read the quotes on the back.

'Chilling.'

'Unbelievable.' That's a back-handed one, thinks Harbinder.

'Brings a gory chapter to life.'

'Inside the mind of a killer.'

'Well-written and empathetic.'

Harbinder looks at this last one again. Not only is its tone slightly different from the others but, through accident or design, it's printed in a smaller typeface. So small that the author's name is hardly visible.

Melody Chambers.

Chapter 8

Natalka: a good murder

'Let's go through your stories again,' says Natalka. 'I think you should limp, Benny.'

'Why?' says Benedict.

'It makes you look mysterious.'

'I'll forget and limp with the wrong leg,' says Benedict.

'I don't want to look any more decrepit than I am,' says Edwin. 'I'm hoping to pass for a spritely eighty.'

'And I don't know why we can't just be honest,' says Benedict.

'And say you're a private detective?' says Natalka. 'That's crazy. They'd chuck you out.'

'I'm not a private detective,' says Benedict. 'I sell coffee from a shack.'

Natalka thinks he sounds rather bitter (like his coffee some-times – ha!). They are at the Coffee Shack although the shutter is down and the blackboard with the prices on it – and sometimes a line of poetry – is packed away. It's one of Natalka's favourite times of the day. The golden hour, it's called in England. The period between sunset and dusk when the shadows are sharp and the sea and sky are a hundred different shades of blue. It's kind to faces too. Benedict looks troubled rather than sulky and Edwin noble rather than old.

Natalka is making sure Benedict and Edwin rehearse their aliases before their trip to Battle House tomorrow. Edwin is, in her opinion, very well-prepared.

'I've wanted to write all my life,' he tells them, in character. 'But, what with my job at the BBC and everything, I've never had the time. I've always scribbled down stories in the back of notebooks and, now that I'm retired, I want to have a proper go at writing a book. I've got the ideas. I just need the push to get started.'

'It takes more than time to become a writer,' says Benedict. Natalka thinks he's being very obstructive.

'This weekend is important,' she says. 'Battle House links Melody, Don and Malcolm. And I told you that Melody wrote a – what are they called? Blurb? – for that writer of Harbinder's. The woman who died. The Jack the Ripper woman.'

'I thought Harbinder said she died of natural causes,' says Benedict.

'That's what they said about Melody.'

'Well, maybe it's true.'

Natalka takes a breath of sea-scented air. She's determined not to lose her temper.

'Her daughters think she was murdered,' she says, 'and Don's friend Richard thinks *he* was murdered. They've paid us to investigate. And that's what we should do.'

'Besides,' says Edwin, 'it'll be fun.'

Benedict groans and runs his hands through his hair. 'I'm sorry. It's just I hate all this . . . all these false pretences.'

'It's only a very mild lie,' says Edwin. 'I don't think even Father Brendan would count it. After all, we *are* both interested in books and writing.'

Father Brendan is the parish priest at the church attended by Edwin and Benedict. Natalka has met him a few times in the course of her care work. He's very good at attending deathbeds.

'What sort of books are you interested in writing, Edwin?' says Natalka. 'I'm being one of the tutors,' she adds.

'Crime fiction,' says Edwin immediately. 'I love a good murder.'

Natalka laughs but then she sees Benedict's face. He looks positively shocked.

'Lighten up,' she says. 'It's funny. 'Besides, one of the tutors, Imogen Blythe, is a crime writer. That should appeal to her. What sort of books are you going to say you write, Benny?'

'I don't know,' says Benedict.

Natalka is just about to lose it when Edwin says, 'That's a good answer. An honest answer. After all, we've come on the weekend to find out what sort of writers we are. What did it say on the advertisement? "Start your writing journey today. No experience necessary."'

'Just as well,' says Benedict. 'I wonder what the other students will be like?'

'The house only sleeps eight,' says Edwin. 'So there won't be that many of them. Six students and the two tutors – Leonard Norris and Imogen Blythe. I wonder whether one of us should have read Leonard's book to prepare. I couldn't face it somehow.'

'Remember to ask about Melody and Don,' says Natalka. 'But make it sound natural. Benny, you can say you were a friend of

Don's. Edwin, maybe you knew Melody from the library or a writers' group.'

'We'll think of something,' says Edwin. 'I'm looking forward to it. I'm going to go home and pack my most writerly clothes. What time's the train, Benedict?'

'You can take my car if you want,' says Natalka. No one can say that she's not supporting her fellow sleuths. She'd love to go to Battle House but doesn't think she could pull off the writer thing. 'Besides,' Edwin told her, 'we're meant to be undercover and people always remember you because of being so beautiful.' Natalka sees his point.

'You'll need it,' says Benedict. 'To take Valentyna to mass and so on.'

Other evidence of Natalka's saintliness is that this weekend is Orthodox Easter. Valentyna will want to attend church – there's a Ukrainian priest in Rottingdean – make *paska*, decorate eggs and cook mounds of traditional Easter food. Natalka has little patience with religion at the best of times but this Easter, with Dmytro in the middle of a war, will require almost Christ-like levels of patiently borne suffering.

'Your reward will be in heaven,' says Edwin, reading her mind as he sometimes does.

'That's a great comfort,' says Natalka.

Back at the flat Valentyna is cooking supper but she has already assembled some provisions from the Polish market. Benedict is full of questions about Easter food

'We'll save some for you,' Valentyna tells him. 'You'll be back on Sunday night. I want you to try *holubtsi*.'

'That's the meat wrapped in cabbage leaves, isn't it?' says Benedict. 'I'm looking forward to it. The olivier salad too.'

'I'm going to make *paska* tomorrow,' says Valentyna. 'Shall I give some to John and Brenda next door, Talia?'

'No,' says Natalka. It's traditional to offer *paska*, Ukrainian Easter bread, to your neighbours but Natalka doesn't think she can bear the chorus of, 'Oh, how quaint! Isn't it terrible what's happening in your country? We can hardly bear to watch the news.' She has nothing against her neighbours but she wants to keep it that way.

After supper, Natalka leaves Benedict and Valentyna watching *The Repair Shop* and goes into her bedroom to do some work. She can't understand why you would watch a programme about mending old clocks and ornaments. They don't even sell the things for a profit afterwards. Her dad used to think he was good at fixing things. Natalka can still remember the new wheels he added to her scooter. They were too big and jacked it up like an American racer. She'd been delighted at the time, though, mug that she was. Only a year later, her father had left his family.

Natalka opens her laptop. She is in the process of researching Melody Chambers and her family. Facebook is where she usually starts. A few days ago, she found Alan Franklin's page. He hasn't posted for six years but it told her that he was born in Hayes, Middlesex, and studied pharmacy at the University of Greenwich. There were no other personal details and his last post was about Brexit (he's a Remainer). Natalka checked his contacts and sent a couple of friend requests to the most likely ones. Two accepted her, which surprised Natalka. Beware of blonde foreign-sounding women, she wants to tell them. They were both at university with Alan. Arjan is from Glasgow, married with several children. He mostly posts about politics and the family's labradoodle. Steve is from Bradford but lives in London. He only posts about football. Natalka checks on them both daily but, unless there's a pharmacists' reunion, she's not sure how much use these contacts will be.

Melody's Facebook page still exists. Her daughters haven't posted about her death or turned it into a memorial. It's poignant to see the photos of her books and her spaniel, the comments to ailing friends ('thinking of u hon') or celebrating grandparents ('congrats to all!!'). Melody joined the social media site in 2008. Natalka's not sure when she married Alan but he starts to appear in photographs from about 2016, mostly in the background of dog posts. There's an elderly Labrador in several pictures and, in 2019, 'Frodo!' and a photo of a spaniel puppy. There are no pictures of Tony, Melody's first husband.

Harmony and Minnie both have Facebook pages. Minnie's is full of pictures of her children. Natalka hopes that, when they grow up, the children will sue their mother for breach of their privacy. There's even a photo of a milk tooth, bloody and revolting, on someone's palm. Caption: 'Tooth Fairy coming tonight.' Natalka is very tempted to add a vomit emoji. Harmony posts less; a few of her garden, a courtyard full of tasteful plants and statuary, and one of her arm-in-arm with a man who must be her husband. 'Twenty years and counting.' Followed by several hearts. Honestly, some people are just asking to get divorced.

'Hi.' Benedict appears in the doorway. 'How are you doing?'

'OK. People's Facebook pages make me sick.'

'You should see Celia's. It's like an advertisement for being middle class.' Celia is Benedict's sister-in-law. She has made a few overtures of friendship towards Natalka and she accepted some of the invitations, mostly out of curiosity. A morning at a spa that smelt of lemongrass and despair, Ladies Day at Ascot and an evening with her 'girlfriends' where they drank Prosecco and complained about their husbands. The whole experience left Natalka feeling profoundly grateful that she was with Benedict and not his brother.

'I can't imagine sharing stuff about my life,' says Natalka.

'You're a secret agent at heart,' says Benedict. He says it lightly but he must know that there's some truth behind the words. When Natalka first left Ukraine, she was also escaping.

'You're not on Facebook either,' says Natalka.

'Only because there's nothing interesting about me,' says Benedict. 'Why don't you stop working and watch TV? There's a programme about a serial killer.'

'Now you're talking,' says Natalka.

Chapter 9

Benedict: battle stations

'Battle station,' says Edwin. 'Battle stations. Get it?'

He's been making the same joke throughout the extremely tedious train journey, changing at Brighton and St Leonard's Warrior Square.

'I get it,' says Benedict. 'Have you got a contact number for the retreat? Didn't they say that someone would meet us at the station?'

Battle is one of those branch stations that looks as if it's the end of the line, possibly the end of the world. Two platforms, linked by a bridge, the tracks stretching into infinity and, after the St Leonard's train has moved away, an eerie silence, broken only by birdsong. Benedict carries his own bag and Edwin's wheelie suitcase over the bridge. There's not a soul to be seen. They were the only people to alight at Battle and there are no cars in the car park. Benedict stares, rather desperately, at the bus timetable. It's only six p.m. but the last bus left an hour ago.

'What about an Uber?' says Edwin, who's an old urbanite at heart.

'I haven't got the app. Have you?' Natalka has but Natalka is miles away in Shoreham, though not as far as the trains made it seem.

'Can you look up local taxi firms?' says Edwin, now sitting on his suitcase. 'I think Battle House is only a couple of miles away.'

Can't you look them up? Benedict wants to say. Aren't you the one who's meant to be the silver surfer? But, instead, he clicks on his phone. He's just typing in 'taxi near me' when there's the sound of a car approaching and a voice says, 'Mr Cole? Mr Fitzgerald?'

A woman is leaning from the window of a Range Rover. Not a smart, yummy-mummy Range Rover, but the authentic farmyard version, with mud on the wheels and a retriever in the back.

'Yes,' says Benedict. Edwin is already opening the rear door.

'I'm Georgina from Battle House,' says the woman, getting out of the car. She's a tall blonde in jeans and authentic-looking wellingtons. She makes short work of their cases, tossing them into the boot with a casual 'Stay, Buster!' to the dog. Benedict feels that he has been overpowered by a stronger personality, a sensation that is both pleasant and slightly alarming. He gets into the front seat as Georgina drives off in a series of jerky gear changes.

'Sorry. I'm used to my little automatic. This is David's car really.'

Benedict wonders if they're meant to know who David is. He asks if Battle House is full this weekend.

'I think so. I don't really get involved in the courses. David and I own the house, but we live in the farm up the road. Is Buster bothering you?' This last to Edwin, who has the dog breathing in his ear.

'Not at all. Friendly old fellow.'

'I expect most people come by car,' says Benedict. He really should have his own car. *Ridiculous, a man of your age going by public transport*, says the voice in his head that is a mixture of Hugo and his father.

'No, I was saying to Leonard only the other day, it's funny how lots of authors can't drive.'

'I can drive,' say Benedict and Edwin in unison. Georgina laughs as if this is a joke. They are travelling along a tree-lined lane. Benedict watches the speedometer move to fifty. Buster whines from the back.

Benedict closes his eyes and, when he opens them again, they are bumping along a track through a wood: bracken, log stacks, signs warning of deer and the dangers of fire. Then the Range Rover turns a corner and Battle House stands in front of them. The spring afternoon is still sunny but the house is in shadow. The small windows give the façade a closed, sullen look. With a nice sense of atmosphere, the rooks start cawing in the trees.

'Reminds me of the parsonage at Haworth,' says Edwin, buttoning up his jacket.

'Not a great omen.'

'Well, it is if you're thinking about writing,' says Edwin.

Georgina helps Benedict get the bags out of the boot. Then she strides to the door and knocks loudly. Buster disappears around the side of the house, nose down in hunting mode.

'Hallo!' The man appears so quickly that Benedict suspects he was lying in wait. He recognises Leonard Norris from his publicity photos, although this version is a good ten years older.

'Come in. Come in. I'm Leonard, one of your hosts.'

Benedict and Edwin introduce themselves and Georgina exits with a cheery, 'Good luck!' Benedict wonders to whom this is addressed. They are in a large, square hall with a staircase in front of them. A stained-glass window provides diffuse, ecclesiastical light. A grandfather clock ticks meaningfully in the background.

'Your other host is Imogen, but she's teaching at the moment. Now,' Leonard goes to a roll-top desk and takes out two keys, 'Benedict, you're in Duncan Grant.' Edwin laughs and turns it, unsuccessfully, into a cough. 'Edwin, you're Enid Bagnold. Supper is at seven-thirty. Peter and Frances are on duty, so it'll be a good one.'

Benedict and Edwin exchange glances. It had never occurred to them that the guests would be expected to cook.

Benedict is relieved to see that his room is large and comfortable with all the essentials of a hotel room: en-suite bathroom, tea-making facilities, blackout blinds and a plug close enough to the bed for him to be able to charge his phone while he sleeps. The bedspread and curtains are a rather frenzied version of a William Morris print and there's an etching of the fishing net huts at Hastings over the bed. Benedict fills the mini kettle and switches it on to boil, then goes to inspect the view. The windows are bigger at the back of the house and they show a walled kitchen garden and a rather untidy lawn with a hammock stretched between two trees. Otherwise the forest looms as if it has reluctantly allowed the house this small clearing in its ranks. It's not a cosy prospect, exactly.

Benedict feels more cheerful after a cup of tea. There's proper china too, and home-made biscuits. He lies down on the bed and scrolls through his phone. He hasn't even done Wordle yet. He's still stuck on five when a text from Edwin pops up. 'Supper ?' Why do old people always put a space before a question mark or exclamation point?

'Coming!' Benedict texts back.

Edwin is waiting on the landing. He has swapped his cardigan for a tweed jacket, shirt and bow tie. Benedict feels underdressed in comparison. He knows that his blue jumper is unravelling slightly at the hem.

'Got it in three,' is Edwin's greeting. 'Rather an easy one today.'

Benedict is tempted to ask for a clue but feels that would give Edwin too much satisfaction.

They follow the cooking smells along a corridor to a large kitchen. The low ceiling and hanging herbs give the impression of entering a woodland glade. The Forest of Arden? *Sermons in stones and good in everything*.

'Welcome!' The voice belongs to Leonard Norris but his face is lost in a clump of thyme. 'Everyone. This is Benedict and Edwin.'

'Well met,' says Edwin. Has he also been thinking along Shake-spearean lines? Benedict wonders what the other writers will make of the new arrivals. Surely the age difference is too great for them to be a couple? Do they look like father and son? Uncle and nephew?

'Hi!' A small woman with closely cropped brown hair pops up from the table. 'I'm Imogen Blythe, the other tutor. Let me pour you a drink and then we'll do introductions. Red, white, beer?'

Benedict and Edwin both ask for white wine. Imogen pours generous glasses whilst telling them that she writes 'crime stuff mostly'. This is self-deprecation because Imogen is a well-known writer, often seen on the bestseller lists. Benedict has read several of her books about folk-singing detective Samantha Copper. He remembers, with a stab of guilt, that he gave the latest only three stars on Goodreads.

'Peter and Frances are doing the cooking today,' says Imogen.

'Peter's a children's author. Wonderful stuff. And Frances is a fab poet.'

A man with a grey crew cut and a woman with long white hair wave from the Aga.

'And this is Sue, who writes short stories.' A narrow face framed by dark hair peeps from behind the herbs.

'And Johnnie, who's another crime writer.'

It's a moment before Benedict registers that Johnnie is a woman. She has a tanned face and short grey hair. She's the only one who shakes hands and it's a formidable grip.

'Imogen's too kind,' she says. 'I'm not published yet. Probably never will be.'

'I write crime too,' says Edwin. 'Also unpublished. Sadly.'

It was a shock when Edwin announced that his alias would be that of a crime writer. Benedict, who had been about to come clean about his unpublished manuscripts, was forced to fall back on a nebulous literary persona.

'I don't know what I write really,' he says now.

'That might be one of the things you find out this weekend,' says Imogen. 'And it's not about getting published,' she says, with a note of rebuke, 'it's about telling your story.'

'And getting a two-mil advance,' says Johnnie, clinking glasses with Edwin.

The vegetable terrine is much praised but Benedict thinks it's rather tasteless. Edwin is particularly admiring but Benedict notices that he doesn't eat much and hides his couscous under the moulded vegetables. Benedict isn't too worried because he knows Edwin prefers to eat at midday but he is rather concerned when his friend lets Imogen fill up his glass again. Is that his third or fourth? Benedict tries to catch Edwin's eye but he looks away, deliberately, Benedict thinks.

'I wonder if you knew a friend of ours?' Edwin asks Imogen over the cheese and biscuits. 'Melody Chambers. She died recently. Very tragic.'

Benedict is alarmed. They had agreed that they would tackle Leonard and Imogen individually about Melody and Don. To do so over a crowded table seems bordering on reckless.

'Oh, I loved Melody,' says Imogen. 'She came here a few times. She was lovely, wasn't she, Len?'

'Lovely,' agrees Leonard. He's been quiet during the meal but this could be because he hasn't drunk any wine. Benedict wonders whether he's an alcoholic. Not that you need a reason to abstain. Benedict was an expert on abstention in his time. But there's something rather watchful and sad about Leonard's face as he sips his elderflower cordial.

'I met her husband recently,' says Edwin. 'He's devastated, of course.'

'I never met her husband,' says Imogen. 'Her daughter came once.'

'Which daughter?' asks Edwin, cutting a minuscule sliver of pecorino.

'Harmony,' says Imogen. 'She was nice. She even joined my book club for a while.'

'Harmony and Melody,' says Peter. 'How ridiculous.'

'There's a sister called Minim,' says Edwin. Benedict gives him a look. This is betraying too much inside information. But no one seems to notice and a lively discussion about pen names follows.

'I'm choosing a pseudonym,' says Sue. 'Something exotic like Seraphina.'

'I'm going to keep Johnnie Newton,' says Johnnie. 'Useful to have a gen neut name.'

After a few seconds Benedict decodes this as 'gender neutral'. He decides this is his cue. 'I had a friend called Don who published as Donna. It's not usually that way round, is it? Think of George Eliot and the Brontës. Acton Bell and all that.' He realises that he's rambling and stops talking, with some difficulty. Across the table, Edwin raises an eyebrow.

'Don Parsons?' says Imogen. 'He came here too. But wasn't he a vicar?'

'So was I once,' says Benedict. 'Well, a priest. A monk.'

This, of course, is far too interesting. The table erupts into questions. What's it like to be a monk? Did he have to wear robes? Chant? Flagellate himself? Benedict is so flustered that he allows Imogen to fill his glass again.

'I loved being a monk,' he says, aware that he's slurring slightly. 'The community, the prayers, the gardening.' Why did he say gardening? 'But then I realised that I wanted to have a partner and a family, maybe even get married, so I had to leave.'

'And did you?' asks Imogen. 'Get married, I mean.'

'No,' says Benedict. This suddenly strikes him as very sad.

'But you've got a lovely girlfriend,' says Edwin. Benedict turns and is surprised to see Edwin sitting next to him. The dots on his bow tie seem to be moving.

'She is lovely,' he says, 'isn't she?'

'If you find someone you love,' says Sue, 'stick to them like glue.'

This is almost the first thing Sue has said all evening. It strikes Benedict as very emphatic.

'Stalker alert!' Johnnie's loud laugh seems to be coming from very far away.

'Don't bother about love,' says Leonard, 'concentrate on writing.'

'The two aren't mutually exclusive,' laughs Imogen. 'I've managed to crank out a few books whilst remaining happily married.'

Benedict takes a gulp of water, trying to sober up. He knows that he should be listening intently to these possible clues.

'It was sad Don didn't find love,' he says.

'He seemed slightly asexual to me,' says Imogen.

'I don't know,' says Leonard. 'I thought there was something odd about him.'

'In. What. Way?' says Benedict. Trying not to slur, he only succeeds in sounding aggressively staccato.

'Like he was trying to hide something,' says Leonard.

'We're all trying to hide something,' says Imogen. 'We're writers, after all.'

This strikes Benedict as a very significant remark but he's had too much wine to work out why. He takes another sip of water and listens to the conversation eddying and swirling in a way that makes him feel slightly sick. Then Imogen says something about not staying up too late on the first night. People start to stand up and say goodnight. Benedict closes his eyes.

'Benedict. Time for bed.' The voice sounds fatherly, which means it couldn't possibly be Benedict's father. He opens his eyes. The kitchen is almost empty. It's just Edwin, Benedict and the herbs.

'I must have dropped off for a minute,' says Benedict.

'It's been a long day,' says Edwin.

'I'll take a glass of water to bed with me,' says Benedict.

'Good idea,' says Edwin.

Benedict gets up and manages to walk fairly steadily to the sink. He turns on the tap, which is either retro or genuinely rusty. He's waiting for the water to get cold when there's a sound at the door. Benedict swivels round to see Sue, already dressed for bed in pyjamas and blue dressing gown.

'I just wanted to say,' she says, 'I know it's your first time here, but you need to be a bit wary of Imogen.'

'Wary?' says Edwin. 'In what way?'

But the vision in blue has disappeared.

Chapter 10

Edwin: deep water

Edwin wakes to the sound of birdsong. Even as this phrase occurs to him, he thinks it's the wrong one. He's woken by a pandemonium of birds. A chaos, a clamour, a racket. A gang of football hooligans couldn't have made a more uncivilised uproar. There's one particular avian who sounds like he's blowing a whistle on a picket line. Edwin's been on a few marches in his time. *Maggie, Maggie, Maggie. Out, out, out.* He looks at his travelling alarm clock. Six a.m. He might as well get up.

Edwin pads to the bathroom in his slippers. His essential travel kit – towelling slippers, alarm clock, emergency teabags, aspirin and Gaviscon – hasn't changed much since his BBC days. He used to bring a transistor radio but now his phone provides Radio 4 at the touch of a button and the kit includes two chargers and an extra-long wire. As it's Saturday, there's no *Today* programme yet, just two women talking earnestly about farming. Edwin feels that he's had enough of the countryside and switches to Radio 3. As Benedict often tells him, Edwin is a townie at heart. He was born in Surrey, an unsatisfactory liminal zone between urban and rural, and went to prep and boarding school in Yorkshire. But, as soon as he could, he escaped to London, sidestepping both university (his parents' ambition for him) and music college (his own). He joined the BBC as a trainee and worked his way up. Even now, his heart thrills at the sight of a black cab or a red bus. It was in London that he'd had his first relationship with a man. David from Sotheby's, specialising in ceramics. Edwin often thinks of him when he watches *Antiques Roadshow*; the sight of a porcelain plate can spark quite a reminiscent glow.

Edwin makes himself a cup of tea and sits on the window seat, listening to Mozart competing with the screaming birds, art definitely trumping nature. There's mist on the ground and the treetops emerge out of it, spiky and threatening. A dog barks, adding to the cacophony, and Edwin wonders if it's Buster, the retriever who had panted down his neck yesterday. As he watches, a figure appears from the house and crosses the lawn. Edwin recognises Sue by her black hair and slightly hunched posture. He remembers her sudden reappearance last night, the warning about Imogen, Benedict staring owlishly with the tap still running. Poor old Benedict, he really was quite squiffy. Edwin decides to get dressed and go for an early morning walk himself. Someone has got to do a bit of detecting around here.

The mist has almost cleared by the time Edwin opens the back door, wearing his jacket and scarf as protection against the early morning air. As he walks across the lawn, he can feel the wet grass through his suede shoes. Two apple trees, bowed down with blossom, give a triumphal, bridal look to the garden which, otherwise, seems rather unloved. The flower beds are overgrown, and a bird bath stands forlornly in the centre of a paved area where weeds are pushing up between the stones.

Even so, there's something rather primal and mysterious about being in a garden so near dawn. Edwin finds himself humming 'Morning has Broken' and thinking about Eden, the agony in the garden, Judas arriving with the soldiers to betray Christ. At the edge of the wood, Edwin looks back at the house. All the curtains are drawn but smoke is rising from the chimney so someone must be awake.

There's no sign of Sue but, earlier, she seemed to be heading for the wood so Edwin walks in that direction. A robin follows him, bright with curiosity. It's alarming how quickly the trees seem to close around him. Soon the house is no longer visible. At least he's now on a gravel path so his shoes are safe. It seems to be going downhill, zigzagging around trees and shrubs until it arrives, without any warning, at a large expanse of brackish water. Edwin stops, slightly out of breath. There's a woman in front of him, leaning forwards, her hair actually touching the dark water. It's a few seconds before he realises that this is a statue, its grey stone back mottled with lichen.

A voice says, 'Hallo.' Edwin swings round. Sue is sitting on a tree stump at the edge of the pond – or is it meant to be a lake?

'Good morning,' says Edwin. 'Sorry to disturb you.'

'I didn't think anyone would be up this early,' says Sue, rubbing her eyes. Edwin can see the track marks of tears on her face.

'I don't sleep very well,' says Edwin, lowering himself onto another stump. 'One of the curses of old age. Not that you'd know anything about that.' No harm in trying to be charming. He suspects that Sue's hair is dyed but, even so, she's at least twenty years younger than him.

'I don't sleep well either,' says Sue. She throws a stone into the water. The sound it makes seems disproportional to the size of the missile. Edwin watches the ripples widen. It's a strangely unattractive pond, sunless and sullen, its edges dark with trailing leaves. A sign, almost hidden by reeds, says, 'Deep Water'. Edwin can't imagine that it's the perfect place for a spot of nature contemplation.

'I lost my boyfriend a few months ago,' says Sue. 'I haven't slept well since then.. I thought it would be better here but . . . well, it isn't. It's worse if anything.'

'I'm so sorry to hear that,' says Edwin, trying to project interest and sympathy. Not easy when you're balancing on a tree stump.

'We came here last year,' says Sue. 'I thought it might be easier being somewhere where we'd been together. But with Malcolm . . .'

'Malcolm?' says Edwin, too sharply.

But Sue seems not to notice. She's talking into the air. 'With Malcolm it was different. We'd go walking in the woods and be full of ideas for our writing. Malcolm was going to write his book at last. I had at least a dozen short stories planned. I remember Imogen said . . .'

She stops. Edwin says, 'Last night you were saying something about Imogen . . .'

But Sue is looking beyond him. Edwin follows her gaze and sees a figure moving on the other side of the water. It walks towards them, hooded and menacing. A bird flies out of the trees, making them both jump.

'Hallo, Imogen,' says Sue.

'Hi.' Imogen is in dark leggings and hoodie. She has obviously been on her morning run and is panting gently.

'Lovely morning for it,' says Edwin. It strikes him as a very phatic, and very English, comment.

Imogen eyes them both and Edwin thinks she's on the verge of saying something. But then she looks at her watch, a clunky affair that probably monitors her steps and heart rate.

'I'd better go. I'm meant to be helping Len with the breakfasts.'

When Edwin enters the kitchen, Leonard is at the stove frying pancakes. 'Imogen and I do breakfasts,' he explains, demonstrating some rather expert flipping. 'There's a rota for the other meals. It's pinned up on the noticeboard.'

'We're doing Sunday lunch,' says Benedict, who is sitting at the table.

'There are provisions in the larder,' says Leonard, 'but if you want to cook something special, you can always pop into Battle. Now, what would you like, Edwin? Pancakes? Full English? Eggs? Bacon? All the other meals are vegetarian so now's your chance to have some meat. Or there's fruit and muesli on the table. And coffee in the cafetière.'

Edwin asks for bacon and a poached egg. The cooked breakfast smells delicious and he's not sure if his slightly wobbly back teeth can cope with nuts. Benedict, the only other person present, is already attacking the full English but, when he looks up at Edwin, his face is stricken. Edwin's heart flutters. Is it just a hangover or has Benedict had some bad news? Surely it can't just be the thought of cafetière coffee?

'Are you OK, dear boy?'

Benedict runs a hand through his hair. 'I've lost my streak.'

For a moment, Edwin doesn't understand.

'You've lost what?'

'My streak. At Wordle. I was stuck before we went to supper. I meant to get back to it before I went to sleep but I forgot. And now I'm back at zero.'

This last word is almost a wail. Edwin almost laughs but composes his face in time. 'Bad luck but it happens to us all in the end.'

'It hasn't happened to you.'

'No, but it will. And when it does, it will be quite a relief.' He crosses his fingers behind his back. Edwin is not going to lose his unblemished two hundred and fifty-three without a fight. It's the same with Duolingo, which he started during lockdown. He hasn't got any better at French but he's not going to lose his streak.

'You're up early, Edwin,' says Leonard, whisking boiling water before cracking an egg into it.

'I went for a walk in the grounds,' says Edwin. 'Lovely place.'

'It's going to rack and ruin,' says Leonard. 'The garden was beautiful when I first started coming here. Miriam still lived at Battle House then. Miriam Fry. Georgina's aunt. She was a poet and she used to invite writers here for weekends. It was magical. We'd swim in the lake and read our stories aloud by candlelight. I wrote most of *Hopes* here. Sometimes we'd just lie on the lawn and listen to opera. There's a really superior sound system in the drawing room.'

It's the warmest and most enthusiastic Leonard has ever sounded.

'I love opera,' says Edwin. 'Especially Verdi and Puccini.' It's been a long time since he's heard anyone say 'drawing room'.

'So do I,' says Leonard. 'The whole wonderful feeling of being swept along by fate. *La Forza del Destino*.'

'I love *La Forza*,' says Edwin. 'The overture is magical. So doom-laden and beautiful. But the opera's considered unlucky. Pavarotti refused to perform it for that reason.'

'Pavarotti.' Leonard dismisses the famous tenor with an appropriately Italianate hand gesture. 'I prefer Di Stefano. Anyway, those weekends with Miriam, they were the start of the retreats. Georgina and David only keep them going for the money. They're not interested in Art.' The word is definitely invested with a capital letter but Edwin assumes that money is also the reason why Leonard is flipping pancakes and teaching creative writing. It's been some years since he published a book, after all.

Leonard slides the perfect poached egg onto a piece of toast, adds a slice of bacon and some mushrooms and presents the plate to Edwin with a flourish.

'Thank you,' says Edwin. 'Looks delicious.'

'Did you see Imogen on your travels?' Leonard asks.

'Yes. She was coming back from a run.'

'We were meant to start prepping breakfast at seven,' says Leonard. The clock over the Aga hood says seven-thirty. Edwin knows, from the handout in his bedroom, that the day's activities start at nine-thirty with a 'sound walk'. He wonders where all the other writers are.

Imogen arrives just as Edwin is finishing his toast. She is followed by Sue, who has changed her clothes since Edwin saw her by the lake, and Johnnie, resplendent in a purple tracksuit.

'Sorry,' says Imogen to Leonard. 'Sorry. Sorry. I'll take over here. You grab some breakfast.'

'You're forgiven,' says Leonard, though he does not sound very forgiving.

Sue puts a tiny helping of yoghurt and muesli in a bowl. Johnnie expresses a preference for a 'big slap-up'.

'More coffee?' says Leonard, putting the kettle on. Edwin says yes, even though his last cup had tasted bitter and slightly rancid. This is a chance for more detecting.

Frances and Peter appear together, which makes Edwin wonder if they're a couple. Peter asks for a 'bacon butty' although he's not noticeably northern. Frances peels an apple and tells them about a dead crow she saw on the lawn.

'Its plumage was iridescent, shiny, life-enhancing. But its eyes were plucked clean away. Eyeless in Gaza. I might write a poem about it.' She eats a grape.

'The birds were very loud this morning,' says Edwin. He's not sure if he's offering this in sympathy with the crow or its attacker.

'That's what our first session will be about,' says Imogen from the Aga. 'We'll walk in the grounds just noting the sounds we hear. Our breath. Birdsong. Our feet on the grass.' Edwin glances at his shoes. He's changed into what he calls his 'trainers', fabric shoes with thick soles. He doesn't want to ruin another pair.

'Well, this bird wasn't about to sing,' says Frances.

Chapter 11

Benedict: overheard voices

Benedict thinks that he'll be good at the sound walk. At the monastery, every day had started with silent prayer. He woke up at five and often walked in the gardens before Vigils at six. He remembers feeling a great sense of oneness with nature that he hasn't been able to capture since. Sometimes he walks by the sea with Natalka but even the wind and the waves can't compete with her presence, which is all he is ever aware of. Today, he thinks, he will try to recapture that transcendental rapture. 'It's mindfulness for writers really,' Imogen said, when outlining the exercise. St Thérèse would approve, thinks Benedict. He finds a bench in the walled garden, sits down and closes his eyes.

But rapture evades him. He's conscious of his closed eyelids, of the eggs and bacon rearranging themselves in his stomach, of the sun beating down on his unprotected face. Natalka is very keen on suncream but he always forgets. He tries to concentrate on the birdsong. Skylarks. Rooks. A conversation chirping in the hedge beside him. But, instead of losing himself in the moment, his thoughts wander to Natalka finishing her morning rounds, talking cheerfully to her clients whilst helping them to dress or shower. Benedict knows some of her regulars from his days as a carer during the pandemic. Harriet, who knows the plot of every soap opera. Paddy, who lost a leg aged eighteen but still likes to joke about finding it one day. Freda, who sings snatches of opera in a soprano that is still surprisingly loud and true. A couple of his favourites died recently, which is one of the worst and most inevitable things about the job. After her rounds, Natalka will go for a run or a swim. Then she'll have lunch with Valentyna, borscht again or *okroshka*. Natalka and Benedict used to have lunch together in the Shack but Natalka knows her mother likes to make this meal for her. Then it's paperwork in the afternoon, maybe some evening rounds, supper, TV, night-time yoga. In the old days, the sight of Natalka in her lycra was often too much for Benedict and they'd make love on her yoga mat.

With difficulty, Benedict wrenches his mind away from sex and back to the wonders of nature. The birds are still chatting in the hedge but the skylark is no longer right above him. He can hear sounds from the house, doors slamming, Leonard's voice calling, 'Have you got the . . . ?' The answer is inaudible but then there's a laugh and another door opening and closing. Concentrate, Benedict tells himself. A mechanical whine coming from the wood, a dog barking, footsteps crunching over gravel. These seem to be coming closer. Benedict opens his eyes. The footsteps are on the other side of the wall. Then Benedict hears a male voice, presumably talking into a phone.

'Have you done it yet?'

Something staccato and sharp about the words makes Benedict think this isn't a casual Saturday morning call to a loved one.

'There's not much time,' says the voice. 'We have to be brutal. It's the only way.' Then, 'OK.' And again, 'OK, OK.' The footsteps speed up. Benedict stands up and then climbs carefully onto the bench. He sees Peter, the children's writer, hurrying away in the direction of the trees.

'Right,' says Imogen. 'Let's share.' She laughs, presumably at the shocked faces in front of her. 'Come on, there are no wrong answers. Benedict, what did you hear on your walk?'

Benedict clears his throat. He's sure that Imogen has asked him first because of the whole 'meditative monk' thing.

'Birds,' he says hoarsely. Imogen pauses for a second before saying, brightly, 'Did anyone else hear birds?'

'Skylark,' says someone. Imogen writes it on the flipchart. This, and an overhead projector, are the objects that turn the sitting room into a classroom. Otherwise the writers are seated casually on sofas and armchairs. Edwin, Benedict notes, has secured the most comfortable of these. Benedict is wedged into a sofa with Johnnie and Sue. Peter and Frances face them. Leonard is sitting at the upright piano as if he is about to lead them in a hymn, although the instrument looks as if it is locked.

'Rooks,' says Frances. 'I saw a dead one earlier.'

'Collared doves,' says Sue.

'Chiffchaffs,' offers Edwin. 'Such a nice onomatopoeic word.' There's a murmur of approval and assent. Benedict needs to suppress a feeling of what he knows is jealousy. He, the author of two and a half almost-complete books, can only come up with the pathetic 'birds' but Edwin, who only writes reports on erring husbands, is suddenly the darling of the room.

'Wheatears,' says Johnnie. 'From an old English word meaning "white arse". And blackbirds. *Turdus merula*.' She nudges Benedict in the ribs and grins around the room.

'Excellent,' says Imogen. 'Solidity of specification. Details anchor our narratives to reality.'

At the end of the sofa, Sue is earnestly writing this down.

Imogen continues. 'It's far more powerful to say, "I heard chiff-chaffs in the garden,"' she smiles at Edwin, 'than to say simply, "I heard birds singing." Of course, it depends on your character's point of view. If it was my husband, for example, he'd notice types of car, not species of birds.'

There's some laughter, which sounds sycophantic to Benedict.

'If you know some interesting folklore, as Johnnie obviously does,' Imogen continues, 'then this can help fix your story in time and place.'

They go on to discuss the distant whine of traffic, something Benedict hadn't heard, though apparently others had.

'In the UK, it's very hard to get away from that sound,' says Imogen. 'Remember, your setting doesn't have to be completely isolated in order to be sinister. The juxtaposition of so-called civilisation can bring added tension and atmosphere. Blackwater Park in *The Woman in White* is near the railway station and the village, yet it's a prison for Laura.'

'That's a great name, Blackwater,' says Edwin. 'I love Collins.'

'So do I,' says Imogen. 'There's no one better at atmosphere. Think of the Shivering Sand in *The Moonstone*.'

Benedict hasn't read Wilkie Collins for years – nor has Edwin, to his knowledge – but he remembers Marian Halcombe in *The Woman in White*, one of his favourite heroines, edging her way along a roof in the dark and overhearing the villains plotting her downfall.

'Overheard voices,' he says now. 'You can never quite make out the important words.'

This goes down better than 'birds' and there's a lively debate about whether mobile phones, EarPods and lack of social inhibition have made eavesdropping obsolete.

'My teens are *glued* to their phones,' says Imogen.

'Mine too,' says Frances. 'I have to text them if I want a reply.'

Benedict looks over at Peter, the supposed expert on children, who hasn't taken any part in the discussion. Peter is gazing into the distance, his expression unfathomable. In his head, Benedict replays the one-sided conversation he heard earlier.

Have you done it yet?

There's not much time.

We have to be brutal. It's the only way.

OK. OK. OK.

Before the coffee break, Imogen gives the authors their first writing task. She goes to the flipchart and writes: 'If only I hadn't . . .'

'Take this as your starting point,' she says, 'and write two to three hundred words, about a sheet of A4. Don't think too much about it. Just write. Leonard and I look forward to reading your pieces. I set this exercise every time but students always come up with something different.'

She smiles at Leonard, who seems to be concealing any excitement he might feel. The older writer has not taken any part in the first teaching session. Benedict wonders if this will be the pattern of the weekend: Imogen teaching and Leonard observing, maybe occasionally chipping in with a wise word. Not that any wisdom has been forthcoming yet. Leonard had seemed more at home making pancakes.

'You can go anywhere to write,' Imogen continues. 'There's the library and the smaller sitting room or you can go into the grounds or up to your room. Meet for lunch at one.'

In the kitchen, Benedict avoids the cafetière and makes himself a peppermint tea. He is surprised to see Edwin both drinking the vile coffee and chatting to Sue. When Benedict joins them, Sue is saying, 'Malcolm always said that journalists make the worst writers . . .' At the name 'Malcolm' Benedict looks at Edwin who gives an almost imperceptible nod.

'Had Malcolm finished his book?' asks Edwin, in his most sympathetic tones.

'No,' says Sue. 'That's what was so tragic. He'd only really made a few notes.'

'Do you have those?' says Edwin. 'Maybe you could carry on where he left off? What was it about?'

'It's hard to explain but basically it's about a musician—'

'A musician?' says Imogen, who is standing by the kettle. 'Like my Samantha Copper?'

'Oh no,' says Sue. 'Not a folk singer. A classical musician.'

There's a brief silence. 'I love the Samantha Copper books,' says Benedict.

Perhaps Imogen notices the insincerity because she gives him only a perfunctory smile before turning to address the room at large. 'You need to be getting on with your writing, people. You've only got two hours until lunch.'

Benedict goes upstairs to collect his laptop and is not surprised to see Edwin following him. They have a whispered conversation on the top landing.

'Was Sue talking about Malcolm Collins?'

'Yes! He was her boyfriend. They used to come here together. I met her by the lake this morning and she told me.'

'Did you ask what she meant about being wary of Imogen?'

'I was just about to when Imogen appeared. Gave me quite a jolt.'

'See if you can get Sue alone again. You seem to be getting on with her.'

'Just being a detective,' says Edwin.

Slightly stung, Benedict says, 'I heard something interesting this morning.' He repeats Peter's conversation. 'It sounded important. I mean, it didn't sound trivial.'

'Let's trail him too,' says Edwin. 'This is fun, isn't it?'

Benedict agrees that it is.

Armed with his laptop, Benedict descends the stairs. He plans to choose a strategic spot in the garden where he can write and keep an eye on his housemates. There's no one around as he crosses the hall. The grandfather clock ticks ponderously and a bee is buzzing somewhere in the rafters. Benedict leaves by the front door and skirts the house. He sees Sue in the small sitting room and hopes Edwin manages to join her there. Frances is on the bench by the kitchen garden scrolling through her phone. She doesn't seem to notice Benedict passing. He crosses the lawn and finds a wooden seat at the edge of the woods. From here he can see almost the entire house and gardens. There's a movement in one of the upstairs rooms and a curtain is drawn. Has someone nipped upstairs for a quick nap? The skylarks are still singing and a ginger cat appears from the undergrowth, tail puffed up in outrage. Benedict opens his laptop.

'If only I hadn't . . .'

If only he hadn't what? If only he hadn't entered the monastery? If only he hadn't waited almost a year before kissing Natalka? If only he hadn't packed too many T-shirts and not enough jumpers? None of these will do for his two hundred words.

Just write, Imogen had said. But Benedict can't think of a single word in the English language. He types 'If only' again and, trying to take himself by surprise, adds his name and Natalka's, then what he had for breakfast.

If only
Benedict
Natalka
Eggs, bacon, tomatoes, mushrooms.

It looks like the start of a poem but, although Benedict loves poetry, he's never tried writing any. If only he had. If only he could think of the next line. Maybe a quotation will help? But he can only think of hymns and prayers. Natalka always complains that, whatever Benedict starts singing in the shower, it always ends up as a hymn.

Oh Lord my God, when I in awesome wonder
Thine be the glory, risen conquering son
We blossom and flourish as leaves on a tree—

'How are you getting on?' Benedict jumps. He hadn't heard Johnnie approaching. Has she come from the house? Surely not or he'd have seen her purple tracksuit looming up.

'Not very well,' he confesses.

'Don't overthink it,' says Johnnie. 'I've already written mine.'

'Already?' Benedict looks at his watch. It's nearly twelve. Later than he thought but surely not enough time to have written a complete piece?

'I get on with things,' says Johnnie. 'You learn that when you've been in an institution. I'm off to prep lunch now. Toodle-pip.' And she strides away, following the woodland path.

Lunch, prepared by Sue and Johnnie, is quiche and salad. Benedict is relieved that it seems fairly basic so he and Edwin won't have too hard an act to follow. Benedict still feels full from breakfast so he doesn't eat much. He has a headache which he thinks is partly creative writing and partly hangover. He drinks a pint of water and surreptitiously slides some aspirin out of his pocket.

'Feeling under the weather?' It's Johnnie, proffering a basket of rolls.

'Just a bit of a headache.'

'Maybe it's hay fever,' says Sue. 'My eyes have been stinging.'

'Too early for hay fever,' says Johnnie.

'Maybe too much sun,' says Edwin, who is looking remarkably perky. 'Try and have a rest before the afternoon session. I had a little lie-down before lunch and it worked wonders.'

'Have you finished your piece?' Benedict can't help asking.

'Of course.' Edwin looks surprised.

'It was fun,' says Johnnie.

'I turned mine into a poem,' says Frances, sounding smug, as if poetry trumps prose.

'What about you, Peter?' Benedict thinks it might be time to bring the children's author into the conversation.

Peter looks startled to be addressed. 'I did it,' he says. 'Two hundred words are nothing to me. I write two thousand words every day.'

'I suppose kids' books are quite short,' says Johnnie.

'I don't write that sort of children's book,' says Peter. 'Flopsy Bunny meets the Calico Cat and they have tea with Mr Fox. I write about murder, drug abuse and cannibalism.'

'Goodness,' says Edwin. 'More quiche?' He passes the plate whilst managing to wink at Benedict, who forgives his friend for being the class goody-goody. Things would be a lot worse without Edwin.

The afternoon consists of Leonard lecturing them about character and motivation, which mostly involves criticising writers who have got it wrong. 'Don't deal in stereotypes like so-and-so, even though they do end up on so many shortlists; none of us understood the motivation in such-and-such, which must be the author's fault, not ours.' Benedict dozes, listening to the bees buzzing in the ivy. Through the open window comes the scent of grass and the faint drone of a lawnmower. After an hour of this, Imogen chips in, 'Why don't we listen to some of your writing from this morning?'

Benedict freezes. When no mention was made of the task, he had assumed it was forgotten, despite Imogen's earlier promise to read the pieces.

'Who wants to start?' says Imogen.

Benedict often finds himself volunteering for things, sometimes just to break an awkward silence. 'Don't put your hand up,' Natalka hisses at him, during residents' association meetings. There's no chance of him doing that now. He looks down at his feet.

'I'll go if you like.' Sue speaks up from the other end of the sofa. They have kept their same places from the morning. Benedict was amused to see the others leaving the best armchair for Edwin.

Sue opens her laptop and puts on a pair of glasses.

'If only I hadn't met Malcolm. I was, after all, well past the age of having a boyfriend. Even the word seems absurd when applied to us. I was fifty-five when we met, he was sixty. We met in a library. Of course we did. Shoreham Library on a wet Monday afternoon. I was exchanging books, he was using the microfiche. He loved old newspaper cuttings, did Malcolm. The librarian introduced us – our own teenage matchmaker – by saying, jokingly, that we were her best customers. I was embarrassed, I remember, thinking that she was implying we didn't have anything better to do. But the truth was, I didn't. I'd taken early retirement from my job as a primary school teacher. "You'll never be busier in your life," people said, but the truth was that I was bored and lonely. My only hobbies were reading and writing short stories, neither of which were exactly sociable. So when Malcolm looked up, smiled, and said, "Sounds like we have a lot in common," it was like manna from heaven.

'We went for a coffee (my mum always said it was common to say "a coffee" but she was a snob like that) and we talked. We met again the next day and the next. My mum said, "You've got a new beau," and the silly Scarlett O'Hara-ish word made me laugh. But really it wasn't until Mum died that Malcolm really became my boyfriend. I was suddenly free to spend the night with him, even to go on holiday together (Belgium and Italy). The best thing, though, was coming here, to Battle House, for weekend courses. We spent lockdown together and, honestly, I wish it had been longer. But I missed our writing weekends and, when Battle House opened again, for "socially distanced courses" with lots of handwashing and temperature checks at the door, we were the first to sign up. That was in October 2021 and, the first evening, Malcolm turned to me and said, "I know what my book is going to be about, a musician who's murdered by his own instrument." You must write it, I said. He died two weeks later. Now I suppose I'll have to write it. Now that I know the real story. If only I hadn't met him.'

There's a silence. The lawnmower has stopped and even the bees seem to be holding their breath. Benedict sneaks a look at Sue and she seems perfectly composed, taking off her glasses and holding them in her lap. Johnnie pats her shoulder, so hard that she jerks forward. Imogen looks across the room at Leonard before saying, 'I really enjoyed that, Sue. I liked the asides about your mum and Scarlett O'Hara. Maybe in a longer piece you could make more of that?'

Leonard speaks from the piano stool. 'Are you northern?' he asks.

Sue looks surprised. 'I was born in Halifax.'

'Thought so,' says Leonard, 'because of the "did Malcolm". It's OK to use colloquialisms in your writing if it's genuinely regional. Even "I was sat" seems acceptable now, though I don't agree with that one. Also, you repeat the phrase "the truth was".'

There's a pause while everyone waits for Leonard to continue but it seems he's said his piece. He leans back against the piano. Imogen says, 'Has anyone else got feedback for Sue?'

'I'm so sorry about Malcolm,' says Frances. 'I met him here once – well, I met both of you – and I thought he was really lovely.'

'He was,' says Imogen. 'A good writer too.'

'Thank you,' says Sue.

'I loved the parts about your mum,' says Edwin. 'A coffee. My mother would have said the same. It's a real skill to be funny and poignant at the same time.'

'That's so true,' says Imogen, smiling at Edwin. Once more, Benedict feels a stab of jealousy. It's very childish to be jealous because the teacher prefers your friend to you but there it is.

'"Manna from heaven" seems a bit esoteric,' says Peter. 'I mean, I know the reference because I've read the Bible. The Israelites being fed in the desert. But would others get it?'

'Good point,' says Sue. 'I had a rather religious childhood.'

To Benedict's embarrassment, several people turn to look at him. He says, 'I always think a religious background is a boon to a writer. Look at T.S. Eliot, Graham Greene . . .' He tries to think of a female example and fails.

'Jeanette Winterson,' offers Edwin.

'Great example, Edwin,' says Imogen.

There's a creaking sound as the clock in the hallway prepares itself to strike. Three o'clock. Imogen says, 'Let's have a break now. Back at three-thirty for some thoughts on plotting. Oh, and if you want me and Leonard to look at your pieces from the morning, just email them to me.'

Benedict stands up. He has no intention of emailing his free verse to Imogen.

The session on plotting is actually quite fun. They work in groups and Benedict, Johnnie and Sue come up with a narrative that includes a haunted caravan, bungee jumping and a murderous postman. Peter, Frances and Edwin take it more seriously and (of course) Imogen praises Edwin's contribution of a retired hitman who just can't stop killing people. Both groups were instinctively drawn to the crime genre, Benedict notices.

They end at five. Imogen tells them that supper is at seven-thirty and gives them a voluntary writing exercise. 'Two hundred words on arriving at a new place.' Benedict doesn't think he'll be handing anything in. Really, he's not proving a very promising student.

Benedict goes to his room and is surprised at how tired he feels. All he's done the whole day is sit around and fail to write. How can that be so exhausting? His bed, with its swirling cover of trees and flowers, looks extremely inviting. To stop himself going to sleep, he sits in his desk chair and makes some notes.

Peter Abbot – overheard talking about having to be brutal, writes books on cannibalism.

Imogen Blythe – knew Melody and Don. Sue warned us to be wary. Doesn't seem to like me much.

Sue Hitchins – Malcolm Collins' girlfriend, warned us about Imogen. Why? Thinks she needs to finish Malcolm's book.

Johnnie Newton – mentioned that she'd been in an institution. What sort?

Leonard Norris – ex-alcoholic? Knew previous owner of B House. Says he thought Don Parsons was 'odd'.

Frances O'Toole – seems to like dead birds.

Benedict sighs and crosses out 'doesn't seem to like me much'. It's not about him, after all. He wishes that he was getting more out of the course. All the creative writing sessions have done is instil a deep sense of inadequacy. Maybe he just isn't an author. Maybe he should just carry on at the Coffee Shack, brightening people's days with mindful cappuccinos. Or maybe he should do something entirely different. He's still trying to think what when Edwin knocks at the door.

'Ready for supper?'

Edwin has changed again and is wearing his favourite pink bow tie. He has certainly brought a lot of clothes with him, thinks Benedict. No wonder his suitcase was so heavy. Benedict changes into his only other jumper, which is olive green. At least it's not unravelling but that's really all that can be said for it.

He shows Edwin his notes. Edwin laughs at the crossed-out line.

'Of course Imogen likes you. Why wouldn't she?'

'I don't know. Because I couldn't come up with any interesting birds?'

Edwin laughs again but there's a rather uncomfortable amount of understanding in his voice when he says, 'Imogen's not judging us.'

'She is,' says Benedict. 'That's exactly what she's doing. She's trying to see who's a good writer and who's not. She obviously thinks you are.'

'She hasn't read anything I've written,' says Edwin. But Benedict thinks he looks rather pleased all the same. 'Imogen likes you. Everyone always does. And Johnnie seems to have taken to you.'

'She said she used to be in an institution. Maybe she thinks I should be in one too.'

'That's interesting,' says Edwin. 'We must find out more. You concentrate on Johnnie and Sue. I'll take Imogen and Leonard. We can save Frances and Peter until later.'

'There was that suspicious conversation that Peter had. About being brutal.'

'That's true. We can't rule anyone out.'

Edwin sounds very cheerful about this.

Supper has been cooked by Imogen and Leonard. The vegetarian lasagne is really very good; Benedict bets that Leonard made most of it. Imogen circles the table, filling up wine glasses. Benedict is sitting next to her and takes the opportunity to compliment her on her teaching skills.

'Thank you,' she says. 'I actually used to be an English teacher. I sometimes think children are much easier to teach than adults. You seem like you could be a good teacher.'

'Really? What makes you say that?'

'You listen,' says Imogen. 'That's rare.'

Benedict is mollified, despite himself. It's funny how even the smallest compliment can cheer you up. Then he wonders if Imogen is referring to his comment about overheard conversations. Maybe she just thinks he's an eavesdropper.

Across the table, Frances is talking about her teenagers. 'They're super bright, they scare me sometimes.' Peter says that he doesn't like children much.

'Even though you write for them?' says Benedict.

Peter gives him an unfriendly look. 'I don't write for children. I write children's books. That's very different.'

Is it? thinks Benedict. But he doesn't pursue the subject. Leonard is handing out slices of delicious-looking carrot cake.

'That's all I come here for,' says Johnnie, on Benedict's other side, adding a generous helping of cream. 'The grub.'

'How many times have you been to Battle House?'

'This is my third time. I've been to Leonard's course for new writers and Imogen's crime-writing weekend.'

'That sounds fun,' says Benedict. 'I love crime fiction.'

'It was great fun. We played a murder game. Turned all the lights out. It was quite scary.'

'Sounds it,' says Benedict. 'What did that teach you about writing a crime novel?'

'The element of surprise,' says Johnnie, grinning at him. She has a gold tooth which glints in the candlelight.

'Did you ever meet Melody Chambers?' asks Benedict. 'Or my friend Don Parsons?'

He really should know more about Don, if he's going to continue pretending to be his friend. He must ring Don's actual friend Richard for some information.

'I don't think so,' says Johnnie vaguely.

'I remember Melody,' says Frances suddenly. 'You were close to her, weren't you, Leonard?'

Leonard doesn't answer. 'Seconds, anyone?' he says to the table in general. When he stands up, his shadow is suddenly monstrous against the wall.

Benedict is careful not to drink too much but, when he goes to bed, he still can't sleep. He makes himself a camomile tea from the selection provided and thinks of Natalka as he drinks it. She and Valentyna love herbal tea although Benedict sometimes longs for PG Tips. He texts her, 'Goodnight. Love you xxx', but she doesn't answer. She's probably asleep. It's nearly midnight.

Benedict goes to the window and looks out. There's no moon

and the garden is dark but, as he watches, a security light comes on. What has triggered it? A fox? The cat again? Benedict has taken off his glasses but can make out a figure walking across the lawn, which sparkles with a slight frost. From the person's height, he thinks it's Leonard. Another figure emerges from the trees. A woman, too tall to be Imogen and too willowy to be Johnnie. He has an impression of long hair tied back in a ponytail. Benedict puts on his spectacles but he still can't make out the faces. The two people stand talking for a few minutes before melting into the darkness of the woods. Why go that way and not into the house? thinks Benedict. Although he stands watching for some time – until his tea is quite cold – the couple do not return.

Chapter 12

Natalka: a bad feeling

Natalka is woken by an insistent humming sound. At first she thinks it's Benedict snoring but, when she stretches out her hand to shove him, the bed is smooth and empty. Natalka reaches for her phone. Five-thirty a.m. Who would be making noises this early? As the hum harmonises with a series of bangs, Natalka identifies it. Her mother is cleaning the house.

She pulls on her kimono and goes into the sitting room. Valentyna has upended the sofa and is hoovering the cushions.

'What are you doing? It's practically the middle of the night.'

'The sun's up,' says Valentyna. This isn't quite true but streaks of light are making their way through the open curtains. Now that the vacuum cleaner is silent, Natalka can hear the birds singing.

'But no one else is,' says Natalka. 'You're disturbing the neighbours. You're disturbing *me*.'

Valentyna looks momentarily stricken at the mention of the neighbours. She tries very hard to get on with the people in the flats below and above. When she first arrived in England, she was shocked that Natalka had never invited them over for a meal.

'I couldn't sleep,' says Valentyna.

Natalka softens slightly. She can imagine her mother's dreams – Dmytro dying in some eastern field – because she has them too. All the same, though, it's Saturday morning in Shoreham. English people don't spring clean their houses at this hour. In fact, from what Natalka has seen of their homes, they don't spring clean them at all.

'I've got to go to work at seven,' she says. 'You could have waited until six at least. We're short-staffed. I've got three calls to do this morning.'

Valentyna, who had been looking apologetic, now takes on a mulish expression that Natalka remembers from her childhood.

'I need to keep busy.'

Natalka sympathises; she is the same. But she knows what's coming.

'You should let me work for you. I could be a carer.'

Natalka knows that this is true. Her mother once trained as a nurse and looked after her parents until their eventual deaths. Natalka remembers daily trips to see her grandparents. She looked forward to the visits because her grandmother gave her sweets and her grandfather called her 'vnuchka'. Now she realises that her mother was cooking and cleaning for her parents as well as bringing up two children on her own. Later on, Valentyna managed various geriatric ailments and nursed her mother through Alzheimer's. Natalka admires and loves her mother, but she doesn't want to work with her.

'You need special papers to work in England,' she extemporises.

'But we went to Croydon to do the . . .' Valentyna searches for the English word, 'biometric tests. That means I can work here.'

This is true. 'I'll talk to Maria,' says Natalka. Maria is her deputy manager and an ex-nurse herself. Natalka knows that Maria will jump at the chance of taking on such a qualified carer. If Natalka asks her, that is.

Valentyna is mollified and shows this by offering to make tea. Natalka accepts and goes to have a shower. As the water runs she thinks of Benedict and Edwin in their rural retreat. When Edwin first mentioned Battle House she couldn't think of anything worse than a weekend of talking about books but now she feels moment-arily envious. At least it will be peaceful there.

Natalka's first call is to one of her favourites, Harriet Hartington. She is bedbound and so it takes two carers to hoist her upright in the morning and evening. Despite this, and many such indignities, Harriet and her husband, Douglas, are two of the most cheerful and positive people Natalka knows. She looks forward to her visits to them, not just because Douglas gives her chocolate bars (memories of her grandmother?). But today Natalka knows immediately that something is wrong. Maria, the second carer, has not yet arrived but Natalka goes upstairs to the second floor flat because Harriet dearly loves a chat. Time to talk is a precious commodity. Natalka's previous boss called it 'wasting time' but Natalka sometimes thinks that ten minutes' gossip about a soap opera does more good than an occupational therapist.

But Harriet is not up to a *Coronation Street* update this morning. She is a terrible colour and is having difficulty breathing. Douglas hovers nervously.

'She's been like it ever since I came in this morning.' Douglas now sleeps on the sofa because his wife needs a hospital bed.

'Can you hear me, Harriet?' Natalka bends close to the recumbent woman, hearing the ominous rattle in her throat.

'Natalka,' gasps Harriet. Natalka feels her pulse, it's galloping.

'I think we need to get her to hospital.'

'Can't we call the doctor?' says Douglas.

'No one will come out on a Saturday,' says Natalka. She, too, is reluctant. She's seen too many clients disappear in an ambulance and never return. Alive, that is. Hospital is almost the unhealthiest place for an elderly person but Harriet needs medical help.

Maria arrives as Natalka is phoning 999. She's as matter-of-fact as ever but, when Douglas goes to pack a bag for Harriet, she says, 'I've got a bad feeling about this.'

'Don't say that,' says Natalka, fighting an urge to cross herself.

'Are you OK to wait with them? I can do your other morning calls.'

'Thanks,' says Natalka. 'Any more luck with getting agency staff?'

'No,' says Maria. 'I'm going to ring round a few nursing friends. See if anyone fancies earning some extra money. Very likely with nursing pay the way it is.'

Natalka takes the plunge. 'My mum might be able to help. She's an ex-nurse.'

'That would be great,' says Maria. 'I'd better go now. Bye, Harriet,' she bends over the bed, 'God bless.'

Maria is Polish and has no problem with the G word.

*

By the time Natalka has waved goodbye to the ambulance, she is in a thoroughly gloomy mood. She decides to jog to the Care4You offices and catch up with some paperwork but, before she can set off, her phone throbs with a text. It's Benedict.

Morning! Just about to do a sound walk.

Whatever that is, thinks Natalka, she's sure it won't be as bad as seeing a woman carried down two flights of stairs on a stretcher. She doesn't know what to reply so contents herself with a heart reaction.

Another message. This time it's from Minnie Barnes, Melody's daughter.

Any news?

Natalka sighs. Melody's daughters, especially Minnie, phone and text continually. 'These things take time,' Natalka tells them, but Minnie can't understand why Alan Franklin hasn't been arrested immediately. The lack of evidence doesn't seem to be a problem.

Natalka decides to call the woman's bluff. It's nine a.m., she can imagine the Barnes household getting ready for a day of sports activities and visits to the garden centre.

I'll be over in 40 mins. Put the kettle on.

In fact, it takes Natalka almost an hour to drive, through Saturday traffic, to Preston Park. Sure enough, when she arrives at the house, a man she assumes is Mr Minnie is shepherding two boys in football kit out of the house. Minnie, in the doorway, is holding the dog in her arms. 'Bye, darlings! Good luck!'

'Sorry,' she says to Natalka. 'It's crazy here on Saturdays. I've got to take Phoebe to ballet in an hour.'

'Why doesn't Phoebe do football?' asks Natalka. She'd loved

football as a girl and still resents the fact that it was Dmytro who got to go to soccer camp in the holidays. To be fair, she used to go to maths camp which, at the time, was her idea of fun.

'She's a real girly girl,' says Minnie. 'However much I discourage stereotypes.'

Natalka isn't sure how much Minnie, dressed today in leggings and a pink T-shirt embroidered with stars, actually discourages them but she likes pink herself so is prepared to be generous.

They retreat to the kitchen, where the dog settles into its bed. It's the wheezy sort and its breathing reminds Natalka of her mother's vacuum cleaner.

'He's called Percy,' Minnie tells Natalka. 'He's a Chug.'

'A what?'

'A Chihuahua–pug cross. They cost a packet these days. Especially after lockdown when everyone decided to get a dog.'

Minnie is very aware of how much things cost, Natalka notices. She tells her that the house has recently gone up in value, that her husband, Nick, is facing 'downsizing' at work and that school fees are seven thousand a term.

'Why not a state school?' asks Natalka.

'That's what Harmony says. She teaches at one. Honestly, it's a dump.'

Natalka has been thinking of the sisters as a pair but now she sees that they are very different. Harmony is a teacher, Minnie is (appropriately) an accountant. It's Minnie who has been nagging for daily updates, Minnie who says now that Alan is 'the devil incarnate'. Harmony is too soft, she says, too willing to give Alan the benefit of the doubt. Natalka also thinks that Minnie is both richer than her sister and more worried about money. She remembers the comment made by Lydia, Melody's author friend, about the sisters wanting their mother 'to fund their husbands' business schemes'. Does Nick, shortly to be downsized, have any entrepreneurial plans?

Having promised an update, Natalka tells Minnie that Edwin and Benedict are undercover at Battle House.

'Edwin is your partner, right?' says Minnie, who is going through the coffee-making ritual again.

'My business partner. Benedict is my . . . er . . . life partner.' It sounds wrong, somehow, but Natalka feels the need to explain the relationships.

'Why do you think Battle House is relevant?' asks Minnie, rather pugnaciously. 'I don't think Alan ever went there.'

Natalka wonders if it's worth introducing the idea that not all roads necessarily lead to Alan. She says, 'There's a possible link between your mum's death and the death of two other writers, Don Parsons and Malcolm Collins. Do either of those names ring a bell?'

'I don't think so,' says Minnie, putting a cup in front of Natalka. 'But I don't get much time for reading.'

'Do you remember your mother visiting Battle House?' Natalka asks.

'Yes,' says Minnie. 'She went a few times. She knew the woman who used to own it. In fact, I think she – or her niece – introduced Mummy to Alan. Something to thank her for, I don't think.'

This is interesting. Natalka remembers Alan saying they had met at his chemist's shop. Quite a 'meet cute', as she believes it's called in movie circles.

'What was the woman called?' The only name Natalka can remember from the website is the tutor, Leonard Norris.

'Miriam, I think. Hang on, I've got a picture of her.'

To Natalka's surprise, Minnie goes to a cork board which is propped up behind the door.

'We had this done for Mummy's funeral,' she says. 'I don't know what to do with it now. Upsets me to look at it.'

Natalka can understand why. Melody's face smiles up at her, as a schoolgirl, graduate, young bride and a mother with two smiling babies in a pushchair. She's cuddling dogs, laughing on the beach and reading in a hammock. In one picture, she is standing between a man and a woman in front of a square, solid-looking house.

'That's Mummy at Battle House with Miriam. The man is one of the tutors, I think.'

The man is handsome in a self-important way, longish hair falling over his face. The woman is older, wearing a Panama hat and dungarees. Melody looks young and happy, her hair long, wearing a flowery dress.

'Can I take this?' says Natalka. 'I promise I'll bring it back.'

'Please do,' says Minnie, unpinning the photo. 'I see her face and I see myself. It shocks me sometimes when I look in the mirror. Is your mother still alive?'

'Yes,' says Natalka. 'She's living with me at the moment.'

'You're very lucky,' says Minnie, wiping her eyes on the seabirds tea towel. 'Remember that.'

Chapter 13

Benedict: on the Sabbath day

It still feels odd not to go to mass on Sunday. When he was a teenager, Benedict used to sneak away to church while his siblings were being ferried to their various sports activities. His parents, who were strictly Christmas and Easter people, were appalled when they found out and threatened to send him to a psychiatrist. As a monk, Benedict attended mass every day but there was still something special about Sundays, not least because visitors were allowed into the chapel and there was coffee and biscuits afterwards. Even lay people honour the Sabbath, Benedict often thinks, although they might not be aware of it. The papers are thicker and full of glossy advertisements, Radio 4 is tuned to the moral high ground and television showcases its most tasteful murder mysteries. Public transport takes the fourth commandment extremely seriously and trains can hardly bring themselves to run.

Benedict wakes at Battle House, knowing that the day is different somehow. Light streams through the Morris-patterned curtains and the birds are singing as if they are practising for the choir. Benedict lies in bed for a few minutes, enjoying the strangeness of the room, the unfamiliar hulking wardrobe, the way the window and door seem to have changed places. Then he makes himself a cup of proper tea, has a shower and gets dressed, clean T-shirt but old jumper. He texts Natalka and she messages that Valentyna has been cleaning the house 'like mad woman'. It's always a sign of stress when Natalka starts to forget her articles. 'What are you doing today?' texts Benedict. Natalka answers that she's taking her mother to mass, which makes Benedict feel guilty all over again. He should be taking Valentyna to mass. It's Orthodox Easter Sunday, he should be sharing the celebration with her. He should be going to mass himself. 'Have fun,' he texts, rather lamely. Natalka answers with an emoji that could be a wink or a grimace.

Most of the guests are already assembled when Benedict comes down to breakfast. There's a more collegiate atmosphere than yesterday, partly because everyone knows each other better. Leonard is cooking, turning from the stove to laugh and joke with the writers. Imogen is pouring coffee and putting bread into the eight-slice toaster.

'Good morning,' says Edwin. 'Sleep well?'

Edwin looks as bright as ever. He's wearing a cream jumper with a navy-blue gilet and looks the epitome of smart casual.

'Yes, thank you,' says Benedict, although he remembers rather confused dreams about birds and bungee jumping.

'Don't forget, you two are doing lunch,' says Leonard, putting eggs, bacon and mushrooms in front of Benedict.

That's another thing that's more significant on a Sunday: lunch. No other meal has quite the same power to soothe and terrify.

Yesterday, Benedict and Edwin agreed on tagliatelle with a simple tomato sauce. There's plenty of pasta in the larder and fresh basil in a pot on the windowsill. *Isabella and the Pot of Basil*. Today, that menu seems dull and unadventurous. It will also be their last meal together. There are no afternoon sessions, just 'general discussion' and the day ends, officially, at five.

Imogen outlines the morning programme. They are going to do an exercise in pairs, which involves coming up with a scene where one character is active and the other passive. Halfway through, the roles have to change. Benedict hoped to be paired with Edwin but Leonard picks the names out of a battered Panama hat. Benedict gets Sue. He exchanges a look with Edwin, who smiles encouragingly. Edwin gets Frances.

Benedict and Sue go outside to discuss their scene. They can hear Peter and Johnnie, in the walled garden, bellowing at each other. Either they have got into their roles extremely quickly or they are having a humdinger of an argument.

Sue and Benedict sit on the bench at the edge of the wood. The ginger cat appears again and starts a thorough all-over wash in the sunshine. Benedict asks who it belongs to.

'I think he's Georgina's,' says Sue. 'Georgina from the farm. She loves animals. Leonard doesn't like him. He says he's allergic.'

There's a rather awkward silence.

'I don't like these exercises,' says Sue, the words coming out in a rush. 'We had to do a murder thing another time. I hated it. I didn't even like murder in the dark as a child.'

'Johnnie was telling me about that. What happened?'

'Someone was the murderer and they had to catch the others by saying The Word. But no one knew what the word was. It was night and all the lights were switched off. I tried to stay with Malcolm but Imogen told us we had to split up. I was hiding in the little sitting room by the front door and suddenly Declan, Imogen's husband, came in and bellowed 'Parsnip!' That was the word, you see.'

Benedict wants to laugh – the word is such an anticlimax – but Sue's anguished face tells him not to. Instead he says, 'Imogen's husband was there?'

'He wants to be a crime writer,' says Sue. 'I don't know if that's just because Imogen's done so well at it.'

Interesting, thinks Benedict. He wouldn't have thought you could catch writing talent by osmosis. He says, 'On Friday night you said something about being wary of Imogen . . .'

Sue doesn't look at him. The cat seems to be absorbing all her attention.

'Oh, that. I just meant . . . she comes over as all encouraging but she doesn't really help new writers. Malcolm sent her some pages he'd written and she didn't even bother to answer.'

'That's not good,' he says. 'Did she . . .' He stops because Imogen and Leonard are walking across the lawn, deep in conversation.

'Shall we get on with this scene?' says Sue.

They come up with a cross-examination in court. Not very original but Benedict thinks they have incorporated quite a good twist. The barrister, Benedict, turns out to be a student practising with his pupil master, Sue. Benedict knows this rather archaic term because of his sister's training for the bar. He thinks it adds to the power imbalance. Sue is surprisingly enthusiastic and comes up with some interesting ideas. Benedict finds himself almost looking forward to the session.

After coffee, they regroup in the large sitting room. Johnnie and Peter act out a scene of a police officer arresting a drug dealer, which involves a lot of shouting. The switch – the police officer is also on drugs – doesn't really work because both are still as aggressive as ever. Sue puts her hand over her eyes, as if shielding them. Benedict feels his headache coming back.

Edwin and Frances are more interesting. Edwin is interviewing Frances, a famous writer. Eventually it transpires that Edwin thinks Frances stole his idea for a book. The interview becomes at first cutting and then downright accusatory. Edwin, who has conducted a few interviews in his time, does the move from ingratiation to anger extremely well. Then it's Benedict and Sue's turn. Benedict thinks he's quite good as the supercilious barrister, 'Would you have us believe . . .' etc, but Sue is unexpectedly brilliant when the tables turn.

Sue: All that posturing. Where does it really get you?
Benedict: It's going to get me the verdict I want.
Sue: You don't know what you want.

Afterwards, Imogen asks them what they've learnt about dialogue. Sue says repeating another person's words can be powerful. Benedict, remembering Imogen last night, says that he's learnt to listen.

'Excellent,' says Imogen. 'A lot of dialogue is about mirroring, but you'll never be a writer unless you learn the power of silence.'

Benedict doesn't know quite what this means. Perhaps it's a reference to Leonard, who hasn't said a word all morning.

Benedict and Edwin get to leave early to prepare lunch but,

before they can escape, Imogen asks if anyone wants to read their piece about arriving at a place for the first time. Benedict assumes that no one will have bothered with this additional homework but almost everyone offers to read. Edwin writes about his first day at prep school, Sue about going to an intimidating book club, Johnnie about starting a new job. Benedict finds it hard to concentrate. He's wondering how much pasta to cook.

The meal is quite successful. The sauce, made from fresh tomatoes and basil, is light and aromatic. Benedict doesn't think they've made enough tagliatelle but he found some garlic bread in the freezer, which fills everyone up. The other writers help clear the table and then they drift away. Benedict and Edwin are left loading the dishwasher.

'I could never run a restaurant,' says Benedict.

'Isn't that the next step after the Shack?'

'I don't know what's next after the Shack.'

By the time they've packed everything away, it's nearly three-thirty. The closing session is not until four so Benedict and Edwin go for a walk in the grounds. The air is very still, with that expectancy that sometimes comes before rain. Benedict thinks of the Wordsworth quote he loves: *It is a beauteous evening, calm and free, The holy time is quiet as a nun . . .*

'Where is everyone?' says Edwin, because the garden seems empty. Even the cat has disappeared.

'Maybe they're packing,' says Benedict.

'It won't take me a minute to pack,' says Edwin. 'I only brought a capsule wardrobe.'

As they take the path through the trees, the sun disappears.

Benedict shivers in his scruffy blue jumper, Edwin zips up his gilet. A bird cries out, loudly, as if sounding an alarm. The lake appears very suddenly. Benedict sees the warning sign and the kneeling statue before he notices the body, floating face down in the water.

Chapter 14

Edwin: something awful

Edwin recognises the black hair. He shouts, 'Sue!' The birds fly into the air and Benedict wades into the water.

'Call an ambulance!' yells Benedict.

Edwin's fingers tremble but he dials 999 and the operator's calm voice brings him to his senses. He gives the address, even remembering the postcode, then he texts Imogen. By now, Benedict has Sue's body in his arms. She's clearly dead and Edwin knows he should tell Benedict not to disturb the crime scene but, instead, he goes to help his friend. The water is freezing. Edwin catches his foot in some weeds and falls to his knees but he gets himself upright again. He hears people calling from the bank, but he still struggles forward. He's hardly aware that another man has joined Benedict and together they are carrying Sue onto dry land.

'Edwin!' Someone is pulling him back. It's Imogen, her thin arms surprisingly strong. 'Edwin, you're shaking.' A coat is put round his shoulders. He sees Benedict and the other man, Leonard, bending over the waterlogged body. Benedict is attempting mouth-to-mouth but Leonard says, almost harshly, 'She's gone.'

'You need to get back to the house,' Imogen tells Edwin. He doesn't argue. He wants to get away from the accursed lake and the listening trees. As they cross the lawn, he sees Johnnie and Frances running towards them.

'What's happened?'

'It's Sue,' says Imogen. 'She fell in the lake.'

'Is she OK?' says Frances. With her pale hair blowing around her face she suddenly looks like a figure from Greek tragedy, Cassandra perhaps, or some other voice of doom.

'No,' says Imogen. 'I don't think she is.'

She shepherds Edwin into the house and tells him to get out of his wet clothes. 'I'll make tea.' In a daze, Edwin goes up to his room and, mechanically, puts on new trousers, shirt and jumper and slips his feet into suede shoes still water-marked from yesterday's early walk. His phone was in the pocket of the waterproof gilet and, miraculously, seems unharmed. He texts Natalka, 'Something awful has happened. Think it's murder. We're both OK.' As he presses 'send' Edwin hears sirens approaching the house, getting louder and louder until they stop with a suddenness that is even more deafening. He goes to the window and sees paramedics running across the lawn, carrying a stretcher. They are followed by two uniformed police officers. He wonders who contacted the police.

When he goes downstairs, Johnnie, Frances and Peter are sitting round the kitchen table. They all look up when Edwin comes in and Imogen puts a cup of tea in front of him. Edwin is finding her a soothing presence although he can hear Natalka's voice in his head: *trust no one*. Benedict and Leonard must still be at the lake.

'Drink your tea,' says Imogen. 'You must still be cold.'

'I'm fine,' says Edwin but the mug is very comforting to hold. He takes a sip and almost chokes. Imogen has obviously put in about ten sugars.

'Did you actually find her, Edwin?' Frances asks.

'Yes,' says Edwin. 'Benedict and I were walking by the lake and we saw her . . . in the water.'

'Was she . . .' Frances stops, obviously – despite the gruesome poetry – unwilling to say the word.

'She was dead,' says Imogen. 'Benedict tried CPR but I could see it was useless.'

'Do you think she . . .' Frances stops again.

'Committed suicide.' Peter says it for her. 'I think so. I mean, she was very upset about Malcolm.'

'I don't know,' says Imogen, 'and I don't think we should speculate.'

This has the effect of silencing everyone in the room and they are still silent when Benedict and Leonard appear, mud-stained and dripping. They are followed by two people in plain clothes who are, nonetheless, obviously police officers.

Imogen gets up. 'I'll make tea while you get changed.'

One of the officers, a young black woman, raises a hand. 'We'll need the clothes you were wearing. Take them off, touching them as little as possible, and leave them outside your room. SOCO will want to examine them.'

Scene-of-the-crime officers, Edwin translates in his head. It occurs to him that the police seem very sure that a crime has occurred.

Leonard obviously thinks the same thing. 'What's all this about? The poor woman obviously drowned herself. Or fell in by accident.'

'It's a sus death,' says Johnnie.

The woman officer gives her a look before continuing, 'It's an unexplained death at present. We're just following procedure.' She addresses the room as a whole. 'I'm DS Liv Brennan and this is DS Sam Malone. We will need to talk to all of you. In the meantime, can I ask you all not to make any phone calls, leave any messages or post anything on social media.'

'I've got to get home to my kids,' says Frances, although Edwin remembers that they are teenagers and so, presumably, able to fend for themselves for a few hours.

'Me too,' says Imogen.

'Then we'll talk to you two first,' says DS Brennan. 'Is there anyone else who was at the scene?'

'Me,' says Edwin.

'I'll need your clothes too,' says DS Brennan. 'You shouldn't really have changed out of them.'

'He was freezing,' protests Imogen. Edwin thinks there's an unspoken 'and he's old' on the end of the sentence.

Brennan ignores this. 'Can you leave your clothes outside your room, Mr . . . ?'

'Fitzgerald. Edwin Fitzgerald.'

Brennan looks at her colleague who makes a note.

'Shall I find some bin liners?' says Imogen, still anxious to be helpful.

'Plastic contaminates,' says Brennan. 'SOCO will bring paper bags. Now, is there a room where we can do some interviewing?'

Imogen suggests the small sitting room and the detectives escort her there. Benedict goes to change and comes back in his green jumper and jeans with a hole in the knee. He's holding his phone.

'It was in my pocket,' he says. 'Probably ruined.'

'You could try putting it in rice,' says Frances. 'That can dry it out. I think there's some in the larder. I remember from when Peter and I cooked supper.' The vegetable terrine seems years ago, thinks Edwin. Frances fetches a large bag of rice and a bowl. Benedict inserts his iPhone into the wholemeal grains.

'I can't contact Natalka,' says Benedict to Edwin. 'Have you texted her?'

'Yes,' says Edwin. 'Before we were told not to.'

'They can't stop us ringing home,' says Frances.

'I suppose it could be obstructing an investigation,' says Edwin.

'You seem to know a lot about it,' says Peter. 'Are you ex-police?'

'No,' says Edwin. 'I've just watched a lot of TV.'

Frances brings over more tea. Edwin thinks this is a very English way of dealing with death. At least this second cup doesn't contain any extra sugar. He takes a gulp and starts to cough.

'Are you all right?' asks Frances. 'It must have been such a shock.'

'It was rather,' says Edwin.

'I knew Sue was upset about Malcolm,' says Frances, 'but I never thought she'd kill herself. I mean, she seemed all right this morning. You worked with her, didn't you, Benedict?'

This is said rather accusingly. Benedict takes a sip of tea before replying, 'Yes, she seemed fine this morning.'

'We don't know that it is suicide,' says Johnnie.

'Of course it was,' says Peter. 'Suicide while the balance of the mind is disturbed. That's what they say, don't they?'

'It's what they say in TV dramas, certainly,' says Edwin.

'It's ghastly,' says Leonard suddenly. 'Poor, poor Sue. It brought it all back.'

'Brought what back?' asks Edwin. Leonard doesn't answer and, before Edwin can ask again, the door opens and Imogen reappears, colour slightly heightened.

'All done. You can go in now, Frances.'

'What was it like?' says Johnnie.

'OK,' says Imogen. 'They just asked what I was doing this afternoon. I said that, after lunch, I had a meeting with Leonard to go over the weekend and plan for the final session.'

This is an answer to a different question, thinks Edwin. Or is Imogen telling Leonard what she said so that his version will agree? Now Imogen is on her phone. 'Darling? Can you come and get me? Yes, now. Can't explain. Thanks, darling. Love you.'

'Are we free to leave when we've been interviewed?' asks Peter.

'They can't stop us,' says Imogen.

Edwin and Benedict are the last people to be interviewed. By now it's dark outside and raining hard. They can see lights amongst the trees where, presumably, the scene-of-the-crime team is hard at work. Frances and Imogen have been collected by their husbands. Johnnie drives away in her Mini Cooper. Edwin and Benedict wave her off, sheltering under the porch, and then go back into the kitchen. There's no sign of Leonard.

'What do you think Leonard meant by "it brought it all back"?' asks Benedict.

'I don't know,' says Edwin. 'He seemed very cut up.'

'Well, he must have known Sue quite well. She's been on a few of his courses.'

'Peter seemed very certain that it was suicide,' says Edwin. 'He's an unpleasant man, don't you think?'

'Horrible,' says Benedict. 'And I keep thinking about that conversation I overheard, Peter telling someone they had to be brutal.'

'Will you tell the police?'

'I think I have to. Will you tell them about being a private investigator?'

'I think I have to,' says Edwin.

DS Brennan appears a few seconds later, looking impatient.

'Leonard Norris was meant to send you in, Mr Fitzgerald.'

'We haven't seen Leonard,' says Edwin. 'Perhaps he's gone home.'

'He lives here, apparently,' says Brennan. 'This way, please.'

The small sitting room, which had previously seemed quite cosy, seems mysteriously to have become a place of interrogation. The two armchairs are facing each other with a hard chair from the dining room to the side. The central light is harsh, nothing like the diffuse glow from the standard lamps. From the hall, the clock strikes seven. The rain falls on the porch roof with an urgent, drumming sound.

Brennan and Malone introduce themselves again. Brennan has a classically beautiful face, thinks Edwin, with braided hair drawn back into a ponytail. Malone is still young enough to have spots. Edwin feels sorry for him.

'We're asking everyone the same questions,' says DS Brennan. 'Can you tell me what you did from two p.m. until three-thirty p.m.?'

From the end of lunch until the discovery of the body, thinks Edwin. It strikes him that the window of opportunity is very small. He explains about loading the dishwasher and going for a walk with Benedict.

'So you and Mr . . .' Brennan consults her list, 'Cole were in each other's company all the time.'

'That's right,' says Edwin.

'And you came here together, I understand.'

'Yes.' Edwin takes a deep breath. 'Look, I think I should tell you something. I'm a private investigator and, well, I'm here undercover.'

Malone smothers a laugh but Brennan just stares, her large eyes round. 'Undercover?' she repeats.

'My partner and I are investigating the suspicious deaths of two writers, called Melody Chambers and Don – he wrote as Donna – Parsons. We knew that they'd both come here on a writing retreat so we decided to investigate.'

'And your partner is Mr Cole?'

'No, it's actually Benedict's partner – in the girlfriend sense – Natalka Kolisnyk. I came with Benedict because he's a writer himself.' If Benedict thinks that Edwin doesn't know about the crime novels, he's sadly mistaken.

Brennan shakes her head, as if ridding it of the whole notion of private investigators. 'And do you suspect anyone in particular?'

'No, we just wanted an idea of the set-up.'

'Did you know Sue Hitchins before this weekend?'

'We didn't know anyone. I first met Sue on Friday night at dinner.'

'Did you talk to her over the course of the weekend?'

'Yes. On Saturday morning, I went for a walk and, by chance, met her by the pond, lake, whatever it is.'

'How did she seem?' asks Brennan. 'In herself?'

'She told me that she used to come to Battle House with her boyfriend, Malcolm Collins,' said Edwin, 'but he died last year.'

'Did she seem distressed?' asks Malone. Edwin wonders if the police, like Peter, are trying to establish the death as suicide.

'I would say sad rather than distressed,' he says.

'Did she say anything else of interest?' asks Brennan. 'In your opinion as an investigator.'

She might be mocking him but Edwin elects to take this at face value.

'On Friday night she told Benedict and me to be wary of Imogen, one of the tutors.'

'What did she mean by that?'

'Benedict asked yesterday – no, today – and Sue said that she meant that Imogen didn't support other writers. Malcolm once sent her a story he'd written and she didn't even reply.' Benedict had told Edwin this over the washing up.

'Let's go back to today. After you finished tidying the kitchen, you went for a walk?'

'Yes. We crossed the lawn and took the path to the lake. I don't know why really.'

'And when you got there, what did you see?'

'A body. Floating. Almost in the centre.' Edwin shuts his eyes but he can still see it. The dark hair fanned out in the green water, the cardigan spread like grey wings.

'Would you like a glass of water?' asks Brennan.

'No, thank you. I'm fine.' Edwin is determined to seem professional. He sits up straighter.

'What did you do then?'

'Benedict went into the water to try to save her. He shouted to me to call an ambulance and I did. Then I texted Imogen. Something like "come to the lake quickly". I tried to get into the water to help Benedict but I couldn't manage. While I was still floundering, Imogen and Leonard arrived. Leonard went to help

Benedict. Imogen took my arm and pulled me out of the water. Benedict and Leonard had got Sue out by then. Benedict tried to do mouth-to-mouth but it was useless.'

'He shouldn't have tried,' says Malone. 'It was contaminating the scene.'

'I know but it's awfully hard to do nothing.'

'We understand,' says Brennan. 'Was there anything else about the scene that struck you? Any footprints leading to the lake, for example.'

'I can't think,' says Edwin. 'Sorry. I'm being a frightfully bad witness. I think the earth seemed churned up on the shore.'

'Churned up?' says Malone. 'Like there'd been a struggle?'

'I can't say but I thought the mud at the edge looked more trodden than I remembered the day before. But, as I say, I can't be sure.'

'Thank you, Mr Fitzgerald,' says DS Brennan. 'You've been very helpful. Is there any chance that we could talk to this Natalka Kolisnyk?'

Edwin thinks there's every chance.

Chapter 15

Natalka: so many suspects

Natalka is determined to make Orthodox Easter Sunday a happy day for her mother. She gets up early and takes her tea in bed. The gesture is slightly spoilt because Valentyna is already up and dressed at six and doing some light dusting. But Natalka says nothing about the dawn cleaning. She tells her mother that she is going out for a run and that she'll join her afterwards for a proper breakfast. After her shower Natalka even puts on a *vyshyvanka*, the embroidered top that Ukrainians wear on special occasions. Natalka feels slightly stupid in hers, which was made by her mother, like a child dressing up for a party. But Valentyna is touched by the gesture.

'You look beautiful, Talia.'

'It's a bit tight,' says Natalka. 'I've been eating too many of Benedict's brownies.'

'You've always loved chocolate,' says Valentyna, not contradicting her.

After breakfast they drive to Rottingdean for mass with the Ukrainian priest. Valentyna takes a basket of *paska* because the blessing of food is an important part of the service. Natalka doesn't go inside the church. She walks through the picturesque village until she reaches the seafront. The sun is shining and a few brave souls are paddling, shrieking when the waves break against the shingle. There's a folk band playing on a stage in front of a pub and the whole scene has an eccentric British atmosphere that Natalka very much enjoys. On her way back to the church she finds a greengrocer that sells local free-range eggs and chooses six white ones, which means the colour will show better when they've been dyed. Let no one say she's not trying . . .

Back home, Valentyna boils the eggs and, as they cool, she and Natalka talk about Easter at home, about holidays in Odessa, travelling in their camper van, about the beaches in Yalta and the time Dmytro tried to join the circus. When the eggs are ready, they start decorating, both keeping up a stoically cheerful manner. Valentyna is delighted with the white shells but whereas, in Ukraine, she'd use beautiful gold decorations of crosses and chalices, here she's only been able to find stickers of rabbits and ducklings. The Disneyesque faces seem strangely sinister to Natalka but she keeps this thought to herself.

At midday, Dmytro FaceTimes them. Her brother's face is so familiar, and, to Natalka, still so boyish, that it seems impossible – a horrific joke – to see him grinning in a field with a rifle slung round his neck. 'All the boys are here,' he says, angling his phone to show distant figures in army fatigues, 'we're going to have a feast later. So many people have sent us *paska*.'

'How are your boots?' asks Valentyna.

'Great,' says Dmytro. Army boots are in short supply but Natalka has found an army surplus store in Brighton and has bought supplies for Dmytro and his comrades. There's a man called Tomasz who makes regular trips in his van from Brighton to Kyiv. Natalka and Valentyna are his best customers.

'Are you getting enough sleep?' says Valentyna. Dmytro glances quickly at Natalka before replying, 'I'm sleeping fine. The open air agrees with me.'

'If you snore like you usually do,' says Natalka, 'they'll probably throw you out of the army.' I wish they would, she thinks. She has barely forgiven her brother for joining up in 2014, being taken prisoner by the Russians and disappearing for several years. And now, after finding safety in Aberdeen, as part of a prisoner exchange, here he is again, standing in a muddy field like a boy playing soldiers. Natalka is the oldest – though only by eighteen months – and, in her opinion at least, the bravest and cleverest. It should be Dmytro in the kitchen, sticking rabbits on eggs, and Natalka leading her troupe into battle.

They talk about Benedict and Dmytro's Scottish girlfriend Kelly, who is also furious with him. Valentyna tells him about the Ukrainian priest in Rottingdean and how she has joined the library. 'It's a place for people who can read, Dmytro,' says Natalka. Dmytro tells them that he's now a captain and not to worry because, as an officer, he will keep out of trouble. Both women agree enthusiastically with this blatant untruth. They wave goodbye, smiling broadly.

Valentyna turns away when the FaceTime session ends. Natalka knows her mother is crying but she also knows that, if she comforts her, she will cry too.

'Let's get on with these eggs,' she says, in the manic tones of a children's TV presenter.

'Let's!' says Valentyna, with matching jollity.

Natalka looks down at her phone. Benedict has texted that he and Edwin are cooking lunch. Benedict is quite a good cook, especially now that he's been having lessons from Valentyna. Natalka can imagine that Edwin will have his own ideas, though, probably taken from some Radio 4 programme about good food.

Good luck. Hows yr day?

OK. Morning quite fun. Looking forward to getting home though. How about you? I miss you xx

All OK. Heard from Dmytro. He seems well. About to paint eggs.

She adds a yawn emoji. Benedict is not fooled. He texts back.

Glad you could talk to him but must be hard. Sending loads of love xxx

The coloured eggs don't look so bad when they are finished and rubbed with oil. When Natalka and Dmytro were children they used to play a game which involved cracking the eggs against each other. Now they just arrange them in a bowl, where they glow like a memory of the past. Valentyna and Natalka then eat a selection of Easter food for lunch. Neither of them has much appetite but they make up for this by talking animatedly. Valentyna drinks a glass of red wine but Natalka sticks to water in case she has to make some care calls later. It's silver birch water, a Ukrainian delicacy said to possess endless health-giving properties and available at the Polish market. The slightly sweet fermented taste reminds Natalka of home. They raise their glasses and make the toast '*Khrystos Voskres*', Christ is Risen, although, to Natalka, these are just words. Benedict actually believes it.

After lunch, Natalka jogs to the Care4You office to catch up on paperwork. There are several requests from the local hospital for them to take on more clients. It's a vicious circle really: geriatric patients don't do well in hospital and they take up much-needed beds but they can't be discharged without care plans and, because there's a shortage of both social workers and money, these plans often take weeks to complete. Natalka knows that people prefer to stay in their own homes but private care firms like hers need to get money from somewhere. Clients pay a certain amount every week and the government is meant to make up the shortfall, except that payments are almost always late. With a pang Natalka thinks of Harriet being lifted into the ambulance. She must ring Douglas this evening.

To cheer herself up, Natalka looks at her phone. At two-thirty Benedict texted: 'Lunch went well I think. Nearly over. Can't wait to see you xxx.' Natalka replies, 'Any clues?? Suspects??' but there's no reply. The next message comes at three-fifteen. Benedict writes: 'Going for a walk in grounds with Smartypants (ie Edwin). He's teacher's pet.' Natalka replies: 'Are u jealous?' When Benedict does not reply she wonders if he's offended. Benedict is easy to tease because he takes everything so seriously but it's unlike him to be sulky. On the walk home, Natalka texts, 'Tell me more about yr day', an invitation Benedict can't usually resist. But the message stays on 'Delivered'.

At the flat, Valentyna is watching a Miss Marple film. Natalka spots the murderer in five minutes, following Benedict's theory that it's always the most famous actor, but even this can't lift her spirits. At 5.01 her phone buzzes with another text. It's Edwin: 'Something awful has happened. Think it's murder. We're both OK.'

'Edwin says there's been a murder,' says Natalka to Valentyna.

'Is he joking?' says Valentyna. She likes Edwin, whom she thinks of as the perfect English gentleman, but she's been caught out by his sense of humour more than once. So has Natalka so she texts back, 'Is this a joke???' There's no reply until seven-thirty when Natalka and Valentyna are eating potato pancakes in front of a *Downton Abbey* repeat. Natalka's phone vibrates with a call. Edwin.

'What's going on?' she says.

'Someone's been killed,' says Edwin. 'A woman called Sue. Benedict's phone fell in the water. That's why I'm ringing.'

Water? thinks Natalka. The two facts don't seem connected somehow. 'Are you both OK?'

'Fine. The police are here and they've interviewed me. Benedict's with them now.'

'Who was the woman who died?'

'She was called Sue Hitchins. She drowned in a lake in the grounds. Benedict and I actually found her.'

'Drowned? You said you thought it was murder.'

'That was my initial reaction, I must admit, but some people here think she might have killed herself. Sue's boyfriend died last year and she's obviously still very upset. But guess who the boyfriend was? Malcolm Collins.'

Natalka whistles. 'Suspicious.' On the TV screen people in dinner jackets are drinking Champagne. Valentyna has turned the sound down but is still watching, entranced.

'Yes. Look, the thing is, I had to tell the police about being a private detective.'

Natalka stands up. 'Do they want to see me?'

'If possible. You could go into the police station in Hastings tomorrow but, to be honest, Benedict and I could do with a lift home.'

'I'm on my way.'

The sunny day has given way to a rainy evening. Natalka's windscreen wipers battle as her satnav takes her on a convoluted route of unlit country roads. But Natalka is a confident driver and she keeps up a steady speed, trusting in technology, her headlights picking out signposts and the occasional fox, eyes gleaming. Even so, she almost misses the entrance to the house and needs to make a last-minute swerve. A uniformed policeman is standing by the gate.

'Can I ask your name and business, miss?'

'Natalka Kolisnyk. I'm here to see DS Brennan.' Edwin told her to say this. It does the trick and the officer waves her through. Natalka drives along an unmade-up track with trees on either side. The rain has stopped now but, under the leafy canopy, water drips steadily. After a few twists and turns, she is driving over gravel that widens out into a driveway. A police van, a hatchback and a sports car are parked in front of the house, which is in darkness apart from one light downstairs and one upstairs. Natalka knocks on the door and, seconds later, it is opened by Benedict. He hugs her fiercely. 'Thank God you're here.'

In the background, Natalka can see Edwin, holding the handle of his wheelie suitcase. He looks elderly and vulnerable but his voice is as jaunty as ever.

'Welcome to the crime scene. I like your top.'

Natalka had forgotten that she was still wearing the *vyshyvanka*, visible under her denim jacket. It doesn't really add to the professional detective image. She pulls the edges of her jacket together to hide the embroidery.

'Where's the lake?' she says.

'At the back of the house,' says Edwin. 'In the woods.'

'Can we look?'

'The whole area's been sealed off,' says Edwin. 'The scene-of-the-crime team are there now. That's the police inner cordon, apparently. The outer cordon starts at the gate.'

'Yes, there's a policeman there. Are you the last guests to leave?'

'Yes,' says Benedict. 'Only Leonard Norris is still here. Turns out he actually lives in Battle House.'

'He's the tutor, isn't he?'

'One of them. The other one, Imogen, left as soon as she could. Her husband came to pick her up.'

'So many suspects,' says Natalka.

'Miss Kolisnyk, I presume?' Natalka looks round. Two people are standing in the open doorway, a black woman and a white man. Both are wearing high-viz waterproof jackets. It's the woman who spoke and Natalka is impressed because her name was pronounced correctly.

'That's me,' she says, a shade too brightly for the circumstances perhaps.

'I'm DS Liv Brennan,' says the woman. 'And this is DS Sam Malone. Can we have a word?'

They step into the hall and, rather to Natalka's surprise, indicate that Edwin and Benedict can stay. Edwin sits on the only available chair.

'I understand that you're a private investigator,' says Liv Brennan.

'And that Mr Fitzgerald and Mr Cole were at Battle House under false pretences.'

'Not exactly false pretences,' says Natalka. 'I mean, they're both interested in books and writing.' She knows that Benedict has several novels in his desk and assumes that, one day, they will either be published or he'll forget about them.

'But you're investigating the deaths of Melody Chambers and Don Parsons?'

'That's right.'

'I've looked in the files,' says Malone, speaking for the first time, 'and her death was classified as natural causes.'

'Her family thinks differently,' says Natalka. 'And we know Melody came on courses here. One of her daughters gave me this.' She produces the photograph taken from Minnie's cork board.

Brennan and Malone examine the picture. Benedict comes to look over their shoulders.

'That's Leonard,' he says. 'He's younger here but I'm sure that's him. I wonder who the woman is?'

'Minnie thought it was the woman who used to own the house,' says Natalka. 'Miriam something.'

'I've seen that hat before,' says Edwin. 'I think we drew the names out of it this afternoon. I do like a Panama.'

Natalka thinks they are straying from the point. 'It's a clue,' she says.

Brennan gives Natalka a hard stare. She has the sort of immovable face that's good at this sort of thing. Natalka stares back, chin lifted.

'We appreciate you were approached by this woman's family,' says Brennan at last, 'but we don't need you interfering on this case. There's nothing that links the deceased with this Melody Chambers or Don Parsons.'

'Nothing except this house and the people in it,' says Natalka.

'And we know that another writer connected to Melody, Malcolm Collins, came here too,' chips in Edwin. 'He died in 2021. Sue Hitchins was his girlfriend.'

'Yes, we've heard that Sue was grieving her boyfriend,' says Malone. 'Points to suicide, in my view.'

Now it's his turn to get the Brennan stare. The two officers might be equal in rank but Natalka knows who's in charge.

'This is a police investigation.' She's addressing all three of them now. 'I don't want amateurs getting involved.'

'We're hardly amateurs,' says Natalka. 'We've been in business three years, ever since we worked on a case with DI Harbinder Kaur.'

She's not prepared for the effect this name has on DS Brennan. She actually takes a step backwards.

'Harbinder Kaur from West Sussex?'

'The one and only.'

'Isn't she your heroine?' says Malone, then stops. Even in the semi-darkness Natalka knows Brennan is giving him a look.

'Even so,' says Brennan. 'I must ask you not to involve yourself in this case. Do I make myself clear?'

They agree that she is crystal clear. The officers then walk them to Natalka's car. Brennan asks Natalka if she's Ukrainian. She says that she is.

'It's great that you've been able to come to England,' says Malone. 'To get away from the war.'

'I've lived in England for ten years,' says Natalka. 'I'm a British citizen.' She married her student boyfriend, Daniel, after leaving Bournemouth University. Her motivation had been citizenship but she'd been fond of him, though not fond enough to have kept in touch. Natalka is always stung by the suggestion that she is here because of the war although it is true, in a way. She escaped a different war or, rather, the same war that has been continuing since 2014.

Brennan seems not to hear. 'It's good that Ukrainians have had such a warm welcome here,' she says. 'A bit of a contrast to the welcome afforded to refugees that look like me. Goodnight now. Drive safely.'

In the car, Benedict says, 'I'm glad to get out of that place. I thought it had a sinister atmosphere from the start and I was right.'

Edwin is sitting in the back. 'Poor Sue,' he says. 'It's easy to fool oneself about things like this but I had an uneasy feeling about her that morning that I met her by the lake.'

'You need to tell me all about it,' says Natalka. 'We'll have a proper meeting tomorrow.'

'We'll have to tread carefully,' says Edwin. 'I think the police meant it about not interfering.'

'We'll see what Harbinder says about that,' says Natalka. 'I've asked her to join us.'

Chapter 16

Harbinder: simultaneous translation

Harbinder is, in fact, already in Shoreham. Harbinder and Mette went to Denmark for Easter so Harbinder knew that her mother would expect them for the following weekend. Bibi Kaur is as keen on Sunday lunch as any Christian. Also, Harbinder's nephew is playing in a football match and Mette wants to be there. She loves the game and, in consequence, is adored by the younger members of the family. When Natalka rang, babbling about bodies in lakes, Harbinder agreed to delay her departure and meet the gang in Edwin's flat the next morning. Mette has an early meeting so she gets the commuter train back to London. Harbinder will drive back later.

Harbinder doesn't like to admit it, even to herself, but there is something both exciting and comforting about going sleuthing in Shoreham again. The air has the fresh feel of a morning after rain and a bright blue sky is reflected in the puddles as she walks along the promenade. The windows of Seaview Court sparkle in the sunlight. It was here that Harbinder first encountered Benedict and Edwin, here that she first witnessed the amateur detectives in pursuit of their friend Peggy's killer. Harbinder remembers being impressed by Benedict's methodology, Edwin's observational powers and Natalka's frankly terrifying lack of scruples. The trio had driven her mad on the Peggy Smith case but somehow they had also become friends. Harbinder wasn't surprised when Natalka set up a detective agency or when Edwin joined her. As far as she can see, they have run it professionally and have had good results. Neil says that they are well-respected by the local force.

Harbinder presses the buzzer and Edwin tells her to come up. He greets her at the door, not looking like an eighty-four-year-old who, yesterday, found a dead body in a lake. He's wearing a checked shirt, cream trousers and a rather smart blue cardigan. 'Harbinder! How lovely to see you.' He kisses her on both cheeks.

Benedict and Natalka are sitting at a table equipped with what Harbinder recognises as Edwin's detecting tools: pens, pencils, notepads, a large map of East Sussex. Benedict jumps up and gives her a hug. He looks more haggard than Edwin, which doesn't surprise Harbinder. Benedict always takes things to heart. Natalka doesn't bother to get up. 'Hooray, the detective's here,' she says. 'Now we can get on.'

'I've brought some snacks.' Harbinder proffers a paper bag. Her mother has insisted on sending her with an assortment of Indian sweets – *mithai* and coconut *laddoos*.

'Snap,' says Natalka. 'My mum sent *paska*. Ukrainian Easter bread.'

When Valentyna first arrived in Shoreham, Harbinder's parents invited her to lunch. Bibi greeted her by taking her hands in hers and saying, 'I'm so sorry about what is happening in your country.'

Harbinder hadn't known whether to be embarrassed or impressed. She had managed to avoid mentioning the war to Natalka. It seemed too huge a subject somehow. But here was Bibi wading straight in. Harbinder's father, Deepak, added, 'I remember my parents talking about partition, the horror of neighbour turning against neighbour. To have an invader in your land is a terrible thing.' Harbinder wondered whether Deepak was equating Britain's presence in India with Russia's in Ukraine. At any rate, Valentyna had clearly been deeply moved.

'How is your mum?' she asks now.

'OK,' says Natalka. 'We heard from Dmytro yesterday. Happy as anything, standing in a muddy field carrying a machine gun.'

Harbinder doesn't know how to reply to this. She suspects that her mother would have had the words, despite English not being her first language. Harbinder, like many second-generation immigrants, is skilled at simultaneous translation but she doesn't know how to respond to someone whose brother is actually fighting in a war.

'It must have been nice to see him,' is all that she can manage.

'It was,' says Natalka, with one of her dazzling smiles. 'Now let's talk about this murder.'

'Do we know for a fact that it is a murder?' says Harbinder, taking her seat at the table. She knows from experience that it's important, with Natalka, to ask these questions at the outset.

'Let me put it like this,' says Natalka. 'A woman on a writing course says to be wary of one of the tutors. A day later she's floating in the lake. What do you think?'

'Why don't we start at the beginning?' says Edwin, putting a cup of coffee beside Harbinder. The china is so fine it's almost translucent.

'Why don't we?' says Harbinder.

'Very well,' says Edwin. 'Benedict and I arrived at Battle House on Friday afternoon. Later that evening one of the guests, Sue Hitchins, told us to be wary of Imogen Blythe, a crime writer who was one of the tutors. I met Sue by chance the next morning and she told me that she had been to Battle House before with her boyfriend, Malcolm Collins.' He pauses impressively but the name means nothing to Harbinder.

'He was a journalist,' says Benedict. 'An obituary writer and a friend of Melody Chambers, the romance writer whose death we're investigating.'

'Malcolm also died in mysterious circumstances,' says Natalka.

'Well, we think he had a heart attack,' says Edwin. 'It happens. But we didn't tell you, Harbinder, that Don Parsons, the other writer whose death we're investigating, also visited Battle House several times.'

'Don Parsons was one of the names I asked you to check,' says Natalka.

'I remember,' says Harbinder, 'and I remember we didn't find anything suspicious.'

'But it's interesting that he was at Battle House too,' says Edwin. 'At the very least it's an odd coincidence.'

Harbinder admits that it is.

'So what happened next?' she asks Edwin.

'The weekend went on,' says Edwin, 'and we observed various things. Benedict has made a list. Then, on Sunday, after lunch, Benedict and I went for a walk in the grounds and we found Sue floating face down in the lake. It was where I met her that first morning, actually. It was all rather horrible. Benedict and Leonard, the other tutor, got her body out but there was nothing anyone could do. I called an ambulance and the police came too. There were two CID officers who interviewed us all.'

'Really?' says Harbinder. This is interesting. And potentially alarming. 'What were their names?'

'DS Liv Brennan and DS Sam Malone.'

'Brennan was the clever one,' says Natalka, 'and she more or less told us to stay out of the case.'

Harbinder groans inwardly. 'Did you tell her you were private investigators?'

'Yes,' says Natalka brightly. 'And we told her we knew you.'

'Great,' says Harbinder. 'Thanks.'

'Does the presence of CID mean that the death is considered suspicious?' Benedict asks.

'Not necessarily,' says Harbinder. 'I imagine they are treating it as an unexplained death. Unexplained is playing it safe. But you're right that they obviously don't think it's an open-and-shut natural death. Did forensics attend the scene?'

'Yes,' says Benedict. 'They took our clothes and everything. They were very thorough.'

'I'll see if I can talk to the officers involved,' says Harbinder. 'But they're under no obligation to tell me anything.'

'I bet they will,' says Natalka. 'You're famous.'

'Hardly,' says Harbinder.

'Can I show you my list?' says Benedict.

'Please do.'

It's very neat, organised in alphabetical order.

Peter Abbot
50s. Children's author, but 'dark stuff'. B overheard him talking about having to be brutal, writes books on cannibalism.

Imogen Blythe
45. Crime writer. Married to Declan, a lawyer and would-be writer. Two children. Has been teaching at BH for 5 years. Knew Melody and Don. Sue warned us to be wary of her.

Sue Hitchins
60s? Ex-teacher. Lives in London. In a relationship with Malcolm Collins.
Warned us to be wary of Imogen. Why? Thinks she needs to finish Malcolm's book.

Johnnie Newton
Mid-50s? Aspiring crime writer. Mentioned to B that she'd been in an institution. Where?

Leonard Norris
61. Ex-alcoholic? Writer though hasn't published anything since 1992. Lives at Battle House and knew previous owner Miriam Fry. Has been teaching at BH for 10 years. Knew Don Parsons and said he thought he was 'odd'.

Frances O'Toole
50s or even 60s. Poet. Seems to like dead birds.

Georgina and David Potter-Smith
Farmers. Own Battle House. Miriam was G's aunt.

'If you had to suspect one of these people,' says Harbinder, 'who would it be?' She often finds, with her team, that first impressions are surprisingly prescient. Not counting Tory's, of course.

'Imogen,' says Benedict.

'Peter,' says Edwin.

'That's interesting,' says Harbinder. 'Why?'

'Peter kept going on about Sue's death being suicide,' says Edwin. 'Almost like he wanted to convince us. Plus, Benedict heard him talking on the phone about being brutal to someone. I thought he was a nasty character. He talked about writing cannibalism books for children.'

'To be fair,' says Harbinder, 'those sound like the kind of books my nieces and nephews would love. Why did you say Imogen, Benedict?'

Benedict sounds slightly defensive. 'Well, Sue did warn us to be wary of her.'

'I thought she explained that all she meant was that you couldn't trust Imogen's feedback,' says Edwin. 'I have to admit I quite liked Imogen. She's invited me to join her book group.'

'That's probably why I picked her,' says Benedict. 'I could tell she liked you and thought I was an idiot. But, also, she tried too hard to be relatable. All that chat about her husband and kids.'

'My sergeant, Kim, does that too,' says Harbinder. 'Very hetero-normative but useful sometimes.'

'Actually, I don't really see Imogen as a murderer,' says Benedict. 'Whoever killed Sue must have acted on the spur of the moment, seized their opportunity. That's a rare sort of person, isn't it, Harbinder? Almost a psychopath.'

'Psychopaths can behave in an impulsive or risky manner,' says Harbinder. 'They also lack guilt or empathy. Pushing a stranger into a lake could be seen as psychopathic behaviour but, if this was planned, it would depend on very exact timing. Remind me of the timeline again.'

'Lunch finished at around two-fifteen,' says Benedict. 'People helped clear the table. Annoyingly I can't remember exactly who. Then the other guests left and Edwin and I loaded the dishwasher and tidied up. By the time we'd finished it was three-thirty.'

'I'm not surprised,' says Natalka, 'you're obsessive about the way you load the dishwasher.'

'Well, if you don't stack all the plates the same way, they don't wash.'

Harbinder clears her throat.

'Sorry,' says Benedict. 'The last session wasn't until four so we decided to go for a walk. We didn't see anyone on our way. In fact, Edwin said how quiet the place was and I said I thought people were packing. We went to the lake and, well, you know what we saw.'

'Imogen said that she and Leonard were having a meeting,' says Edwin. 'That sounded a bit like an alibi to me at the time. And Leonard said something strange in the kitchen, when we were waiting to be interviewed by the police. He said Sue's death "brought it all back".'

'I'd forgotten that,' says Benedict.

'Frances said that Leonard was close to Melody Chambers,' says Edwin. 'I think we ought to follow that up.'

'So the murder happened between two-fifteen and three-thirty,' says Harbinder. 'It's a very small window of opportunity.'

'What about this Johnnie?' says Natalka. 'What institution do you think she'd been in?'

'She made it sound like it was prison,' says Benedict. 'But I could see her doing that just to shock. She might just as well have been a nurse or a teacher.'

'Or in the army,' says Edwin. 'I can see her as a trained killer.'

'Can you?' says Harbinder.

'Well, maybe not exactly,' Edwin backtracks. 'But she had rather a brusque manner.'

'That's not quite enough for a conviction,' says Harbinder. 'I'll see what I can find out about the investigation. It's worth remembering that the killer – if there is a killer – could have been an outsider. How secure was the site?'

'Not secure at all, as far as I could see,' says Benedict. 'Anyone could approach via the woods or the fields.'

'Were there any houses nearby?'

'Only the farmhouse where Georgina and David live.' Benedict points at his precious list.

'Could they have got to the lake without being seen?' asks Harbinder.

'I think so,' says Benedict. 'But I can't think why either of them would kill Sue.'

'We're thinking about means, not motive,' says Harbinder. 'If I was the SIO, I'd ask for a search of all the surrounding countryside. But it's hard when the area is so wide and there are animals around to contaminate the scene. The rain last night won't have helped either.'

'So what's our next step?' says Natalka. 'Should we concentrate on Sue or on Melody and Don?'

'Is it worth reminding you that the police asked you not to get involved?' says Harbinder.

But no one, not even law-abiding Benedict, pays any attention.

Harbinder arrives back in West London at one. When she gets to her office, she sees that Kim has left a sandwich on her desk. It's very hard not to have favourites, thinks Harbinder, when one of your team does things like this. She's just eating it, and sifting through her messages from Freya, her PA, when the outside line rings.

'A call from Hastings CID,' says Freya.

Harbinder hastily swallows her mouthful.

'DI Kaur.'

'Hallo,' says a voice that sounds young but not lacking in confidence. 'This is DS Liv Brennan from Hastings CID. I'm investigating the death of a woman called Sue Hitchins. She was found last night in the grounds of a residential centre called Battle House. She had drowned in a lake.'

Harbinder wonders if she should just wait to see how much Liv Brennan is prepared to tell her but then she thinks that this isn't very professional and, besides, she hasn't much time. As succinctly as possible, she tells Liv that she has already spoken to Natalka.

'I can't believe it,' says Liv, sounding much less measured. 'I specifically told her not to get involved.'

'Well, Natalka isn't the best at obeying orders.'

There's a pause and then Liv says, 'Confidentially, we're treating this as a suspicious death.'

'Really?' says Harbinder. 'I thought it might have been suicide.'

'That's what we thought at first but SOCO found two sets of footprints at the water's edge. It was raining hard which made conditions difficult but there are definite signs indicative of a struggle. Also animal prints, probably a dog.'

'So, someone attacked Sue Hitchins and pushed her into the lake?'

'It looks like that. The post-mortem will tell us more, of course. Could have been a random attacker. We're looking at anyone with previous who might have been in the area on Sunday afternoon. There are a couple who live in the nearby farmhouse but they were together all afternoon and evening. So you can see why we're also going to have to look carefully at everyone who was at Battle House that weekend.'

'I can see that,' says Harbinder. She waits.

'So I was thinking . . . Edwin Fitzgerald was actually on the writing course. Benedict Cole too. Technically they're suspects. But I've been looking into the detective agency. K and F, it's called. They seem legitimate. If we can rule out Fitzgerald and Cole – and they seem to have a solid alibi for Hitchins' death – they could be quite useful to us. So what I wanted to ask you was – should we trust them? Should we trust this Natalka Kolisnyk? She's the one who's a partner in the agency, not Benedict Cole.'

'I know,' says Harbinder. She has always wondered why Benedict, who seems to have the best detective's brain of all of them, didn't want to be involved in the agency.

'I wondered what you could tell me about K and F,' says Liv. 'I know you know them from the Peggy Smith case.'

Harbinder is impressed that Liv has done her homework. She hesitates. On the one hand, she knows the gang are desperate to be involved but, on the other, is it fair to embroil them in another murder case, one that is potentially dangerous? She thinks of

Benedict with his list, Edwin with his pens and notepads, Natalka being brave about her brother.

'They're a good team,' she says. 'Natalka is very bright, Edwin doesn't miss a trick and Benedict, even if he's not officially part of the company, has excellent detective's instincts. I think they could be very helpful to you.'

Chapter 17

Edwin: next steps

Edwin loves holding meetings in his flat. It makes him feel like he's at the centre of the investigation instead of the elderly person on the sidelines, holding the youngsters' coats. The presence of Harbinder had helped make it feel official. He remembers from previous cases the way she can cut through the detail to the important matters. 'Timeline?' 'How secure was the site?' It's a matter of pride with Edwin to be able to answer these questions calmly and carefully. He's not emotional, like Benedict, or impulsive, like Natalka. In Edwin's own mind, he's the perfect combination of the two.

When Harbinder leaves to go back to London, Benedict says that he must go and open the Shack.

'Benny!' says Natalka. 'What's more important? Serving coffee or solving crimes?'

'Well, serving coffee is my job.' Edwin thinks he looks rather crestfallen. He knows Benedict doesn't want to be a café-owner for ever but it must be hard to hear Natalka dismissing his business like this.

'Why don't you ask Kyle if he'll open it?' says Edwin. Kyle is the son of Alison, who manages Seaview Court. He's a student – no one knows of what – and often helps out at the Shack.

'Good idea,' says Benedict, brightening.

'I am going to have to go into work in a minute,' says Natalka. 'We're still short-staffed.'

'Is Valentyna going to join the team?' asks Benedict.

'She's shadowing Maria this morning,' says Natalka. 'Then she's going to take on her own clients. That should help, if she doesn't drive me crazy, but, until she's working on her own, I still need to do some shifts. So, we must move quickly. What are our next steps?'

'There's a WhatsApp group for people who were on the course,' says Benedict. 'At the moment it's just everyone saying how shocked they are, but I think we should maintain a presence.'

'Definitely,' says Natalka. 'And it would be worth interviewing them all separately if you can. Edwin, aren't you going to Imogen's book group?'

'Yes, but she hasn't given me a date yet.'

'When she does, it'll be a great chance for some sleuthing. Do you think any of the others will be there?'

'I don't know,' says Edwin. Imogen told him that she only invited the most promising students but he doesn't want to repeat this in front of Benedict. 'Maybe Frances or Johnnie? They've both been to Battle House several times.'

'Hang on,' says Benedict. 'Are we actually investigating Sue's death now or are we still concentrating on Melody and Don? That's what we're being paid to do, after all.'

Natalka looks mutinous but Edwin thinks Benedict has a point.

'You're right,' he says, 'but I think there are some potential cross-overs. I thought I'd do some more research on Malcolm. I'll go to the library today and look up all his recent obituaries. There might be clues there. And, given that Sue and Malcolm met at Shoreham Library, I might be able to find out more from the staff.'

'Maybe I should talk to Don's friends and parishioners,' says Benedict. 'It seems unlikely that he was connected to Sue or Malcolm, but he was at Battle House last year. And my friend Richard definitely thought there was something suspicious about his death.'

'You should do it immediately,' says Natalka. 'You can borrow my car if you want.'

Benedict looks taken aback. Edwin sympathises. Natalka's preference for instant action can be exhausting sometimes. 'What about the Shack?'

'Weren't you going to ask Kyle to look after it?'

'OK,' says Benedict. 'Looks like I'm off to Surrey.'

'Excellent,' says Natalka. 'Let's meet here again this evening, after I've done my last rounds. Is that OK with you, Edwin?'

'Perfect,' says Edwin.

Edwin still feels full of energy as he washes up the coffee cups. He doesn't think it's worth having a dishwasher when he mostly just uses one plate, glass and cup a day. He smiles when he remembers Benedict with the monster dishwasher at Battle House. Natalka was right: he was a bit neurotic about it. But, while they were arguing about whether knives should go blade upwards, someone had murdered Sue Hitchins. Or she had killed herself. Edwin remembers the crouching figure at the water's edge. The statue of a woman leaning forward with her hair touching the water. 'I thought it would be better here,' Sue had told him, 'but it isn't. It's worse if anything.' If that had been the last Edwin had seen of Sue, he could well believe that she had yielded to the temptation of the still, green water. But, for the rest of the weekend, she'd seemed fine. She wrote a piece on the theme 'If only I hadn't' and offered to read it aloud. She'd performed in a sketch with Benedict on Sunday. In fact, she'd been unexpectedly good. She had complimented Edwin on his pasta sauce. Was this the behaviour of someone who, only hours later, would take their own life?

By the time Edwin has tidied everything away, he is flagging slightly. He almost has a chocolate biscuit for the energy but resists. He doesn't fancy the walk to the library, though, so he calls the local taxi firm, where he has an account. He's lucky. It's Ali, his favourite driver, and they chat about books for the short journey. Ali averages a book a day, reading between jobs, and he's actually far better read than Edwin.

The sight of the library revives Edwin again. The church and the library are his favourite communal places and, in Edwin's mind, they fulfil the same function: worship of the unknowable. He remembers Peggy with her beret and 'Books are My Bag' tote bag, searching out volumes on Russia and the Balkans while Edwin scanned the biographies. Dear Peggy. It's not the same without her.

Even the lobby, with its posters for computer clubs and amateur dramatic groups, soothes Edwin. He recognises the woman behind the desk from his trips with Peggy. There's a tricky moment when he can't remember her name but, luckily, a colleague calls over with a question about an event tonight.

'Hallo, Sally. Long time no see.'

'Edwin!' Full marks to Sally. 'I was just talking about you and Peggy the other day. I still miss her.'

'So do I.'

They exchange Peggy memories for a while and then Edwin says, leaning casually on a pile of Richard Osmans, 'Did you ever meet a woman called Sue Hitchins?'

To his surprise, Sally says immediately, 'Writes short stories? Yes, she used to come here a lot at one time. How's she doing?'

'There's no easy way to say this,' says Edwin, 'but she's dead. I was at a writing retreat at the weekend and she . . . she drowned in a lake.'

'Oh my God.' Sally puts her hand up to her mouth. 'That's so awful.'

'Yes,' says Edwin. 'Isn't it?'

'You must be really shaken.'

'I am,' says Edwin although, truthfully, this last exchange has invigorated him. He feels that he's close to a discovery of some kind. 'Sue mentioned that she met her boyfriend, Malcolm Collins, here.'

'Yes. We were all so pleased when they got together. It was young Rosalind who introduced them, I think. She's not here any more.'

Rosalind must be the 'teenage matchmaker' mentioned in Sue's piece, thinks Edwin.

'It was so unfair,' says Sally. 'I think Sue was quite lonely after she retired and her mum died. Then she met Malcolm and they seemed so happy. Then that wretched Covid.'

'Covid?' says Edwin. 'Did Malcolm die from Covid? I thought it was a heart attack.'

'I'm pretty sure it was Covid. I remember thinking – people are still dying from it.'

'Yes, they are,' says Edwin. He's thoughtful as he makes his way to the computer room. If Malcolm died from Covid, then his death was from natural, if tragic, causes. There can't be a link with Melody Chambers or Battle House. All the same, he's reluctant to let go of the connection. It can't hurt to do a bit of googling.

He starts with 'Malcolm Collins death' and comes up with a round-up in the *Guardian*, the only paper that is still tracking Covid cases. 'Malcolm Collins, journalist, 63, from complications resulting from Covid-19.'

Next, Edwin searches 'Malcolm Collins obituaries'. He reads about opera singers and TV producers, actors and ballet dancers. How much some people achieve in their lives, thinks Edwin. If he'd really persevered at his clarinet, could he have been a professional musician? Probably not. Edwin suspects that he was always born to be a dilettante, on the edges of the art world and now on the edges of the crime world. Well, at least he's still alive. A depressing number of obits are for people who were born in the 1950s or even 60s.

Just when Edwin thinks that he needs a break and a sandwich, he catches sight of an obituary from 2021 for Felix Marshall, 'The Artist who made the Flute Cool'. That's quite an achievement, thinks Edwin, remembering the derision he got at school for playing a woodwind instrument. This obituary follows Malcolm Collins' usual pattern: straight in with a description of the deceased, brief biography, then a summary of descendants. Edwin reads that Felix Marshall, 82, a classical flautist who was also a famous folk musician, died at his home in Kensington, flute in hand. He was a widower and is survived by three adult children, one of whom works for the BBC. Nothing very surprising there (though very sad, of course), until Edwin remembers Sue's description of the book Malcolm was planning to write if his own death hadn't intervened. The book about a classical musician.

A musician who's murdered by his own instrument.

Chapter 18

Benedict: live and let live

Don Parsons' parish church, St Mary's, is in a village outside Banstead in Surrey. It's the kind of picture-postcard building, lychgate, Norman tower, ivy-covered graveyard, that prompts Catholics, including Benedict's mother, to comment 'it was ours once'. Benedict usually replies by saying that the Reformation was a good thing (the clue is in the name) but, thinking of some of the concrete and glass churches where he had been a curate, he feels a slight pang for evensong, choir practice and the picturesque life of a country vicar. Even the monastery had been a relatively new construction because all the beautiful old abbeys were destroyed by Henry VIII or given to his rich friends. If he'd been a Protestant, wonders Benedict, as he parks the car and walks under the gate towards the very closed-looking wooden door, would he have left the priesthood? After all, vicars can get married, although Don never had.

To Benedict's surprise, the door is unlocked and the smell that greets him is the aroma of churches everywhere: candles, flower-stalks and damp. The interior is beautiful with stained glass windows casting pools of light onto the stone floor, which is being swept by a woman in dungarees.

'Hallo,' says Benedict.

The woman doesn't hear him so, when she turns and sees a strange man by the baptismal font, she gives a squeak of surprise. Benedict sees the white tips of AirPods in her ears.

'I'm sorry to disturb you,' he says. 'I'm looking for the vicar.'

The woman, who is quite young with short blonde hair, touches an ear, presumably to silence the speakers, and says, 'Lucy will be doing Knit and Natter now. It's in the parish hall next door?'

Somehow Benedict hadn't expected the incumbent of this traditional-looking church to be a woman.

'I was a friend of Don's, the previous vicar,' he says. It's not exactly a lie. They were brothers in Christ, after all. 'Did you know him?'

'Oh yes,' says the woman. 'Father Don was lovely. Everyone liked him. But Lucy's more dynamic, you know?'

She has the modern habit of ending sentences on a question mark. Even Benedict's sister does it, although she's never questioned anything in her life.

'It was so sad about Don,' says Benedict.

'Yes,' says the woman. 'Just when he'd nursed his mum through all that and finally got his life back? I didn't even know that he was ill.'

As far as Benedict knows, Don wasn't ill. Until he dropped down dead of a heart attack.

'Did you ever read his books?' he says, trying for a friendly bookish tone.

The woman laughs. 'Not my sort of thing. I'm more of a horror girl. I mean, when the news got out, some people in the parish were shocked. A vicar writing as a woman! But live and let live, you know?'

'Did Don have any close friends in the village?' asks Benedict.

The woman moves her broom across her chest in a gesture that looks both protective and slightly threatening.

'I thought you were meant to be his friend?'

'I am but we haven't seen each other in years.' That, at least, is true.

'Lucy's next door,' says the woman and, with a touch of her headphones, she turns her back on him.

Lucy, a jolly woman who is probably in her mid-fifties, is far more forthcoming. 'By all accounts, Don was a sweet man but he really did no outreach of any kind. I've started Knit and Natter, Bitch and Stitch, Sow and Sew – that's gardening *and* needlework, by the way.'

'Gosh,' says Benedict. The parish hall, a converted barn in the grounds of the church, contains six women in various stages of wool construction. Lucy's own knitting, a pink square, doesn't resemble any item of clothing Benedict can think of. The room is too large to be cosy although some efforts have been made to cheer the place up: colourful beanbags, a table with coffee and plastic cups, a rainbow banner on the wall.

Benedict and Lucy are drinking the coffee and sitting on the beanbags. The knitters carry on nattering in their corner. Benedict sips the drink cautiously. Has he finally found it? The worst coffee in the world?

Benedict asks Lucy if she's ever read any of Don's books.

'I haven't got much time for reading,' she replies, 'though I did start the Words and Wine Club. We meet in the library after it closes on Fridays. It's more wine than words, though.'

'I understand some people were shocked by Don writing as a woman?'

'This is a small rural village,' says Lucy. 'Some people are stuck in the old ways.'

'When did the news get out that Don was Donna Parsons?'

'I think a reporter found out about it. As I understand it, Father Don then put a message in the parish newsletter.'

'Was there a backlash?'

'I wouldn't go that far. More of a gentle ripple of disapproval. Like I say, Don was a nice man. Most people liked him.'

'Did he have any close friends in the village?'

'I think he kept himself to himself after his mum died. Just him and his cat. I inherited her. A terrifying beast called Sybil.'

Benedict likes Lucy for taking on Don's cat. He asks the vicar if she has heard of a writers' retreat called Battle House. Unexpectedly, she says she has. 'They got in touch a few weeks ago. Said that Don was meant to send them a short story, or something like that, and it hadn't arrived. I had to break it to the man on the phone that Don was dead. He sounded awfully upset.'

'This man, was he called Leonard Norris?'

'I don't think he gave a name. Sorry.'

'I don't suppose you found Don's short story? I'd love to read it, if so.'

Benedict wonders if Lucy, like the cleaner, will start to distrust this inquisitive stranger but she says, with unruffled amiability, 'I didn't look but you're welcome to search his laptop. It's still at the vicarage. I'll walk you back there. I've got an hour before Sing and Sign.'

On the walk to the outskirts of the village, Lucy tells Benedict that Don was a very traditional Christian, 'Almost Anglo-Catholic. You know, the rosary, the true presence, confession. Don was a great one for confession. I haven't been since 1982. I'd have to set aside a whole day. Ha.'

'I used to be a monk,' says Benedict. 'We went to confession every week. Honestly, it was hard to think of enough sins. I've read that Pope John-Paul the Second used to go every day.'

'The cloistered life has never appealed to me,' says Lucy. 'I like being part of the community. I'm not married and this is my family. Here we are.'

Benedict knows that the days of Victorian vicarages, for the vicar, his wife and their solid Victorian family, are over but, even so, the small, brick bungalow seems particularly soulless. But, inside, the house is a tribute to Lucy's many interests: muddy hiking boots by the front door, bicycle in the hallway, boxes full of jumble and bric-a-brac, a dryrobe hanging on a hook.

Lucy bends down to pick up her post and a cat appears, miaowing accusingly. It's the largest domestic feline that Benedict has ever seen, tortoiseshell with round, disconcertingly human-looking eyes.

'That's Sybil,' says Lucy. 'Don's cat. I think she hates me.'

'I'm sure she doesn't,' says Benedict. Sybil gives him a look of pure contempt.

'The laptop's in the study,' says Lucy. 'Don had his study in here too. It's the smallest bedroom really.'

The room is indeed small and full of clutter. There's an exercise bike and a confusing tower of wicker baskets that Lucy says is an 'activity centre' for Sybil. 'She never uses it, of course.'

Bookshelves line one wall. Benedict sees bound volumes of what look like parish records mixed with an extensive selection of paperbacks. He spots the Agatha Christies – with his favourite Tom Adams covers – by their spines. Were these Don's books if Lucy doesn't have time for reading? Lucy reaches above the Georgette Heyer collection to take down a slim, silver MacBook Air. It strikes Benedict as slightly strange that Don, who according to Richard had not owned a mobile phone, possessed such a high-tech computer. Lucy's own preference is clearly for a desktop, which takes up almost half the old-fashioned partners' desk.

Benedict flicks open the laptop.

'It might need charging,' says Lucy. 'There's a lead somewhere.' She rummages in a drawer. Benedict takes the opportunity to look at his phone. It's working again after its immersion in rice, but the screen has a marbled look that suggests this might not continue for long. One message from Edwin saying, 'Possible clue !' Nothing from Natalka.

'Here you are.' Lucy brandishes a length of cable. Benedict plugs in the computer and, a few seconds later, the Apple logo appears. 'Password' it prompts.

'I don't suppose you know the password?' he asks.

'Try Don's name,' said Lucy. 'Or the word password. That's what I always do.'

Hoping the village does not contain a Hack and Track club, Benedict tries Don's name in various forms, including the feminine version, without any success.

'Take it with you,' said Lucy. 'One of his other friends might know.'

Was this a pointed remark? But Lucy's face is as friendly and guileless as ever.

'Thank you,' says Benedict. 'That's very kind.'

From the window ledge, Sybil turns away in disgust.

'This is his actual laptop?' says Edwin. 'I can't believe the Rev Lucy just gave it to you.'

'I know,' says Benedict. 'I couldn't work out if she was trusting or just not very interested. A bit of both, I think.'

They are in Edwin's flat in Seaview Court for their debriefing session. Edwin has looked up Malcolm Collins' obituary for Don Parsons and has found his date of birth, but this doesn't reveal the laptop's secrets. When Natalka arrives, she suggests the names of Don's – or Donna's – books. Edwin looks on Wikipedia and comes up with *Red as the Rose*, *A Rose for Remembrance*, *A Rose by Any Other Name*, *A Country Girl*, *Golden Lads and Girls* and *A Deadly Bargain*. None of them provides a password.

'So many roses,' says Natalka, biting into one of Edwin's posh biscuits.

'Of course one of them's a Shakespeare quotation,' says Edwin. 'Hang on, I wonder . . .'

He goes to the bookcase and comes back with a thick, leather-bound volume.

'Is that a Bible?' asks Natalka.

'Better,' says Edwin. 'It's the complete works of Shakespeare. Let me have a look . . . it'll be near the end . . .'

He leafs through the thin, gilt-edged pages until he evidently finds the play he's looking for.

'Here it is . . . *Golden lads and girls all must, As chimney-sweepers, come to dust . . .*'

He looks at them triumphantly. Benedict and Natalka exchange glances.

'What does it mean?' says Natalka.

'I read somewhere,' says Benedict, 'that "golden lads" was an old Warwickshire name for dandelions. They're chimney-sweepers when they turn white and you blow on them . . .' He stops because Natalka is looking at him with bafflement and Edwin with impatience.

'It's from *Cymbeline*,' says Edwin. 'Oh, come on. *Imogen*.'

'Imogen in *Cymbeline*?' says Benedict. He tries to remember what happens in the play. Does Imogen survive or is she one of Shakespeare's many dead girls? He thinks of Imogen Blythe, her intent look when listening to the students read their work, her eagerness to fill wine glasses, her reluctance to talk books with Benedict.

'Do you think there could be a link to the Imogen at Battle House?' he says. 'It's a bit tenuous.'

'Is it? We know Don went to Battle House and someone there is pretty keen to get hold of his writing.'

'When was Golden Whatsits written?' asks Natalka.

'2019,' says Edwin. '*A Deadly Bargain* was his last book. It came out in January this year.'

'Try Imogen as a password,' says Natalka.

Edwin does but with no success. After trying variations on Cymbeline, Imogen, Shakespeare and dandelions, he shuts the laptop.

'We'll never be able to open it.'

'Let's leave it for now,' says Natalka. 'What else have you found out? You said there was a possible clue.'

'Well, for a start,' says Edwin, 'Malcolm Collins died from Covid, not a heart attack. So his death isn't suspicious.'

'Shame,' says Natalka. Benedict wonders if she knows she said it aloud.

'But I did find something. It might be nothing . . .' Benedict can tell Edwin doesn't think so, he has the modest look that usually comes with a revelation of some kind. 'I looked through Malcolm's obituaries and I came up with one for Felix Marshall, a flautist who died in 2021. Nothing suspicious about his death except that he had his flute beside him. And I remembered what Sue had said about the book Malcolm was going to write. It was about a musician *murdered by his own instrument*. Well, what better way to kill someone who plays the flute than by poisoning the mouthpiece?'

'Do you think this Felix was murdered?' asks Benedict.

'Well, maybe Malcolm thought he was, and that's why he wanted to write a story about it and mentioned his suspicions to Sue. And, a few minutes after describing this story, Sue was also killed. And do you remember what else she wrote? *I know the real story*. That implies there was more to tell. Anyway, I thought it was worth checking up. I rang one of my old BBC friends. Felix's son, Ivan, works there. I've arranged to meet him in London on Wednesday. Pretending to be an old friend of Felix's.'

'Well done, Edwin,' says Natalka. 'Now, if we could just get into Don's computer and find a link to this Felix. What do we know about Don, Benedict?'

'Not much,' says Benedict. 'Richard said he was devoted to his mother and his . . .'

He stops, opens the laptop and types, 'SYBIL'.

'Welcome Don,' says the screen.

Their task is made easier by the neatness of Don's files. There's one for each of his books plus PARISH (in scary capitals), Donna, Sybil and Work in Progress. In the latter file Benedict finds notes for a book called *The Lily and the Rose* (Don really did like that flower) and a document entitled 'I'm Scared'. He opens it.

'"I'm scared, they're trying to kill me. For weeks I've been telling myself it's impossible. They're my friends. They wouldn't hurt me. Even if I know their secret, they know mine. Surely, we are even. But one day I'll be found dead and no one will know or care. But they will have killed me."'

Benedict reads this aloud and looks up at Edwin and Natalka.

'He was found dead,' he says. 'And no one cared. Except his friend Richard. That's what Don wrote to Richard. He said, "They're trying to kill me." I wish Richard had kept the letter.'

'They,' says Edwin. 'More than one person.'

'Unless it's a non-binary person who uses the pronoun "they",' says Natalka. 'I had to explain pronouns to my mum the other day. It was very hard.'

'He said "They're my friends,"' counters Edwin. 'In the plural.'

'Don's friends were plotting to kill him,' says Benedict. 'He knows their secret, they know his.'

'We must show Harbinder,' says Natalka.

'She'll just say it's too vague,' says Benedict. 'And she'd be right.'

'Could it be part of a story?' asks Edwin.

'That's what Alan Franklin said about Melody Chambers writing that her husband was trying to kill her,' says Natalka. 'I think we need to talk to Alan again.'

'There's no link to Don, though,' says Benedict.

'Except that Don and Melody both went to Battle House,' says Edwin.

They all jump when Edwin's phone, which is always kept on the loudest setting, pings. Edwin looks at the message, which Benedict knows will be displayed in a size 20 font.

'It's Imogen,' says Edwin. 'Sue's funeral is on Friday.'

'We'll be there,' says Benedict.

'Oh, and there's another message too.' Benedict can feel Natalka growing impatient as Edwin finds and enlarges the text.

'It's from DS Brennan at Hastings CID. She wants to talk to us.'

Chapter 19

Natalka: a bit of detecting

Natalka and Benedict are having breakfast together. Valentyna is
working the early shift at Care4You. She has not yet been there
two full days but Maria already says she doesn't know how she ever
coped without her. Despite her earlier misgivings, Natalka finds the
flat is a happier place now that they're all working. This morning
Valentyna had left before Natalka returned from her run and now
she can sit with her boyfriend in the sunlight eating muesli. Natalka
wants to talk about the case but Benedict seems distracted, crum-
bling his toast and looking past Natalka, out of the window. Last
night, Natalka had found him in the kitchen at two a.m., staring
out to sea. His face, briefly illuminated by the strobing lighthouse
beam, had looked pale and haggard.

'I used to look at the lighthouse before I met you,' said Benedict,
'and wonder if I'd die alone.'

'Come back to bed,' said Natalka.

He had acquiesced and they had made love silently, conscious of Valentyna in the next room. But, this morning, Benedict still seems troubled.

'Are you OK?' says Natalka.

'Of course.' Benedict gives her his nicest smile, his eyes softening behind his glasses. That's as it should be, thinks Natalka. Her boyfriend should look at her like that. But he shouldn't get up in the night and talk about being alone. And the other day he had shocked Natalka by asking her if she ever imagined her own obituary. 'No,' she'd said, 'I don't think about death.' Not her own, anyway.

'Are you thinking about Sue?' she says.

'A bit,' says Benedict. 'I don't like this side of detection work.'

'The deaths, you mean?'

'Yes. In the murder mysteries I like – the golden age ones – the deaths are almost incidental. But Sue was alive and now she's dead. I saw her body in the water.'

'That must have been awful.'

'I keep replaying it in my head. Thinking I could have done more.'

'She was dead already. The police said so.'

'I know. But I keep thinking I should have guessed that something was going to happen to her that weekend. There were clues. Her comments about Imogen, her piece on "If only I hadn't" when she wrote about knowing the real story. I keep thinking: if only I *had*. Done something, I mean.'

'You can't think that way. You'll drive yourself mad.'

'I know. I'll pull myself together. But this is why I wouldn't be a good private detective. You and Edwin are tougher.'

'I have to be tough,' says Natalka, suddenly impatient. 'My brother's at war.'

'I know,' says Benedict. 'I'm sorry.'

Natalka decides it's time for action. She stands up.

'Come on,' she says. 'Let's get ready. We need to pick Edwin up at ten. Doing something will make you feel better. I think it's great that the police want to involve us.'

'Why do you think they do?'

'Because Harbinder told them how good we were.'

'How good *you* are,' says Benedict, but he smiles again.

Benedict does seem to cheer up when they collect Edwin, spruce in a pale blue V-neck and chinos. They even play 'Who Am I?' in the car, as they did on the road trip to Scotland four years ago. Natalka could have predicted the results. Edwin: Maria Callas. Benedict: Agatha Christie. Natalka: Stormzy. She knew the others wouldn't get hers in twenty guesses and they didn't.

Hastings is looking its best in the sunshine. They park by the huts that were once used for drying fishing nets and look like elongated garden sheds. They walk through the old town which is full of cafés and antiques shops. The police station isn't picturesque, though, it's a brick and glass modern building that manages to look both dreary and menacing.

'It was voted the most sexist police station in the country last year,' Liv Brennan tells them, 'so that's nice.'

Natalka knew that she'd like Liv and she does. She reminds her of Harbinder with her deadpan humour and no-nonsense manner. Sam Malone, who is waiting in the meeting room, seems quite over-awed by her. All the same, Natalka wonders what it's like being a woman, and a black woman too, in the most sexist police station in Britain.

After offers of tea and coffee – politely refused – Liv faces them across the round table.

'Thank you for coming. I've spoken to DI Harbinder Kaur and she says that she worked with you on a previous case. She vouches for your professionalism and discretion.' Is it Natalka's imagination or does Liv glance, slightly doubtfully, in her direction?

'Very kind of her,' says Edwin.

'So I'm . . . we're . . .' an apologetic glance at Sam, 'interested in your impression of the other guests at Battle House last weekend. Anything that you might have noticed.'

'Does this mean that you're treating Sue's death as suspicious?' asks Natalka.

Liv exchanges a look with Sam before answering, a shade repressively, 'Confidentially, we are treating this as a suspicious death. We can't give you any more information at this time.'

'We've made some notes,' says Benedict. He hands over his list of suspects. Both Sam and Liv lean forward to look at it. Natalka knows it by heart.

'Was there any animosity between Sue and any of the other guests over the course of the weekend?' asks Liv.

'Not that I could see,' says Benedict. 'Sue was fairly quiet in the group but she seemed on friendly terms with everyone. She cooked a meal with Johnnie. Imogen and some of the others gave Sue positive feedback on a piece she'd written.'

Edwin coughs discreetly. 'Speaking of that piece. In it, Sue mentioned a book that her partner Malcolm, who died in 2021, was writing. I did wonder if that had any bearing . . .'

'Any bearing on her death?' says Liv, brows knitted.

'How could a book have anything to do with it?' says Sam.

'It was just a thought,' says Edwin. He doesn't say anything about the flautist.

'Did either of you have any contact with Sue over the weekend?' asks Liv.

'As I told you,' says Edwin, 'I talked to her by the lake on Saturday morning. She seemed sad about Malcolm but didn't mention anyone else on the course.'

'Did she mention being wary of Imogen Blythe?' asks Liv.

'Not again,' says Edwin. ' I was about to ask her about Imogen when Imogen herself turned up. But, as Benedict says, there didn't seem to be any animosity between them.'

'And did Sue seem well in herself?'

'I think so,' says Benedict. 'She complained of hay fever. That was all.'

'What about Peter Abbot's "potentially suspicious conversation"?' asks Liv, her voice putting fastidious quotation marks around the words.

Benedict blushes. 'I overheard him talking on the phone. He said, "There's not much time. We have to be brutal."'

'Did you ask him what that meant?'

'No. How could I? He didn't know I'd overheard.'

'Which of the guests knew Sue from previous courses?' asks Sam.

'Imogen and Leonard, the tutors,' says Benedict. 'And Frances too, I think. Frances mentioned knowing Malcolm too.'

'Johnnie Newton?'

'I can't remember but she'd been on a few previous courses. It's possible they knew each other.'

Liv says, in a casual voice, that immediately puts Natalka on alert, 'Were there any animals at Battle House?'

'Animals?' Benedict looks at Edwin. 'There was a cat I saw a few times. I think it belonged to the farmhouse.'

'And the dog that breathed all over us in the car,' says Edwin. 'Buster, his name was. He belonged to Georgina Potter-Smith.'

After a few more questions, Liv thanks them for their help and says she'll be in touch.

'Are any of you attending Sue's funeral on Friday?'

'Benedict and I will be there,' says Edwin.

'So will we,' says Liv. 'But we'll have to be discreet. Keep your eyes open.'

They have lunch in a Hastings pub, a lopsided building full of twisted beams and secret staircases, where the floor is so uneven that your glass slides across the table. Natalka loves English places like this. She has a ploughman's lunch and a lemonade, because she's driving. Benedict and Edwin both have half pints of beer. They discuss Liv and Sam.

'Liv reminds me a bit of Harbinder,' says Natalka.

'Sam said something on Sunday night about her being Liv's heroine,' says Edwin. 'I expect she's a real role model for women on the force. Especially women of colour,' he adds, in the slightly nervous tone he reserves for this phrase, hoping it's the right one.

'Who do you think they suspect?' asks Benedict, cutting into the crust of his steak-and-kidney pie. The smell stops Natalka wanting to eat her ploughman's. She pushes her plate to one side.

'I think Liv was suspicious of Imogen,' says Natalka. 'She mentioned that thing about being wary of her.'

'I can't see Imogen as the murderer,' says Edwin. He keeps saying this. It makes Natalka feel curious about the woman who led the course. Imogen Blythe's Facebook page shows a thin wispy creature, not a likely killer, but she's a crime writer which must mean that she's thought a great deal about means and motive. The Peggy Smith case taught Natalka not to underestimate authors.

She says, 'They dismissed any connection with books and writing but I think that's the key. Malcolm was going to write about a murder but then he died – even if it was from natural causes. Sue took over and she was killed. That has to be the link. It'll be interesting to see what your flute player has to say, Edwin.'

'Flautist,' says Edwin. An unnecessary correction, in Natalka's opinion. 'And it's his son. But, yes, it will be interesting.'

Natalka's phone buzzes. She guesses before she looks at the screen. 'Minnie.'

'What does she say?' says Benedict.

'The same as always. "Any news?"'

'Well, we do have news,' says Benedict. 'Are you going to tell her about Sue?'

'I don't see why not. I mean, it'll be in the papers soon.'

Natalka texts. 'Yes. Are you up for a chat?'

The answer comes back immediately. 'Can you come to Harmony's house this afternoon?' A map reference follows.

'Interesting,' says Natalka.

Natalka drops Edwin at his flat and Benedict at the Shack. Then she pops home to change into more comfortable clothes. She put on black trousers and a white shirt to impress the police officers and now feels too hot. Valentyna is sitting on the sofa, still in her scrubs.

'Are you going out again, Talia?'

'Yes. I've got a bit of detecting to do.' Natalka looks at her mother. She looks tired but Natalka knows that a change of scene always perks her up. 'Want to help?'

'Me?' Valentyna jumps to her feet immediately. 'Help with detective work? Just give me ten minutes to shower and change.'

Mother and daughter drive to Steyning, under the flyover, horses grazing unconcernedly, then along country roads, hedges on one side, foaming with cow parsley, fields on the other. As they near the village they pass an abandoned cement factory with monstrous towers and rusting machinery.

'Why don't they knock that down?' says Valentyna.

'You know the British,' says Natalka. 'It's probably a listed building.'

She has often wondered this herself. Harbinder's friend Clare lives in one of the smart houses nearby. What must it be like to live with that nightmare edifice in your back garden? Natalka suspects that Clare, an annoyingly self-possessed headteacher, hardly notices.

In Steyning, Natalka parks behind the High Street and gives Valentyna her instructions.

'Go into the pharmacy. It's just through that alleyway there. Ask to see the pharmacist. He's called Alan Franklin. Ask for him by name if necessary. Say you're having trouble sleeping and see what he recommends.'

'Do you suspect him of something?' asks Valentyna, wide-eyed.

'Other people suspect him,' says Natalka. 'I just want to see whether he's a bit free and easy with prescriptions. Or if he offers you something dodgy. Be pathetic. See if you can push him.'

'I can cry if you like,' offers Valentyna. 'I'm good at acting.'

'Go for it,' says Natalka. She has never heard her mother make this boast before.

Natalka sits in her car listening to Lizzo and ignoring the parking attendant who keeps walking slowly past her. After ten minutes, Valentyna is back.

'I saw him,' she says. 'I thought he was very charming.'

'Did he offer you sleeping pills?'

'He said he was reluctant to give them, except as a last resort. He suggested a milky drink before bedtime and not looking at my phone too much.'

This sounds like good advice – Natalka knows she spends too much time doom-scrolling on her phone – but it doesn't help with finding out whether Alan Franklin killed his wife. Natalka can just imagine Minnie's reaction. 'Well, of course he'd say that. He's diabolically clever. Can't believe you fell for it.'

'I've got a visit to make,' she tells Valentyna. 'Would you mind waiting in the car?' It doesn't scream 'modern detective' to turn up with your mother in tow.

'Why don't you leave me here,' says Valentyna, 'and pick me up afterwards? There are some lovely shops. Even a bookshop. I could buy a present for Benedict.'

'OK,' says Natalka. 'I don't think I'll be more than an hour.'

Harmony and her husband Patrick Skelton live in a terraced house on the outskirts of Steyning. It's very pretty and obviously decorated with great care but you could have fitted the whole ground floor into the kitchen of the house where Alan Franklin is now living, or Minnie's place in Brighton, for that matter. Patrick is apparently an 'entrepreneur' and Harmony is a science teacher. Patrick is out but Harmony says she does supply work and can be flexible. The couple have no children.

They sit in the courtyard garden next to a water feature and a perfectly positioned statue of a nymph. Natalka recognises it from Harmony's Facebook page. She worries about being overheard but this doesn't seem to be a concern with the sisters.

'Have you found anything on Alan yet?' asks Minnie. She is wearing exercise clothes and looks as if she has a lot of pent-up energy. She would be pacing if the backyard were big enough. As it is, she contents herself with scuffing gravel.

'I've got a contact in the police,' says Natalka. 'I checked and he's never been convicted of any crime. There have never been any complaints against him as a pharmacist either.'

'That doesn't mean he's innocent,' says Minnie, predictably. 'It just means he's cunning.' Natalka doesn't tell her about Valentyna's visit to the pharmacy. 'He's probably got another woman by now,' Minnie adds. 'He's that type.'

'You said you had some news,' says Harmony, rather hastily.

'Yes. Remember I told you that Edwin and Benedict my . . . er . . . associates . . . went to Battle House at the weekend?'

'Minnie told me,' says Harmony. 'I went there with Mummy once. Funny old place.'

'It seems so,' says Natalka. 'A woman called Sue Hitchins was killed there on Sunday.'

Harmony puts her hand in the vague area of her heart. 'Killed?'

'She drowned,' says Natalka. 'The police are investigating.'

'What's that got to do with Mummy?' says Minnie, single-minded as ever.

'Sue was in a relationship with Malcolm Collins,' says Natalka. 'I think he was one of your mum's friends?'

'Malcolm?' Harmony knits her brow. 'Oh, the journalist. He died last year, didn't he?'

'He did,' says Natalka. 'Though I read an obituary written by him the other day.'

'I think they write those things years in advance,' says Minnie. 'And they don't always get the facts right. Mummy's obituary said I was forty-five.'

'But do you think this Sue's death could be linked to Mummy's?' says Minnie.

'It's a line of investigation,' says Natalka.

'Well, it shouldn't be,' says Minnie, taking another turn around the statue. 'We've told you what happened. Alan Franklin killed our mother and now he's squatting like a toad in her house.'

It's an arresting image. Natalka remembers Dmytro finding a toad in their uncle's allotment. The creature had been oddly beautiful. She notices that Harmony is looking rather troubled. Now she says, with a nervous look at her sister, 'There is one thing . . .'

'What?' says Natalka, leaning forward. 'Any little thing could help.'

'Was Leonard Norris at Battle House? When the woman was killed?'

'Yes,' says Natalka. 'Do you know anything about Leonard Norris?'

'Only that I think he had an affair with Mummy,' says Harmony.

Chapter 20

Edwin: the youth project

Edwin starts out quite jauntily on his trip to see Ivan Marshall, son of Felix the Flautist. He takes a taxi to Shoreham-by-Sea station, changes at Brighton and gets one of the fast trains to Victoria. He even buys a *Private Eye*, to read alongside Leonard Norris's novel, *The Hopes and Fears of All the Years*. He's looking forward to being in London. It's his happy hunting ground, the place where he lived for thirty-odd years before moving to Brighton. Then he had prided himself on knowing every Tube and bus route, he knew which Underground stations had too many stairs and when it was just easier to walk. It was on foot that he knew the city best: the antiques shops around Shepherd's Market, where high-class prostitutes walked tiny dogs on leads, the drinking dens of Soho, the secret parks and graveyards.

But, when he emerges from the train, he finds Victoria station quite changed. There are shops everywhere and banks of ticket machines, interspersed with strange circular seating areas. Edwin has trouble finding his way to the Underground. He descends the steps, clinging tightly to the rail (it's been raining and the ground is slippery) to find a solitary ticket machine whose display reads 'Out of Order'. Edwin looks around and eventually locates a man in Transport for London uniform.

'Excuse me, where can I buy a ticket to Oxford Circus?'

'Use your card,' says the man. 'It's contactless.'

'My card?' repeats Edwin. But the man has moved away to help a woman with a pushchair. Does he mean a travel pass? But Edwin doesn't have one. He stands, hopelessly, as better-informed passengers stream past him.

'Can I help you?'

'Er, yes,' Edwin replies nervously. This man is not an official. He's young – almost a *youth* – with tattoos and multiple piercings. Is he about to mug Edwin? But, terrifying as he is, tattooed boy is the only person offering assistance.

Edwin says, 'I'm trying to get through the barrier.'

'Use your card.'

'What card?'

'Your debit card.'

Edwin gets out his wallet and finds his Barclaycard.

'Wave it at the machine,' says the youth.

Edwin does so but nothing happens. Impatient commuters divert on either side of them.

'Give it here.'

Edwin is amazed to find himself handing over the precious piece of plastic. Is *this* how the mugging is about to happen? But the young man waves the card at the barrier and, as it opens, hands it back. 'You can go through now.' Edwin walks forward, too flustered even to thank his saviour. How does the machine know how much to charge him when it doesn't know where he's going? Is this how he's going to be robbed today? In a contactless, digital way? But there's no time for questions and no one to give him any answers. Edwin continues on his way to the Victoria Line.

The walk seems endless, many more tunnels and escalators and meaningless walkways than Edwin remembers. He's exhausted by the time he gets on the train. Even the Tube map looks different because the Elizabeth Line has been added. Edwin has read about this new route in the papers and knows it's opening next month. What else will have changed? Edwin sits upright in his seat, scared to open his book in case he misses his stop.

Edwin gets out at Oxford Circus, tapping his debit card nervously at the barrier, and, after initially taking the wrong exit, heads for Portland Place. His old Radio 3 entrance, topped with the now-controversial Eric Gill statue, is closed for repairs so he walks around the corner to the impressively curved façade of Broadcasting House, recognisable from countless self-referential TV programmes. In the reception area Edwin submits to having his photograph taken for a security pass. When it arrives, it shows a scared-looking old man in a pink bow tie. Edwin hangs the lanyard around his neck without looking again. Then his lightweight backpack (a present from Natalka) is passed through something like an airport scanning machine. Edwin imagines the X-ray image of his book, notepad and indigestion tablets. There's evidently nothing to alarm the bored-looking attendant who attaches a purple tag and hands the bag back to Edwin.

He takes a seat on a long sofa beneath a huge TV screen showing rolling news. A seemingly endless stream of humanity passes in and out of the revolving doors. Rolling news, revolving people. Edwin is starting to feel slightly dizzy. What if no one comes to claim him? But a few moments later someone is saying his name. A large red-faced man is standing on the other side of the security gates.

'Edwin? I'm Ivan Marshall. Do you want to come through? Just wave your pass at the reader. No, that way. A bit higher. Hang on, I'll ask the receptionist to let you in.'

Eventually Edwin, slightly ruffled, is in the lift with Ivan. There's not a lot of space and Edwin keeps his eyes fixed on Ivan's security pass. It was taken when he was a lot thinner.

But Ivan is very friendly, considering he doesn't know Edwin from Adam. He gets coffees for them both and they sit in Ivan's office. Its glass walls show people hurrying to and fro, intent on the business of news. Edwin feels a stab of nostalgia for the days when he was one of the worker ants with his own security pass and a file full of interview notes.

'So you were a friend of Dad's?' says Ivan.

'Yes. I knew him in my BBC days,' says Edwin. At least, if Ivan checks, Edwin's name will be in the annals somewhere. 'I was so sorry to learn that he'd passed away.'

'Yes, it was a shock,' says Ivan. 'Even though he was a good age. We just thought he'd go on for ever, living in that Kensington flat that was far too big for him, having lunch at the same restaurant every day, playing his flute for the grandchildren.'

'He was a great musician.'

'He really was. Decca are bringing out a CD of his early record-ings.'

'So it was a shock when Felix died?'

'Yes, it was. My sister, Henry, had seen him the day before and she said he was on good form. He was even learning a new piece.'

'I read the *Guardian* obituary,' says Edwin. 'It said that Felix died with his flute in his hand.'

'Yes, the coroner thought he was actually playing it when he died. What a way to go, eh?'

'Definitely the way he would have wanted it,' says Edwin. 'The obituary writer was Malcolm Collins, another old friend of mine. Did you ever meet him?'

'I don't think so. No.'

'Was it your sister who . . . er . . . discovered the . . . found your dad?'

Ivan gives Edwin rather a keen look. Is this going too far, even for a supposed old friend?

'It was Margot, his cleaner,' says Ivan. 'Did you say you were writing a book about Dad?'

'About my days at the BBC,' says Edwin. He is so taken by this cover story that he can almost see the book. *Music to My Ears* by Edwin Fitzgerald. A tastefully blurred image of a piano and an old-school microphone.

'I've found some old photos of Dad at the Beeb,' says Ivan. He hands over a brown envelope. 'I'd like them back but take your time.'

'Thank you,' says Edwin. 'That's very kind.'

'It's good to meet someone who knew the old boy in his prime. As you say, he really was an important musician. It's funny. Neither Henry nor I can play a note on any instrument.'

'What about your children?'

'They only play computer games, as far as I can see.'

'It's the modern world,' says Edwin.

'Tell me about it,' says Ivan.

The two men sit in silence while the modern world revolves around then.

By the time Edwin gets the train home, he's feeling rather pleased with himself. He negotiated London, interviewed Ivan Marshall and has some interesting photos to look through. What's more, he eschewed the easy option of Pret for lunch and found a backstreet restaurant where he consumed delicious ravioli and drank a glass of red wine. He used his debit card on the Tube and now has a comfortable forward-facing seat for the journey back.

Maybe he'll read a few pages of *The Hopes and Fears of All the Years*. Edwin got it out of the library on Monday and has only got to page ten. In his private review he has deducted points for the words 'inchoate' and 'rebarbative'.

Now he opens the book at page eleven.

. . . his destination, should he have put the quest in those terms, was the soft inside of her thighs, that liminal zone between quietude and desire . . .

Edwin shuts the book. He's just falling into a pleasant doze when his phone pings loudly. Edwin looks round guiltily but no one else in the carriage seems to have noticed. He expects it to be a WhatsApp message from Natalka on their Super Sleuths chat. They use this method of communication because Benedict says it's secure although Natalka always laughs hollowly and says the Russians can hack anything. But it's from Imogen.

Don't forget about book club! We're meeting next Monday. The Youth Project.

It's a few seconds before Edwin realises that this is a book choice. He googles it.

A dystopian novel about a world where elderly people are executed when they are deemed to have outlived their useful purpose.

Edwin wonders what the criteria are. Failing to negotiate a security barrier? Inability to type on a mobile phone? He shuts his eyes again and falls into an uneasy sleep.

Chapter 21

Benedict: wreath bearer

Benedict's friend Francis – Father Francis now – says that funerals are in danger of becoming his hobby. And it's true that Benedict has attended more than his fair share. As a curate he'd helped officiate at funerals and, at the monastery, had said farewell to several of the older monks. They all seemed to live to a great age but they had to go eventually, helped on their way by Latin chanting and fulsome prayers. Since leaving the priesthood, Benedict has attended several parish funerals, especially those of older people where he's worried that there won't be enough mourners. They are sad occasions, of course, but there has always been something redemptive about them. I am the way, the truth and the life. The thurible swinging. The handheld cross leading the coffin on its last journey.

But try as he might, Benedict can find nothing consoling about Sue Hitchins' funeral at Worthing Crematorium. It's a grey day and the small group gathers outside the chapel, waiting for the previous service to finish. Imogen is there, next to a tanned, grey-haired man who must be her husband. Benedict also spots Leonard

Norris, Johnnie Newton and Frances O'Toole. Johnnie, who is uncharacteristically subdued in a black trouser suit, gives Benedict and Edwin a wave but doesn't come over. Frances, who is wearing purple, doesn't seem to have recognised them. Benedict notes that Peter Abbot is the only person from the writing weekend not to have attended. Apart from the writers, the only other mourners are an elderly couple in black. They must be family because the undertakers confer with them before lifting the coffin from the hearse. An aunt and uncle? Benedict remembers Sue saying that her mother was dead. No partner, no children. It's no wonder that the mood is bleak, even for a funeral.

As they file into the chapel, following the plywood coffin topped by a single wreath, Benedict turns and sees Liv Brennan and Sam Malone taking their places at the back. Both are in black, which Benedict thinks is a nice touch. He joins Edwin in one of the middle rows.

The service is led by one of the undertakers who does a good enough job but is hampered by obviously not knowing much about Sue. He mentions her job as a teacher but not her writing. He says that her partner, Malcolm, sadly died last year but refrains from suggesting any heavenly reunion. There are no eulogies and, after barely five minutes, there's a taped recording of *Pie Jesu* and the curtains draw together in a soundless and sinister way.

Outside, Edwin gravitates towards Imogen and Benedict hears her introducing her husband Declan. Benedict wants to talk to Johnnie, who seems the friendliest face, but feels that he ought to offer condolences to Sue's relatives, who were introduced by the celebrant as Auntie Dora and Uncle Keith. They are standing by the doors, holding the wreath.

'I'm so sorry,' says Benedict, trying to put priestly warmth into his voice.

'Thank you,' says Dora. 'Were you a friend of Sue's?' She has a northern accent and Benedict remembers Sue saying that she was born in Halifax. Have the couple come all the way from Yorkshire?

'I was on the writing course with her,' says Benedict.

'The one where she died?' says Keith.

'Yes,' says Benedict. 'It was so sad. She seemed like a lovely woman.'

'The police still haven't closed the case,' says Keith, who seems to find this a personal insult.

'They're just doing their job,' says Dora.

'Did you know Sue's boyfriend, Malcolm?' Benedict asks.

'Met him a few times,' says Keith, but he doesn't elaborate. Dora says that Malcolm seemed very nice and it's all very sad.

'So sad,' says Benedict. 'And I think Sue's mother died fairly recently?'

'A couple of years ago,' says Dora. 'I'm her younger sister. Much younger,' she adds. Benedict had the couple in their seventies, which fits.

'We need to get going,' says Keith. 'The taxi will be here soon. What are you going to do with that?' He gestures at the wreath. 'You can't take it on the train.'

'I don't know,' says Dora, looking round rather helplessly.

'Shall I take it?' says Benedict. 'There might be a special place for flowers.'

'Thank you,' says Dora, who hands over the circle of greenery as if she is performing a ceremony at the cenotaph. Then the couple hurry away.

Carrying the wreath, *bearing* it, thinks Benedict, makes him feel semi-official somehow. He walks over to the others, who are now gathered in a circle around Imogen. There's no sign of the police officers. Have they already left or are they waiting in a car somewhere?

'Poor Sue.' Imogen is dabbing her eyes. 'Not much of a send-off.'

'Nothing like a requiem mass,' says Declan, who has an Irish accent.

'Maybe Benedict can say a few words,' says Frances. 'Didn't you used to be a priest?'

'A monk,' says Benedict. 'Let's find somewhere to lay the wreath and I'll say a prayer if you like.'

They follow the signs to the garden of ashes, which is actually a tranquil and attractive space, a smooth lawn with memorial stones placed on the grass like a child's game of stepping stones. There are several wreaths under a flowering cherry tree. Benedict adds Sue's and says, 'Eternal rest grant unto her, oh Lord, and let perpetual light shine upon her. May she rest in peace. Amen.'

'Amen,' echo Declan and Edwin.

'I don't know about the rest of you,' says Johnnie, 'but I could do with a drink.'

They go to a modern pub in the middle of a roundabout. It's midday but feels much later. Benedict is driving so he has mineral water but most of the others drink wine or beer. Johnnie picks up a laminated menu and says, 'Anyone up for lunch?' Benedict suddenly realises that he's starving, a common post-funeral affliction, he knows. It seems that everyone feels the same and the writers take up a long table in the dining area. It reminds

Benedict of the first evening at Battle House, Imogen pouring drinks and performing introductions, Sue peering from behind the dried herbs. He remembers Leonard abstaining from alcohol that time and checks his glass. Looks like tomato juice but maybe Leonard, too, is driving.

There's a palpable sense of relief, a feeling of duty done, amongst the group. Leonard and Frances are talking about books, Declan and Johnnie have discovered a possible mutual friend. Only Imogen is drinking her white wine in silence.

'Did anyone notice the police pres?' asks Johnnie, taking off her black jacket.

There's a noticeable change in atmosphere, almost a tremor around the table.

'What do you mean?' asks Imogen.

'DS Brennan and DS Malone. They were at the crem. They sat at the back of the chapel. Maybe they were taking notes.'

'Taking notes?' says Imogen. 'Do you think we're *suspects*?'

'Maybe they were just there out of respect,' says Benedict.

'It's ridiculous,' says Declan, rather heatedly, Benedict thinks, for someone who wasn't at the writing weekend. 'Sue fell in the pond. It was either an accident or suicide.'

He speaks rather loudly and Benedict sees other diners looking round. He lowers his own voice. 'The case is still open. I suppose they're covering every angle.'

'Does going to the funeral make us look guilty or innocent?' asks Johnnie, taking a swig of Guinness.

'Innocent, surely,' says Frances.

'I don't know,' Benedict can't help adding. 'Murderers often return to the scene of the crime.'

'What do you know about it?' ask Frances. Rather rudely, in Benedict's opinion.

'I read a lot of crime novels,' says Benedict.

'So do I,' says Johnnie. 'And the crematorium wasn't the scene of the crime.'

'Well, you know who isn't here?' says Imogen. 'Peter.'

'He hates death,' says Frances.

'Don't we all, ducky?' says Johnnie.

The arrival of the food halts this conversation. Benedict's scampi is brightly coloured – orange breadcrumbs, glowing tomato, star-tlingly green peas – but tastes of very little. Even so, Benedict clears his plate and notes that Edwin does the same with his Day-Glo Caesar salad. Benedict overhears Edwin telling Leonard that he's reading *The Hopes and Fears of All the Years*.

'Are you enjoying it?' asks Leonard. 'Not that it's a book that was written to be enjoyed, of course.'

'No, I can see that,' says Edwin. 'I'm finding it quite an ex-perience.'

Leonard preens slightly and Edwin gives Benedict the ghost of a wink.

'I hope you haven't forgotten the book club, Edwin,' says Imogen. 'We're meeting on Monday at my place.'

'I'm looking forward to it.'

'I love chatting about books,' says Benedict. Imogen smiles vaguely but no invitation is forthcoming.

There's no further mention of Sue until they are having pudding (Johnnie), coffee (Benedict and Leonard) and more drinks (everyone else).

'It's so awful about Sue,' says Imogen, who seems to be slightly slurring her words. Surely she's only had two glasses of wine, thinks Benedict. At least Declan is now on diet Coke.

'Awful,' says Leonard. 'I can't stop thinking about it. Especially when you remember what happened to Miriam.'

'What happened to Miriam?' asks Benedict, remembering that this was the name of the woman who originally owned Battle House. He thinks of the photograph of Melody, Leonard and Miriam in front of Battle House, Miriam wearing the Panama hat.

'She drowned,' says Frances, with what feels like unnecessary relish. 'In that very lake.'

Chapter 22

Natalka: hell's angel

Natalka is slightly disappointed to miss the funeral although, she tells herself firmly, what sort of person gets FOMO about a funeral? But any detective knows that funerals are an excellent place for picking up clues. So, after her morning calls, Natalka decides to spend the rest of her day detecting. She thinks it's time to talk to Alan Franklin, the devil incarnate, in his lair. She checks with the pharmacy and learns that Alan doesn't come in on Fridays. Remembering Minnie's remark about Alan having another woman by now, Natalka wonders if his door will be opened by a nubile young thing. But no, Alan's only companion is the spaniel, Frodo, who seems delighted to have a visitor.

'Natalka.' Alan is slightly less welcoming. 'To what do I owe this pleasure?'

'I thought you'd like to hear how the investigation is progressing,' says Natalka brightly.

Alan looks dubious but steps aside to let her in, Frodo panting at their heels.

This time they go into the sitting room which is huge but – despite a grand piano and two giant sofas – comfortable rather than intimidating. French windows lead into the garden and Frodo runs in and out as if demonstrating their effectiveness.

Alan doesn't offer refreshment and Natalka doesn't blame him. They sit on different sofas and Alan says, 'So have Goneril and Regan given up the case?'

Someone else called them this but Natalka can't remember who. She says, 'You'll have to explain the reference. English isn't my first language.'

'It's from *King Lear*,' says Alan. 'I'm no Shakespeare expert, though. Melody was. She knew loads of the plays almost by heart.'

'Edwin's like that,' says Natalka. 'My partner in the detective agency. It's very annoying sometimes.'

'I remember Edwin,' says Alan. 'He seemed like an interesting chap. And I loved Melody quoting Shakespeare. It was very sexy.'

He gives Natalka a grin that is, in her opinion, both inappropriate and rather attractive.

'What is your first language?' asks Alan. 'Ukrainian?'

One of the only positive things about Ukraine being in the news so much, thinks Natalka, is that most people guess her nationality correctly. Pre the invasion, people usually assumed she was Polish or (far worse) Russian. Also, there's some understanding that Ukrainian is different from Russian. Natalka is actually fluent in Russian too but, now that her country's sovereignty is threatened, the distinction between the two languages has become more important than ever. Like the Ukrainian communion separating itself from the Russian Orthodox Church (which supported the war), it's more than symbolic.

'Yes,' says Natalka. 'I'm a poor Ukrainian refugee. Are you sorry for me?'

'I can't imagine you as a poor anything,' says Alan, 'but I am sorry about what's happening in your country. Very sorry.'

'Thank you,' says Natalka. The conversation seems to have strayed into different, albeit potentially interesting, territory. 'I've been trying to trace you on social media,' she says, 'but you haven't got much of a profile.'

'I hate all that stuff,' says Alan. 'Who's interested in what I think or do? I only joined because an old university friend asked me to.'

'Arjan or Steve?' asks Natalka.

Alan laughs. 'You have been thorough. I think it was Arjan.'

'I'm not on social media either,' says Natalka. 'But your Facebook page is very boring. I couldn't even see any previous girlfriends.'

'Are you asking me about previous relationships?' asks Alan. 'I've never been married before but I lived with a woman called Jill for several years. Jill Butler. I'm sure you can find her on Facebook.'

His smile isn't exactly warm but it's not unfriendly either.

'Do you know a man called Leonard Norris?' asks Natalka.

'I don't think so.'

'He's a writer.'

'I told you before, I don't know any of Melody's writer friends.'

'Do you know if Melody knew him?'

'I've said I don't recognise the name.'

'It's just that I heard a rumour that Melody once had an affair with Leonard.'

'A rumour? Let me guess. Goneril or Regan?'

'I can't say who told me,' says Natalka, realising that she has probably already given away her informant. But Alan doesn't seem offended. He's laughing – *chuckling* would be the English word, Natalka thinks – with, it seems, genuine amusement.

'No, Melody didn't have an affair with this Leonard person. Not to my knowledge, anyway. Of course, I can't say what happened before I knew her. I suppose it's possible.'

'Did you ever visit Battle House with Melody?'

'No. Writers' retreats are not my thing.'

'Did you know Miriam Fry? She used to own Battle House.'

'I don't think so.'

'Minnie gave me a picture of Melody with Miriam and Leonard. She said it was from a display at Melody's funeral.'

'I remember those pictures. Not one of me in the whole lot. Minnie tried her hardest to erase me from Melody's life.'

It was true there were no pictures of Alan on the board, thinks Natalka, but there were none of Tony, the first husband, either. The emphasis had been on Melody the individual. As it should be.

Natalka remembers something else. 'Minnie said she thought Miriam had introduced you and Melody.'

Alan laughs again. 'That's not true. We met when she came into my shop. I told you before.'

'Why would Minnie say that about Miriam?'

Alan shrugs. 'Search me. I'm a pharmacist, not a psychologist.'

Time to get back to the case.

'Have you heard what happened at Battle House last weekend?'

'I'm sure you're going to tell me,' says Alan, leaning back with a smile.

'A woman called Sue Hitchins was killed there. Her funeral's today.'

'Killed? What do you mean?' The smile vanishes.

It's not a very obscure word, thinks Natalka.

'She drowned in the lake. Police suspect foul play.'

'Poor woman. Well, I suppose that's one death Minnie can't blame on me.'

'Why do Harmony and Minnie hate you so much?' asks Natalka.

Alan pauses before answering. Natalka can hear the birds in the garden. It's nesting season and they're particularly vocal. Frodo gazes hopefully at a wood pigeon on the bird table, probably wondering if it wants to be his friend.

'They thought I was taking their dad's place,' says Alan at last. 'Though Tony, their father, died ten years before I met Melody. He was ex-army, apparently very strait-laced. Melody met him when she was quite young, they got married when she was twenty-three and he was thirty.'

Quite an age difference, thinks Natalka. Though not as big as the gap between Melody and Alan. Maybe, after marriage to a stuffy-sounding older man, Melody just felt like some fun?

'Minnie and Harmony refused to come to the wedding,' says Alan. 'It probably didn't help that I'm only ten years older than Harmony. Also, I've got long hair and I used to ride a motorbike. I think they thought I was a Hell's Angel even though it was a harmless Honda and not a Harley.'

'They disapproved?' says Natalka, thinking that disapproval is probably one of the sisters' specialities.

'Well, they're quite strait-laced too. Everything Daddy did was perfect and, as far as I can see, they've tried to be as much like him as possible. They were even both army cadets as teenagers. Then they went to respectable universities and picked nice, sensible careers – a teacher and an accountant.' He smiles and Natalka can't help wondering what he thinks about private detective as a job description.

'When did you and Melody get married?' asks Natalka. She thinks of Melody's Facebook page, Alan suddenly appearing in the background.

'2015,' says Alan.

The wedding didn't appear on Melody's Facebook page, Natalka muses, but, thinking of Minnie and her saccharine posts, Natalka is inclined to think the author was right to concentrate mainly on dog pictures.

'Seven years,' says Natalka. 'You'd think they'd be used to you by now.'

'They'd come round a bit in recent years,' says Alan, 'but when they found that Melody had left me the house, all hell broke loose.'

'Is that what it's about?' says Natalka. 'The house?' She looks round at the room with its gracious lines and faded fabrics. It's beautiful but watching entire Ukrainian cities crumble to dust has made Natalka impatient with the British worship of home ownership.

'It's about who Melody loved the most,' says Alan. 'And I can't help it if that was me.'

'Will you stay here for ever?' asks Natalka.

Alan shrugs. 'Maybe. Or I might travel. Go abroad. Australia maybe. I could get a medical visa.'

'I've never been to Australia,' says Natalka.

'I should imagine it's your sort of place,' says Alan.

This is disconcerting because Natalka thinks it might be true.

★

Benedict and Edwin are already sitting outside the Shack when Natalka gets there. Kyle, who has worked there all day, is at the counter reading a book. It's golden hour again. Natalka thinks how handsome Benedict looks in his black suit, tie loosened, hair standing up in a crest where he has run his hand through it. Natalka thinks that the only other time she has seen him so formally dressed was at Peggy's funeral. Even Edwin looks rather wonderful, an elder statesman with his white hair, starched shirt and black jacket. The two of them give a rather surreal look to the beach, dark-suited undertakers under a rainbow umbrella, like a Magritte painting come to life.

'How was the funeral?' she asks.

'Depressing,' says Benedict. 'No prayers, no ritual, hardly any flowers.'

'I want the full requiem mass when I go,' says Edwin. 'Make a note, both of you.'

'Don't,' says Benedict just as Natalka says, 'Who says you're going to die first?'

'Statistically speaking,' says Edwin, 'I'm next for the grim reaper.' But he sounds quite cheerful about it, lifting his face up to catch the last rays of the sun.

'Did you get any clues?' asks Natalka. 'I've just been to see Alan Franklin.'

'Minnie will be pleased,' says Edwin. 'Did you find anything helpful?'

'Not really. He says he didn't know Sue Hitchins or Leonard Norris but then he would say that, wouldn't he?'

'Did you ask him about Melody having an affair with Leonard?' asks Edwin.

'Yes,' says Natalka.

'You're always so brave,' says Edwin.

'Didn't take much bravery,' says Natalka. 'He laughed. Said it wasn't true unless it was before his time.'

'Do *you* think it's true?' asks Benedict.

'I think we should ask Leonard,' says Natalka. 'Let's go to Battle House. I'd like to see the crime scene again.'

'We learnt something interesting about Battle House today,' says Benedict. 'Miriam Fry, the woman who used to own it, the woman in the photo with Melody and Leonard, she died by falling into the lake.'

'The same lake that Sue drowned in?'

'The very same,' says Benedict. 'That must have been what Leonard meant when he said Sue's death "brought it all back".'

'That was the warmest Leonard ever was,' says Edwin, 'talking about Miriam. He wrote his god-awful book when he was staying with her. Maybe that's why.'

'I thought so too,' says Benedict. 'Miriam and opera were the only things he mentioned with any affection.'

'There was a statue by the lake,' says Edwin. 'It showed a woman kneeling by the water, her hair falling over her face. I wonder if that was a memorial to Miriam.'

'I remember that,' says Benedict. 'It was the first thing I saw that evening. I almost didn't notice Sue floating in the water. Rather a macabre memorial for someone who died from drowning.'

'Battle House was rather macabre,' says Edwin. 'I agree with Natalka. We should go back there. I think the retreats must be the key to all this. After all, they're the only thing that links Melody,

Don, Malcolm and Sue. And I'd like to talk to Leonard. I don't understand why he lives at the house, for one thing.'

'Maybe it's just because he runs the courses,' says Benedict.

'He didn't do much teaching the weekend we were there,' says Edwin. 'That was all Imogen. I bet he didn't even read our pieces.'

'Imogen was a good teacher,' says Benedict. 'I told her so. She said she thought that I'd be a good teacher too.'

'You would,' says Natalka. Benedict smiles but Natalka can't tell if he's offended.

'I wonder if Imogen is as happy as she appears to be,' says Edwin. 'She seemed distracted today. Though a funeral can do that to you. And I think she might have a drink problem.'

'Do you?' says Benedict. 'I wondered. She was slurring her words a bit, but I only saw her have two glasses of wine.'

'Hip flask,' says Edwin knowledgeably.

Natalka thinks it's time she took charge. 'You can observe Imogen at the book club, Edwin. Plenty of chance for her to drink there.'

'I've been thinking about the book group too,' says Edwin. 'Remember the piece Sue wrote at Battle House?'

'The "If only I hadn't" piece?' says Benedict.

'No, the other one. The one about going to a place for the first time. Sue wrote about going to a book club.'

'So she did,' says Benedict. 'I wonder if she meant the one at Imogen's house. As I remember, she said it was intimidating.'

'I won't be intimidated,' says Edwin. Natalka believes him.

'What did you write about, Benny?' she asks.

'I didn't do the exercise,' says Benedict. 'I told you I was a washout.'

'I wrote about prep school,' says Edwin. 'Boarding school is very useful if you want instant trauma. Mind you, I loved prep school by the end.'

'I loved school too,' says Natalka. 'I was the best at maths and my hair came down to my waist.' She knows she's said this before but the memory seems to grow stronger, not weaker, with the years.

'Should we tell the police if we're going to talk to Leonard?' asks Benedict.

'I don't see why,' says Natalka.

'Brennan and Malone were at the funeral,' says Edwin. 'They didn't speak to anyone but it seemed to spook some people. Imogen in particular.'

'Who else was there?' asks Natalka.

'All the writers except Peter Abbot,' says Edwin. 'Does that make him more or less likely?'

'Peter "hates death".' Benedict puts ironical quotation marks round the words. 'That's what Frances said.'

'Frances seems to know a lot about Peter,' says Edwin. 'Do you think they're having an affair? They're both married, I think.'

'I wonder,' says Benedict. 'Peter could have been talking to Frances on the phone that day. "Have you done it yet?" Maybe he meant – has she told her husband yet?'

'But why talk to her on the phone?' says Natalka. 'I mean, she was there. At Battle House.'

'Lovers are not always rational.' Benedict smiles at her.

'As I recall,' says Edwin, 'Peter also talked about time running out. I wonder what he meant by that?'

'I think our time is running out,' says Benedict, looking at his watch. 'Kyle will be wanting to get home.'

He goes to the counter and speaks to the young man, who looks so much the typical student (glasses, scruffy clothes, earnest expression) that Natalka always suspects him of subterfuge.

Edwin stands up, brushing down his black trousers. 'I'd better get back to reading *The Youth Project*. What a depressing book it is.'

'Well, keep your eyes open at the book club,' says Natalka. 'We're relying on you.'

How easy it is to make people happy, she thinks. A little praise does it every time.

When they get home, Valentyna has made risotto.

'Funerals make people hungry,' she says, one of the unanswerable sayings that probably originated with Natalka's grandmother. Benedict certainly eats well but Natalka hasn't got much appetite. But, then, she wasn't at the funeral.

After supper, Benedict and Valentyna watch *Bake Off*, one of their favourite programmes. Natalka goes to her bedroom and listens to music with her headphones on. Every song reminds her of Dmytro, the only person who shares her love of pop and hip-hop. What is he doing now, her sweet, hapless brother? Once, before, she had thought him dead but had found him again. She can't bear the thought of losing him again. The fear is with her all the time, a horrible churning sensation that makes her feel sick and shaky, but talking about it is worse, even with her mother.

Her phone buzzes. Unknown number. Could it be one of Dmytro's comrades? But the message is in English.

Hi, Alan here. I wondered if you'd like to go for a walk with me and Frodo one day?

Natalka looks at the message for a long time. Then she goes into the sitting room and suggests to Benedict that they visit Battle House tomorrow. She doesn't tell him about the text from Alan Franklin.

Chapter 23

Benedict: gun dog

Benedict feels guilty about asking Kyle to cover for him again, and on a Saturday too, but the student seems quite happy to have another day's work. Even so, there's a feeling of skiving, heading off with Natalka in her car just as the Shack is at its busiest. Natalka has left Maria in charge of the care agency but Benedict is sure that she too is feeling, not guilty exactly (Natalka doesn't do guilt), but excited at the thought of a morning that is outside their usual routine.

Benedict also feels bad about Edwin. It was his idea to go to Battle House, after all. They did invite Edwin but he said that he ought to get on with reading *The Youth Project*. Benedict knows that this is Edwin being tactful, leaving the couple alone to have quality time at a crime scene. And it does feel inappropriately jolly. Natalka sings along to Radio 1 and Benedict tries to make the satnav talk to him. They stop for coffee in Alfriston and Benedict allows himself a brief daydream about living in the picture postcard village, just him and Natalka in a terraced cottage with uneven beams and hollyhocks in the garden. Maybe he could get a job at Much Ado Books or even start a new Coffee Shack. But he doesn't think that Natalka would want to leave her mother.

Eventually they are approaching Battle, trees on either side of the road allowing glimpses of timbered houses and modern bungalows.

'Welcome to 1066 country,' says Natalka, passing another sign proclaiming this. 'Why are the English so obsessed with 1066? Wasn't the Battle of Hastings a defeat?'

'It was the last time England was invaded,' says Benedict. 'That's what we were always taught at school. It was a revolving door before that. The Romans, the Vikings, the Danes. But, after 1066, the Normans took over and it was the start of modern England, I suppose.'

'Lucky you,' says Natalka. 'My country was invaded this February.'

'I know,' says Benedict. He wishes he hadn't mentioned the I word.

The satnav, having been very bossy about roundabouts, completely misses the turning to Battle House. Natalka sees it just in time and the car swerves into the tree-lined tunnel, the canopy of leaves dense and green. Benedict thinks he sees a flutter of yellow crime-scene tape but, otherwise, it's as if the woods have absorbed the events of the last week. The track seems almost overgrown in places. Have the trees moved even closer? But there's the house, looking as dour and blank-faced as ever. The door is firmly shut but there's a red sports car parked outside.

'The Porsche was there last time,' says Natalka. 'Is it Leonard's?'

'I suppose so,' says Benedict, 'but he doesn't seem the Porsche type to me.'

'He does to me. Probably means he's impotent,' says Natalka.

Benedict approaches the door but Natalka calls out to him to stop. 'Let's look round first.'

This goes against all Benedict's law-abiding instincts, but he follows Natalka around the side of the house. The garden, too, looks more overgrown than it did a week ago. The hammock is swinging as if someone has just left it but there's no sign of Leonard. Benedict walks across the lawn to the bench where he sat and tried to listen to nature. He's looking back at the house when there's a tremendous rustle in the undergrowth and a large animal appears in front of him. He jumps back before he recognises Buster, the golden retriever that was in Georgina Potter-Smith's car. This time the dog is accompanied by a man and the only thing Benedict notices about him is that he's carrying a gun.

'Who are you?' says the man.

'I'm Benedict,' says Benedict, rather ridiculously, he feels. 'I'm here to see Leonard.'

'We're friends of Leonard's.' Natalka has crossed the lawn and is patting Buster. Benedict watches the man's aggression drain out of him as he looks at Natalka, her blonde hair glowing in the spring sunlight. He's not sure how he feels about the effect his girlfriend has on every member of the male sex but he supposes it's useful if it stops them being murdered.

'There was no answer when we knocked,' says Natalka, with one of her best smiles. 'But his car's outside.'

'He's probably asleep,' says the man. 'Or drunk. I'm David, by the way. David Potter-Smith. I own the place.'

So this is Georgina's husband, the farmer. It all makes sense now. Even so, Benedict still eyes the gun warily. It's the type with a long barrel which he thinks is used for murdering wildlife rather than humans, but he can't be sure. David sees him looking. 'Just out to shoot pigeons. Buster here is a great gun dog.'

Buster is rootling around in the garden, head down. Are you allowed to just go out and shoot things? wonders Benedict. It appears that you are. Natalka doesn't seem surprised but Benedict remembers her once saying that her father, who left the family more than twenty years ago, was 'a hunter'.

'Wasn't it terrible what happened to Sue?' says Natalka, still looking at David. 'It must have been such a shock for you all.'

'It was terrible,' says David. 'We had the police trampling all over the land, putting up the pheasants. I told them we'd got a shoot in two weeks' time.'

Benedict wonders what DS Brennan made of that. David himself seems to realise that he has struck a wrong note because he changes the tune. 'I mean, it was a tragedy. Of course it was. Georgie was very upset. It brought it all back, you see. Her aunt, the woman who used to live in this house, drowned in that same lake ten years ago.'

'How awful,' says Benedict. 'I think I remember Leonard talking about Georgina's aunt. Was her name Miriam?'

'That's right,' says David, resting the gun more easily on his arm. 'She was a poet. Quite famous if you like that sort of thing. Can't say I do. Leonard was very fond of her. He was the one who discovered her body, actually. I don't think he ever got over it. Georgie thinks he had a nervous breakdown. That's why she lets him stay here. Rent free, too. She's far too soft-hearted. He's not short of a bob or two. I mean, look at his car. Anyway, Leonard put up this statue as a memorial to Miriam. Don't know if you saw it. Woman kneeling by the water. Gives me the creeps.'

'I saw it when I was here last weekend,' says Benedict.

'Bloody eyesore,' says David. 'And now another woman has drowned herself in the same place.'

'The police don't think Sue's death was suicide,' says Natalka.

David's rather pale eyes bulge. 'Of course it was. Another woman killing themselves over bloody Leonard . . .' His face changes and he says, 'Hallo there, Sleeping Beauty.'

Leonard Norris is walking towards them. He's wearing a jacket over what could conceivably be pyjamas. Was he, as David suggested, still in bed at midday?

'Hallo, Leonard,' says Benedict loudly, hoping to conceal the fact that Natalka is a stranger to the man.

But Leonard just blinks at him. 'Hallo. What are you doing here?'

'Just came to see how you were.'

Leonard looks quite touched. 'Thank you. It's been a hell of a few days.'

'I'll leave you to it then,' says David. 'Come on, Buster.' The dog, who has been lying in the overgrown flower bed, heaves himself up and follows his master.

They walk back to the house and Benedict is able to introduce Natalka. Leonard gives her the familiar glazed look as if he is wondering how on earth such a woman can be with Benedict. You and me both, thinks Benedict.

In the kitchen, Leonard makes coffee. The room, which had seemed cosy during the writing weekend, now feels cold and neglected. There's washing up in the sink – despite the dishwasher – and several days' worth of *Guardian*s on the oak table. Benedict remembers Leonard making pancakes and thinking that he seemed at his happiest when cooking. There's not much sign of cookery today. Leonard opens the fridge in search of milk and asks hopefully if they mind having black coffee. They both say that this is fine.

When they are sitting at the table, Natalka looks at Benedict and then addresses Leonard.

'Leonard, it's true that we came to see how you are. Benny was worried about you. But there's another reason. You see, I'm a private detective.'

Leonard obviously thinks this is a joke because he laughs and then, looking at Natalka's face, apologises.

'I'm investigating the death of a woman called Melody Chambers. Do you remember her?'

'Yes.' Leonard runs a hand across his chin, scraping the stubble. 'She came on a writing retreat. With her daughter, I think.'

'Melody died earlier this month and her daughters suspect foul play.'

Natalka loves expressions like 'foul play'. Those Ukrainian translations of Agatha Christie have a lot to answer for, Benedict reckons.

'We've also been asked to look into the death of Don Parsons. The vicar who wrote romances under a woman's name. The only thing that links the two of them is this place.'

Natalka pauses and Leonard looks at Benedict. 'Is that why you came here last week? You and Edwin?'

'Partly,' says Benedict, feeling embarrassed. 'But we're interested in writing too.'

'I could tell Edwin was a real writer,' says Leonard, 'but I wasn't sure about you.'

Given his failure to complete any of the writing tasks, Benedict can't really blame Leonard for his opinion, but he feels hurt all the same. I've written two and a half completely unsuccessful books, he wants to say. I'm not a complete fraud.

'You knew Sue,' says Natalka. 'You knew Malcolm and Melody too. You've met Don. Can you think of anything – or anyone – that links them?'

'I don't know.' Leonard rubs his face again. 'Writing, of course. Though they all wrote in such different genres. Melody was a successful romantic novelist but she wasn't a bad writer for all that. Don had great success with his books. I can't say I ever read any of them. Sue wrote a few decent short stories but she wasn't a writer per se. Malcolm was really just a journalist.'

So much literary snobbery in one go makes Benedict feel quite dizzy.

He says, 'Someone . . . I think it was Imogen . . . said that you were close to Melody.'

'Her daughter said the two of you were having an affair,' says Natalka, abandoning subtlety.

Leonard blinks. He looks as if he no longer finds Natalka quite so attractive.

'I never had an affair with Melody. We were friends, I suppose. Melody was a professional writer so we had that in common.' Leonard's tone is casual, almost bored, but Benedict notices that he's picking at a piece of loose wood in the table.

'Did Melody know Miriam Fry?' asks Natalka.

'I don't think so.'

Natalka produces the photograph from the cork board.

'That's you and Melody with Miriam Fry, isn't it?'

'Where did you get this?' The splinter comes off in Leonard's hand.

'Minnie gave it to me.'

'Minnie? Oh, that's the other daughter, isn't it? Minim and Harmony. Ridiculous names.'

Edwin said that same thing, thinks Benedict, but it sounds nastier coming from Leonard.

'That's Battle House in the picture, isn't it?' says Natalka.

'Yes. Now I come to think of it, I think Melody came to some of the early retreats. Just Miriam and a few like-minded friends.'

'You must have been very upset when Miriam died,' says Natalka. 'David said that you actually found her body.'

There's a pause and then Leonard says, 'I'll never forget it. Miriam floating in the water. And then for Sue to die in the same way . . . I'm starting to see the place as cursed. Like the dreadful hollow in Tennyson. You know.'

Benedict is not sure that he does. Edwin would get the reference, he thinks resentfully, because *he's* a real writer.

'David implied that you'd had a relationship with Sue,' says Natalka. Benedict admires her cool, he would not have had the heart to continue with this line of questioning. This time, there's a definite flash of anger from Leonard.

'I wouldn't trust anything David says. The amount he drinks.'

He said the same thing about you, thinks Benedict. He and Natalka both wait and, after a few seconds, Leonard says, in a much quieter voice, 'Sue was . . . Look, she had a bit of a crush on me. I think it was because I'm a successful literary author. Booker Prize and all that. At one time, she kind of convinced herself that we were in a relationship. I gather she did the same thing with Malcolm Collins.'

Benedict remembers Leonard's taciturn comments on Sue's 'If

only I hadn't' piece. And what was it that Sue had said, the second evening? 'If you find someone you love, stick to them like glue.' Someone – Johnnie? – had said at the time that this was stalkerish. Could Sue have been harassing Leonard? But Benedict thinks that Leonard is just the type to imagine that women are in love with him, although he was quick to deny any liaison with Melody. He also wants to remind Leonard that being on the Booker longlist is not the same as winning the prize. Instead he says, 'So you don't think Sue and Malcolm were romantically involved?'

'I think she romanticised their friendship,' says Leonard. 'As I say, she had a tendency to do that.'

But Sue's relatives had met Malcolm, thinks Benedict, the library staff knew about their relationship. He very much wants it to be true.

'Did Miriam leave Battle House to you?' asks Natalka.

Leonard snaps the splinter in two. 'No, the house belongs to Georgina. Miriam left it to her. I just stay here to run the courses. Not that anyone will come any more when the news about Sue gets out.'

Apart from a paragraph in the local paper, Sue's death has not been covered by the press. Benedict thinks that Leonard is taking too gloomy a view. Natalka obviously thinks so too because she says, 'People forget very quickly. What does the other teacher – Imogen? – think?'

Leonard laughs, a sound which seems to contain both affection and derision. 'Oh, she thinks crime writers will come *because* of the deaths. You know what genre fiction's like. Not that Imogen wasn't sad about Sue.'

'She seemed very upset yesterday,' says Benedict, remembering Imogen's tears at the funeral.

'We were all upset,' says Leonard, though that's not quite how Benedict remembers it.

'Did Imogen know Miriam?' asks Benedict.

'No. Imogen only started teaching here about five years ago. I didn't know her before then. She's a good enough teacher. A bit lazy sometimes.'

Benedict thinks this is unfair. Imogen may have been late to cook breakfast but she had certainly worked far harder than Leonard in the teaching sessions.

'Imogen's asked Edwin to join her book group,' he says.

'Yes,' says Leonard. 'I thought she would.'

Benedict doesn't know what to make of this. Natalka, obviously tired of the book talk, leans forward and says, 'What do you think happened to Sue? Did she take her own life? Like Miriam?'

'Yes,' says Leonard, giving her a very direct look. 'I think that's exactly what happened.'

As they leave the house, Benedict hears a shot coming from the woods. Birds rise into the air, cawing desperately.

'I hope he misses,' says Benedict. 'Funny that the dog didn't bark.'

'Gun dogs don't bark,' says Natalka. 'They just pick up the dead bodies.'

On the way home, Benedict looks up the Tennyson quotation on his phone.

I hate the dreadful hollow behind the little wood,
Its lips in the field above are dabbled with blood-red heath,
The red-ribb'd ledges drip with a silent horror of blood,
And Echo there, whatever is asked her, answers, 'Death'.

Chapter 24

Edwin: archetypes

Benedict offers to drive Edwin to the book club but Edwin prefers to take a cab. He doesn't want Benedict hanging round waiting to drive him home and, besides, he likes taxis. It's Ali again tonight and they have an interesting chat about Charles Dickens. Ali's favourite novel is *David Copperfield* which Edwin hasn't read for years. He struggles a bit when they're talking about Barkis. Who was he again? Edwin thinks he's the stagecoach driver who's in love with David's nurse, Peggotty. He'd like to check on his phone but he'd never be able to see Wikipedia in the dark.

'I didn't really get on with the book we're reading tonight,' says Edwin. 'It's about how people should be killed as soon as they reach seventy.'

'Goodness,' says Ali. 'Well, at least you and I have a few years left.'

Edwin is charmed that Ali, whom he places in his fifties, thinks that Edwin is at least fourteen years younger than his actual age.

Imogen lives in a Georgian terrace on the road to Worthing. The handsome curve of the street makes Edwin think of Brighton – one of his favourite places – but here the houses look slightly more weathered, the balconies leaking rust and the arched windows blurred with salt.

Ali is impressed, though. 'Nice place. You'd pay a million for one of these.'

Did Imogen pay a million? wonders Edwin, as he climbs the steps to the front door. A few years ago he encountered a best-selling crime writer who lived on so-called Millionaire's Row, a highly exclusive seafront enclave. He wouldn't have put Imogen quite in that category, though.

The door is opened by Declan, Imogen's husband. Edwin remembers him from the funeral but, in his own home and on a less sombre occasion, Declan is far more outgoing. He's holding a glass of red wine but manages to pat Edwin on the shoulder, remove his coat and usher him towards an inner room without spilling a drop.

'The gang are all in the sitting room. What can I get you, Ed? Wine? Beer? G and T?'

'White wine, please,' says Edwin. He's exactly on time and finds it slightly sinister that everyone is already assembled, waiting for him. Plus, he hates being called Ed.

The room, which has high moulded cornices and a marble fireplace, seems very full of people. In an echo of the first evening at Battle House, Imogen rises from the sofa and begins introductions. She's wearing a green garment that Edwin thinks is called a jumpsuit.

'You know Johnnie, of course. And did you meet George? I can't remember.'

'Yes,' says Edwin. 'Georgina kindly gave us a lift from the station.' Once again, Georgina Potter-Smith is accessorised by a dog but Edwin assumes that this animal – a fluffy poodle type – belongs to Imogen and Declan.

'Oh yes,' says Imogen. 'This is Felicity.' She gestures towards a blonde woman. 'Orla.' A younger female in oversized spectacles. 'And Pietro.' This last is a man of about Edwin's own age with suspiciously dark hair.

'This is Edwin,' says Imogen, leading him towards an armchair upholstered in red brocade. 'He's a super writer.'

Edwin has no idea how Imogen knows this. The only thing she can have read of his are two short pieces: 'If only I hadn't' and the one about his first day at prep school. He sits down and Declan puts a glass of wine on the table next to him. Imogen wordlessly holds out her own glass to be refilled. Edwin notes this, remembering the suggestion that Imogen might have a drink problem. Declan pours the wine without a word or even a glance.

'I'm off now, book lovers,' he says, to the room at large. 'Don't do anything I wouldn't.'

Edwin wonders why Declan is making such a strategic retreat. Benedict had said something about Imogen's husband wanting to be a crime writer like her. If so, wouldn't he want to stay for the literary chat?

'I'm not a real writer,' says Edwin, thinking that humble is the way to go. Just like Uriah Heep, another great character in *David Copperfield*. 'Nothing like Imogen.'

'Imogen is wonderful,' says Orla. There's a murmur of agreement. Edwin discovers that Orla is Imogen's agent, which might account for the mutual admiration. Felicity is a yoga instructor who has come all the way from London. Pietro is a retired chef who runs what is apparently Imogen's favourite pastry shop.

'Coffee and *cornetto* from Pietro's. You can't beat it.'

'Just one Cornetto,' sings Johnnie.

'*Cornetti* are actually Italian pastries,' says Pietro. 'But I appreciate the cultural reference.'

Rather to Edwin's disappointment, he has no trace of an Italian accent.

'Now,' says Imogen, tapping her glass with a pen. 'Let's talk about the book.'

'Can I take a photo first?' says Edwin. 'I'm trying to get better with my phone.'

He's rather proud of the fuss he makes pretending not to know which way to point the camera. As a matter of fact, he has already taken several surreptitious snaps but he wants a good picture of everyone's face. Eventually Imogen, with obvious impatience, helps him and then arranges herself in the corner of the group photo.

'You young people are so good with technology,' says Edwin, swiftly zooming in and out. 'Say cheese! Say book club!'

'Book club,' they chorus.

'Now,' says Imogen, with a slightly forced laugh. 'Can we get on with the actual business of the book club? What did we all think of the book?'

Edwin has actually taken notes, which are tucked inside his paperback copy, but he waits to see what the others say. He doesn't want to sound pretentious – or not pretentious enough.

'I think it's an important book,' says Orla. 'Blue Fraser is a force to be reckoned with.'

Blue Fraser is the author, whose black-and-white photograph adorns the back page. He looks about fifteen.

'Such spare muscular language,' says Imogen.

'The characters are archetypes,' says Felicity, 'which only makes them more powerful.'

'As someone nearing eighty-five,' says Pietro. 'I found it offensive.'

Edwin notes that the Italian is exactly his age. He is emboldened to say, 'I have to say I agree. The fact that it's written from the point of view of the inventor of the so-called youth project, someone we're meant to admire, only makes it worse.'

'But Bardyweb's mother is one of the first to die,' says Imogen. 'Didn't you find that an incredibly powerful situation?'

'Not really,' says Edwin, 'because Bardyweb doesn't seem more than mildly inconvenienced and we're never given the mother's point-of-view. Do we even know her name?'

'Old Woman 1,' says Pietro.

'They're archetypes,' says Felicity again. 'Not characters.'

'Is that a good thing?' says Edwin. 'I like to read about characters.' He thinks about Barkis, a minor character who nevertheless has clearly stayed with Ali, the taxi driver, for many years.

'Netflix have bought the rights,' says Orla, as if this settles the matter. Which perhaps it does.

Edwin assumes that the book is Orla's choice, given that she seems to know everything about it, but it turns out to have been Felicity's. Next week will be Pietro's turn, *The Leopard*.

They discuss the book for a bit longer. Orla speaks the most and Georgina the least, although she does say that she prefers books that use quotation marks. 'Otherwise it's so difficult to know who's talking.' Georgina herself speaks with difficulty because Barty, the cockerpoo, insists on sitting on her lap with his head under her chin. 'He likes you,' says Imogen, her tone implying that this is a huge honour. There are photos of the animal all over the room, interspersed with two children, a boy and a girl. Edwin wonders where they are because there's no other sign of teenage presence. Imogen says they're both at boarding school, 'Which they love.' Edwin is sceptical although he'd loved his boarding school by the end.

At nine o'clock Declan comes in with pizza. Edwin takes a slice of margherita. It tastes both too wet and too dry. Pietro refuses politely when the plate comes his way.

'I thought you were Italian.' Johnnie seems determined to establish this.

'I'm from Florence, not Naples,' says Pietro.

'Were you born in Italy?' asks Edwin. He once had a wonderful holiday in Florence with his French boyfriend, François.

'Yes,' says Pietro. 'In 1938, which wasn't the best time to be in Italy. My father was a prisoner-of-war and my mother, who was actually a princess, had to take in washing.'

'Who took your father prisoner?' asks Felicity. 'The Germans?'

'No,' says Pietro. 'The British. We were on the wrong side of history.'

'Pietro makes delicious *bombolini*,' says Imogen.

After the pizza, Edwin asks the way to the loo. Imogen says there are two, one by the kitchen and one on the first floor. Edwin opts to go upstairs because he wants to do a bit of light sleuthing. The house is tall and narrow. Edwin thinks it's probably three storeys high, maybe with a loft conversion. The first-floor bathroom is large and slightly grungy, with mould creeping into the corners. Edwin is willing to bet that Imogen and Declan have their own immaculate en-suite somewhere. He opens the medicine cabinet and finds only treatments for adolescent ailments like spots and swimmers' ear. There's one bottle of penicillin with a label on it. Edwin squints and thinks he sees the word Steyning. That seems a long way to go for antibiotics. And isn't Alan Franklin's pharmacy in Steyning? He takes a photo on his phone.

Descending the steep stairs carefully, Edwin sees Johnnie in the hall, typing on her phone. She looks up. 'Hallo. Haven't had a chance to chat to you. What do you make of all this? I'm just messaging my husband and telling him about old Bardyweb.'

Edwin wonders why Johnnie feels the need to offer an explanation. What did Harbinder say about people mentioning their husbands?

'I can't say I enjoyed the book,' he says, 'but the company is very pleasant. Have you been coming long?'

'About three years. After my first weekend at Battle House. It's quite an honour to be asked, I think.'

'Who else was asked?' asks Edwin. 'Frances? Peter? Sue?'

'Sue came once or twice,' says Johnnie. 'I don't remember her saying much, though. I think she was intimidated by Orla.'

'I don't blame her.'

'Nor do I. A few people have come and gone over the years. Henry came for a bit. And Don.'

'Don? Don Parsons? The vicar?'

'That's right. Did you know him? He was a nice man. Quite shy. I was sorry to hear that he'd died.'

'I've never met him,' says Edwin, 'but he was a friend of Benedict's.'

'Oh yes. Benedict was a priest, wasn't he? He said a prayer at Sue's funeral.'

'A monk. Yes.'

'I had enough of priests and do-gooders in my old job but Benedict seemed quite normal.'

Edwin treasures this glowing endorsement to pass on to Benedict.

'I was surprised Imogen didn't invite Benedict,' he says.

'Oh, she only invites the best writers,' says Johnnie, with more than a trace of smugness.

'I don't know how she can know what sort of writer I am. She's only read a few paragraphs of mine.'

'Oh, she knows,' says Johnnie.

'Is Georgina a writer too?'

'No, she was a teacher but now she just works on the farm. I honestly think she comes here to get away from David. He's a bit of a bore and he drinks too much. Passes out in front of the TV every evening. George once said she only stays with him because of Buster, her dog.'

'Imogen's dog certainly seems to like her.'

'Yes, he's a nippy little thing too. He bit Orla once. I'm hoping it'll happen again.'

Ali comes to collect Edwin at ten. He's tired by then and not in the mood for another discussion about Dickens. But, as often happens, when he's in bed, Edwin finds he can't sleep. This is one of those times when having a pet would help. A creature to chat to in the dark hours. Edwin had once cohabited with a beautiful cat called Barbra. 'People are either dogs or cats,' Nicky, an ex-boyfriend, once told him. 'You're all cat, Edwin.'

Edwin has a headache and the pizza is churning in his stomach. After thinking about these afflictions for a while, he decides to do something about them. He gets two aspirin and a Gaviscon from his bathroom cabinet, thinking, as he does so, about the mysterious pill bottle in Imogen's house. At least he will have something to tell Natalka and Benedict tomorrow.

In his towelling slippers, Edwin pads into the kitchen to get a glass of water, even though he fears this will mean multiple trips to the loo. As he runs the tap, Edwin opens the window and breathes in the night air. Although his flat doesn't face the sea, he can smell it and hear the waves rustling against the shingle. And, in a rush of memory, he remembers something said at Barkis's deathbed in *David Copperfield*, that people along the coast can't die until the tide is out. What's the tide doing now? Edwin doesn't think he wants to know.

But, when he finally sleeps, he dreams not about the sea, but about Italian pastries and François' awestruck face when he saw Michelangelo's *David* for the first time.

Chapter 25

Harbinder: small world

Tuesday, 3 May

Harbinder arrives at work to hear that she has a visitor waiting in her office. Freya, her PA, tells her it's DS Brennan from Hastings CID. Harbinder's detective senses, temporarily dulled by breakfast with Mette, immediately swing into action. Liv Brennan is the detective investigating what she thinks of as Natalka's case. But what is she doing in West London at eight-thirty in the morning?

Freya says that she's made coffee for the visitor, which implies she's been there for some time. Harbinder, who is carrying her reusable mug of Costa cappuccino, pushes open the door.

'Hi. Sorry to keep you waiting.'

'Hi. Sorry to turn up without an appointment. I was in London anyway and I thought it might be easier to talk in person.' Harbinder had not realised that Liv was another woman of colour – still rare in CID – so she is well-disposed towards her colleague, although she's not sure she buys the 'in London anyway' story.

'How's the case going?' says Harbinder.

'Frustrating,' says Liv. 'We asked your friends in for a chat and they were very helpful.'

'I'm glad. They're very good, very professional. You can trust them.' Harbinder hopes so, anyway.

'Benedict Cole had a whole list of suspects and clues.'

'Yes, Benedict likes a list.'

'The trouble is, there are too many of both suspects and clues.'

'Anything from SOCO?' asks Harbinder. She is still not sure why they are having this discussion, in person. And she's not sure if she likes Liv's reference to 'your friends'.

'Post-mortem shows that Sue was hit over the head before entering the water. There are footprints leading along the farm track towards the pond and definite signs of an altercation at the water's edge. Whether it was planned or not, we don't know. Sue's phone records don't show that she was on her way to meet anyone. But, if it was a spur-of-the-moment killing, that points to some kind of psychopath and there are no known offenders in the area.'

'Something will come up,' says Harbinder. 'It always does. A number plate, a text message, someone being where they shouldn't be.'

'Yes,' says Liv. 'That's what I'm telling myself.' There's a pause and then she says, 'I'm here on false pretences really. This is my day off.'

'Is it?' is all Harbinder can think of to say.

'I came to ask your advice, I suppose.'

'About the case?'

'That too. But, really, it's my boss.'

'I see,' says Harbinder. She's beginning to.

'DI Derek Poole. He's one of the old school.'

'Sexist and racist then?'

'A bit.' Liv gives her a reluctant grin. 'He's a good copper. Everyone at the station respects him. But he makes these comments to me, asking where my family are from and all that.'

'I used to get that. Where are you really from? I kept telling people "Shoreham" but, of course, that wasn't what they were asking.'

'I'm the deputy SIO on this case,' says Liv. 'But Poole undermines me at every turn. He keeps deferring to my partner, Sam, who's nice enough but not the sharpest tool in the box. And he's younger and less experienced than me.'

'Tell me about it,' says Harbinder. She feels extremely weary. How long are woman officers going to have to put up with this sort of thing?

'I *am* telling you,' says Liv, 'because you've always been . . . well, a hero of mine. You solved the Peggy Smith case. You went to London and solved the murder of that politician. People say you might be commissioner one day.'

'I doubt that,' says Harbinder. But she knows that this is not the moment for false modesty. This is the time to give Liv advice, to help keep a good officer on the force.

'First of all,' she says, 'keep a list . . .'

When Liv has left Harbinder rings Natalka. Through the glass walls of her office, she can see her team arriving: Jake swaggering in like an even shorter Tom Cruise, Kim halfway through her breakfast, Tory apparently engaged in a riveting exchange of texts.

'Hi, Natalka. I've just seen Liv Brennan.'

'Oh, have you? Did you like her? She reminds me a bit of you.'

'Do all people of colour look the same to you then?'

It's a tease, although Harbinder also thinks it might be true.

'I don't mean in looks,' says Natalka. 'I mean in character. She doesn't suffer fools gladly. That's a good English phrase, isn't it? I'm bilingual now.'

Harbinder thinks that Liv might not suffer fools gladly but she definitely has one as a boss. She says, 'I've been telling DS Brennan that she can trust you.'

'Thank you. I think she liked us when we went to see her in Hastings but she was still a bit wary. We've made some progress here. Edwin went to the book club at Imogen's house last night. Remember Imogen Blythe, one of the teachers at Battle House? Anyway, turns out that both Sue and Don Parsons were members of the club.'

'Remind me who Don Parsons is again?'

'He's a vicar who wrote books under the name Donna Parsons. He died last month and a friend of Benedict's called Richard Fraser asked us to investigate because Don had written him a letter before he died saying someone was trying to kill him.'

'And you really think the deaths could be linked?' Harbinder's head is swimming, an effect Natalka often has on her.

'I think it's possible. There are links all over the place. And Melody wrote a quote for the book by the other woman who died, Eileen O'Rourke, about Jack the Ripper. It's a small world, the book business. We learnt that last time.'

The book is still on Harbinder's shelves. She can see the spine with its shiny red letters. *My Name is Jack* by Eileen O'Rourke.

'That wasn't a suspicious death.' It feels important to remind

Natalka of this. 'We only investigated because the daughter, Felicity, said—'

'What was that name?'

'What name?' Harbinder asks. The dizzy feeling is back again.

'The daughter's name.'

'Felicity.'

'There was a Felicity at the book club last night. I'm almost sure of it. I'll check with Edwin. If I know Edwin, he'll have taken a photo. I'll send it to you. If it was Eileen O'Rourke's daughter, then there's definitely a link.'

'It's not very likely, is it?' Harbinder says, trying to cling on to rationality.

'I don't know,' says Natalka. 'It's as likely as Don Parsons being there. Anyway, I'd better go. Got a busy morning.'

'Are you out on a run?'

There's a slight pause. Harbinder can hear Natalka breathing. 'That's right. Speak soon. And thanks for the heads-up.'

Heads-up, thinks Harbinder. Natalka really is bilingual.

Chapter 26

Natalka: the marrying kind

Natalka is not on her usual seafront run. She is jogging towards the car park at Ditchling Beacon where she has arranged to meet Alan Franklin. It's work, she tells herself. I'm interviewing a suspect. She does want to ask herself why she hasn't told Benedict that this is how she is spending the morning. She didn't tell Harbinder either and she has left her car at the bottom of the hill, rather than parking it near Alan's. She is behaving, in other words, like someone with something to hide.

She sees him when she is still some way away. He's standing by a stile with Frodo on the lead. He's wearing jeans and a black T-shirt and his long hair is lifting in the breeze. Natalka remembers looking up the word 'beacon' when she first came to live in Sussex. It means, according to the Cambridge Dictionary: 'a light or fire in a place that is easy to see, a warning or a signal.' Alan is easy to see, silhouetted against the sky. Is he a warning or a signal?

Alan doesn't say anything about the fact that Natalka is on foot.

He greets her casually, unlike Frodo who jumps up, pawing at her leggings.

'Down, dog.' Alan pulls him away. 'Sorry. He gets overexcited.'

'Downward facing dog,' says Natalka, walking through the gate that Alan holds open. 'That's a yoga pose.'

'I bet you do yoga.'

'I do.' Natalka is slightly put out, both by Alan's familiar – almost affectionate – tone and by the idea that she is so predictable.

They walk across the Downs, the city spread out below them, sea on one side and, on the other, the curves of the Amex, the rather beautiful stadium where Brighton play their increasingly beautiful football. It's an exposed landscape, just grass and the occasional stunted tree, blown into crouching position by the wind. They walk in silence for a few minutes, Frodo running on ahead, nose down, plumy tail up.

'He's very cute,' says Natalka.

'He's a nutcase,' says Alan, but he says it lovingly, she thinks.

'Frodo was Melody's dog, wasn't he?'

'Yes,' says Alan. 'Harmony and Minnie wanted to take him after she died but her will explicitly left him to me.'

That must mean that Melody revised her will not long before she died, thinks Natalka. She remembers the Facebook post 'Frodo!', and the picture of the adorable puppy. She thinks it was dated 2019, three years ago.

'Those women really hate you,' she says. 'Harmony and Minnie.'

'They do,' says Alan. 'It's uncomfortable being hated that much.'

'I don't mind being hated,' says Natalka. 'It shows you made an impression.'

'But a wholly negative one,' says Alan, calling Frodo away from a tempting cow pat.

'You know who doesn't hate you?' says Natalka. 'Your ex-girlfriend Jill.'

Natalka spoke to Jill yesterday. It had been fairly easy to find her via Facebook. Natalka sent a message asking if she could call for a 'quick chat about Alan' and Jill had phoned her back within the hour. 'We had a good few years together,' Jill said. 'No major rows or anything. It was very civilised. Too civilised, if anything.' 'Why did you split up?' asked Natalka. 'Simply because I wanted children and he didn't,' said Jill. 'The old biological clock and all that.' Natalka doesn't know if Jill succeeded in having children. There are none in evidence on her Facebook page.

'You followed up on that lead, then,' says Alan, once again sounding amused.

'Of course,' says Natalka. 'I'm a detective.'

'How did you become a detective?' asks Alan.

'A friend of mine was murdered,' says Natalka. 'A client. I was just a carer then, not a detective. I thought there was something suspicious about her death from the first. The police didn't seem interested – apart from one woman detective. My friends and I, we thought we'd try to solve the case.'

'And did you?'

'Oh yes,' says Natalka. She doesn't mention the danger, the foolish decisions, the horror of death seen at close range.

They walk through another gate and there in front of them, like a mirage, is a pink catering van. Several dog walkers, obviously in on the secret, are drinking coffee at a picnic table. A wire-haired terrier comes up to Frodo and sniffs him briskly.

'They even do gin,' says Alan, laughing at the surprise on Natalka's face.

'It's a bit early for me,' says Natalka, although, for a minute, she is tempted. She asks for coffee and she and Alan move to the most remote table.

Natalka is finding Alan easy company as they chat about their respective jobs and laugh at Frodo's antics. She's caught off guard when he suddenly says, 'So, Natalka. Are you in a relationship?'

'Yes,' says Natalka. 'I live with my boyfriend, Benedict. And with my mother at the moment. Unfortunately.'

'Has she come over from Ukraine?'

'Yes. I'm very happy that she's safe but it's a small flat for three people.'

'What does Benedict do?'

'He runs a coffee shop,' says Natalka, rather defiantly. She doesn't think there's anything wrong with Benedict's job but she knows how snobbish English people can be. She gets enough of that from Benedict's family.

'That's not what I expected,' says Alan.

'What did you expect?'

'I don't know. A firefighter, a martial arts expert, a brain surgeon.'

'I don't think I'd like to be in a relationship with any of those people.'

'No. Me neither.'

There's a short pause and then Natalka says, 'Harmony and Minnie think you'll find a new girlfriend soon.'

Alan laughs but there's obviously something slightly wrong with the sound because Frodo looks at him anxiously. 'Typical,' he says. 'I'm in no rush. And, anyway, the best ones are all taken.'

Natalka is not sure what to make of this.

Natalka has arranged to meet Edwin for lunch in Shoreham. She doesn't have time to go home, shower and change and wonders if Edwin, who notices everything, will comment on her exercise clothes. But Edwin, who is sitting outside their favourite café with a view of the harbour, doesn't comment on her appearance. She loves the way he still stands up when he sees her and tips his Panama hat. Dear Edwin. Who needs a father or grandfather when she has him?

Natalka orders a ham sandwich but finds she isn't hungry. Edwin sympathises.

'I'm still tasting the wretched pizza from last night.'

'How was it?' says Natalka, opening her diet Coke. 'Tell me everything.'

Edwin has already given her a quick debrief on the phone. But now he gets out his notebook, puts on his glasses and clears his throat.

'Here's a list of the people present. Imogen and her husband Declan. Orla, Imogen's agent. Johnnie. Georgina, who owns the farm. A woman called Felicity. A man called Pietro.'

'A man! He was brave. How old was he?'

'About my age.'

Natalka thinks that Edwin says this slightly too casually.

'Boyfriend material?'

'Really, Natalka.' Edwin looks at her over the top of his glasses. 'I'm far too old to have a boyfriend.'

'Husband then.'

'Steady on. I've only met him once. Besides, I've told you before, I'm not the marrying kind.'

'Nor am I,' says Natalka. Daniel doesn't count, she tells herself. 'I'm interested in Felicity. Did you manage to take a photo?'

'I certainly did,' says Edwin. 'You should have seen me pretending I didn't know which button to press.'

He passes the phone to Natalka, who enlarges the picture. 'Is that her? The blonde next to Johnnie?'

'Yes. Why are you interested in her?'

'You know Harbinder told us about that author in London who died? Eileen something. Wrote the book about Jack the Ripper. Her daughter was called Felicity.'

'It's a bit of a long shot,' says Edwin. 'Although this Felicity was from London. I thought at the time it was a long way to go for a book club.'

'I'll send Harbinder the picture,' says Natalka, doing so. 'Well done for taking it. Pietro looks cute.'

'He doesn't,' says Edwin, retrieving his phone. 'He's a handsome man of a certain age.'

Natalka registers this but decides it's time to drop the subject.

'So, what did you think? Is there a link between the book club and what happened at Battle House?'

'There are some cross-overs, certainly,' says Edwin. 'Sue used to go to the book group. So did Don Parsons. Johnnie said a few people have been and gone over the years—'

He stops. Natalka looks up, concerned. Now's not the time for Edwin to have a mini-stroke.

But it seems that Edwin is thinking. 'I'm almost certain that Johnnie mentioned the name Henry.'

'Who's he?'

'I think it could be a she. Remember I went to see Ivan, the son of Felix Marshall, the flautist? Well, he mentioned his sister Henrietta. Except he called her Henry. Now, if she also went to the book group, there's a link to all the deaths.'

'Great,' says Natalka. 'We're getting somewhere at last. You must ask your friend.'

As she speaks, Edwin's face changes again. This time it is beautified by a sudden smile. 'Benedict! Dear boy. This is a nice surprise.'

Natalka turns and sees Benedict loping between the tables. He, too, is grinning broadly.

'The Shack wasn't busy,' says Benedict. 'So I thought I'd have lunch with you two.' He stoops to kiss Natalka, smelling of soap and coffee.

'Did you have a good run this morning?' Benedict asks her.

'It was OK,' says Natalka. 'Just the usual. You know.'

'Back to usually,' says Benedict, which is a joke between them.

Natalka doesn't laugh. 'We're talking about the case,' she says. 'Get a chair and join us.'

Chapter 27

Benedict: another word for fate

Benedict has put the evening aside for reading Don Parsons' computer files and Melody's notebook. He thinks that Natalka slightly resents being left in the sitting room with her mother while he escapes to the bedroom but he doesn't think that he can concentrate with *Downton Abbey* (Valentyna's favourite show) playing in the background. Besides, it's normally Natalka who puts her headphones on and leaves him to endure the travails of Lady Mary and co.

Natalka has been slightly distant today, thinks Benedict. She looked surprised but not pleased when he turned up at lunchtime. Had she been looking forward to time alone with Edwin? Benedict must remember to give them more time together. He thinks that Edwin is a surrogate father to Natalka, even more important because her own father seems lost for ever. He doesn't think that Edwin is a father figure to him, partly because his male parent still looms large in his life. He's more like a much-older brother or a kind uncle, the sort who takes you to the opera or to Camden Market. The sort Benedict didn't have.

Benedict starts with Don's laptop files. PARISH is full of rotas for church cleaning and flower-arranging. Benedict remembers the woman he met sweeping the church. Should he have talked to her for longer? 'Don't forget the carers,' Natalka always says, 'they know everything that goes on in a house.' Could the same be said for cleaners? He looks at the list of names. He's willing to bet that the dungaree-clad woman with her AirPods was Chelsea and not Edna or Mavis. There's nothing else of interest in this file, just the mundane business of maintaining a parish. Presumably Lucy's computer is full of outreach groups with rhyming or alliterative names.

The folder called Sybil is more interesting. There are about twenty photos of the tortoiseshell cat, lying in the sun or on armchairs, turning accusing amber eyes at the camera. But there are also several letters. One to someone called Jelli, who is presumably Don's agent. 'If Seventh Seal don't want the new book, can't we find a more adventurous publisher who will appreciate it? Isn't that your job?' The tone is querulous and demanding, decidedly unvicar-like. Did Don ever send this letter or email? The name Jelli also seems to ring a bell. He thinks it's short for Angelica and that she was involved in the Peggy Smith case somehow. There's also a letter to a certain M. Flowers in which Don defends himself from the accusation of Anglo-Catholicism. 'The church has a side-altar that was, in its Catholic days, dedicated to the Virgin Mary. I never use it as such . . . I certainly don't remember ever, consciously, turning to the east during the Creed . . .' Lucy had also called Don an Anglo-Catholic. Is it really such an awful thing to be? Benedict wonders whether Don ever sent the email. Are these the missives that Don wrote but never sent?

Another file is called, simply, 'Donna'.

Donna Parsons was born in Hastings in 1960. She excelled at school and studied English at Girton College, Cambridge, where she was a prominent member of the Footlights. After graduating with a double first, she worked in publishing, eventually becoming editorial director of Seventh Seal. Her first novel, Red as the Rose, *won the 2007 Romantic Novel Award. Donna is married to Tony, an architect, and has three grown-up children.*

This is interesting, on many levels. As far as Benedict remembers from Malcolm Collins' obituary of Don Parsons, he didn't go to Cambridge or work in publishing. Is this the biography Don really wanted for himself, marriage to Tony and all? Benedict has been wary about assuming that the pseudonym meant that Don wished that he could identify as a woman but did he, at heart, wish that he was Donna? Benedict also thinks it's significant that Donna worked at Seventh Seal, Don's publishers who apparently turned down the 'new book'. And the word Hastings gives Benedict a jolt too. He thinks that Don was born in Surrey. What is the link to Hastings, where Battle House is situated? 1066 country and all that.

The last folder is the biggest. 'Work in Progress' contains 39,127 words of something called *Absolution*. Benedict starts on the first page, to discover it's set in a very different world from the flower-named romances. This, as far as he can tell, is a novel about a lonely bachelor living with his mother in an English village. It reminds Benedict a little of Barbara Pym but without that author's leavening wit. It's a bleak read but it is, Benedict thinks, rather well-written.

It wasn't that he didn't want to pass the time of day with his neighbour. Rather that he didn't know how to start the conversation and, by the time that

he'd thought of an inoffensively genial remark, said neighbour was a speck in
the distance, a smug silhouette with acquiescent dog at his side. Passing the
time of day was more than a mere pleasantry. It was essential.

Blimey, thinks Benedict, poor old Don. On the spur of the
moment, he rings Richard.

'Hallo, Ben. What's up?'

'Sorry to disturb your evening.'

'No problem. Madeline's trying to make me watch something
on Netflix but I can't make head or tail of it. Hang on, I'm going
into the kitchen.'

There's a sound of voices, then movement and a dog barking.
Benedict didn't realise Richard had a pet.

'Right,' says Richard, sounding out of breath even from that
small exertion. 'I'm all yours.'

'I went to Don's parish the other day,' says Benedict. 'There's a
nice new vicar called Lucy.'

'Oh yes. I hear she's one of the happy-clappy sort. Find anything
out?'

'Lucy very kindly gave me Don's laptop.'

'That was helpful of her. I can't imagine Don with a laptop. I
imagined him writing with a quill somehow.'

'I thought that too. Anyway, on the computer there's an unfinished novel called *Absolution*. I wondered if Don had ever mentioned
it to you?'

'No,' says Richard. '*Absolution*. That sounds rather Catholic,
doesn't it?'

'Yes, it does,' says Benedict. He knows that 'absolution' means
the forgiveness of sins, something that, in the Catholic Church,

happens after confession. When you leave the confessional, you are free from sin, as pure as the day you were born (not counting original sin, of course). The word, Benedict remembers, comes from the Latin *absolutus*, to set free. He also remembers it being impressed on him that this special forgiveness comes not from the priest hearing the confession, but directly from God.

'I gather Don was a bit of an Anglo-Catholic,' he says.

'He was,' says Richard, 'but he didn't have the courage to go all the way.' Like the neighbour in Don's book, he sounds rather smug. Benedict wonders whether Don's secret wish to become Donna was the reason he didn't 'go all the way'.

'Have you discovered anything else?' asks Richard.

'Don used to go on writing retreats to a place called Battle House. I went there for a weekend and, well . . . it was rather eventful . . .' As succinctly as possible, he tells Richard about Sue's death.

'Oh my goodness. The poor woman.' Benedict can almost hear Richard crossing himself. 'But there's no link between her and Don, is there?'

'Not that I can see. Although they both used to go to the same book group.'

'I can't imagine Don at a book group.'

'Why not?'

'He was so shy he could hardly speak. Especially in mixed company. The only women in his life were his mum and his cat.'

'I've met the cat. A terrifying beast.'

Richard laughs and the dog barks again. After promising to keep in touch, Benedict rings off. There's a tap on the door and Natalka appears.

'I thought I heard voices.'

'I was talking to Richard, my priest friend. I found a slightly odd manuscript in Don's files.'

'Odd? Why?'

'It was quite good, for one thing. And very depressing.'

He turns the screen towards Natalka.

'I hate that sort of book,' she says. 'The kind where they go for walks and take their books back to the library and nothing else happens. I like a proper plot.'

'Talking of plots, how's *Downton Abbey*?'

'I had to get away. Sybil's giving birth.'

'I wonder if Don's cat was named after Lady Sybil in *Downton Abbey*,' says Benedict.

'Probably,' says Natalka. 'Everyone in England seemed to watch it. Even now, there are repeats all the time. Find anything else interesting?'

'Do you remember someone called Jelli from the Dex Challoner case?'

'Yes, she was his agent. It's short for Angelica, I think. I remember Harbinder talking about her.'

'She was Don's agent too. Or rather Donna's. Look at this.'

He shows her the Donna biography.

'Don wanted to be a woman,' Natalka says immediately. 'I've always thought so. Sad that he couldn't transition. I suppose those were different times.'

'Yes, it is sad,' says Benedict. 'I wonder if that was what the unfinished manuscript was going to be about. Eventually. There's a letter from Don to Jelli saying that his publishers didn't want the new book. I suppose it was too different from the Donna books. I'll have to read to the end, or as far as Don got.'

'Rather you than me,' says Natalka. 'But I've got something to tell you. I've just had a text from Harbinder. The Felicity at Imogen's book club *was* the daughter of the writer in London that died. Eileen O'Rourke, remember? That can't be a coincidence, can it?'

'Coincidence is only another word for fate,' says Benedict. 'I read that somewhere.'

Natalka ignores this, probably hoping that he doesn't come up with the source of the quotation.

'I need to infiltrate the book club,' she says.

'I could do it,' says Benedict. 'I know Imogen after all.'

'I think I should do it,' says Natalka. 'Imogen knows you but she won't be suspicious of me.'

Want to bet? thinks Benedict. But he agrees that Natalka should try to get an invite to the book club. Natalka looks pleased and offers to make him a cup of tea.

With a cup of peppermint tea to hand, Benedict scrolls through the remaining files of Work in Progress. It's interesting to see Don's planning process. There's one file which just seems full of random words: sisters, friendship, flowers, blooming, weeds, sun, flames, death, rebirth. Death comes as a bit of a shock, thinks Benedict, but then it always does. There's a synopsis for *The Lily and the Rose*, which sounds much more like the rest of Donna's oeuvre. 'Two girls, brought up together as sisters. Two lives that take very different directions . . .' There's no synopsis or plan for *Absolution*.

Finally, Benedict opens the document entitled 'I'm scared'.

I'm scared, they're trying to kill me. For weeks I've been telling myself it's impossible. They're my friends. They wouldn't hurt me. Even if I know their secret, they know mine. Surely, we are even. But one day I'll be found dead and no one will know or care. But they will have killed me.

Is this the beginning of a short story, the one requested so urgently by someone at Battle House? Is it a plan for the letter eventually sent to Richard? Either way, it has the feel of genuine desperation.

Benedict turns, with some relief, to Melody Chambers' notebook. There's something intimate about seeing her actual handwriting, with its loopy y and indistinguishable n and u. Unlike Don with his chapter plans, Melody obviously uses the book to jot down ideas as they come to her.

Babies swapped at birth? Cliché? Rich family/poor family. Black & white?
Dead husband returns. Wife happy with new life. Or is she?
Romcom from POV of dog??

POV means point of view, Benedict remembers that from the writing weekend. He can't help feeling disappointed that Melody never progressed with this idea. The notebook also contains several sketches of Frodo, some recipes and a plan for a vegetable patch. Reading these pages makes Benedict like Melody very much.

The piece of writing that convinced Melody's daughters of her husband's guilt is frustratingly short and broken up by a shopping list and what looks like an attempt to solve a Wordle. Benedict feels another twinge of empathy.

I think my husband is going to kill me. I can't tell anyone. He watches me all the time. I'm scared of him. What can I do? I'm a prisoner here.
Chicken thighs
Lime
Ginger
Coconut milk
**Y*Y

'Coyly', Benedict wants to tell Melody. And, two goes later, she gets it.

Then:

I used to love him and I thought he loved me. Is this what becomes of love? Of course, once he loved her. Does he still? I thought I knew him so well. Twin souls. But it seems we know nobody in this life. Our loved ones least of all.

This last does sound a bit like the strapline of a book. But Benedict is not sure about the rest of it. Could Melody have sandwiched a cry for help between a recipe for Thai chicken curry and an attempt to solve a tricky Wordle? And who is 'she'? After staring at the page for several more minutes, Benedict gives up and goes into the sitting room where he finds Natalka and Valentyna in tears, *Downton Abbey* having proved unexpectedly tragic.

Chapter 28

Edwin: little jackals

Monday, 6 June

It was surprisingly easy to get Natalka invited to the book group. Edwin simply told Imogen that he had a Ukrainian friend who liked reading and Imogen said why didn't he bring her along. 'It's guilt,' said Natalka. 'Your friend Imogen feels guilty that she didn't offer to host a Ukrainian in her home but she didn't want her comfortable life upset. So she invited me to her book club instead.' Edwin said nothing. He thought that Natalka was probably right, but he knew that she hated the idea that people might feel sorry for her.

They seem to have made very little progress over the last few weeks. Harbinder followed up on the Felicity clue but was told that Felicity had been at school with Georgina and knew of the book club through her. Edwin phoned Ivan Marshall on the pretext of discussing the photos and managed to get the conversation round to his sister Henrietta or Henry. 'Is she musical? Or does she prefer reading? Does she go to a book group?' 'How should I know?' snapped Ivan, sounding irritated. Edwin didn't blame him.

Natalka has been very busy with the care agency. Valentyna is also working there which seems to have given her a new lease of life but clearly irritates Natalka. She's looking rather pale and tired recently, Edwin's lovely Natalka. It's probably anxiety about her brother combined with overwork. Edwin wonders whether to discuss it with Benedict but he doesn't want to interfere in the couple's relationship. Benedict, too, has seemed slightly distracted. He keeps talking about an unfinished manuscript called *Absolution*, which he found amongst Don Parsons' papers. 'Give it a rest about that boring book,' Natalka had snapped, at one of their meetings at the Shack.

Over the past few weeks, Edwin has been adding to their list of names.

Peter Abbot
50s. Children's author, but 'dark stuff'. B overheard him having a potentially suspicious conversation.

Imogen Blythe
45. Crime writer. Married to Declan, a lawyer and would-be writer. Two children. Has been teaching at BH for 5 years.

Felicity Briggs
Daughter of Eileen O'Rourke, a true crime writer who died of a heart attack. Felicity first claimed that it was murder but seemed to retract. Attends Imogen's book group.

Melody Chambers
70. Writer, married to Alan Franklin. Daughters found a letter/unfinished story saying that she was scared her husband was trying to kill her.

Malcolm Collins
Journalist and obituary writer. Died of Covid in 2021. Attended courses at Battle House. In a relationship with Sue Hitchins.

Alan Franklin
55. Pharmacist. Melody's second husband. Inherited her house, to the anger of her daughters Harmony and Minim.

Sue Hitchins
60s? Ex-teacher. Lives in London. In a relationship with Malcolm Collins. Warned us to be wary of Imogen. Drowned in lake at Battle House. Police treating as suspicious.

Ivan and Henrietta Marshall
Adult children of Felix Marshall, famous flautist. Might have been the inspiration for Malcolm Collins' book idea 'a musician poisoned by his own instrument'. Henrietta possibly attended Imogen's book club.

Johnnie Newton
Mid-50s? Aspiring crime writer. Mentioned to B that she'd been in an institution.

Leonard Norris
61. Writer though hasn't published anything since 1992. Lives at Battle House and knew previous owner Miriam Fry. Has been teaching at

BH for 10 years. Says that Sue fantasised she had an affair with him. Ex-alcoholic?

Don Parsons
62. Vicar who wrote romantic fiction as Donna Parsons. Supposedly died of a heart attack. Before he died he wrote to Richard Fraser (Catholic priest friend) saying he thought 'they' were trying to kill him. Unfinished manuscript (not a romance) called Absolution *that was rejected for publication. Attended the book club.*

Frances O'Toole
50s or even 60s. Poet.

David Potter-Smith
Farmer. Georgina's husband. Appears to have a grudge against Leonard Norris.

Georgina Potter-Smith
Vet. Owns Battle House. Miriam Fry was her aunt. Attends Imogen's book group.

There are recurring themes, thinks Edwin, reviewing the list as he dresses for book group. 'Leitmotifs' he would have called them in his Radio 3 days. Battle House, the book group, unfinished manuscripts. They just need the one clue that unites them all. Edwin ties his bow tie carefully. It's Italian. He wonders if Pietro will notice.

Edwin expected Natalka to drive them to Imogen's house, but she suggested that they get a taxi. 'That way I can have a drink.'

Edwin was surprised – Natalka isn't a big drinker – but he booked the cab. The driver's not Ali this time but a taciturn Scotsman called Bob. Edwin soon gives up trying to engage Bob in conversation and talks to Natalka about *The Leopard*. He has taken a lot of care with this month's book, partly (he has to admit) because it was Pietro's choice. His paperback classic bristles with post-it notes.

Natalka says she read the book on her Kindle but Edwin begins to suspect that she didn't finish it.

'The prince is a bit of a Don Quixote, don't you think?' says Edwin. He's trying the observation out before offering it to the group.

'For God's sake, don't give me any more names,' says Natalka. 'There are quite enough in the book.'

'And Don Ciccio is Sancho Panza.' Edwin is determined to finish the thought. He's worried about his Italian pronunciation. It used to be considered quite good at the BBC but will it be good enough for Pietro?

'I liked the parts about Garibaldi,' says Natalka. 'He was a real freedom fighter. Like President Zelenskyy.'

Of course, thinks Edwin, war and invasion are not just words in a history book to Natalka. She probably understands the book in a way that he, sheltered on this smug little island, never can.

'Does he die in the end?' asks Natalka. 'I got bored.'

'He dies in the section called Death of a Prince,' Edwin can't help saying. 'There's a very beautiful description of the last rites.'

'You and Benedict with your Catholic stuff,' says Natalka. 'It gets on my nerves.'

Edwin doesn't want Natalka to be irritated with Benedict. He's still trying to think of something uplifting to say when the taxi pulls up outside Imogen's town house.

'Here ye are,' said Bob. 'Don't do anything I wouldn't.'

Imogen greets Edwin with a careless affection that implies they are old friends. She then takes Natalka's hand in both of hers. 'You're *very* welcome.'

'Thanks,' says Natalka. She gives Edwin a 'what did I tell you?' look.

Once again, the company are all assembled, like actors at the start of a play. Orla and Felicity are sitting on the sofa, apparently looking at a photo album. Georgina is sharing the armchair with Barty, the dog. Johnnie is on her phone and Pietro is staring intently at his glass, as if suspecting it of containing New World wine.

'Here's Edwin and his lovely Ukrainian friend, Natalka,' says Imogen.

'Well, you don't know if I'm lovely yet,' says Natalka.

'I'm sure you are,' says Declan, who has appeared in the doorway. He gives Natalka what Edwin considers an inappropriately speculative glance. Maybe Imogen sees it too because she quickly dispatches her husband to get drinks. Natalka sits on the sofa beside Orla, allowing Edwin to take the place next to Pietro.

'Back again?' says Pietro. 'Didn't we scare you off last time?'

'I don't scare easily,' says Edwin.

Pietro seems to give Edwin his own speculative glance. Edwin hopes he isn't blushing. It's too ridiculous in your eighties.

Edwin is surprised that Natalka asks for mineral water. Wasn't the whole point of getting a taxi so she could drink? He asks for white wine. 'It's French,' says Pietro, in a sorrowful whisper.

The book discussion seems more cursory than it did last time. Orla has less to say, although she does remark that *The Leopard* is 'of its time'.

'Obviously,' says Pietro. 'So am I. So are you.'

Edwin gets in his Don Quixote quip and has an interesting conversation with Pietro about the depiction of ageing and death.

'"We were the leopards, the lions,"' quotes Pietro. '"Those who take our place will be the little jackals, hyenas . . . and sheep." It reminds me of the Mussolini quote. "*Meglio vivere un giorno da leone che cento anni da pecora.*"'

'What does that mean?' asks Georgina. 'We don't all speak Italian.'

'Edwin will translate,' says Pietro.

'Better to live one day as a lion than a hundred years as a sheep,' says Edwin. He hopes that Pietro isn't a fascist.

'What about living a hundred years as a lion?' asks Natalka.

'That's my preferred option too,' says Pietro.

Johnnie says that she found the description of the three sisters, at the end of the book, rather sad. 'We remember them as young and beautiful and now they're just old ladies going to mass every day.'

'It happens to us all,' says Pietro. 'Though not the going to mass part.'

Is Pietro not a practising Catholic then? wonders Edwin. He'll have to keep quiet about his own mass attendance.

'Reminds me of my auntie,' says Georgina. 'Living all on her own in a big house, gradually losing her marbles.'

'My mother too,' says Felicity. 'She just sat in one room while rubbish piled up around her.'

Wasn't Felicity's mother a successful author living in a beautiful town house? thinks Edwin. He's surprised to hear Natalka say, 'My mother's living with us at the moment. It's difficult. We've only got a one-bedroom flat.'

'I can imagine,' says Imogen. 'I dread Declan's mother coming to live with us.' She casts a guilty look at the door.

'That's the good thing about not having children,' says Pietro. 'You don't have to worry about them growing up to despise you.'

'I love my mum,' says Natalka. 'It's just . . .'

'I know,' says Imogen soothingly. 'It must be so difficult.'

What does Imogen know about the difficulties of Natalka's life? thinks Edwin. He's surprised when Natalka gives her a sweet smile and says, 'Thank you.' What game is she playing?

Edwin decides it's time for a little detecting. 'I think a friend of mine used to come to this group,' he says. 'Well, the daughter of a friend. Henrietta Marshall?'

'Oh, Henry,' says Johnnie. 'She was great fun.'

'She was,' says Orla. 'Why did she stop coming?'

'I think she'd outgrown the group,' says Georgina.

Imogen bristles. 'No one outgrows the group.'

It sounds like a declaration of war.

Bob arrives promptly at ten. When Edwin is putting on his jacket, Pietro follows him into the hall and asks if he'd like a coffee one day. Edwin says that he would. Pietro says that he'll pop in with some pastries and they exchange details. Imogen hugs Natalka and says that she hopes she'll be back soon. Natalka says she's had a lovely time but, in the taxi, turns to Edwin and says, 'What an awful evening!'

'I don't know,' says Edwin. 'We found out about Henrietta. And Pietro asked me out.'

'Good work!' Natalka offers a high five and, for once, he meets her hand with a satisfying slap.

'I'll tell Benny we're on our way back,' says Natalka.

Edwin is pleased by this evidence of togetherness. Natalka only calls Benedict Benny when she's pleased with him. But, when she looks down at her phone, she frowns.

'What the hell is he doing now?' she says.

Chapter 29

Benedict: evil in the air

Benedict and Valentyna have a plan for the evening of the book club. They are going to watch *Love Actually*. Benedict loves the film and Valentyna has always wanted to watch it. 'I'm not sitting through it again,' said Natalka. 'Lots of annoying people and toxic workplaces.' Benedict can see Natalka's point, a lot of the characters seem rather creepy now and he's past the point when he can find a prime minister lovable, but he's still a sucker for the idea that love is all around us. It's a Christmas film really but he hopes that Valentyna will find it entertaining and comforting, even in summer. She needs comfort right now. They haven't heard from Dmytro for a week.

Benedict cooks pasta, to give Valentyna a break, and they settle down to watch. Benedict is hyper-alert at first (he'd forgotten how much swearing and sex there is in the first few scenes) but relaxes when Valentyna starts to laugh. They are just enjoying Colin Firth being adorable in a France that is strangely populated by Portuguese women when Benedict's phone buzzes. It's a WhatsApp message.

At first he thinks it's his Super Sleuths chat with Edwin and Natalka but then he sees the name Battle House Gang. It's the group with the writers from that ill-fated weekend, created at breakfast that first day when their biggest problem was how to eat enough of Leonard's pancakes. Edwin has long since muted the chat but Benedict likes to keep track of what's happening. Now it seems like there's been a burst of activity.

Leonard: Is anyone there i'm scared
Frances: ??
Peter: whats up m8
Leonard: can you come theres evil in the air
Frances: ringing you now

There's no reply from Imogen or Johnnie but Benedict supposes that they are both at the book club. Poignantly, Sue is still tagged in the group.

Benedict types, 'R U OK @Leonard?'

There's no reply. He rings Leonard but it goes to voicemail. On the screen Colin and his Portuguese cleaner are simmering with unexpressed sexual tension.

'I have to go out,' Benedict says to Valentyna. 'Will you be OK?'

'Do you want me to . . . to stop film?' She waves the remote.

'No. Don't worry. I know what happens.'

'Is it a happy ending?'

'Wait and see.'

Benedict gets the keys to Natalka's Golf. He'd wondered at the time why she didn't drive to the book group but now he's grateful for it. He texts: 'Going to B House. Will explain later. Hope OK to take car.' Too late if it's not, of course, but Natalka is always generous about her belongings. Benedict hopes she'll be too intrigued to mind.

The drive, in the dark, is very different from the carefree journey with Natalka. The roads seem unfamiliar, almost malign, signposts lost in the undergrowth or appearing with terrifying suddenness at crossroads. Natalka's car is ten years old and doesn't have hands-free technology. Benedict puts his phone on the passenger seat and looks down when he dares. There are several angry-looking question marks from Natalka but nothing from the Battle House Gang. His heart jumps when the screen lights up just before Battle but, when he pulls into a lay-by, it's only someone making a move in Words with Friends. He doesn't check after that.

The turning to Battle House is a plunge into darkness. Benedict's headlights illuminate the trees, a baleful moon caught in their branches. There are no lights on in the house and Benedict feels the first stirrings of fear. Is he mad, to come here on his own? Should he have called the police? His footsteps crunch over the gravel. Leonard's car is parked by the front door. Benedict knocks and, as he does so, hears music coming from the house, something operatic and somehow doom-laden. Maybe Leonard is listening on his superior sound system and can't hear the knock. At any rate, there's no reply. Benedict tries the handle. Locked.

Benedict switches his phone onto the torch app. Then, as he did with Natalka, he walks around the side of the house. Only this time, he can almost hear his heart beating above the swell of the opera. The garden is grey in the moonlight and the music is louder here. Benedict sees that the French windows are open and his apprehension increases.

A soprano voice soars into the night.

Benedict enters the sitting room. Waves of sound crash and break around him. For a moment he can only pick up sounds, as if his other senses have deserted him. Then he sees Leonard sitting in an armchair, his head slumped onto his chest.

Benedict knows it's too late, even before he sees the bullet hole in Leonard's chest, a surprisingly neat entry point surrounded by charred cloth and very little blood. He listens for a heartbeat, all the same, but can hear nothing apart from opera. Leonard's skin is warm but already has a waxy, unreal texture. One hand is on the CD player next to him, which is still belting out the soprano aria, the other is hanging down. Looking closer, Benedict sees that this hand is clutching a scrap of paper. He observes all this whilst calling for police and ambulance. He's pretty sure that the second won't be needed but it seems callous to leave them out.

He hears his voice, sounding unnaturally calm, giving the address. Then he rings Natalka.

'Don't worry,' she says. 'We're on our way.'

'On your way to Battle House? Who's driving you?'

'Bob,' says Natalka. 'We'll be with you soon.'

Benedict puts his phone in his pocket and looks around the room. It has only just occurred to him that the assailant could still be present. Should he wait outside? It's hard to concentrate with the music still blaring but he doesn't want to touch anything, not even the off switch. He goes to the French windows. There's a path through the long grass as if trodden by an animal. Did Leonard's killer enter and leave by this route? As Benedict stares into the night he hears a new sound, something more modern and mechanical than grand opera. A car – or maybe a motorbike – is approaching at speed. Is it the emergency services? Or could it be the gunman coming back?

Benedict retreats into the room, looking for a weapon. He finds a brass statuette and, feeling ridiculous, holds it in readiness. Footsteps approaching. A voice says, 'Leonard?' Benedict raises the statuette. There's a scream. And the music stops.

Frances stands in the doorway, hand to her mouth. Benedict puts down his impromptu weapon and moves forward.

'It's OK. It's me.'

'Benedict? What's happened?'

'Leonard's been shot. I've called the police.'

'Oh no! Is he dead?'

'I'm afraid so.'

'Oh my God. Did you get the messages? About being scared and there being evil in the air?'

'Yes. That's why I came.'

'Me too. I was sitting around feeling worried then I just got on my bike and came over. I only live in Hastings.'

It's quite a long explanation, Benedict can't help noticing. Also, he can't imagine Frances on a motorbike. She's wearing leathers, though, and carrying a helmet.

Frances approaches Leonard. The body, thinks Benedict. That's how the police will see him.

'Don't touch anything,' he says.

But Frances has pulled the scrap of paper from Leonard's hand. She smooths it out and shows it to Benedict. There are only four printed words.

If only I hadn't.

Their eyes meet. They are still staring at each other when a siren breaks the silence. It grows louder and louder and then doors slam, torchlight fills the garden and two uniformed police officers crash into the room, accompanied by two paramedics.

The paramedics approach the body. Benedict and Frances are ignored until a voice behind them says.

'What's this? A reunion?'

It's DS Liv Brennan. She's accompanied by DS Sam Malone. Already the house feels like the centre of an incident, serious and tragic but under control.

'We both got messages from Leonard,' says Benedict. 'We were worried so we came over. Separately,' he adds.

Brennan confers with the paramedics. Benedict hears the words 'life extinct'. Then the two green-suited figures back out of the room.

'OK,' says Brennan. 'This is a crime scene now. Let's get SOCO here. Sam, can you call them?' Then she turns to the uniformed officers. 'Let's get tape up. I don't want anyone else entering the house.'

On cue, Edwin and Natalka appear in the doorway.

Chapter 30

Benedict: the force of destiny

'What are you two doing here?' says Brennan. She does not sound happy.

'Benedict called us,' says Natalka. 'Has Leonard been killed?'

'This is a police matter now,' says Brennan. 'I'm securing the scene. Please stay where you are.'

But Edwin moves closer to where Leonard's body now sits in isolation. Benedict wonders at his nerve. Edwin doesn't touch anything but he looks sadly at the dead writer and then turns his attention to the CD player, peering to look through the tinted plastic.

'*Tosca*,' he says. 'Leonard did love opera. He told us so that first morning. We talked about *La Forza Del Destino*. The force of destiny,' he translates kindly.

'It was still playing when I arrived,' says Benedict. He looks down at the bronze statue on the table beside him. It's a hand with a quill and the inscription reads: *Miriam Fry, T.S. Eliot Prize 1997*.

'Then he must have been killed quite recently,' says Edwin. 'Even a full recording will be less than two hours long.'

Benedict thinks this is a very intelligent remark, but DS Brennan ignores it.

'Move away from the deceased,' she says. 'PC Andrews, can you show the witnesses into another room? I'll need statements from all of them.'

The officer, who looks young and slightly scared, ushers them out of the room. Then he stands in the hallway, obviously unsure of the layout of the house. It's Edwin who leads them into the small sitting room. PC Andrews shuts the door and leaves them alone. He's probably waiting outside but Benedict doesn't know how much he can hear. Frances sits down heavily on the sofa. Natalka takes Benedict's hand.

'Are you OK, Benny?'

'I'm fine,' he says, 'it was just a shock. I'm glad you're here. Did you take a taxi all the way?'

'Yes,' says Edwin. 'It's lucky I have an account. I gave Bob my last tenner as a tip. I don't think he was too impressed.'

'Did you just find Leonard there?' says Natalka. 'Sitting in the chair?'

'Yes,' says Benedict. 'There was no answer when I knocked on the door but I could hear the music playing. I thought Leonard might just not have heard. So I walked round to the back garden. The French windows were open and the music was blaring out. Leonard was in his chair. I knew something was wrong immediately but it was a few seconds before I saw the bullet hole in his chest.'

'One shot,' says Natalka. 'Sounds like a professional. I wonder where David the farmer was last night?'

Benedict remembers the large man with a gun. *We've got a shoot in two weeks' time.* Hunting is different, Natalka would say. Or is it?

'David wouldn't shoot Leonard,' says Frances. 'They were friends. Georgina and David often used to come over for meals during the writing weekends.'

David hadn't seemed particularly friendly when Benedict met him. Or very enamoured of Leonard. He'd called him 'bloody Leonard' and speculated that he might be drunk.

'This was in Leonard's hand.' Frances shows them the crumpled piece of paper.

'You have to show that to the police,' says Benedict, aware that he is sounding slightly hysterical.

'"If only I hadn't,"' says Natalka. 'What does that mean?'

'It was a writing exercise we had to do,' says Edwin. 'Maybe Leonard was reading them. Although he didn't seem very interested at the time.'

'I wondered if it was a suicide note,' says Frances.

'People don't write suicide notes on scraps of paper,' says Natalka. 'You'd need a whole sheet for something like that.'

'Maybe it was a whole sheet,' says Benedict, 'and someone – the killer – tore the rest out of his hand?'

'You're right, Benny,' says Natalka. 'It's a clue.'

'Please leave the clues to us,' says DS Brennan from the doorway, 'and give me that. You should never have touched it.'

She takes the paper with gloved hands. Frances looks suitably abashed, Benedict guilty by association.

'Can I have a few words, Mr Cole?' says Brennan.

They go upstairs, into Duncan Grant, the bedroom where Benedict stayed all those weeks ago. Sam Malone is there, along with an older man whom Brennan introduces as 'DI Poole, the officer in charge.'

Poole has a lugubrious, lived-in face, all the lines drooping downwards. He says, 'Is this the private investigator?'

'One of them,' says Brennan.

'Actually, the agency is run by Edwin and Natalka,' says Benedict.

'That's his girlfriend, guv,' Brennan explains.

Poole grunts. 'I can't stand PIs. Even if this one is a friend of your heroine DI Kaur.'

Benedict thinks that Brennan looks slightly discomfited but it doesn't show in her voice. She's all professionalism now. There's none of the camaraderie she showed the day they visited her at Hastings.

'We need to take a witness statement from you, Mr Cole. I'm recording it on my body cam. Is that OK?'

'Yes,' says Benedict. 'Of course.'

He sits on the bed, remembering the exact feel of the quilt, both stiff and slithery. He only spent two nights in the room but now it feels quite home-like. Liv Brennan pulls up a chair opposite. Malone and Poole stand by the window, bulky shapes against the Morris-patterned curtains.

'I'm DS Liv Brennan,' says Brennan, talking into her chest. 'With me are DS Sam Malone and DI Derek Poole. This is a witness interview with Benedict Cole, dated seventh of June. Zero hours ten.'

For the first time, Benedict realises that it's past midnight.

'Tell us, in your own words, Mr Cole, what happened on the night of sixth of June 2022.'

Benedict explains about the WhatsApp messages and driving to Battle House. He thinks that he sounds reedy and anxious to please.

'When I got to the house I saw that Leonard's car was outside so I thought he was in. I knocked on the door but there was no answer. I could hear music playing and thought that Leonard might be listening to CDs – he said he liked to do that – and hadn't heard my knock. So I went round the side of the house. The French windows were open. I saw Leonard in his chair. When I went closer I saw that he'd been shot.'

'Did you touch the deceased?'

'I listened for a heartbeat and touched his face. I knew I probably shouldn't touch him but just wanted to be sure . . .'

'What did you do next?'

'I phoned 999 for the police and ambulance. Then I phoned Natalka. My girlfriend.'

'Why did you phone Natalka?'

'To let her know where I was. The last thing she heard was that I was driving to Battle House. I thought she'd be worried.'

'Did you ask Natalka to join you at Battle House?'

'No, but she must have been worried because she was already on her way. In a taxi. With Edwin. They'd been on their way home from their book group.'

'What happened next?'

'Frances arrived. She'd seen the same WhatsApp messages. I told her what had happened. Well, she could see . . .'

'Did Frances touch the body?'

'I don't think so,' says Benedict, 'but she took a piece of paper from Leonard's hand.' He feels rather disloyal but thinks this needs to be said.

'Why did she do that?'

'I don't know. Probably in shock.'

'What did the note say?'

'Just "If only I hadn't."'

'Does that phrase mean anything to you?'

'It was the title of a writing exercise we had to do on the weekend that I was here.'

He thinks that Poole snorts contemptuously at the idea of a grown man spending time like this. He'd get on well with Benedict's father.

'Did you touch anything else in the room?' asks Brennan.

Feeling more ridiculous than ever, Benedict says, 'I picked up a bronze statuette. I was scared when I heard a motorbike approaching, I thought it might be the killer coming back.'

'You were going to hit the killer over the head with a bronze statuette?' says Poole.

'I wasn't thinking clearly,' says Benedict. 'When I saw it was Frances, I put the statue down.'

'We'll need to take your fingerprints and a DNA sample to eliminate them from the scene,' says Brennan. 'If you leave your contact details with DC Andrews, we'll ring to make an appointment. But, for now, you're free to go. Thank you.'

'Don't leave the country,' says Poole.

Natalka drives them home. Benedict protests but he's actually grateful. Natalka and Edwin both seem energised by the situation and, although it's now well past midnight, converse animatedly throughout the journey. Benedict sits silently in the back. He feels as if he can still hear the opera playing, still see Leonard's body in the chair, facing the doors as if expecting his appointment with death.

'The note is definitely a clue,' Natalka is saying.

'I agree,' says Edwin. 'I'll ring Imogen and see if I can get hold of the "If only I hadn't" pieces that people wrote that weekend. She should have them all.'

'Good idea,' says Natalka. 'Of course, Imogen doesn't know about Leonard yet. I wonder if we should tell her?'

'Maybe we should,' says Edwin. 'But let's wait until the morning. Of course, it's morning already. What a night. It seems that only a few minutes ago we were talking about *The Leopard*.'

'Edwin's got a new boyfriend,' says Natalka. 'Benny, did you hear me? Edwin's got an admirer.'

'Hardly,' murmurs Edwin, sounding delighted.

Benedict makes an effort to rouse himself. 'That's great. Who is he?'

'He's a pastry chef called Pietro,' says Edwin, 'and he's just a friend although Natalka's trying hard to marry us off. But let's get back to tonight. Who killed Leonard? I suppose Imogen and Johnnie are in the clear because they were both at the book group. Frances took her time getting to Battle considering she only lives in Hastings. She could have killed Leonard and then doubled back.'

'Why would she do that?' says Benedict.

'Perhaps to explain away any DNA that was at the scene,' says Natalka. 'The police said they were going to eliminate your DNA. Presumably they'll do the same with hers. Maybe that was why she was so quick to grab the paper.'

This is a good point, Benedict has to admit. Natalka definitely has a detective's mind.

'What about Peter?' he says. 'He certainly saw the WhatsApp message. Could he have driven straight round and shot Leonard? But why?'

'Maybe we'll find out when we read the creative writing pieces,' says Edwin.

Benedict scrolls through his phone to find the messages. He has already given screen shots to DS Brennan.

Leonard: Is anyone there i'm scared

Frances: ??

Peter: whats up m8

Leonard: can you come theres evil in the air

Frances: ringing you now

'Did Frances ring him?' wonders Edwin. 'And, if so, what was said?'

'Did he read through the pieces and see something that scared him,' says Natalka, 'or was it something else entirely? Maybe he heard a noise outside. He does say "Is anyone there?" Maybe it was an intruder.'

'Hard to hear anything with the music playing that loudly,' says Benedict.

'Farmer David must be the prime suspect, though,' says Natalka. 'He didn't seem to like Leonard that much.'

'The dog,' says Edwin.

'What dog?' Benedict is starting to feel dazed again.

'The dog. Buster. It didn't bark tonight. I wonder if that's significant.'

They have now reached Shoreham, the sea calm and clear in the moonlight. They drop Edwin at his apartment block and wait until the light goes on in his flat. Then they drive home. Valentyna is waiting for them. She speaks in Ukrainian to Natalka whose face changes entirely in that instant. She turns to Benedict.

'It's Dmytro. His brigade has disappeared. There are rumours they have all been killed.'

Chapter 31

Harbinder: every contact leaves a trace

When Harbinder comes out of the morning briefing, Freya hands her a message to ring DS Brennan at Hastings CID. What can be happening now in leafy Sussex?

'Leonard Norris is dead,' says Liv. 'Murdered.'

'Remind me who he is again?'

'One of the tutors at Battle House. He was shot as he sat in his chair.'

'Shot?' Harbinder realises that she's now enough of a Londoner to be surprised about gun crime in the provinces.

'Single bullet in his chest,' says Liv, sounding, in her turn, grimly satisfied at the effect of her words. 'From a Glock 17 pistol. Body was discovered by your old friend Benedict Cole. Natalka and Edwin turned up just as we did.'

'Benedict? Why was he there?'

'Apparently he was on a WhatsApp group with Leonard. Last night Leonard sent a message to say he was scared. Benedict drove over from Shoreham and found Leonard dead. That's his story, anyway.'

'I'm sure he's telling the truth. Benedict's the most honest person I know.'

'Yeah, he checks out, although my boss thinks anyone who goes on a creative-writing course is deeply suspicious. He's not mad on PIs either.'

'Lots of people in the force feel that way. Mind you, lots of ex-coppers become PIs. Maybe that's why.'

'Maybe. Leonard was found with a piece of paper in his hand saying, "If only I hadn't". Apparently, that refers to an exercise they had to do on the course.'

'So you think there's a link?'

'It's possible. We can't find Norris's phone. That would tell us if he called anyone before he died. Our prime suspect was the farmer next door, David Potter-Smith. He's got a gun and he wasn't a fan of Leonard's, who was living rent free in his wife's house. Unfortunately, David's got a cast-iron alibi. He was in Scotland looking at cows. To buy, not in a romantic way. He took his dog with him too.'

Harbinder laughs. She hasn't previously suspected Liv of possessing a sense of humour. She also wonders why she is ringing. Is she having trouble with her boss again? But when Harbinder asks, Liv says that he's actually been slightly better than usual. Maybe Harbinder's tactic of remaining calm and keeping a journal has helped. She asks what the plan is.

'We'll have to see if SOCO come up with anything at the house,' says Liv. 'Every contact leaves a trace and all that.'

It's something Harbinder often says to her team. Especially when she's not sure what to do next.

When Liv rings off, Harbinder phones Natalka. She assumes that she will be delighted to talk about this new development. But when Natalka speaks, her voice is so flat that Harbinder wonders if she's ill.

'Are you OK?'

'Dmytro's missing,' she says, 'I can't think of anything else.'

'I'm so sorry,' says Harbinder. She thinks of her brothers, Abhey and Khushwant, both thoroughly irritating and suddenly very dear to her.

'His brigade has disappeared,' Natalka continues, still in the same mechanical tone. 'Gone off the radar. There are rumours of a big battle out east but it's hard to get information.'

'I'm sorry,' says Harbinder again. 'Is there anything I can do?'

'No,' says Natalka, adding, 'It's just awful – not knowing.' Harbinder knows that Natalka's preference is always for action. She will be wishing she could get in a car and drive to Ukraine, searching the beautiful, war-torn country for her brother. Harbinder passes on her good wishes again and rings off. Then she phones Edwin.

In contrast to Natalka, he sounds bright and eager, although he starts by saying isn't it terrible about Dmytro. 'Benedict rang me this morning. Poor Natalka. And poor Valentyna.'

'I suppose there's a chance he's still alive?'

'There's always hope,' says Edwin, 'but it's so hard to get information. Most parts of Ukraine only have internet for a few hours a day. And we don't hear about the casualties but I think they're pretty heavy.'

'That's awful,' says Harbinder. 'I rang to give Natalka some information about the case but, understandably, she wasn't interested.'

'Tell me,' says Edwin. And Harbinder can almost see him sitting up straighter. 'I'm in charge now.'

Harbinder tells him about her conversation with Liv Brennan. 'Looks as if the farmer has an alibi.'

'Interesting,' says Edwin. 'I rang Imogen this morning to give her the news about Leonard but she already knew. I've asked her for all the pieces we wrote that weekend beginning "If only I hadn't". There might be some clues there.'

'I'll let you know if I hear any more from Liv. I really don't know why she keeps telling me this stuff.'

'From something Benedict said, I think she's a great admirer of yours. Her boss – who seemed rather an oaf – referred to you as her heroine.'

'That's nice,' says Harbinder.

And it is a pleasant thought that she's someone's heroine. It gets her through several dull meetings and an acrimonious discussion with the chief super about staffing levels.

Chapter 32

Edwin: If only I hadn't

'I'm in charge now.' As soon as Edwin says these words he feels years – decades – younger. Of course, he's terribly upset about Natalka. He almost cried when Benedict told him the news. It shouldn't still be happening in 2022, a date that seemed un-imaginable when Edwin was young. Young men shouldn't be going into battle and dying. Humanity ought to be beyond such horrors. But there's nothing Edwin can do to help Dmytro or Natalka. Or even Leonard Norris. What he can do is try to solve this case.

After Harbinder has rung off, Edwin looks at his 'to do' list.

Ask Imogen for creative writing pieces
Read and look for clues
Ring Henrietta Marshall
Ring Pietro

Edwin ticks number 1 as Imogen, showing typical efficiency, has already emailed him the pieces and, to delay the possibly enjoyable

2 and 4, he telephones Henrietta. He obtained her number from a now rather impatient Ivan and has managed to concoct a fairly plausible cover story.

'Hallo? Henrietta? Henry? This is Edwin Fitzgerald. I was a friend of your dad's and I'm writing a book that features him. Ivan might have told you that I visited him at the BBC.'

'I think he mentioned you,' says Henrietta. Like her brother, she has a deep, patrician voice.

'Ivan gave me some photographs and I think you're in a couple of them. Is it OK if I email them to you to be sure?'

Henrietta spells out her email address. Edwin looks at the photographs in front of him. He has no idea if Henrietta is in any of them. There are very few women and those that appear seem too old. Still, it's a decent excuse.

'Funnily enough,' Edwin rattles on, 'I think we might have a mutual friend. Imogen Blythe?'

There's a pause. 'I do know Imogen slightly,' says Henrietta. 'Haven't seen her for years, though.'

'I think you used to go to her book group? I'm a new recruit. It's great fun, isn't it?'

'I've never been to a book group,' says Henrietta. 'I'm not much of a reader. Email me those pics and I'll have a look when I get a minute.'

Curiouser and curiouser, thinks Edwin, ticking number 3 on his list. Why would Henrietta deny being a member of a book group? Surely it's one of the most innocuous gatherings possible?

Next, Edwin prints out the 'If only I hadn't' documents. He might be a silver surfer but he prefers to read physical pages. Besides, he needs to make notes and he's never worked out track changes. He gets a glass of water and, though he has no idea why, brushes his hair and straightens his cravat. Then he sits at his desk and starts to read.

If only I hadn't
By Peter Abbot

If only I hadn't called my first book *The Balkan Adventure*. It was the A word that tied me for ever in the straitjacket of a children's author. That and the fact that my hero, Hector, was fifteen. But Scout's a child and no one calls *To Kill A Mockingbird* a children's book. But I was young and naive. I was stupidly delighted to be published but didn't realise that I would be endlessly shelved in the primary colours section alongside such literary luminaries as Enid Blyton and A.A. Milne.

But my books aren't for children. Hector has his first affair at sixteen and is on drugs by seventeen. He's a man in a child's body. My editor refuses to listen. She keeps droning on about sensitivity readers and not upsetting people. Listen, love, I tell her, a writer's job is to upset as many people as possible. She tells me not to call her love. She's that sort. I parted company with my agent Alastair recently. He's a nice guy and I suppose we were friends but there's no room for nice guys in this business. My new agent's nickname is The Assassin.

My next book will definitely *not* be for children.

Edwin writes: 'Poor Hector! Who has Peter upset? Next book??'

If only I hadn't

By Sue Hitchins

If only I hadn't met Malcolm. I was, after all, well past the age of having a boyfriend. Even the word seems absurd when applied to us. I was fifty-five when we met, he was sixty. We met in a library. Of course we did. Shoreham Library on a wet Monday afternoon. I was exchanging books, he was using the microfiche. He loved old newspaper cuttings, did Malcolm. The librarian introduced us – our own teenage matchmaker – by saying, jokingly, that we were her best customers. I was embarrassed, I remember, thinking that she was implying we didn't have anything better to do. But the truth was, I didn't. I'd taken early retirement from my job as a primary school teacher. 'You'll never be busier in your life,' people said, but the truth was that I was bored and lonely. My only hobbies were reading and writing short stories, neither of which were exactly sociable. So when Malcolm looked up, smiled, and said, 'Sounds like we have a lot in common,' it was like manna from heaven.

We went for a coffee (my mum always said it was common to say 'a coffee' but she was a snob like that) and we talked. We met again the next day and the next. My mum said, 'You've got a new beau,' and the silly Scarlett O'Hara-ish word made me laugh. But really it wasn't until Mum died that Malcolm really became my boyfriend. I was suddenly free to spend the night with him, even to go on holiday together (Belgium and Italy). The best thing, though, was coming here, to Battle House, for weekend courses. We spent lockdown together and, honestly, I wish it had been longer. But I missed our writing weekends and, when Battle House opened again, for 'socially distanced courses' with lots of handwashing and temperature checks at the door, we were the first to sign up. That was in October 2021 and, the first evening, Malcolm turned to me and said, 'I know what my book is going to be about, a musician who's murdered by his own instrument.' You must write it, I said. He died two weeks later. Now I suppose I'll have to write it. Now that I know the real story. If only I hadn't met him.

Edwin writes: 'Who was at BH with Sue and Malcolm?'

If only I hadn't
By Johnnie Newton

If only I hadn't answered the advertisement. Isn't that how crime novels traditionally begin? The naive young woman (ha!) answers an ad for a governess. Two children, no mother, absent father, isolated house in the middle of nowhere. What could go wrong? She travels there on a train or maybe even by boat for the last bit (islands are always good value). It's snowing and her clothes aren't warm enough. When she arrives, the door is opened by a sinister retainer seething with unspoken resentment. She is shown to her room, which is in a tower accessible only by a rickety staircase. The children, when she meets them, are sullen and possibly traumatised. Yet she feels an unspoken pull towards them and want to protect them at all costs. But whose is the mysterious portrait in the hall? And why do all the clocks strike thirteen?

Well, none of that happened to me. But I did answer an advertisement. I was fresh out of the hospital and I needed a new challenge. Matron in a girls' school. I had visions of Enid Blyton, Angela Brazil, maybe even Nancy Spain. *Poison for Teacher*. I thought too of *Miss Pym Disposes*, a favourite book of my mother's. The evil that can fester in an all-female environment.

The school wasn't in an isolated location. It was situated in the leafy suburbs of London. You could get a bus to the West End and I frequently did. There was no need for me to be met at the station by a horse and carriage driven by a surly groom. I simply walked up the hill and presented myself at reception. Far from being in a sinister tower, my quarters were a sunny suite on the ground floor with a view over the playing fields. I remember sitting there that first night with a gin in a tin and thinking: I've fallen on my feet. Yet that's where I met her. And I wish I hadn't.

Edwin writes: 'Where is this school? And who is "her"?'

If only I hadn't
By Frances O'Toole

If only I hadn't killed it
The bird
Once so majestic in flight
Now only feathers and bone
Beak and sad scrawny
Feet

Like pipe cleaners
My father had a pipe
Puffing away while Rome burned
Who killed Cock Robin?

Edwin writes: 'Morbid? Father?'

To be strictly fair, Edwin includes his own piece.

If only I hadn't
By Edwin Fitzgerald

If only I hadn't worn my best suede shoes. It was vanity, of course. I didn't want to seem like a little old man. Though I am. Old, I mean. I think I'm still just about average height, although you shrink a little with each passing year. But I didn't want to turn up in slip-on shoes with non-slip soles. They would instantly place me in the world of walk-in baths, stair-lifts and buzzers around necks. Press in case of an emergency. Give up your seat for the elderly and infirm. Care: old people crossing. People would guide my steps, speak extra loudly, ask if I need help on the stairs. But, in my suede loafers, I felt like a man about town. Bertie Wooster perhaps, on my way to the Drones.

And, this morning, when I set out on my walk I felt, if not Woosterish, then at least the hero of my own story. I strode across the wet lawn, the birds performing a raucous background number. I took the path to the lake and had a pleasant conversation while a stone woman stared at her reflection. But, as I retreated to the house – it felt like a retreat – I saw that my shoes were sodden, the beige material now quite dark brown. I was forced back to my room to change into lace-up footwear that were almost trainers. I descended the stairs with one hand firmly on the banister. I think I might even have shuffled a bit.

Vanity of vanities. All is vanity.

Edwin writes: 'Trying too hard.'

If only I hadn't
By Benedict Cole

If only
Benedict
Natalka
Eggs, bacon, tomatoes, mushrooms.
Oh Lord my God, when I in awesome wonder
Thine be the glory, risen conquering son
We blossom and flourish as leaves on a tree . . .

Edwin smiles. Benedict hadn't handed in his piece but agreed to give it to Edwin to complete the set. Edwin knows that Benedict is embarrassed not to have completed the task but, after reading the other authors' work, Benedict's feels like a palate cleanser. It's a better poem than Frances's really. It has it all: love, food and God.

It's interesting how different the pieces are, thinks Edwin. They have nothing in common apart from a desire to impress (Benedict aside). The connections are hard to find. Enid Blyton is mentioned twice, as is naivety. Sue and Johnnie talk about their mothers.

Frances's father makes an appearance, puffing balefully on a pipe. Edwin and Sue both reference scripture. Edwin remembers Sue saying she had 'a rather religious childhood'. That certainly hadn't been in evidence at her funeral.

A few points definitely call for further investigation. Who was at Battle House when Malcolm had his brilliant idea for a new book? Where was Johnnie working as a matron and what happened there? What is Peter's next book about? What does Frances do with her time, apart from riding a motorbike and writing poems about dead birds?

Edwin wonders what Imogen made of their writing. Were they better or worse than the average group? It's funny how much he wants them to be better. Then, as clear as the clock striking at Battle House, he hears Imogen's voice.

I set this exercise every time but students always come up with something different.

They were not the only people to write about 'If only I hadn't'. Whose was the piece Leonard was holding when he was killed?

Chapter 33

Benedict: as long as she dies

Benedict is feeling useless. For a change, sneers his inner voice which is even more vituperative than usual this morning. Natalka and Valentyna are frantically trying to contact the Ukrainian authorities but, as Benedict can't speak Ukrainian (beyond his few carefully learnt phrases), he can't really help. He offered to stay at home to provide support and herbal tea but Natalka told him, quite brusquely, to go and open the Shack. So here he is, dispensing coffees to people in a hurry and trying not to think about Dmytro, of whom he is very fond, lying dead on some desolate wasteland in Crimea. The very name sounds like something from a history book. Images of Florence Nightingale, Balaclava, the Charge of the Light Brigade. *Into the jaws of death, into the mouth of hell.* Benedict remembers that, in one of the first Sherlock Holmes stories, John Watson had recently returned from the war in Afghanistan. How terrible that they are still fighting the same wars.

'I asked for a grande,' says an impatient voice. She pronounces it Gran Day.

'Sorry,' says Benedict, though the only sizes he offers are large and small. He makes a fresh coffee in a bigger cup. The woman takes it without thanking him. By now Benedict has a queue so he decides to dispense with some of the smiles and eye contact.

'Yes?' he says, head bent over the coffee machine.

'Hallo, Benedict.'

It's Frances. She has obviously just taken off her motorbike helmet and her long hair is flat and sweaty. She fluffs it up with one hand while Benedict stares at her. He wants to say, 'What are you doing here?' but settles for, 'Would you like a coffee?'

'Espresso, please,' says Frances. 'With some milk on the side.'

Interesting, thinks Benedict. He often tries to match people to their coffee choice and had thought that Johnnie was more espresso than Frances. Mind you, an espresso is a poem of a drink – short, dark and bitter – so maybe it suits Frances. Imogen is a decaf latte.

'Take a seat,' says Benedict. 'And I'll join you when there's a lull.'

As he serves the next customers, he sees Frances out of the corner of his eye, her hair now looking white in the sun. She's wearing leathers so must be feeling very hot.

Eventually Benedict is able to make himself a flat white and join Frances. He brings her another espresso and a glass of water. He considered brownies but thought they might be too frivolous.

'I hope you don't mind me coming,' says Frances. 'I just kept thinking about it. About finding Leonard like that. And I had to talk to someone.'

'Of course I don't mind,' says Benedict, 'but how did you know where to find me?'

'You said you ran a coffee stall near Shoreham Beach,' says Frances. 'I asked around.'

Benedict can imagine the conversation. 'Do you know a tall, skinny guy with glasses? Runs a coffee stall? A bit odd?' 'Oh yes, that'll be Benedict . . .'

'The thing is,' says Frances, 'I've never seen a dead body before. I'm sure you see them all the time in your line of work.'

She makes him sound like a grave robber. 'You mean selling coffee?' says Benedict.

'No, being a private detective. Leonard told me that's what you do. You and your girlfriend. The one who was there last night.'

This is interesting. Benedict wonders when Leonard told Frances this. 'My girlfriend runs the agency with Edwin,' he says. 'I really am just a coffee seller.'

Frances seems hardly to take this in. 'I know I write a lot about death,' she says, 'but it really hasn't touched my life. My parents are both still alive, both still in good health. I know I'm lucky.'

How old is Frances? Initially Benedict placed her in her sixties but that might just be the hair. Her skin is smooth and unlined, though with the burnished look of someone who spends a lot of time outdoors. She could easily be fifty, with parents in their seventies. He remembers Frances talking about having teenage children. Heteronormative, Harbinder had called it.

'I don't think you ever get used to death,' he says. 'Especially violent death.'

'That's just it,' says Frances. She tips her head back to drink the last coffee dregs. 'Leonard was *shot*. I mean, who would do that?'

'I don't know,' says Benedict. 'It's hard to imagine. You knew Leonard better than me. Did he have any enemies?'

'I didn't know him that well,' says Frances, sounding rather defensive. 'But I've been on a couple of his courses. I didn't like him very much, to be honest. Always going on about his book being shortlisted for the Booker Prize. But he hadn't written anything for ages. And I don't think he knew much about poetry. His favourite poet was A. E. Housman. Imagine!'

Benedict rather likes Housman although he could do without all the lovely lads and lasses. *Golden lads and girls all must, as chimney sweepers come to dust*. He says, 'Was Leonard married?'

'Divorced. I think his marriage broke up around the time his book was published. I've heard that he went off the rails, had a bit of a drink problem.'

'I noticed that he didn't drink,' says Benedict. 'And I wondered. Someone also mentioned a possible affair with Sue.'

'With Sue?' Frances laughs. 'I can't see Leonard fancying Sue. Imogen maybe. Anyway, Sue was with Malcolm. They seemed perfectly matched.'

'Of course, you knew Malcolm too, didn't you?'

'Not really, but I was at Battle House with him a few times. He was very nice but a bit dry, if you know what I mean. The sort who'd spent years writing a boring book about trees.'

'Why trees?' says Benedict. He thinks of the woods closing in on Battle House. Of Housman. *Loveliest of trees, the cherry now Is hung with bloom along the bough*.

Frances shrugs. 'It's just an example.'

'I thought Malcolm was meant to have had a brilliant idea for a crime novel. Sue mentioned it just before she . . .'

'Before she was killed?' Frances finishes the sentence for him. They look at each other. In the distance, an ice cream van plays its siren song.

'Do you think the same person killed Leonard and Sue?' asks Benedict.

'I think so, don't you? Two murders in the same house. It's a bit of a coincidence if not.'

Benedict doesn't think it's the time for 'coincidence is only another word for fate'.

'Do you think it's to do with books somehow?' he asks.

'Why do you say that?'

'Two murders at a writing centre. As you say, that can't just be coincidence. And there have been some other writers who died. Malcolm Collins. Melody Chambers. They both stayed at Battle House.'

'Why would anyone kill a writer?'

'Why did you take that piece of paper out of Leonard's hand?' Benedict counters.

Frances sighs and glances away; the sea breeze whips her long hair round her face. She looks ageless somehow, in this setting. Like a harpy or a mermaid.

'As I said, I write a lot about death. I thought, if he was holding something I'd written, it might be incriminating. But it was just a scrap of paper.'

'Someone else had ripped it out of his hand before you did,' says Benedict.

'I suppose so,' says Frances.

'What do you think Leonard was scared of?' asks Benedict. 'You know, he said in the WhatsApp group that he was scared.'

'I don't know,' says Frances, 'but it can't have been one of us because, if so, why message the group?'

This, Benedict has got to admit, is a good point.

'Maybe he saw something outside,' he says.

'Maybe he heard something.'

'He was playing opera at full blast. I don't think he heard anything.'

'I hate opera,' says Frances. 'You know what they say? A woman can do anything in an opera, as long as she dies in the end.'

Benedict thinks of the swirling music, of the silent auditor in the armchair. He'll have to check with Edwin but he's pretty sure that Tosca dies in the end.

'She certainly does,' says Edwin. 'Throws herself from the battlements of the Castel Sant'Angelo. Cup of tea?'

Benedict has called in to see Edwin on his way home. He doesn't want to admit that he's slightly dreading seeing Natalka and Valentyna. He knows that he would have heard if there had been any news, good or bad. It's soothing, being with Edwin, because he doesn't have to explain this or anything else. Edwin is sad about Dmytro, Benedict knows, but he's also in detecting mode. His desk is covered with papers, annotated in Edwin's beautiful handwriting. Benedict sees the words, 'If only I hadn't . . .'

'Find out anything interesting?'

'Potentially.' Edwin hands the pages to Benedict. 'Have a read. I'll make us some tea. Unless you'd rather something stronger?'

Benedict's hesitation is obviously telling because Edwin says, 'I'll pour us both a glass of Montepulciano.'

Benedict can't remember Edwin drinking this wine before. Is it in expectation of a visit from the mysterious Pietro? He decides not to ask and, while Edwin is out of the room, Benedict skims through the pieces. They tell him nothing apart from the fact that Frances writes about her father as if he's dead but he's apparently still alive and in good health. Also, Peter is a thoroughly unpleasant person.

Edwin puts two glasses of wine and a plate of salted biscuits on the coffee table in front of Benedict.

'What do you think?' he asks.

'I've worked something out,' says Benedict. 'I think Peter was talking to his agent that day at Battle House. Do you remember? *There's not much time. We have to be brutal.* He was probably talking about ditching his old agent or even his editor. What was the new one called? The Assassin.'

'That fits,' says Edwin. 'I must say, I don't feel compelled to read one of Peter's books.'

'But is *he* the assassin? As Frances said earlier, if Leonard was scared of one of the group, why message us?'

'Ah,' says Edwin, sounding smug. 'You've forgotten. Imogen sets this task for all her students. The piece Leonard was reading could have been written by anyone who'd ever attended a course at Battle House. Since Imogen's been teaching anyhow.'

'Good thinking,' says Benedict. 'But isn't that hundreds of people?'

'I've got the list from Imogen,' says Edwin. 'There are a hundred and fifty names on it.'

'That's not that many.'

'No, but lots of people came multiple times. Sue and Malcolm, for example. Also, there were no courses in 2020 because of Covid.'

'It seems to me that we can rule a few people out,' says Benedict. He starts a list on a clean sheet of paper. 'Everyone at the book group. That's Imogen, Johnnie, Georgina, Felicity and the agent . . .'

'Orla.'

'Also, potentially everyone in the WhatsApp group. Peter, Frances and Johnnie. Though we've already ruled Johnnie out.'

'And Harbinder says that David, Georgina's husband, was in France.'

'Who's left?' says Benedict. He takes a gulp of wine and feels its warmth permeating his body. This must be why people become alcoholics.

But Edwin is looking at the list. 'There's something we're missing. I'm sure of it. "If only I hadn't." Why did Imogen set that task in the first place? It's a rather negative way to start a story but maybe that makes it easier.'

'I didn't find it easy,' says Benedict.

'Maybe you haven't got any regrets, dear boy.'

On the way home, Benedict thinks about this. He's always considered his life, up till Natalka anyway, as a complete failure but, when he thinks about it, he doesn't actually regret any of his decisions. He's glad he went into the monastery and glad he left it. He's glad that he came to Shoreham and blesses the day he befriended a couple of elderly customers called Peggy and Edwin. He doesn't even regret going to Battle House.

He's careful to wipe the smile from his face before he enters the flat.

Chapter 34

Natalka: longest day

And that's that. Nothing else matters. Only Dmytro. Natalka can hardly remember Leonard or why, only a few hours ago, she was so interested in finding out who killed him. The other names – Melody, Don, Sue – have vanished into the ether. She would be hard put to recognise them. When Harbinder rang on Tuesday morning Natalka, who hadn't slept, could hardly understand what she was saying. 'Dmytro's missing,' she said, 'I can't think of anything else.' 'I'm so sorry,' said Harbinder, actually sounding it. 'Is there anything I can do?' 'No,' said Natalka. And, after a few more awkward but well-meaning words, Harbinder had rung off.

Natalka doesn't know if Harbinder spoke to Edwin. She knows that Benedict told him about Dmytro because Edwin sent Natalka a loving message, ending with the welcome words, 'Don't feel you have to reply'. Natalka didn't reply. She and her mother have a plan of campaign, ringing all Dmytro's friends and anyone who has any military contacts. It's made difficult by the fact that some parts of Ukraine have no phone service. Benedict showed signs of wanting to stand around looking sad and anxious so Natalka sent him out to work. He came back at seven o'clock, looking guilty but having the presence of mind to bring takeaway pizza. Natalka and Valentyna haven't eaten all day so they sit down for an almost silent meal.

Natalka wants to stay up all night – sometimes the internet connection is better in the early hours – but she's so tired that she goes to bed at nine. She's surprised to find herself wanting to have sex. Benedict is surprised too, she can tell, but as eager as ever. She thinks of the first time they made love. They had been staying in a 'safe house' on the Scottish coast. Halfway through the evening an armed gunman had burst in. Benedict had thrown himself in front of Natalka to protect her. Then, like a miracle, Dmytro had appeared, having been presumed dead for years. Can he pull off a similar miracle this time? It seems unlikely. Natalka falls asleep twisting the silver ring that Dmytro once gave her.

She wakes at five. The room is full of light. Of course, it's June, nearly the longest day. In Ukraine they'd celebrate Ivan Kupala, the summer solstice, by weaving wreaths, dancing, singing and jumping over red cloth meant to symbolise fire. There's something about learning the name of your future husband too but Natalka never bothered with that bit. She wonders what she will be feeling in early July, the traditional time for these festivities. She doesn't think she'll ever be happy again, but she supposes that life will go on. After all, she has mourned Dmytro once. She can do it again.

Natalka gets up and wraps her kimono round her. She takes her laptop and goes into the kitchen. She can hear Valentyna snoring from the sitting room and doesn't want to wake her. She props the laptop on the work surface and switches it on. Through the window the rising sun is turning the sea pink and gold. But Natalka has eyes only for the screen. Fighting in the Donbas region. Civilians killed in Bucha, Irpin and Hostomel. More foreign leaders visiting Kyiv. Talk of Ukraine joining the EU. There's nothing here that points to Dmytro except the obvious fact that he is a soldier in a country at war. Slightly reassured by the lack of messages, Natalka makes herself a cup of mint tea. Maybe she can get word to President Zelenskyy somehow. Her father used to boast about all the important people he knew. Natalka could do with his help now except that she has the feeling that the famous friends were all imaginary.

Valentyna is up at six and soon has her own laptop open. Benedict wakes next and makes them eggs and bacon for breakfast. 'You need to eat.' Then he leaves to open the Shack. By now Natalka has a headache and feels slightly nauseous (possibly from too much breakfast) so she goes for a run. There's something comforting about her feet pounding along the pavement, the glinting view of the sea on one side, the houses on the other. The houseboats are clinking gently in the harbour and seagulls swoop on the fishing nets drying on the beach. I'm still alive, Natalka tells herself. Maybe so, but she has to stop and be sick in a bin by the Ropetackle Arts Centre.

Back at the flat, Natalka opens her laptop again and is surprised to see an email from Imogen.

Dear Natalka

It was SO lovely to meet you the other night. [How long ago was the book club evening? thinks Natalka. It seems a lifetime ago.] I was just wondering if your mum would like to join a group of lovely Ukrainian ladies who meet in Worthing on Wednesday

afternoons. They chat, sew, bake cakes and generally reminisce about the old country. If your mum would like to go, I would be happy to pick her up. Let me know. My number is below.
Much love,
Imogen.

Much love, thinks Natalka. She wouldn't even sign letters to Benny like that. It never ceases to surprise her how profligate British people are with their words and how grudging with their actions. But she supposes that Imogen is at least offering to do something. It's Wednesday today. Natalka doesn't think her mum will want to attend this grim-sounding Ukrainian Mothers' Union but, when she puts the idea to her, Valentyna is surprisingly keen. 'It'll be something to do and at least the other women will understand. They'll have sons and grandsons in the army too.'

Natalka takes the point. She rings Imogen and says that her mother would love to go.

Chapter 35

Edwin: a thin line

Edwin's day starts, as usual, with Wordle and a stretch. He guesses the word, 'trait', on his fifth attempt, by which time his porridge is ready. As he eats it, Edwin looks through his notes on the case. It's up to him to solve it now. He wishes that Peggy still lived across the landing. She would like nothing more than looking through his list of suspects. She'd find the culprit in minutes, the way she always solved the cryptic crossword before Edwin had worked out the first anagram. The new occupant of the flat, Belinda Shepherd, is a very pleasant lady who also once worked at the BBC. Edwin is quite friendly with her but they are not on sleuthing terms.

The papers arrive and Edwin takes them to the Shack. He remembers the day when he read the obituary of Chips Walker and noted that the writer, Malcolm Collins, was also dead. That was the start of it all: Melody Chambers, Don Parsons, Battle House, Sue Hitchins, Leonard Norris, Imogen's book group. A trail of words, writers and clues so subtle that Edwin, with his sub-par crossword skills, can't quite grasp their significance.

He's early today and Benedict is still busy. He doesn't get to sit down with Edwin until nearly ten.

'Do Wordle today?' asks Edwin.

Benedict shakes his head. 'I've got out of the habit since losing my streak. Besides, it's all a bit tense at home.'

'I can imagine,' says Edwin. 'How's Natalka?'

'She's taking it very hard,' says Benedict. 'You know Natalka, she hates not being able to solve things. She wants to find out what happened to Dmytro but she just can't. I think she fears the worst, though.'

'Is it a comfort to her having her mum there?'

'I think it is in a way. At least they can talk in Ukrainian to each other. But, in another way, I think Natalka feels responsible for Valentyna. She was so pleased when she came to England and was out of danger. And then Dmytro had to choose to go back.'

'Mad,' says Edwin. 'Or brave. I think there's a thin line between the two. I'm often glad that I was born in 1938 and didn't have to find out how I'd cope in a war. Very poorly, I suspect. I even managed to escape National Service because of a weak chest.' He thinks of Pietro saying that he was also born in 1938 and that it wasn't the best time to be in Italy. He must summon up the courage to ring him today.

'I think I would have been a conscientious objector,' says Benedict. 'If I'd had the courage.'

'Thou shalt not kill,' says Edwin. 'That's pretty unambiguous. No small print in the ten commandments.'

'Natalka would say – what if your country got invaded?' says Benedict. 'It's all very complicated.'

'Talking of complications,' says Edwin, finishing his flat white and taking a small bite of brownie (for the energy), 'have you had any thoughts on the case?'

'Not really,' says Benedict. 'I still can't see how it all fits together. I mean, what links Melody Chambers, Don Parsons, Sue Hitchins and Leonard Norris? To say nothing of your flautist friend.'

'There must be a link,' says Edwin. 'There always is.'

Back at the flat, Edwin gets his notes out again. Time for some free association.

He writes:

Battle House
Battle Stations
If Only I Hadn't
Murdered with his own instrument
Imogen
Cymbeline
Golden lads and girls
The hopes and fears of all the years
The youth project
The Leopard
We are the leopards, the lions
Better to live one day as a lion.

Why does he keep coming back to the book group? It can't just be because of Pietro. Edwin doesn't like to be so obvious, even to himself. Surely the book club can't be connected because they were discussing *The Leopard* when Leonard was killed. Shot dead whilst listening to *Tosca*. What a way to go. Edwin thinks of the scene at

Battle House, Leonard sitting in his chair, one hand on the play button of the CD player. One hand . . . Leonard must have put on the music just before he was killed. It was still playing when Benedict found him. What if he was listening to *Tosca* for something other than pure auditory pleasure?

Edwin goes to his CD collection, which takes up three shelves. He selects his favourite recording. Maria Callas as the singer Floria Tosca, Giuseppe di Stefano as the revolutionary painter Cavaradossi and Tito Gobbi as evil police chief Scarpia. When was it made? He checks the cover – 1953. Edwin was living in London. He'd just met Nicky, who was a sports reporter. He remembers listening to this CD with Nicky and being furious when the latter went to sleep during *Vissi d'arte*. Well, Nicky is dead now. Sleeping for ever. Edwin chose Cavaradossi's aria, *E lucevan le Stelle*, for Peggy's funeral.

Edwin puts the CD into the hi-fi and presses 'play'. He's too old for Spotify and the like. The orchestra, miraculously conducted by Victor de Sabata, fills the room. Edwin sits on the sofa, temporarily floored by beauty. He knows he'll cry when Maria starts to sing. Edwin saw Maria Callas's farewell concert in London in 1973. He went with his mother because he was still rather miffed with Nicky about the sleeping.

Edwin sits up straighter.

His mother.

He remembers Sue's piece about meeting Malcolm. *We went for a coffee. My mum always said it was common to say 'a coffee' but she was a snob like that . . .*

Edwin had sympathised and said his mother was just the same.

Sue's mother had stood in the way of her romance with Malcolm.

Don Parsons had looked after his elderly mother until she died. What had Ivan said about his father, Felix?

We just thought he'd go on for ever, living in that Kensington flat that was far too big for him . . .

Georgina: *Reminds me of my auntie. Living all on her own in a big house, gradually losing her marbles.*

Felicity: *My mother too. She just sat in one room while rubbish piled up around her.*

Was this what the book club had in common, that they all had inconvenient elderly parents? Did the club somehow help them remove these impediments so that the children could inherit Kensington flats and Steyning houses? With a chill, Edwin remembers Felicity's book choice, *The Youth Project*.

A dystopian novel about a world where elderly people are executed when they are deemed to have outlived their useful purpose.

Ivan's sister Henrietta had been to the book club, though she now denied it. So had Don Parsons and Sue Hitchins. Georgina and Felicity were still in attendance. Melody's daughter Harmony had also been a member. Edwin remembers the pill bottle in Imogen's bathroom. He had checked and the label came from Alan Franklin's pharmacy.

In the background Giuseppe di Stefano begins his first big aria, *Recondita Armonia.*

It's some minutes before Edwin realises that someone is knocking at the door.

Chapter 36

Benedict: presentiment of death

Lunchtime is busy. Benedict has to make more sandwiches than usual. For once, he doesn't have time to check his phone and, at three o'clock, he's surprised to see Natalka materialising in front of him. She's wearing a baseball cap and her face is drawn and pale, but Benedict is still taken aback by her beauty.

'Hallo,' he says. 'This is a nice surprise.'

Natalka has no time to waste on this sort of thing. 'I've had some strange texts from Edwin,' she says. 'I've tried ringing him but there's no answer.'

Benedict feels a sudden chill. Is this the bad news that he has subconsciously been expecting all day?

Natalka hands over her phone. It has a cracked screen and a battered case like a teenager's.

Don't let V go out with Imogen ! Will explain.

Then, a minute later:

I know who killed Leonard.

'He still remembered punctuation and full stops,' says Benedict, feeling slightly reassured. 'Space before the exclamation mark and all. He must have been feeling OK when he sent this.'

'You don't understand,' says Natalka. 'My mum is out with Imogen now. She's taken her to some Ukrainian women's group. I've tried ringing Mum too. And Imogen. But neither of them are picking up. Mum wouldn't turn her phone off because of Dmytro.'

'Let's go round to Edwin's,' says Benedict. 'That's probably the easiest. I can shut the Shack for an hour or two.'

Natalka helps Benedict pull down the shutter and they walk quickly across the beach. Benedict thinks of Edwin taking this same path earlier, so careful in his smart shoes and gallant hat. Despite the punctuation, he is worried. Edwin always answers his phone, especially if Natalka is the one calling.

Seaview Court is directly opposite the sea. Edwin, for reasons of his own, always calls it Preview Court. 'It's a presentiment of death,' he used to say. 'Don't be morbid,' Peggy would tell him. Benedict can see them now, Peggy in her beret, Edwin in his trilby, arguing gently about politics, books and whether Roger Federer was a better player than Rafael Nadal. Peggy didn't like Nadal, Benedict remembers, because of his habit of fiddling with his undergarments. 'He must wear a thong,' was her opinion. 'Roger would never do that. He's a boxer shorts man through and through.'

The flats have an entry phone but Natalka, as a carer, has a pass key. They run up the stairs, the non-slip treads much derided by Edwin. Natalka knocks on Edwin's door. 'Edwin!' There's no answer. 'I can hear music playing,' says Benedict. The chill now pervades his whole body. All he can think of is Leonard, dead in his chair while Puccini played out his tragic themes in the background.

'Edwin!' shouts Natalka again.

A door opens across the landing. 'Can I help?'

It's Edwin's neighbour. Brenda? Belinda? One of those names. Benedict has met her a few times and hopes she remembers.

'We're trying to get into Edwin's flat. Do you have a spare key?'

'Yes,' says Brenda/Belinda. 'I'll get it. I hope he's all right. Such a lovely chap.'

It takes her an agonising few minutes to locate the key. Natalka, hands shaking, opens the door.

In the sitting room, music swells from the hi-fi. And Edwin sits lifeless on the sofa.

'Edwin!' shouts Benedict. He's across the room in seconds. He kneels down by the side of Edwin, his best friend and father figure. Please God, don't let him be dead.

'Don't shout, dear boy,' says Edwin.

For a second Benedict just stares up at him. 'You're alive.'

'Yogic breathing,' says Edwin. 'I slowed my pulse so as to fool Harmony.'

'Harmony?' says Benedict. Words just aren't making sense at the moment.

Natalka, who had been frozen in the doorway, now crosses the room to sit beside Edwin on the sofa. Benedict is still kneeling at his feet like an acolyte.

'Why didn't you answer the door?' she says. Then adds, 'I'm glad you're not dead.'

'Thank you.' Edwin twinkles at her.

'Harmony,' Benedict repeats. 'You said you fooled Harmony.'

'Yes, she turned up trying to get me to kill myself,' says Edwin. 'I worked it all out, moments before. Leonard must have put on the *Tosca* CD just before he died. *Recondita Armonia*. That was the clue. It means "Remembered harmony". Leonard must have known I'd work it out. Unfortunately, Harmony did too. She turned up today with her little bottle of pills. Told me to take them. I'm so old, you see, that I might as well be dead. That's her whole philosophy. Get rid of the old people, the dead wood, so the young can inherit.'

Natalka says, sounding as confused as Benedict feels, 'You said that Harmony came here? Melody's daughter?'

'Yes, I worked out that she killed Leonard. Remember, Harmony went on a writing course at Battle House. She must have written an "If only I hadn't" piece too and Leonard realised it was incriminating in some way. Anyway, it sent Harmony round to silence Leonard. Perhaps she remembered that we talked about opera when we first met. I even said how much I liked Puccini. So Harmony popped round to make me take some pills. It seemed easier to do so, hide them under my tongue and practise shallow breathing for a few minutes. Harmony was sure I was dead and went away, quite happy with herself. I spat out the pills, put on *La Bohème* and went to sleep for a few minutes.'

'You went to *sleep*?' says Benedict.

'Well, they were sleeping pills. I must have swallowed a couple by mistake.'

'We need to tell the police.' Natalka gets out her phone. 'And what did you mean about my mum and Imogen?'

'He was just wittering,' says a voice from the doorway. 'Old people do that.'

A tall, dark-haired woman stands in the doorway. Benedict doesn't recognise her but he thinks he could make a good guess as to her identity. But the main thing he notices is that she's carrying a gun. Not a hunting rifle but a handgun, the kind that kills people.

'Harmony,' says Edwin, with a sprightliness that is admirable, if misplaced. 'Back again?'

'I had unfinished business,' says Harmony. She has a pleasant, low-pitched voice which somehow makes the whole situation even more unreal.

'Surely you're not going to kill us all,' says Edwin. 'Bit hard to pass off as an accident.'

'Not at all,' says Harmony, waving the gun as if to herd them together. 'She,' she points the barrel at Natalka, 'goes mad with all the worry about Ukraine, shoots you both and then kills herself. I can stage it like an accident. I've done it before. In the army.'

Has Harmony been in the army? Benedict remembers something Natalka told him about her being an army cadet but that's not the same at all. But the important thing is that she is completely focused on Edwin. Benedict edges slowly forwards.

'Did you kill Sue?' asks Edwin. Benedict knows that Edwin understands what he's trying to do. Natalka, too, flickers her eyes towards him. This stiffens Benedict's resolve. He has to save Natalka. Harmony is talking to Edwin, almost casually, gesticulating with the gun. Benedict takes another step forwards. What's the time, Mr Wolf?

'Sue said something she shouldn't have,' says Harmony. 'So she had to be dealt with. Go back, you!'

Benedict realises that the gun is now pointing directly at him.

'Stand with the others,' she says. 'I need to decide who to shoot first.'

Benedict moves to stand in front of Natalka and Edwin.

'Don't be an idiot,' says Harmony. 'The old bloke's had his life. People really shouldn't live that long. Eighty's enough for anyone.'

'I really think—' says Edwin.

But no one hears what he thinks because a figure moves swiftly and soundlessly into the room and fells Harmony with a metal tray full of what look like Italian pastries.

Chapter 37

Natalka: supposition

Harmony lies face down on Edwin's prized Turkish rug and there's a delicious smell of almond and orange-blossom in the room.

'We need to get out of here,' says Benedict. He seems to have changed personality, as he did once before when faced with a gun. They all turn to him instinctively.

'Get the gun,' says Benedict. Pietro picks it up carefully and Natalka sees that he's wearing leather driving gloves. 'Let's go,' says Benedict, 'I've got the key.' He ushers Natalka, Edwin and Pietro out of the flat and then locks the door from the outside. Edwin's neighbour is hovering on the landing.

'Is everything OK? I thought I heard raised voices.' Natalka sees her noticing first Pietro, who is dressed smartly in chinos and blazer, and then the gun in his hand.

'Everything's under control, Belinda,' says Edwin. 'We just need to call the police. Can we go inside?'

In Belinda's flat, which reminds Natalka pleasantly of Peggy, Edwin calls 999 and Natalka rings DS Brennan. The uniformed officers and detectives arrive together, the flashing lights and squawking radios probably making curtains twitch all over the building. Natalka thinks it's the most fun the residents of Seaview Court have had in years. As she watches Liv Brennan emerging from her car, Natalka's phone flashes into life. A text from her mother.

Sorry. Was making babushka dolls and left my phone in my bag. Is anything wrong? Dmytro?

'Everything's fine, Mum,' Natalka types quickly. 'Just come home soon.'

DS Brennan appears in the doorway. 'What's going on now?'

'I think you'll find we solved your case for you,' says Edwin. 'Harmony Skelton is next door, temporarily unconscious. She tried to shoot us all with this gun.'

Pietro proffers it with a bow.

'And who are you?' says Brennan. Rather rudely, Natalka thinks.

'Pietro Alighieri. A friend of Edwin's.'

'You never told me that was your name,' says Edwin. 'Like Dante?'

'A distant relative.'

'If I can just interrupt this cosy chat,' says Brennan. 'Does anyone have a key to the flat where this supposed gunwoman is?'

Benedict gives Brennan the key and she turns away without another word. They hear voices next door and then the sounds of several feet descending the stairs. Liv Brennan reappears. She seems slightly, but only slightly, more conciliatory.

'You'll all have to accompany me to the station. Including you, Mr Alighieri. It'll probably remind you of one of the circles of hell.'

Natalka is quite impressed with this literary reference.

★

They go to the local police station. It's the place where Natalka first met Harbinder, four years ago. Now there's Harbinder's ex-detective-partner, the rather bovine Neil Winston, getting in the way and asking awkward questions. It seems that Brennan and Malone were having a meeting with DS Winston when Brennan got the call from Natalka. It explains why they got to Seaview Court so quickly. Natalka wonders what they were discussing and how many times her name came up.

'I always told Harbinder you were trouble,' Winston tells Natalka.

'I always told Harbinder she was too good for you,' says Natalka.

'You're right there,' Winston agrees. 'She's a star, Harbinder.'

'She is,' agrees Brennan.

Natalka has already messaged Harbinder but hasn't had a response. Anyone would think she has other police work to do.

A receptionist ushers Natalka, Benedict, Edwin and Pietro into a room that seems designed to force culprits into confession through sheer boredom. The walls are magnolia with no pictures, the window looks out onto a brick wall, there are no magazines on the stained coffee table.

Natalka asks the question that's still on her mind. 'What did you mean about not letting my mum go with Imogen?'

Edwin pauses for a moment before replying. 'I think something is going on in the book group,' he says at last. 'Sue's mother died. Felicity's mother died. Georgina's aunt died. Someone – probably Harmony – is killing off the old people so their relatives can inherit.'

Natalka thinks of Imogen's house, the warm wine, the earnest discussion of literature.

'Oh my God,' she says. 'I complained about my mother living with me. Did you think that Imogen was going to kill her for me?'

'I must admit, it did cross my mind,' says Edwin. 'But now I think it must be Harmony. Think of what she said just now. "The old bloke's had his life." I think that's her philosophy.'

Pietro, who has been listening carefully, says, 'But this Harmony isn't in the book group. I have never seen her before today.'

'She used to be a member,' says Edwin. 'Imogen told us. And I think I found her old aspirin bottle in the bathroom.'

'Do you think Harmony killed her own mother?' says Benedict. He no longer sounds calm and decisive. In fact, he sounds almost on the verge of tears. Natalka feels the same, weak and emotional after the shocks of the day, but Edwin and his new boyfriend are chatting away quite calmly. Not for the first time, Natalka marvels at the stoicism and resilience of older people.

'I think it's a possibility,' says Edwin. 'She's a science teacher after all. She could have tampered with Melody's pills.'

They all jump as the door opens but it's only DS Brennan, followed by DS Malone carrying a tray of coffees plus several KitKats.

'Sorry to keep you,' says DS Brennan. 'We've charged Harmony Skelton with possessing a lethal weapon and we are going to try to make attempted murder stick. She's claiming to have lost her memory. You must have hit her quite hard with that tray, Mr Alighieri.'

'I do t'ai chi,' says Pietro. 'It gives you fast reflexes.'

'I'll have to conduct interviews with all of you separately,' says DS Brennan, 'but, right now, I just want to make sense of it all. Why would Harmony Skelton attempt to kill you?'

Edwin explains about the *Tosca* aria and Harmony turning up with the sleeping pills.

'She must have worked out that I knew she killed Leonard Norris.'

Brennan and Malone exchange glances.

'The answer was in an Italian opera,' says Malone. 'I've heard it all now.'

'All the answers are in Italian opera,' says Pietro.

'Leonard found out something about Harmony,' says Edwin. 'I believe that it was that she murdered her mother. The clue might have been in something she wrote while at Battle House. Leonard rang Harmony – which was a big mistake – and, when she appeared in the doorway, he just had the presence of mind to put on the opera – the CD must have already been in the machine – knowing it would give us a clue.'

'Not much of a clue,' says Malone.

'I think,' says Edwin modestly, 'that he might have thought I would get it. We'd had a conversation about opera, you see.'

'How come Harmony had a gun?' says Benedict.

'It was her father's, apparently,' says DS Brennan. 'He was in the army.'

'What interests me,' says Pietro, 'is why Harmony didn't just shoot you the first time, Edwin.'

'I'm rather glad she didn't,' says Edwin.

'Me too,' says Pietro, with a sudden, rather sweet, smile. Natalka is sure that Edwin is blushing.

'I think she thought she could persuade me to take the pills and it would look like suicide,' says Edwin. He turns to the police officers. 'I think there was a pattern of killing elderly parents for their inheritance in this very way. Miriam Fry died which gave Georgina control of Battle House. Felicity's mother – the writer – died. Sue's mother died. Don Parsons' mother died.'

'Hang on,' says DS Brennan. 'Those are a lot of allegations.'

'Don's book *Absolution*,' says Benedict, 'I'm willing to bet that it was going to end with the son killing the mother. That's why Seventh Seal didn't want to publish it. I think Don killed his mother. That's why he was so obsessed with confession. And absolution.'

'And you got all that from the book?' says Natalka. 'I apologise for calling it boring.'

Benedict gives her one of his best smiles. 'That's OK. It was boring in places. Depressing too.'

'And remember Don's last published book was called *A Deadly Bargain*,' says Edwin. 'I think Leonard rang the vicarage and asked for Don's unpublished stories because he was beginning to suspect.'

'This is all supposition,' says DS Brennan. 'Can we stick to one attempted murder at a time? We will charge Harmony Skelton and question her about her mother's death. I thought Harmony and her sister were convinced the husband killed her?'

'Misdirection,' says Edwin.

'You have all the answers,' says Brennan drily, once again reminding Natalka of Harbinder. 'As I said, we'll need to interview you all individually and then you can get home. Although SOCO might still be at your flat, Edwin.'

A squad car drives them home. Edwin's flat is still a crime scene so he comes with them. Pietro offers to put him up for the night and Edwin says he'll ring if the police still haven't finished by the evening. That's going a bit far for a first date, Natalka wants to say, but doesn't. They drop Pietro at Seaview Court so that he can collect his car, a vintage Lancia. They all wave goodbye although Pietro probably can't see them through the tinted windows.

Valentyna is waiting for them. She seems surprised, but pleased, when Natalka hugs her fiercely and says she loves her. 'I love you too, коханий.' Benedict and Edwin also get hugs. Valentyna cooks them pasta but no one has much appetite, possibly because they ate too many chocolate bars at the police station. Edwin gets a call to say that the crime scene investigators have finished with his flat so Benedict walks him home. Natalka thinks that Edwin looks disappointed to miss out on a sleepover at Casa Alighieri but, again, with some difficulty, she manages not to say this.

Natalka is almost asleep by the time that Benedict gets back. She's aware of him entering the bedroom and she thinks he says that he loves her but she can't be sure. When she wakes up, it's eight o'clock and Benedict has left for the Shack. She can't remember sleeping so late in years. Valentyna has gone to do her early shift at Care4You.

For months Natalka has wanted the flat to herself but now that she is alone, with the sun streaming through the windows, she feels oddly restless. She turns the radio on but it's something operatic so she turns it off again. She tries Breakfast News on the TV but it's about Ukraine which reminds her too much of Dmytro. Natalka goes into the kitchen and makes herself toast but even eating slowly, in the way that Benedict does sometimes, doesn't calm her jittery mind. Maybe some yoga will help. She gets her mat, selects some ambient music on Spotify and goes back into the sitting room. It's frighteningly tidy, thanks to Valentyna. The cushions on the sofa are standing on their points like ballerinas. There's no sign that this room is also Valentyna's bedroom.

Natalka is in sphynx pose when her phone buzzes.

It's Alan Franklin.

Can't believe it about Harmony.

Natalka uncurls and types.

I know. Weird.

She practises her yogic breathing, thinking about how it saved Edwin's life yesterday. She must check on him today. In, out. In, out.

Another message.

I don't suppose you could come over? Really need to talk it through with you.

In, out. In, out.

OK.

Chapter 38

Natalka: not like a dog at all

It's a beautiful morning and the road to Steyning is miraculously clear. Natalka passes Harmony's cottage and wonders what's going on inside. Is Harmony still in custody? What's Patrick doing, the husband whom Natalka has never met? He was described as an entrepreneur, which always sounds dodgy. Did Harmony kill her mother to fund her husband's business schemes? And what about Minnie, the other sister? Natalka is almost surprised not to have had an 'any news?' text. She suspects that her sister's arrest will be news enough for Minnie.

The house that once belonged to Melody Chambers looks peaceful in the sunshine. The tree-lined street is silent. Natalka supposes that all the adults are at work and all the children are at school. It's odd, though, that even the nesting birds are quiet. She's rather relieved to hear Frodo barking as she approaches Alan's front door.

'Natalka. Thanks for coming.'

Natalka thinks that Alan looks as if he hasn't slept. He is pale and unshaven and his long hair is swept upwards in a crest as if he's been running his hands through it. For a second, she's reminded of Benedict.

This time he does offer her a drink and she opts for coffee. While he's making it, Natalka sits on the sofa with Frodo. He's really very sweet. Maybe she should have a dog. But it would be too difficult with so many people in the flat.

Alan comes back with two coffees and says, 'Minnie rang me this morning and told me that Harmony's been arrested. I thought she was joking at first. Not that she's known for her sense of humour. I can't think why she told me.'

'Maybe she felt sorry for suspecting you of Melody's murder.'

'She didn't sound sorry. And she said that Harmony had been arrested for threatening to kill *you*. Or you and your friends. That's why I asked you to come over. Is it really true?'

'It felt true when she was pointing a gun at us.'

'A *gun*? *Harmony*?'

'Apparently it was her dad's. Nice to keep it in the family.'

'Tony was in the army,' says Alan, 'but I had no idea there was a gun hanging around. Melody would have been horrified. But why did Harmony try to kill you? I'm trying to get my head round it.'

Natalka wonders how much to tell him. Her own head is feeling slightly woozy. She takes another sip of her coffee and pats Frodo. He even smells nice, not like a dog at all.

'Harmony tried to kill Edwin, my business partner,' she says, 'because he'd worked out that she killed Leonard Norris.'

'Harmony killed Leonard Norris? The Battle House guy? Why?'

'It's complicated,' says Natalka. That much is true.

'Edwin's the old chap? The one with the Shakespeare quotations? How did he work it out?'

'Like I said, it's complicated. You'd have to ask him. But Harmony must have suspected something because she came round with some pills and tried to force him to take them.'

'Pills? I thought you said a gun?'

Did I? thinks Natalka. She is feeling stranger than ever, almost light-headed. She hopes she isn't going to be sick. It would be too embarrassing, here in this tasteful room. Had Harmony been prepared to kill for this house? Had she framed Alan Franklin? But Minnie had been the sister convinced of Alan's guilt. Harmony was the one described as 'too soft', reluctant to act against him. The good sister.

'Did Harmony admit to any of this?' asks Alan. 'To killing Leonard Norris? To killing Melody?'

'She's in police custody,' says Natalka, having trouble with the words. 'Excuse me, I have to go. I don't feel well.' But she can't stand up. She seems to have grown roots attaching her to the sofa.

'Stay where you are,' says Alan Franklin.

Natalka stares at him. Mechanically, she is still stroking Frodo. Her sense of smell, very acute these days, registers the scent rising from his fur. It's a perfume she smelled yesterday. Harmony's perfume.

'You drugged me,' she says to Alan.

He laughs. The ironical laugh that she had previously found rather attractive.

'Just like Minnie. I'm a pharmacist so you assume I drug people.'

'But you do, don't you? You killed Melody. You and Harmony. Did you kill Sue Hitchins too? What about Leonard Norris?'

'Stop jabbering,' says Alan. 'And go to sleep.'

Natalka makes a final effort to stand but the sofa is fighting back. She's got to do something. Where's her phone? It's only on the coffee table but it could be a mile away. She looks at Frodo, his ginger fur now a golden mist. 'Help me,' she sends him a thought message. Frodo barks. Alan looks up. There's an explosion and the world shatters.

Chapter 39

Harbinder: drama

'Armed police! Stand away!'

Harbinder and Liv stand back and cover their eyes as the firearms officer smashes the glass door with a pocket ram.

'Armed police! Put your hands on your head.'

Harbinder steps over the glass shards to see Alan Franklin with his hands in the air and Natalka apparently asleep on the sofa, a small dog standing guard over her.

As Liv reads Alan his rights, Harbinder shakes Natalka's shoulder. 'Natalka? Wake up.'

'Harbinder,' says Natalka sleepily. 'Why aren't you in London?'

'Something came up,' says Harbinder. 'We need to get you to a hospital.'

With Harbinder's help, Natalka is able to stand. Liv and Sam are escorting Alan to the squad car. Harbinder wonders what to do with the dog. She doesn't want to leave him in the house with the shattered window and glass on the floor. So she takes off her belt and loops it through his collar.

An ambulance is also outside. Natalka gets in. It's very strange to see her behaving so meekly.

'I'll see you at the hospital,' says Harbinder.

Alan's next-door neighbours, a man and a woman, are standing in the porch of their grand-looking home. Harbinder approaches and shows her warrant card.

'Would you mind looking after the dog for a few hours?'

'Frodo?' says the woman. 'Of course. He gets on well with our two. But what's happening? Is Alan ill?'

'I'm not at liberty to tell you, I'm afraid,' says Harbinder. 'I'll send a dog handler to collect Frodo.'

'We have a right to know,' says the man. 'We pay our taxes.'

'Very good of you,' says Harbinder. 'I'll be in touch.'

It was the angina tablets. The pills seized from the house of Eileen O'Rourke, author of *My Name is Jack*. When Natalka messaged her last night, Harbinder had rung Liv and learnt that Harmony Skelton had been arrested.

'It's all a bit of a muddle,' Liv told her. 'Edwin Fitzgerald apparently worked out that Harmony killed Leonard Norris. Something about an opera. But he's also convinced that all sorts of other people have been killing their elderly relatives. Names like Georgina, Felicity and Henrietta.'

Felicity. Harbinder got up early the next day and went into work. As Eileen O'Rourke's death had originally been classified as suspicious, there were numbered exhibits from her house in the files. Harbinder peered at the photograph of the angina tablets and there was the address of the issuing pharmacy. Steyning, Sussex. She had rung Liv immediately.

'You need to arrest Alan Franklin. I'm on my way.'

But when Harbinder had arrived at Chichester police station, her old stamping ground, she learnt that armed assistance had been requested. This delayed matters and they didn't reach the house until eleven a.m. Harbinder immediately recognised Natalka's car outside.

'Oh my God,' she said to Liv. 'She's in there with him.'

'Suspect believed to be holding a hostage,' Liv had radioed.

Even in her frantic worry, Harbinder had thought how much Natalka would have loved the drama of it all. Well, now Natalka is safe – Harbinder hopes – and Alan is in custody. Enough drama for one day.

Harbinder goes back to the station for a debrief. Then she calls the hospital who tell her that Natalka is fit to be discharged.

Natalka is sitting on a bed in an A and E cubicle. She looks frail, blonde hair loose and her eyes huge.

'It was deadly nightshade,' she greets Harbinder. 'That's why my pupils look so big. Quite the beauty product.'

'Alan Franklin gave you deadly nightshade?'

'Just a few drops in my coffee, apparently. The doctor here gave me something to bring it up. I'm fine. No damage to . . . to anything.'

'I'll drive you home then,' says Harbinder.

'I can ring Benedict.'

'No, I'll take you. I'd like to see everyone. Have a debrief. And I can call in on my mum and dad too.'

'In that case,' says Natalka, sliding off the bed. 'What are we waiting for?'

★

They are all there in Natalka's flat: Benedict, Edwin and Valentyna. Benedict reaches Natalka first. 'Darling, are you OK?'

It's the only time Harbinder has heard Benedict call Natalka darling. It makes her feel unexpectedly tearful.

'I'm fine,' says Natalka, submitting to hugs from her mother and Edwin. 'And guess what? It was Alan Franklin all along. Harbinder worked it all out.'

'Not quite,' says Harbinder. 'But I think I've got most of it straight now, with Liv's help.'

'Let's hear it,' says Edwin.

Valentyna makes herbal tea and Benedict produces brownies. It must be teatime, thinks Harbinder. With any luck, she can call in on her parents in time for the evening meal.

'I checked the angina tablets belonging to Eileen O'Rourke,' Harbinder tells her audience. 'She was the writer who wrote the Jack the Ripper book. The mother of Felicity Briggs.'

'Felicity from the book club,' says Edwin.

'Exactly. We've arrested Felicity. She admitted replacing her mother's angina pills with caffeine tablets, obtained from Alan Franklin, with whom she was having an affair.'

'Felicity had an affair with Alan?' says Natalka, who is sitting on the sofa, holding Benedict's hand.

'I don't think she was the only one,' says Harbinder. 'Felicity met Alan through her old schoolfriend Georgina Potter-Smith. It sounds like they had an affair too and Alan might have helped Georgina dispose of her aunt so she could inherit her house. The place where Benedict and Edwin went on that retreat.'

'What was in it for Alan?' says Edwin. 'Killing Georgina's aunt and Felicity's mother?'

'I'm sure that he profited financially from both deaths,' says Harbinder. 'Felicity's already told us that she gave him a substantial sum of money. '

'He probably shared Harmony's views about old people being a waste of space,' says Edwin. 'I'm sure he saw enough of them at his pharmacy.'

'Minnie told me Georgina introduced Alan to Melody,' says Natalka. 'He denied it. Said they'd met when she came into his shop.'

'I remember him telling us that,' says Edwin. 'It was almost too neat a story. I thought so at the time. I wondered if they'd actually met on a dating app. Most of my cheating husbands meet women that way.'

'They have dating apps for old people?' says Valentyna. Harbinder is impressed at how well she is following the conversation, but she doesn't want to be distracted.

'Interesting,' she says. 'Maybe Georgina even introduced Melody as a possible victim. Hastings police are interviewing her now.'

'It must have been Alan I saw that night,' says Benedict. 'I thought it was Leonard because he was tall, but I wasn't wearing my glasses. I think now that the other person must have been Georgina.'

'If Alan was at Battle House on Saturday night,' says Edwin, 'then he could have killed Sue Hitchins on Sunday.'

'Liv thinks so,' says Harbinder. 'Georgina tipped Alan off and he turned up and disposed of Sue.'

'Georgina was mowing the lawn when Sue was reading her story,' says Benedict. 'I heard the mower stop. Funny how things like that come back to you.'

'I'm betting the traces of dog hair found at the crime scene belong to Alan's dog,' says Harbinder.

'Frodo,' says Natalka. 'He was nice. What's going to happen to him?'

'I think the neighbours will take him in,' says Harbinder. 'I sent a dog handler round to collect him, but they seemed to want to keep him.'

'So I was right about killing off the elderly relatives.' Edwin clearly wants to get back to his theory. 'Felicity killed her mother. Georgina killed her aunt. Do you think Henrietta killed her father Felix, my flautist?'

'That name did come up,' says Harbinder.

'I'm sure she did,' says Benedict. 'A musician murdered by his instrument. That was in Sue's story and must have been why she was killed. She knew too much. The real story, she said. She was at the book club. She knew all the people. I'm sure Don killed his mother too.'

'If so, Alan Franklin facilitated it,' says Harbinder. 'And he was apparently having an affair with Harmony, his own stepdaughter. According to her, they were planning to elope to Australia. On Melody's money, of course.'

'Alan talked about going to Australia,' says Natalka. 'It might have been when I went on that walk with him.'

'You went on a walk with Alan Franklin?' says Benedict.

'I was investigating, Benny,' says Natalka. She leans into him and then freezes. Her phone is buzzing, so insistently that the device is moving across the table. Harbinder sees the words 'FaceTime request'. Natalka looks at her mother. Both their faces are chalk white.

'Shall I?' Benedict reaches for the phone but Natalka snatches it up. For a second she just stares at the screen, her eyes still belladonna wild. Then she says, in a small cracked voice, 'Dmytro?'

Chapter 40

Benedict: the last word

Benedict feels as if he is watching every emotion drift across Natalka's lovely face: fear, joy, anger, bewilderment.

'Dmytro?'

Valentyna lets out a cry and Benedict moves aside to let her share the screen with Natalka. The two speak rapidly in Ukrainian.

'Dmytro,' Benedict mouths at Edwin and Harbinder. Edwin has tears in his eyes and Benedict realises that his own are wet. Harbinder is smiling broadly. Benedict can hear the familiar notes of love and frustration in Natalka's voice when she addresses her brother. Then there's a pause. Natalka's face registers pure shock. Valentyna says 'Artem'. Curiosity overcomes Benedict and he moves behind the sofa so that he can see the screen. A grey-haired man in army fatigues is speaking. And Benedict remembers that Artem is the name of Natalka's missing father.

Natalka is doing all the talking now. Valentyna looks rather grave until Natalka says something that makes them all laugh. Artem has a surprisingly high-pitched guffaw. Dmytro appears again, mud-stained but as cheerful as ever. Goodbyes are said and Benedict recognises 'I love you', one of the first Ukrainian phrases he learnt. Then the phone goes silent and the five people in the room look at each other, all somewhere between laughter and tears.

'He's been on a secret mission,' says Natalka. 'The idiot.'

'It was an honour to be chosen,' says Valentyna.

'And who chose him?' says Natalka. 'Our dad. Apparently he's a general now.'

Valentyna says, 'I think the army suits him.'

It doesn't sound like a compliment but why would Valentyna want to compliment the husband who walked out on her twenty years ago? Valentyna goes into the kitchen and Benedict wonders whether she's overcome with emotion. But, when she returns, she's carrying a bottle of red wine and five glasses.

'To Dmytro!'

They clink glasses and drink. Then Natalka phones Dmytro's girlfriend Kelly, and Harbinder leaves to go and see her parents.

'I'd better be getting back too,' says Edwin.

'I'll walk with you,' says Benedict. He thinks that Natalka and Valentyna will want some time alone. The two men walk in silence for a while and then Benedict says, 'What a day. I feel quite worn out with emotion.'

'Emotion never tires me,' says Edwin, although Benedict thinks he's walking more slowly than usual and pauses to catch his breath on the slight incline towards Seaview Court. 'It's monotony that's exhausting.'

'When I heard what had happened to Natalka,' says Benedict, 'I felt sick.' Natalka hadn't rung him until she was on her way home with Harbinder. The thought that she'd been through all that without him – a cosy chat with a murderer, attempted poisoning, armed raid, hospital visit – while Benedict was making coffee and wrapping sandwiches in clingfilm, still makes him feel quite faint.

'I bet Natalka didn't turn a hair,' says Edwin. 'I'm so pleased about her brother.'

'Yes, it was like a miracle. Funny, you pray for a miracle, but you never think they're going to happen.'

'After all these years,' says Edwin, 'I still expect my prayers to be answered. You would have thought experience would have taught me otherwise.'

'You seem pretty calm yourself,' says Benedict. 'And you've had quite a time of it too. Harmony actually tried to kill you. Weren't you terrified when she turned up?'

'Not at all,' says Edwin. 'Even though I knew by then that she was the killer. She knocked at the door and I let her in. Strange how the old civilised reflexes work. I think I might even have offered her a cup of tea before she told me to kill myself.'

'Did she really expect you to do it?'

'That's the arrogance of it. I think she did. After she'd explained what a drone I was, I think she expected me to take the pills and shuffle off. That's why she didn't even bother to check my breathing properly. God bless yoga. I must post a message on Adriene's website.'

'How dare Harmony say that? I'd be devastated if you died. I *was* devastated when I thought you had.'

Edwin squeezes his arm. 'Thank you, dear boy. Well, I'm in the last chapter now but "something ere the end, Some work of noble note, may yet be done". Tennyson, "Ulysses".'

'I thought I was good at quotations until I met you.'

'I've had more years to perfect them.'

Seaview Court looms up in front of them, looking, with its bulk and lighted windows, like a ship setting out to sea. Benedict doesn't mention this to Edwin because he fears that it sounds too much like sailing into the sunset. 'Crossing the bar', to quote Tennyson again.

Instead he says, 'Maybe there's another relationship still to come for you.'

'Maybe,' says Edwin. 'Ridiculous to think of two old buffers like me and Pietro having a relationship.' But Benedict thinks he sounds rather pleased all the same.

They part affectionately and Benedict waits until he can see Edwin's light shine inside his apartment. Then he walks home.

The next morning Benedict is woken up by the sound of the vacuum cleaner. 'Oh my God,' Natalka puts her head under the pillow, 'she's cleaning again.' Benedict had been hoping for celebratory sex but he knows, from the clattering and tuneless whistling come from the kitchen, that this isn't going to happen. He gets up, showers, and makes toast. He offers some to Natalka but she says she isn't hungry and goes out for a run. Valentyna, apparently, ate some cereal at five a.m.

Benedict walks to the Shack. As he crosses the coast road his phone starts to buzz and continues until he reaches the picnic table and swipes it open. The Battle House Group WhatsApp is going mad.

Johnnie: omg harmony has been arrested!!!
Frances: for L's murder? When did you hear?
Johnnie: Imogen

Peter: never liked her
Johnnie: George too
Frances: George??
Johnnie: Georgina P-T from the farm
Frances: !!!???

After Benedict has opened the shutter and put on the first coffee, he rings Johnnie. He tells her about Harmony threatening them all with a gun and the arrest of Alan Franklin.

'Well, it's usually the husband,' says Johnnie.

She's right, Benedict knows, but, in this case, they had been blinded by the very obviousness of it. And, he suspects, by Natalka's susceptibility to Alan's charm.

'Imogen says Georgina has been arrested too,' says Johnnie. 'I always thought Georgina was nice. A bit quiet in the book group but basically nice. I mean, Imogen's dog loved her and dogs are never wrong.'

'I don't know how much Georgina was involved,' says Benedict. 'But I think the police suspect she tipped Alan off about Sue. Apparently Georgina had an affair with Alan too. And she introduced him to Melody.'

'Blimey,' says Johnnie. 'Why did they all fall for him? Was he gorgeous or something?'

'Whatever he had, I couldn't see it,' says Benedict. 'Actually, I wondered if you suspected about Georgina. I read the piece you wrote at Battle House, the "If only I hadn't" piece, and I wondered if Georgina was the person you were talking about. When you said, "If only I hadn't met her". When you were the matron at a boarding school. Was Georgina teaching there maybe?'

Johnnie laughs, so loudly that Benedict has to hold the phone away from his ear.

'That was made up! Fiction. I never worked in a boarding school. I was a prison warder. I couldn't cope with a school. Children are horrible little buggers. Much worse than convicts.'

After a few minutes' chat, and promises to keep in touch, Benedict rings off. His first customers of the day are striding along the promenade, mobile phones clamped to their ears.

It's a busy morning and it's not until ten that Benedict realises that he hasn't seen Edwin. Normally, he'd be here by now, papers under his arm and a smug expression that says he's solved Wordle in two. Benedict squints into the distance; the windows of Seaview Court flash in the sunlight. He's still staring when a voice says, 'Cappuccino with a heart on it, please.'

It's Natalka, glowing slightly from her run. But, by now, Benedict is too upset to appreciate the vision.

'I'm worried about Edwin,' he says. 'He's normally here by now.'

'Probably having a lie-in after the last few days.'

'Edwin never lies in. He salutes the dawn with yoga.'

Natalka's eyes meet his. 'Let's go and see.'

'OK.' Benedict pulls down the shutter. At this rate he won't have any customers left but he doesn't really care. They run across the beach, Benedict falling behind. He's not nearly as fit as Natalka. Once again, Natalka uses her pass key and they climb the stairs to Edwin's flat. They hear music as soon as they reach the landing.

'I'm starting to hate opera,' says Benedict.

'Edwin!' Natalka bangs on the door.

'Hang on,' says Benedict. 'I've still got the key. DS Brennan gave it back to me yesterday.'

They let themselves in, cross the tiny hall and go into the sun-filled sitting room. Where Edwin is sitting at his desk reading some papers.

'Hallo, darlings! What's all this? I'm afraid I didn't hear you. Maria is singing Norma, you see.'

This doesn't make any sense to Benedict but it doesn't matter. All that matters is that Edwin is alive, in his white shirt and favourite pink bow tie. He looks at Natalka and knows she feels the same.

'You're getting deaf,' she says. 'That screeching is so loud you can hear it from the beach.'

'Screeching?' says Edwin. 'It's Maria Callas.' But he turns the music down. 'I didn't hear you because I was reading something interesting,' he says. 'DS Brennan sent me Harmony's "If only I hadn't" piece. Harmony had Leonard's phone and from Leonard's texts DS Brennan thinks this is what he was reading before he died. Or, rather, before Harmony came round and shot him. I've printed out copies for you.'

Benedict and Natalka sit on the sofa and read. Edwin goes to make coffee.

If Only I Hadn't
By Harmony Skelton

If only I hadn't met him. Or rather, if only she hadn't met him first. To be introduced to my perfect man as someone else's husband. And hers, of all people. Of course I was married myself. A small detail but I knew immediately that he was The One. The only one I wanted. Part of my soul I seek thee and claim my other half.

And the tragedy is — he doesn't love her and she doesn't love him.
She's too old for him. He has such youth, such vitality. Sometimes I
think he's the son I never had. My son, my sun.

I like to think that in some other life, some other universe, we could
be together. Or that, as the credits roll, we could escape on his motor-
bike, heading for the sunset. To completely vanish and be seen no more.
But it's not to be. I can't have him and am left with my sterile little
life. While she, she has it all and doesn't appreciate it, moaning to
her girlfriends over Prosecco. 'Sometimes I wish I'd never remarried.
I'd be quite happy alone with my dog, watching Netflix in bed with
a takeaway.'

Well, I wish it too. You don't know how much.

'Goodness,' says Benedict. 'What can they have thought when
they read this?'

'I'm betting Leonard didn't bother to read it at the time,' says
Edwin, coming in with a tray. 'You know how lazy he was on our
course, leaving all the teaching to Imogen. And Imogen would only
have commented on the split infinitive.'

Benedict thinks of Leonard slumped in his chair. There was
something resigned about the pose as if he knew the terrors he had
unleashed. *i'm scared . . . theres evil in the air.*

He says, 'I wonder what made Leonard read the piece that
evening.'

'Maybe he was thinking about Melody,' says Edwin. 'I know
he denied an affair, but it was obvious that they were close. I
think you and Natalka visiting brought it all back. That and the
photograph.'

Benedict thinks of the picture. Melody, Miriam and Leonard in front of Battle House. They looked so happy and carefree. Yet, if Edwin is right, Miriam was shortly to be killed for that very house.

Natalka is looking at the printed sheet of paper. 'This is awful,' she says. 'Part of my soul I seek thee. What rubbish.'

Melody had said something in her notebook about Alan being her twin soul, Benedict remembers. But she had suspected him too, which gives Benedict a strange satisfaction.

'It's a quotation,' says Edwin. 'Milton. *Paradise Lost.*'

'Alan told me he found quotations sexy,' says Natalka. 'Maybe that's why he liked Harmony.'

Not for the first time, Benedict wonders what went on when Natalka interviewed Alan Franklin.

'She was certainly in love with him,' says Edwin. 'It's almost painful to read. Here, she seems to think she can never have a relationship with him. I suppose, as time went on, that changed.'

'What I don't understand,' says Benedict, 'is why Harmony went along with accusing Alan of killing Melody. I mean, she knew he did it.'

'Maybe she thought it would look suspicious if she sided with Alan,' says Natalka. 'And, looking back, it was Minnie who drove the investigation. She found the notebook and the photograph. She was the one who kept texting and asking if there was news. She called Alan the devil incarnate. Harmony wasn't nearly as angry with him. I thought that meant she was the nice one. Huh.'

She shrugs and rolls her eyes upwards. Natalka is good at this sort of gesture, thinks Benedict. It has an operatic quality that an English person could never achieve.

'So Minnie didn't know anything about Alan and Harmony?' says Benedict.

'I'm sure she didn't,' says Natalka. 'Looking back, I remember Harmony getting upset when Minnie suggested that Alan might have a new girlfriend. And, then, a few minutes later Harmony said about Melody having an affair with Leonard. That must have been . . . what's that thing you say, Edwin? The thing magicians do?'

'Misdirection,' says Edwin. 'It certainly made us look away from Alan Franklin.'

'Alan laughed when I asked him about the affair,' says Natalka. 'He must have known that it came from Harmony.'

'Alan thought he could kill Melody and marry her daughter,' says Edwin. 'If he wasn't the devil, he was something close.'

'I feel very sorry for Melody,' says Benedict. 'Reading her notebook made me like her a lot. I wish she had left Alan and had watched Netflix in bed with her dog.'

'Well, the case is almost closed,' says Edwin. 'Liv Brennan will be delighted to have had that dramatic raid alongside Harbinder.'

'I'm really annoyed that I missed it all,' says Natalka.

'I can't believe he drugged you,' says Benedict, who is surprised by the intensity of rage he still feels.

'Apparently there wasn't enough in the cup to kill me,' says Natalka. 'Alan asked me to go round so that he could find out what Harmony had said to us, whether she'd incriminated him. A corpse in his sitting room would have looked very bad. Maybe he just wanted to disorientate me or make me fall in love with him, like all the other women. The ancient Greeks used belladonna as a love potion.'

Benedict clenches his fists.

Edwin says, 'Georgina has been charged with assisting a crime but I don't know if they'll be able to pin Miriam Fry's murder on her. It happened so long ago. Ditto Henrietta. She'll probably get away with killing her father just to get her hands on a Kensington flat.'

'If she did,' says Benedict.

'Oh, I think she did,' says Edwin. 'Why deny belonging to the book club if not?'

'It was a very strange book club,' says Benedict. 'Makes me glad I was never invited. Well, I suppose I should get back to the Shack. The lunchtime crowd will be here soon.'

'Yes,' says Edwin, 'can't let the customers down.'

'Actually,' says Benedict, 'I'm thinking of shutting the Shack – or giving it to Kyle – and becoming a teacher.'

Now it's out there he feels relieved. He's been wondering how to tell Natalka but this seems right, mid-murder investigation, with their surrogate grandfather present. It's rather galling to realise that it was Imogen who first gave him the idea of teaching as a career but her words have taken root. He can still write in his spare time. If he has any.

'Oh, Benny,' says Natalka. 'I'm so pleased. A teacher is the perfect job for a father.'

Benedict doesn't take this in. The sun is shining through Natalka's hair and she's doing the glowing goddess thing again.

'Oh, are you pregnant?' says Edwin. 'I did wonder. The not fancying food and so on.'

'I think my mum guessed too,' says Natalka. 'Why else would she be making babushka dolls?'

'You're pregnant?' croaks Benedict at last.

'Yes,' says Natalka. 'Are you happy?'

For a moment Benedict can't speak. Everything is transformed. Edwin's bow tie, Natalka's shining eyes, the glass cafetière: they all seem part of an indescribably wonderful universe. He thinks of his imagined obituary. Now there will be someone in the 'is survived by' paragraph. And maybe his students will also remember him.

'Why don't you call the baby Edwin?' says Edwin. 'Or Maria after La Divina?'

Trust Edwin to have the last word, thinks Benedict.

Epilogue

Harbinder

Saturday, 13 August 2022

'I've never been to an English wedding,' says Mette. 'What happens?'

'It depends,' says Harbinder. She is driving and can't see the expression on Mette's face. Sometimes she still doesn't know if she's teasing or not. 'Sometimes it's at a registry office, with only a few people. Sometimes there's a church and a big party afterwards. Recently I've mostly been to registry offices because gay people can't marry in church. Yet.'

'Gay people do weddings best,' says Mette. 'But this is in a church. Is that because Benedict is religious?'

'I suppose so,' says Harbinder. 'Natalka's been married before but apparently that's OK because it wasn't in a Catholic church so it doesn't count.'

'Natalka's been married before? She's full of surprises.'

'I think she was very young. She'd just finished university and got married so that she wouldn't be sent back to Ukraine.'

'Romantic.'

'You can't accuse Natalka of being romantic. Maybe they just wanted to get married before the baby was born.'

Harbinder hadn't been totally surprised to hear that Natalka was pregnant. She'd suspected as much when Natalka said, in A and E, that there was no damage 'to anything'. And Natalka had had that frail, lit from inside quality that Harbinder has noticed before in expectant friends.

'I can't imagine the blonde assassin with a baby,' says Mette.

'Nor can I,' says Harbinder, 'but I think they'll be great parents. And Valentyna will definitely be a doting grandmother.'

Natalka said that her mother was looking for a place of her own but Harbinder suspects that she will still be in residence when the baby arrives in January. Harbinder's maternal grandparents had lived with them when she was young and she has very happy memories of chattering away to them, secure in the knowledge both that they loved her and that they couldn't understand a word.

Now Harbinder parks in her usual spot near her parents' flat and rings the doorbell. Starsky, the German shepherd, barks and Harbinder's brother Khush waves from the shop. He is looking after the store so that Bibi and Deepak can go to the wedding. In a few minutes they emerge, Bibi in a beautiful red sari, a colour which symbolises prosperity and happiness for the marriage. Deepak is elegant in green and gold kurta pyjamas with his gold turban. Harbinder feels very proud of them.

'I've brought Natalka some *choora* bangles for good luck,' says Bibi. 'Do you think that's all right?'

'I think she'll be delighted,' says Harbinder. She has no idea what Natalka will be wearing but she's pretty sure that whatever it is will match bright red bracelets.

They get some stares as they walk from the shop to the church but Harbinder thinks that this would happen anyway because Mette is six foot tall with long blonde hair and wearing a bright green trouser suit. Harbinder herself is wearing cream trousers and a bright pink jacket. She's still enough of a Sikh to want to wear auspicious colours.

The first people they see at the church are Edwin and his new boyfriend, Pietro. The two men are looking extremely smart, Edwin in a sand-coloured suit and Pietro in blue pin-stripe. Both have removed their hats prior to entering the church. Harbinder makes the introductions and Pietro tells Mette that she looks like the personification of spring, which Harbinder thinks is rather poetic.

It's a blisteringly hot day but the church is cool and flower-scented. Harbinder seems to remember that there's a bride's side and a groom's side but no one tells them where to sit so they take their places behind Valentyna. 'There won't be many people there,' Natalka told Harbinder when she invited her, 'not at such short notice. We might do it all over again when Dmytro can be with us.' It's true that the church isn't full. Harbinder recognises Maria, Natalka's deputy at the care agency, and a couple of residents from Seaview Court. A woman in a wheelchair, accompanied by her husband in a smart blazer with medals attached, is introduced by Valentyna as 'Natalka's favourite client, Harriet'. There's also a large man in a dog collar who must be one of Benedict's friends.

Edwin, who is the best man, takes his seat on the other side of the aisle. Pietro sits with Valentyna. She's wearing a floral dress and has one of those flower things on her head. The woman in the shop tried to make Harbinder buy one. Fascinators, they are called. Harbinder's flat cream sandals seem to be cutting into her feet so she eases them off. Across the aisle she sees a red-faced man who can only be Benedict's brother, Hugo. Benedict said, not without satisfaction, that Hugo was furious not to be the best man. Hugo is with a blonde woman and two identical-looking tow-haired children. Behind them sits a hard-faced brunette who must be Benedict's sister; Harbinder has forgotten her name. Benedict's parents look older than she expected, the father grey and stooped and the mother in a brave hat. Benedict says they are delighted about the marriage and the baby.

The music starts and, turning, Harbinder sees Natalka and Benedict entering the church together. Natalka wanted nothing to do with being 'given away' by a man. Harbinder is surprised how moved she feels, partly because Natalka looks so beautiful. She's wearing a simple white dress and there's a circlet of flowers in her hair. Benedict, in a blue suit, seems to be bursting out of it with pride.

The ceremony, conducted by a beaming Irish priest, is quicker than Harbinder expected. She's sure the Church of England service goes on longer and is more cringeworthy. There's none of the exchanging of gifts and tokens that she remembers from Sikh weddings. Edwin produces the rings and Benedict and Natalka make their vows 'before God and the Church.' Then they kiss, rather more enthusiastically than is usual, and process out of the church to some booming organ music. Edwin and Valentyna follow, then

Benedict's parents, then the rest of the guests. Harbinder only just gets her shoes on in time.

Outside, Natalka and Benedict pose for photographs in the sunshine. The reception will be at a seafront restaurant but, according to the invitation, there will be 'Champagne at the Shack' first. Someone called Kyle will be taking over the Coffee Shack when Benedict starts teacher training next month. It's all change in Shoreham-by-Sea.

The photographer gets them all to pose for a group shot. He clearly wants Deepak at the back because of the turban (or ingrained prejudice). Harbinder stands on a higher step so she's the same height as Mette. Afterwards, there's a general scrum of meeting and greeting. Harbinder kisses Benedict.

'Congratulations.'

'Thank you. We're so glad you came.'

'Wouldn't have missed it for the world. Congrats on the baby too.'

'It's incredible, isn't it?' says Benedict, although Harbinder can't quite see what's so unbelievable about human procreation. 'Edwin keeps suggesting operatic names. It was Iolanta yesterday.'

This, Harbinder can believe. She wonders if the name choice means that the foetus is female. Or is it too soon to tell?

Then Natalka is embracing her, all flowers and silk.

'Congratulations,' says Harbinder.

'I don't believe in marriage really,' says Natalka, 'but this is quite fun.'

'Nor do I,' says Mette in Harbinder's ear, 'but we might do it one day, just for a laugh.'

Harbinder watches as her mother slides the bracelets onto Natalka's arm. She must be getting emotional in her old age because tears come to her eyes as the seagulls call their own congratulations high above them.

Acknowledgements

Huge thanks, as always, to my wonderful editor, Jane Wood, and the fantastic team at Quercus Publishing. Special thanks to Katy Blott, Joe Christie, Florence Hare, David Murphy and Ella Patel. You are all wonderful, as are the sales teams who get my books onto so many shelves. Thanks to Liz Hatherell for her meticulous copy-editing and Chris Shamwana for the beautiful cover. Thanks to my amazing agent, Rebecca Carter, and all at RC Literary and at PEW.

Shoreham, Steyning and Battle are all real locations, although Battle House is imaginary. There are churches, shops and pharmacies in these places but the people who inhabit them in my books are entirely fictional. Steyning Bookshop is real, though, and well worth a visit.

Thanks to Sinéad Crowley for telling me about the work of an obituary writer and my son, Alex Maxted, for the information about opera. Any mistakes are mine alone.

Thanks to my crime writer friends for all their support. Special thanks to Lesley Thomson, William Shaw and Colin Scott. Thanks to Lynne Spahl, Leigh Dewis and the Californian branch. Thanks to all the publishers around the world who publish my books with such care.

Thanks to Daria and Viktoriya Miskevych for the information about Ukrainian food and culture. I'm so happy to know you and count you as cousins but so sad about the adversity that has brought us together.

Thanks, as ever, to my husband Andy and our now grown-up children Alex and Juliet. I couldn't do it without you. I could probably do it without our cat, Pip, but thanks to him all the same.

EG

2024